'Archer is on top form'   *Daily Telegraph*

'I was touched and enthralled by this tale of how Harry from the Bristol backstreets rises from obscurity to high society . . . He's about to marry into the upper classes when tragedy strikes on the steps of the altar. I won't spoil it for you by revealing any more. Or the trademark twist, which is gasp-making'
                                                   Daily Mail

'I enjoyed the book and marvelled at both its pace and the imaginative cliffhanger ending, whetting our appetite for volume two'   *Sunday Express*

'The ability to tell a story is a great – and unusual – gift . . . [it] is not something that can be taught or acquired. You have it or you don't . . . Jeffrey Archer is, first and foremost, a storyteller . . . You don't sell 250 million copies of your books (250 million!) if you can't keep an audience hooked – and that's what Archer does, book after book. Archer's audience will stick with him to the last. They want to know what happens next'
                          Erica Wagner, Literary Editor, *The Times*

'I was reading the book on tour and found I was bunking off from my own signing sessions to get back to the story. Sitting in a Starbucks in Oxford, feverishly thumbing the pages to find out what dire machinations Hugo Barrington (a villain straight out of Victorian melodrama) would come up with next, I had to admit I was utterly hooked. It was an absurdly enjoyable read'
                          Anthony Horowitz, *Daily Telegraph*

'This is a cracker of a read. And quite "unputdownable". The whole thing about Jeffrey is that he has always had the knack of producing page-turners . . . This is a tale about love, treachery, deceit, decency and good triumphing over evil. It is quite captivating . . . and just as you sit on the end of your seat expecting all the loose ends to be tied into a neat little bow, Archer drops a bombshell in the last paragraph of the last chapter . . . If I was head of drama at the BBC I'd start planning the first season now'
Jerry Hayes, *Spectator*

Praise for Jeffrey Archer's novels

'If there was a Nobel prize for storytelling, Archer would win'
Daily Telegraph

'Probably the greatest storyteller of our age'   *Mail on Sunday*

'The man's a genius . . . the strength and excitement of the idea carries all before it'
Evening Standard

'A storyteller in the class of Alexandre Dumas'
Washington Post

'Archer has a gift for storytelling that can only be described as genius'
Daily Telegraph

'Back in top form . . . Archer's imagination at its most sublime . . . an entertaining, pacey page-turner'   *Sunday Times*

'Few are more famous than Archer for keeping the pages turning . . . an extravagant romp – possibly his best' *The Times*

MIGHTIER THAN THE SWORD

JEFFREY ARCHER, whose novels and short stories include *Kane and Abel*, *A Prisoner of Birth* and *Cat O' Nine Tales*, has topped the bestseller lists around the world, with sales of over 270 million copies.

He is the only author ever to have been a number one bestseller in fiction (eighteen times), short stories (four times) and non-fiction (*The Prison Diaries*).

The author is married to Dame Mary Archer, and they have two sons and two grandsons.

www.jeffreyarcher.com

Facebook.com/JeffreyArcherAuthor

@Jeffrey_Archer

ALSO BY JEFFREY ARCHER

JEFFREY ARCHER

THE CLIFTON CHRONICLES
VOLUME FIVE

MIGHTIER THAN THE SWORD

PAN BOOKS

First published 2015 by Macmillan

This edition published 2015 by Pan Books
an imprint of Pan Macmillan
20 New Wharf Road, London N1 9RR
Associated companies throughout the world
www.panmacmillan.com

ISBN 978-1-4472-8798-8

A CIP catalogue record for this book is available from the British Library.

Typeset by Ellipsis Digital Limited, Glasgow
Printed and bound by CPI Group (UK) Ltd, Croydon, CR0 4YY

Visit **www.panmacmillan.com** to read more about all our books
and to buy them. You will also find features, author interviews and
news of any author events, and you can sign up for e-newsletters
so that you're always first to hear about our new releases.

TO

GWYNETH

My thanks for their invaluable advice and research to:

Simon Bainbridge, Alan Gard, Professor
Ken Howard RA, Alison Prince, Catherine Richards,
Mari Roberts, Dr Nick Robins and Susan Watt.

And to Simon Sebag Montefiore, author of
Stalin: The Court of the Red Tsar and *Young Stalin*,
for his advice and scholarship.

THE BARRINGTONS

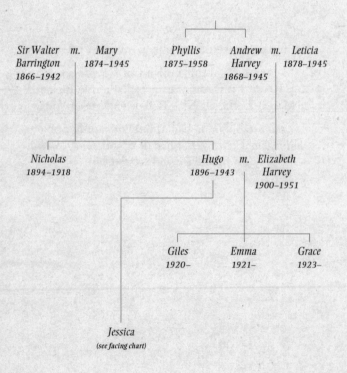

Sir Walter Barrington 1866–1942   m.   Mary 1874–1945   Phyllis 1875–1958   Andrew Harvey 1868–1945   m.   Leticia 1878–1945

Nicholas 1894–1918   Hugo 1896–1943   m.   Elizabeth Harvey 1900–1951

Giles 1920–   Emma 1921–   Grace 1923–

Jessica
(see facing chart)

THE CLIFTONS

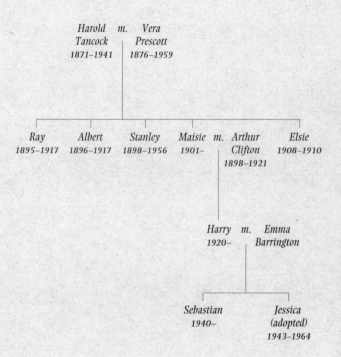

Harold Tancock (1871–1941) m. Vera Prescott (1876–1959)

Ray 1895–1917
Albert 1896–1917
Stanley 1898–1956
Maisie 1901– m. Arthur Clifton 1898–1921
Elsie 1908–1910

Harry 1920– m. Emma Barrington

Sebastian 1940–
Jessica (adopted) 1943–1964

Beneath the rule of men entirely great
The pen is mightier than the sword

EDWARD BULWER-LYTTON 1803–1873

PROLOGUE

Brendan didn't knock on the cabin door, just turned the handle and slipped inside, looking back as he did so to be sure no one had seen him. He didn't want to have to explain what a young man from cabin class was doing in an elderly peer's room at that time of night. Not that anyone would have commented.

'Are we likely to be interrupted?' asked Brendan once he had closed the door.

'No one will disturb us before seven tomorrow morning, and by then there will be nothing left to disturb.'

'Good,' said Brendan. He dropped on his knees, unlocked the large trunk, pulled open its lid and studied the complex piece of machinery that had taken him over a month to construct. He spent the next half hour checking that there were no loose wires, that every dial was at its correct setting, and that the clock started at the flick of a switch. Not until he was satisfied that everything was in perfect working order did he get back off his knees.

'It's ready,' he said. 'When do you want it activated?'

1

'Three a.m. And I'll need thirty minutes to remove all this,' the elderly peer added, touching his double chin, 'if I'm to have enough time to get to my other cabin.'

Brendan returned to the trunk and set the timer for three o'clock. 'All you have to do is flick the switch just before you leave, and double-check that the second hand is moving, then you'll have thirty minutes.'

'So what can go wrong?'

'If the lilies are still in Mrs Clifton's cabin, nothing. No one on this corridor, and probably no one on the deck below, can hope to survive. There's six pounds of dynamite embedded in the soil beneath those flowers, far more than we need, but at least that way we can be sure of collecting our money.'

'Have you got my key?'

'Yes,' said Brendan. 'Cabin 706. You'll find your new passport and ticket under the pillow.'

'Anything else I ought to be worrying about?'

'No. Just make sure the second hand is moving before you leave.'

Doherty smiled. 'See you back in Belfast.'

—◦—

Harry unlocked the cabin door and stood aside to allow Emma to enter first.

She bent down to smell the lilies the Queen Mother had sent to celebrate the launch of MV *Buckingham*. 'I'm exhausted,' she said, standing up. 'I don't know how the Queen Mother manages it day in and day out.'

'It's what she does, and she's good at it, but I bet she'd be exhausted if she tried a few days of being chairman of Barrington's.'

'I'd still rather have my job than hers,' said Emma as

she stepped out of her dress, and hung it up in the wardrobe before disappearing into the bathroom.

Harry read the card from HRH the Queen Mother once again. Such a personal message. Emma had already decided to put the vase in her office when they got back to Bristol, and to fill it with lilies every Monday morning. Harry smiled. And why not?

When Emma came out of the bathroom, Harry took her place and closed the door behind him. She slipped off her dressing gown and climbed into bed, far too tired even to consider reading a few pages of *The Spy Who Came In From The Cold*, by a new author Harry had recommended. She switched off the light by the side of her bed and said, 'Goodnight, darling,' even though she knew Harry couldn't hear her.

By the time Harry came out of the bathroom, she was sound asleep. He tucked her in as if she were a child, kissed her on the forehead and whispered, 'Goodnight, my darling,' then climbed into his bed, amused by her gentle purr. He would never have dreamed of suggesting that she snored.

He lay awake, so proud of her. The launch of the new liner couldn't have gone better. He turned on his side, assuming he'd drift off within moments but, although his eyes were leaden and he felt exhausted, he couldn't get to sleep. Something wasn't right.

―◇―

Another man, now safely back in cabin class, was also wide awake. Although it was three in the morning and his job was done, he wasn't trying to sleep. He was just about to go to work.

Always the same anxieties whenever you have to wait.

Had you left any clues that would lead straight to you? Had you made any mistakes that would cause the operation to end in failure and make you a laughing stock back home? He wouldn't relax until he was on a lifeboat and, better still, on another ship heading towards another port.

Five minutes and fourteen seconds . . .

He knew his compatriots, soldiers in the same cause, would be just as nervous as he was.

The waiting was always the worst part, out of your control, no longer anything you could do.

Four minutes and eleven seconds . . .

Worse than a football match when you're one–nil up but you know the other side are stronger and well capable of scoring in injury time. He recalled his area commander's instructions: when the alarm goes off, be sure you're among the first on deck, and the first in the lifeboats, because by this time tomorrow, they'll be searching for anyone under the age of thirty-five with an Irish accent, so keep your mouths shut, boys.

Three minutes and forty seconds . . . thirty-nine . . .

He stared at the cabin door and imagined the worst that could possibly happen. The bomb wouldn't go off, the door would burst open and a dozen police thugs, possibly more, would come charging in, batons flailing in every direction, not caring how many times they hit him. But all he could hear was the rhythmical pounding of the engine as the *Buckingham* continued its sedate passage across the Atlantic on its way to New York. A city it would never reach.

Two minutes and thirty-four seconds . . . thirty-three . . .

He began to imagine what it would be like once he was back on the Falls Road. Young lads in short trousers would look up in awe as he passed them on the street, their only ambition to be like him when they grew up. The hero who had blown up the *Buckingham* only a few weeks after it had been named by the Queen Mother. No mention of innocent lives lost; there are no innocent lives when you believe in a cause. In fact, he'd never meet any of the passengers in the cabins on the upper decks. He would read all about them in tomorrow's papers, and if he'd done his job properly there would be no mention of his name.

One minute and twenty-two seconds . . . twenty-one . . .

What could possibly go wrong now? Would the device, constructed in an upstairs bedroom on the Dungannon estate, let him down at the last minute? Was he about to suffer the silence of failure?

Sixty seconds . . .

He began to whisper each number.

'Fifty-nine, fifty-eight, fifty-seven, fifty-six . . .'

Had the drunken man slumped in the chair in the lounge been waiting for him all the time? Were they now on the way to his cabin?

'Forty-nine, forty-eight, forty-seven, forty-six . . .'

Had the lilies been replaced, thrown out, taken away? Perhaps Mrs Clifton was allergic to pollen?

'Thirty-nine, thirty-eight, thirty-seven, thirty-six . . .'

Had they unlocked his lordship's room and found the open trunk?

'Twenty-nine, twenty-eight, twenty-seven, twenty-six . . .'

Were they already searching the ship for the man who'd slipped out of the toilet in the first-class lounge?

'Nineteen, eighteen, seventeen, sixteen . . .'

Had they . . . he clung to the edge of the bunk, closed his eyes and began counting out loud.

'Nine, eight, seven, six, five, four, three, two, one . . .'

He stopped counting and opened his eyes. Nothing. Just the eerie silence that always follows failure. He bowed his head and prayed to a God he did not believe in, and immediately there followed an explosion of such ferocity that he was thrown against the cabin wall like a leaf in a storm. He staggered to his feet and smiled when he heard the screaming. He could only wonder how many passengers on the upper deck could possibly have survived.

HARRY AND EMMA

1964–1965

1

'HRH,' MUMBLED HARRY as he came out of a drowsy half-sleep. He sat up with a start and switched on his bedside light, then slipped out of bed and walked quickly across to the vase of lilies. He read the message from the Queen Mother for a second time. *Thank you for a memorable day in Bristol. I do hope my second home has a successful maiden voyage.* It was signed, *HRH Queen Elizabeth the Queen Mother*.

'Such a simple mistake,' said Harry. 'How could I have missed it?' He grabbed his dressing gown and switched on the cabin lights.

'Is it time to get up already?' enquired a sleepy voice.

'Yes it is,' said Harry. 'We've got a problem.'

Emma squinted at her bedside clock. 'But it's only just gone three,' she protested, looking across at her husband, who was still staring intently at the lilies. 'So what's the problem?'

'HRH isn't the Queen Mother's title.'

'Everyone knows that,' said Emma, still half asleep.

'Everyone except the person who sent these flowers. Why didn't they know that the correct way to address the Queen Mother is as Her Majesty, not Her Royal Highness? That's how you address a princess.'

Emma reluctantly got out of bed, padded across to join her husband, and studied the card for herself.

'Ask the captain to join us immediately,' said Harry. 'We need to find out what's in that vase,' he added, before falling to his knees.

'It's probably only water,' said Emma, reaching out a hand.

Harry grabbed her wrist. 'Look more closely, my darling. The vase is far too big for something as delicate as a dozen lilies. Call the captain,' he repeated, with more urgency this time.

'But the florist could just have made a mistake.'

'Let's hope so,' Harry said as he began to walk towards the door. 'But it's not a risk we can afford to take.'

'Where are you going?' asked Emma as she picked up the phone.

'To wake Giles. He has more experience with explosives than I do. He spent two years of his life planting them at the feet of advancing Germans.'

When Harry stepped into the corridor he was distracted by the sight of an elderly man disappearing in the direction of the grand staircase. He was moving far too quickly for an old man, Harry thought. He knocked firmly on Giles's cabin door, but it took a second demanding bang with his clenched fist before a sleepy voice said, 'Who's that?'

'Harry.'

The urgency in his voice caused Giles to jump out of bed and open the door immediately. 'What's the problem?'

'Come with me,' said Harry without explanation.

Giles pulled on his dressing gown and followed his brother-in-law down the corridor and into the stateroom.

'Good morning, sis,' he said to Emma, as Harry handed him the card and said, 'HRH.'

'Got it,' said Giles after studying the card. 'The Queen Mother couldn't have sent the flowers. But if she didn't, then who did?' He bent down and took a closer look at the vase. 'Whoever it was could have packed an awful lot of Semtex in there.'

'Or a couple of pints of water,' said Emma. 'Are you sure you're not both worrying about nothing?'

'If it's water, why are the flowers already wilting?' asked Giles as Captain Turnbull knocked on the door before walking into the cabin.

'You asked to see me, chairman?'

Emma began to explain why her husband and her brother were both on their knees.

'There are four SAS officers on board,' said the captain, interrupting the chairman. 'One of them ought to be able to answer any questions Mr Clifton might have.'

'I presume it's no coincidence that they're on board,' said Giles. 'I can't believe they all decided to take a holiday in New York at the same time.'

'They're on board at the request of the cabinet secretary,' replied the captain. 'But Sir Alan Redmayne assured me it was just a precautionary measure.'

'As usual, that man knows something we don't,' said Harry.

'Then perhaps it's time to find out what it is.'

The captain stepped out of the cabin and made his way quickly down the corridor, stopping only when he reached cabin 119. Colonel Scott-Hopkins responded to the knock on the door far more quickly than Giles had done a few minutes earlier.

'Do you have a bomb-disposal expert in your team?'

'Sergeant Roberts. He was with the bomb squad in Palestine.'

'I need him now, in the chairman's stateroom.'

The colonel wasted no time asking why. He ran along the corridor and out on to the grand staircase to find Captain Hartley charging towards him.

'I've just spotted Liam Doherty coming out of the lavatory in the first-class lounge.'

'Are you sure?'

'Yes. He went in as a peer of the realm, and came out twenty minutes later as Liam Doherty. He then headed down to cabin class.'

'That may explain everything,' said Scott-Hopkins as he continued down the staircase with Hartley only a pace behind. 'What's Roberts's cabin number?' he asked on the run.

'Seven four two,' said Hartley as they hurdled across the red chain on to the narrower staircase. They didn't stop until they reached deck seven, where Corporal Crann stepped out of the shadows.

'Has Doherty passed you within the last few minutes?'

'Damn,' said Crann. 'I knew I'd seen that bastard swaggering up the Falls Road. He went into seven zero six.'

'Hartley,' said the colonel as he charged on down the corridor, 'you and Crann keep an eye on Doherty. Make sure he doesn't leave his cabin. If he does, arrest him.' The colonel banged on the door of cabin 742. Sergeant Roberts didn't need a second knock. He opened the door within seconds, and greeted Colonel Scott-Hopkins with 'Good morning, sir,' as if his commanding officer regularly woke him in the middle of the night, dressed in his pyjamas.

'Grab your tool kit, Roberts, and follow me. We haven't a moment to waste,' said the colonel, once again on the move.

It took Roberts three flights of stairs before he caught up with his commanding officer. By the time they reached the state-room corridor, Roberts knew which of his particular skills the colonel required. He dashed into the chairman's cabin, and peered closely at the vase for a moment before slowly circling it.

'If it's a bomb,' he said finally, 'it's a big one. I can't begin to guess the number of lives that will be lost if we don't defuse the bugger.'

'But can you do it?' asked the captain, sounding remarkably calm. 'Because if you can't, my first responsibility is for the lives of my passengers. I don't need this trip to be compared with another disastrous maiden voyage.'

'I can't do a damn thing unless I can get my hands on the control panel. It has to be somewhere else on the ship,' said Roberts, 'probably quite near by.'

'In his lordship's cabin would be my bet,' said the colonel, 'because we now know that it was occupied by an IRA bomber called Liam Doherty.'

'Does anyone know which cabin he was in?' asked the captain.

'Number three,' said Harry, recalling the old man who had been moving a little too quickly. 'Just along the corridor.'

The captain and the sergeant ran out of the room and into the corridor, followed by Scott-Hopkins, Harry and Giles. The captain opened the cabin door with his pass key and stood aside to let Roberts in. The sergeant walked quickly across to a large trunk in the middle of the room. He tentatively raised the lid and peered inside.

'Christ, it's due to detonate in eight minutes and thirty-nine seconds.'

'Can't you just disconnect one of those?' asked Captain Turnbull, pointing to a myriad different coloured wires.

'Yes, but which one,' said Roberts, not looking up at the captain as he cautiously separated the red, black, blue and yellow wires. 'I've worked on this type of device many times before. It's always a one-in-four chance, and that's not a risk I'm willing to take. I might consider it if I were on my own in the middle of a desert,' he added, 'but not on a ship in the middle of the ocean with hundreds of lives at risk.'

'Then let's drag Doherty up here post haste,' suggested Captain Turnbull. 'He'll know which wire to cut.'

'I doubt it,' said Roberts, 'because I suspect Doherty isn't the bomber. They'll have a sparks on board to do that job, and God knows where he is.'

'We're running out of time,' the colonel reminded them, as he stared at the second hand's relentless progress. 'Seven minutes, three, two, one . . .'

'So, Roberts, what do you advise?' asked the captain calmly.

'You're not going to like this, sir, but there's only one thing we can do given the circumstances. And even that's one hell of a risk, remembering we're down to less than seven minutes.'

'Then spit it out, man,' rapped the colonel.

'Pick the fucking thing up, throw it overboard and pray.'

Harry and Giles ran back to the chairman's suite and took up positions on either side of the vase. There were several questions that Emma, who was now dressed, wanted to ask, but like any sensible chairman she knew when to remain silent.

'Lift it gently,' said Roberts. 'Treat it like a bowl full of boiling water.'

Like two weightlifters, Harry and Giles crouched down and slowly raised the heavy vase from the table until they were both standing upright. Once they were confident they had it firmly in their grasp they moved sideways across the cabin towards the open door. Scott-Hopkins and Roberts quickly removed any obstacles in their path.

'Follow me,' said the captain, as the two men stepped into the corridor and edged their way slowly towards the grand staircase. Harry couldn't believe how heavy the vase was. Then he remembered the giant of a man who'd carried it into the cabin. No wonder he hadn't hung around for a tip. He was probably on his way back to Belfast by now, or sitting by a radio somewhere waiting to hear the fate of the *Buckingham*, and how many passengers had lost their lives.

Once they reached the bottom of the grand staircase, Harry began to count out loud as the two of them mounted each step. Sixteen steps later, he stopped to catch his breath, while the captain and the colonel held open the swing doors that led out on to the sun deck, Emma's pride and joy.

'We need to go as far aft as possible,' said the captain. 'That will give us a better chance of avoiding any damage to the hull.' Harry didn't look convinced. 'Don't worry, it's not too far now.'

How far is not too far, wondered Harry, who would happily have dumped the vase straight over the side. But he said nothing as they progressed inch by inch towards the stern.

'I know just how you feel,' said Giles, reading his brother-in-law's thoughts.

They continued their snail-like progress past the swimming pool, the deck tennis court and the sun loungers, neatly laid out in readiness for the sleeping guests to appear later that morning. Harry tried not to think how much time they had left before . . .

'Two minutes,' said Sergeant Roberts unhelpfully, checking his watch.

Out of the corner of his eye, Harry could see the rail at the stern of the ship. It was only a few paces away, but, like conquering Everest, he knew the last few feet were going to be the slowest.

'Fifty seconds,' said Roberts as they came to a halt at the waist-high rail.

'Do you remember when we threw Fisher into the river at the end of term?' said Giles.

'Could I ever forget?'

'So on the count of three, let's throw him into the ocean and be rid of the bastard once and for all,' said Giles.

'One—' both men swung their arms back, but only managed a few inches, 'two—' perhaps a couple more, 'three—' as far as they could get, and then, with all the strength left in their bodies, they hurled the vase up into the air and over the back rail. As it came down, Harry was convinced it would land on the deck, or at best hit the rail, but it cleared it by a few inches, and landed in the sea with a faint splash. Giles raised his arms in triumph, and shouted 'Hallelujah!'

Seconds later, the bomb exploded, hurling them both back across the deck.

2

KEVIN RAFFERTY had switched on the 'For Hire' sign the moment he saw Martinez step out of his house on Eaton Square. His orders couldn't have been clearer. If the client attempted to make a run for it, he was to assume he had no intention of making the second payment owed for the bombing of the *Buckingham*, and should be punished accordingly.

The original order had been sanctioned by the area commander of the IRA in Belfast. The only modification the area commander had agreed to was that Kevin could select which of Don Pedro Martinez's two sons should be eliminated. However, as both Diego and Luis had already fled to Argentina, and clearly had no intention of returning to England, Don Pedro himself was the only candidate available for the chauffeur's particular version of Russian roulette.

'Heathrow,' said Martinez as he climbed into the taxi. Rafferty drove out of Eaton Square and headed down Sloane Street in the direction of Chelsea Bridge, ignoring the noisy protests coming from behind him. At four in the morning, with rain still pelting down, he only passed a dozen cars before he crossed the bridge. A few minutes later he pulled up outside a deserted warehouse in Lambeth. Once he was certain there was no one around, he jumped out of the taxi, quickly undid the rusty padlock on the building's outer door and drove inside. He swung the cab round, ready for a fast getaway once the job had been completed.

Rafferty bolted the door and switched on the naked, dust-covered light bulb that hung from a beam in the centre of the room. He removed a gun from an inside pocket before returning to the taxi. Although he was half Martinez's age, and twice as fit as he had ever been, he couldn't afford to take any risks. When a man thinks he's about to die, the adrenalin begins to pump and he can become super-human in a final effort to survive. Besides, Rafferty suspected this wasn't the first time Martinez had faced the possibility of death. But this time it was no longer going to be simply a possibility.

He opened the back door of the taxi and waved the gun at Martinez to indicate that he should get out.

'This is the money I was bringing to you,' Martinez insisted, holding up the bag.

'Hoping to catch me at Heathrow, were you?' If it was the full amount, Rafferty knew he would have no choice but to spare his life. 'Two hundred and fifty thousand pounds?'

'No, but there's over twenty-three thousand. Just a down payment, you understand. The rest is back at the house, so if we head back—'

The chauffeur knew that the house in Eaton Square, along with Martinez's other assets, had been repossessed by the bank. Martinez had clearly hoped to make it to the airport before the IRA discovered he had no intention of fulfilling his side of the bargain.

Rafferty grabbed the bag and threw it on the back seat of the taxi. He'd decided to make Martinez's death somewhat more protracted than originally planned. After all, he had nothing else to do for the next hour.

He waved the gun in the direction of a wooden chair that had been placed directly below the light bulb. It was already splattered with dried blood from previous executions. He pushed his victim down with considerable force, and before Don Pedro had a chance to react, he had tied his arms behind his back, but then he'd carried out this particular exercise several times before. Finally he tied Martinez's legs together, then stood back to admire his handiwork.

All Rafferty had to decide now was how long the victim would be allowed to live. His only constraint being, he had to be at Heathrow in time to catch the early morning flight to Belfast. He checked his watch. He always enjoyed seeing that look on the victim's face when they believed there still might be a chance of survival.

He returned to the taxi, unzipped Martinez's bag and counted the bundles of crisp five-pound notes. At least he'd told the truth about that, even if he was more than £226,000 short. He zipped the bag back up and locked it in the boot. After all, Martinez would no longer have any use for it.

The area commander's orders were clear: once the job had been completed he was to leave the body in the warehouse and another operative would deal with its disposal. The only thing required of Rafferty was to make a phone call and deliver the message, 'Package ready for collection.' After that, he was to drive to the airport and leave the taxi, and the money, on the top level of the long-term car park. Another operative would be responsible for collecting it and distributing the cash.

Rafferty returned to Don Pedro, whose eyes had never left him. If the chauffeur had been given the choice, he would have shot him in the stomach, then waited a few minutes until the screaming died down, before firing a second bullet into his groin. More screaming, probably louder, until he finally forced the gun into his mouth. He would stare into his victim's eyes for several seconds and then, without warning, pull the trigger. But that would have meant three shots. One might go unnoticed, but three would undoubtedly attract attention in the middle of the night. So he would obey the area commander's orders. One shot, and no screaming.

The chauffeur smiled at Don Pedro, who looked up hopefully, until he saw the gun heading towards his mouth.

'Open up,' said Rafferty, like a friendly dentist coaxing a reluctant child. One common factor among all his victims was the chattering teeth.

Martinez resisted, and swallowed one of his front teeth in the unequal struggle. Sweat began to pour down the fleshy folds of skin on his face. He was only made to wait a few more seconds before the trigger was pulled, but all he heard was the click of the hammer.

Some fainted, some just stared in disbelief, while others were violently sick when they realized they were still alive. Rafferty hated the ones who fainted. It meant he had to wait for them to fully recover before he could begin the whole process again. But Martinez obligingly remained wide awake.

When Rafferty extracted the gun, his idea of a blow job, the victims often smiled, imagining the worst was over. But as he spun the cylinder again, Don Pedro knew he was going to die. It was just a matter of when. Where and how had already been decided.

It always disappointed Rafferty when he succeeded with the first shot. His personal record was nine, but the average was around four or five. Not that he gave a damn about statistics. He thrust the barrel back into Martinez's mouth, and took a step back. After all, he didn't want to be covered in blood. The Argentinian was foolish enough to resist again, and lost another tooth for his trouble, a gold one. Rafferty pocketed it before he squeezed the trigger a second time, but was not rewarded with anything but another click. He pulled out the barrel in the hope of removing another tooth, well, half a tooth.

'Third time lucky,' said Rafferty as he thrust the muzzle back into Martinez's mouth and pulled the trigger. Another failure. The chauffeur was becoming impatient and was now hoping that his morning's work would be completed on the fourth attempt. He spun the cylinder a little more enthusiastically this time, but when he looked up, Martinez had fainted. Such a disappointment. He liked his victims to be wide awake when the bullet entered their brain. Although they only lived for another second, it was an experience he relished. He grabbed Martinez's hair, forced open his mouth and pushed the barrel back inside. He was about the pull the trigger a fourth time, when the telephone in the corner of the room began to ring. The insistent metallic echo in the cold night air took Rafferty by surprise. He had never known the phone to ring before. In the past, he had used it only to dial a number and deliver a four-word message.

He reluctantly withdrew the muzzle of the gun from

Martinez's mouth, walked across to the phone and picked it up. He didn't speak, just listened.

'The mission has been aborted,' said a voice with a clipped, educated accent. 'You won't need to collect the second payment.'

A click, followed by a burr.

Rafferty replaced the receiver. Perhaps he would spin the cylinder one more time, and if he succeeded, report back that Martinez was already dead by the time the phone had rung. He'd only ever lied to the area commander once, and there was a finger missing from his left hand to prove it. He told anyone who asked that it had been chopped off by a British officer during an interrogation, which few on either side believed.

He reluctantly returned the gun to his pocket and walked slowly back towards Martinez, who was slumped in the chair, his head between his legs. He bent down and untied the rope around his wrists and ankles. Martinez collapsed on to the floor in a heap. The chauffeur yanked him up by the hair, threw him over his shoulder as if he were a sack of potatoes and dumped him in the back of the taxi. For a moment, he had rather hoped he might resist, and then . . . but no such luck.

He drove out of the warehouse, locked the door and set off towards Heathrow, to join several other taxi drivers that morning.

They were a couple of miles from the airport when Martinez re-entered this world, and not the next. The chauffeur watched in the rear-view mirror as his passenger began to come round. Martinez blinked several times before staring out of the window to see rows of suburban homes rushing by. As the realization began to sink in, he leant forward and was sick all over the back seat. Rafferty's colleague wouldn't be pleased.

Don Pedro eventually managed to force his limp body upright. He steadied himself by clinging on to the edge of the seat with both hands and stared at his would-be executioner. What had caused him to change his mind? Perhaps he hadn't. Perhaps only the venue had changed. Don Pedro eased his way forward, hoping to be given just one chance to escape, but he was painfully aware that Rafferty's suspicious eyes returned to the rear-view mirror every few seconds.

Rafferty turned off the main road and followed the signs for the long-term car park. He drove up to the top level and parked in the far corner. He stepped out of the car, unlocked the boot and unzipped the travel bag, pleased again by the sight of the neat rows of crisp five-pound notes. He would have liked to take the cash home for the cause, but he couldn't risk being caught with that amount of money, now there were so many extra security guards observing every flight to Belfast.

He removed an Argentine passport from the bag, along with a first-class, one-way ticket to Buenos Aires and ten pounds in cash, then dropped his gun in the bag; something else he couldn't afford to be caught with. He locked the boot, opened the driver's door and placed the keys and the parking ticket under the seat for a colleague to collect later that morning. Then he opened the rear door and stood aside to allow Martinez to step out, but he didn't move. Was he going to make a run for it? Not if he valued his life. After all, he didn't know that the chauffeur no longer had a gun.

Rafferty grabbed Martinez firmly by the elbow, pulled him out of the car and marched him towards the nearest exit. Two men passed them on the staircase as they made their way down to the ground floor. Rafferty didn't given them a second look.

Neither man spoke on the long walk to the terminal building. When they reached the concourse, Rafferty handed Martinez his passport, his ticket and the two five-pound notes.

'And the rest?' snarled Don Pedro. 'Because your colleagues obviously failed to sink the *Buckingham*.'

'Consider yourself lucky to be alive,' said Rafferty, then turned quickly and disappeared into the crowd.

For a moment, Don Pedro thought about going back to the taxi and retrieving his money, but only for a moment. Instead, he reluctantly headed towards the check-in desk for South America and handed his ticket to the woman seated behind the counter.

'Good morning, Mr Martinez,' she said. 'I hope you've had a pleasant stay in England.'

3

'HOW DID YOU get that black eye, Dad?' demanded Sebastian, when he joined his family for breakfast in the grill room of the *Buckingham* later that morning.

'Your mother hit me when I dared to suggest she snored,' Harry replied.

'I don't snore,' said Emma, as she buttered another piece of toast.

'How can you possibly know if you snore when you're asleep?' said Harry.

'And what about you, Uncle Giles? Did my mother break your arm when you also suggested she snored?' asked Seb.

'I don't snore!' repeated Emma.

'Seb,' said Samantha firmly, 'you should never ask anyone a question you know they won't want to answer.'

'Spoken like the daughter of a diplomat,' said Giles, smiling across the table at Seb's girlfriend.

'Spoken like a politician who doesn't want to answer my question,' said Seb. 'But I'm determined to find out—'

'Good morning, this is your captain speaking,' announced a crackling voice over the tannoy. 'We are currently sailing at twenty-two knots. The temperature is sixty-nine degrees Fahrenheit, and we're not expecting any change in the weather during the next twenty-four hours. I hope you have a pleasant day, and be sure to take advantage of all the wonderful facilities the *Buckingham* has to offer, particularly the sun loungers and the swimming pool on the upper deck that are unique to this ship.' There was a long pause before he continued. 'Some passengers have asked me about a loud noise that woke them in the middle of the night. It seems that at around three o'clock this morning, the Home Fleet were carrying out night-time exercises in the Atlantic, and although they were several nautical miles away, on a clear night they would have sounded considerably closer. I do apologize to anyone who was woken by the sound of gunfire, but having served with the Royal Navy during the war I am aware that night exercises have to be carried out. However, I can assure passengers that at no time were we in any danger. Thank you, and enjoy the rest of the day.'

It sounded to Sebastian as if the captain had been reading from a prepared script and, looking across the table at his mother, he wasn't in any doubt who had written it. 'I wish I was a member of the board,' he said.

'Why?' asked Emma.

'Because then,' he said, looking directly at her, 'I might find out what really happened last night.'

-◄◦►-

The ten men remained standing until Emma had taken her place at the head of the table, an unfamiliar table, but then the ballroom of the MV *Buckingham* had not been built for emergency board meetings.

When she looked around at her colleagues, none of them was smiling. Most of them had faced crises in their lives, but nothing on this scale. Even Admiral Summers's lips were pursed. Emma opened the blue leather folder in front of her, a gift from Harry when she'd first been appointed chairman. It was he, she reflected, who had alerted her to the crisis, and then dealt with it.

'There is no need to tell you that everything we discuss today must remain strictly confidential, because it wouldn't be an exaggeration to suggest that the future of the Barrington shipping line, not to mention the safety of everyone on board, is at stake,' she said.

Emma glanced down at an agenda that had been prepared by Philip Webster, the company secretary, the day before they set sail from Avonmouth. It was already out of date. There was just one item on the revised agenda, and it would certainly be the only subject discussed that day.

'I'll begin,' said Emma, 'by reporting, off the record, everything that took place in the early hours of this morning, and then we must decide what course of action to take. I was woken by my husband just after three . . .'

Twenty minutes later, Emma double-checked her notes. She felt she had covered everything in the past, but accepted she had no way of predicting the future.

'Have we got away with it?' the admiral asked, once Emma had called for questions.

'Most of the passengers have accepted the captain's explanation without question.' She turned a page of her file. 'However, we've had complaints from thirty-four passengers so far. All but one of them have accepted a free voyage on the *Buckingham* at some time in the future, as compensation.'

'And you can be certain there will be a whole lot more,' said Bob Bingham, his usual north country bluntness cutting through the outwardly calm demeanour of the older board members.

'What makes you say that?' asked Emma.

'Once the other passengers discover that all they have to do is write a letter of complaint to get a free trip, most of them will go straight to their cabins and put pen to paper.'

'Perhaps not everyone thinks like you,' suggested the admiral.

'That's why I'm on the board,' said Bingham, not giving an inch.

'You told us, chairman, that all but one passenger was satisfied with the offer of a free trip,' said Jim Knowles.

'Yes,' said Emma. 'Unfortunately an American passenger is threatening to sue the company. He says he was out on deck during the early hours of the morning and there was no sight or sound of the Home Fleet, but he still ended up with a broken ankle.'

Suddenly, all the board members were speaking at once. Emma waited for them to settle. 'I have an appointment with Mr –' she checked her file – 'Hayden Rankin, at twelve.'

'How many other Americans are on board?' asked Bingham.

'Around a hundred. Why do you ask, Bob?'

'Let's hope that not too many of them are ambulance-chasing lawyers, otherwise we'll be facing court actions for the rest of our lives.' Nervous laughter broke out around the table. 'Just assure me, Emma, that Mr Rankin isn't a lawyer.'

'Worse,' she said. 'He's a politician. A state representative from Louisiana.'

'One worm who's happily found himself in a barrel

of fresh apples,' said Dobbs, a board member who rarely offered an opinion.

'I'm not following you, old chap,' said Clive Anscott, from the other side of the table.

'A local politician who probably thinks he's spotted an opportunity to make a name for himself on the national stage.'

'That's all we need,' said Knowles.

The board remained silent for some time, until Bob Bingham said matter-of-factly, 'We're going to have to kill him off. The only question is who will pull the trigger.'

'It will have to be me,' said Giles, 'as I'm the only other worm in the barrel.' Dobbs looked suitably embarrassed. 'I'll try and bump into him before he has his meeting with you, chairman, and see if I can sort something out. Let's hope he's a Democrat.'

'Thank you, Giles,' said Emma, who still hadn't got used to her brother addressing her as chairman.

'How much damage did the ship suffer in the explosion?' asked Peter Maynard, who hadn't spoken until then.

All eyes turned to the other end of the table, where Captain Turnbull was seated.

'Not as much as I originally feared,' said the captain as he rose from his place. 'One of the four main propellers has been damaged by the blast, and I won't be able to replace it until we return to Avonmouth. And there was some damage to the hull, but it's fairly superficial.'

'Will it slow us down?' asked Michael Carrick.

'Not enough for anyone to notice we're covering twenty-two knots rather than twenty-four. The other three propellers remain in good working order and as I had always planned to arrive in New York in the early hours of the fourth, only the most observant passenger would realize we're a few hours behind schedule.'

'I bet Representative Rankin will notice,' said Knowles unhelpfully. 'And how have you explained the damage to the crew?'

'I haven't. They're not paid to ask questions.'

'But what about the return journey to Avonmouth?' asked Dobbs. 'Can we hope to make it back on time?'

'Our engineers will be working flat out on the damaged stern during the thirty-six hours we're docked in New York, so by the time we sail, we should be ship-shape and Bristol fashion.'

'Good show,' said the admiral.

'But that could be the least of our problems,' said Anscott. 'Don't forget we have an IRA cell on board, and heaven knows what else they have planned for the rest of the voyage.'

'Three of them have already been arrested,' said the captain. 'They've been quite literally clapped in irons and will be handed over to the authorities the moment we arrive in New York.'

'But isn't it possible there could be more IRA men on board?' asked the admiral.

'According to Colonel Scott-Hopkins, an IRA cell usually comprises four or five operatives. So, yes, it's possible that there are a couple more on board, but they're likely to be keeping a very low profile now that three of their colleagues have been arrested. Their mission has clearly failed, which isn't something they'll want to remind everyone back in Belfast about. And I can confirm that the man who delivered the flowers to the chairman's cabin is no longer on board – he must have disembarked before we set sail. I suspect that if there are any others, they won't be joining us for the return voyage.'

'I can think of something just as dangerous as Representative Rankin, and even the IRA,' said Giles. Like the seasoned politician he was, the member for Bristol Docklands had captured the attention of the House.

'Who or what do you have in mind?' asked Emma, looking across at her brother.

'The fourth estate. Don't forget you invited journalists to join us on this trip in the hope of getting some good copy. Now they've got an exclusive.'

'True, but no one outside this room knows exactly what happened last night, and in any case, only three journalists accepted our invitation – the *Telegraph*, the *Mail* and the *Express*.'

'Three too many,' said Knowles.

'The man from the *Express* is their travel correspondent,' said Emma. 'He's rarely sober by lunchtime, so I've made sure there are always at least two bottles of Johnnie Walker and Gordon's in his cabin. The *Mail* sponsored twelve free trips on this voyage, so they're unlikely to be interested in knocking copy. But Derek Hart of the *Telegraph* has already been digging around, asking questions.'

'"Hartless", as he's known in the trade,' said Giles. 'I shall have to give him an even bigger story, to keep him occupied.'

'What could be bigger than the possible sinking of the *Buckingham* by the IRA on its maiden voyage?'

'The possible sinking of Britain by a Labour government. We're about to announce a £1.5 billion loan from the IMF in an effort to halt the slide of sterling. The editor of the *Telegraph* will happily fill several pages with that piece of news.'

'Even if he does,' said Knowles, 'with so much at stake, chairman, I think we ought to prepare ourselves for the worst possible outcome. After all, if our American politician decides to go public, or Mr Hart of the *Telegraph* stumbles across the truth, or God forbid, the IRA have a follow-up planned, this could be the *Buckingham*'s first, and last, voyage.'

There was another long silence, before Dobbs said, 'Well, we did promise our passengers this would be a holiday they would never forget.'

No one laughed.

'Mr Knowles is right,' said Emma. 'If any of those three outcomes were to materialize, no amount of free trips or bottles of gin will save us. Our share price would collapse overnight, the company's reserves would be drained, and bookings would dry up if prospective passengers thought there was the slightest chance of an IRA bomber being in the next cabin. The safety of our passengers is paramount. With that in mind, I suggest you all spend the rest of the day picking up any information you can, while reassuring the passengers that all is well. I'll be in my cabin, so if you come up with anything, you'll know where to find me.'

'Not a good idea,' said Giles firmly. Emma looked surprised. 'The chairman should be seen on the sun deck, relaxing and enjoying herself, which is far more likely to convince the passengers they have nothing to worry about.'

'Good thinking,' said the admiral.

Emma nodded. She was about to rise from her place to indicate that the meeting was over, when Philip Webster, the company secretary, mumbled, 'Any other business?'

'I don't think so,' said Emma, who was now standing.

'Just one other matter, chairman,' said Giles. Emma sat back down. 'Now that I'm a member of the government, I have no choice but to resign as a director of the company, as I'm not allowed to hold a post of profit while serving Her Majesty. I realize it sounds a bit pompous, but it's what every new minister signs up to. And in any case, I only joined the board to make sure Major Fisher didn't become chairman.'

'Thank God he's no longer on the board,' said the admiral. 'If he was, the whole world would know what had happened by now.'

'Perhaps that's why he wasn't on board in the first place,' suggested Giles.

'If that's the case, he'll keep shtum, unless of course he wants to be arrested for aiding and abetting terrorists.'

Emma shuddered, unwilling to believe that even Fisher could stoop that low. However, after Giles's experiences both at school and in the army, Emma shouldn't have been surprised that once Fisher had begun to work for Lady Virginia, they hadn't come together to assist her cause. She turned back to her brother. 'On a happier note, I'd like to place on record my thanks to Giles for serving as a director of the company at such a crucial time. However, his resignation will create two vacancies on the board, as my sister, Dr Grace Barrington, has also resigned. Perhaps you could advise me of any suitable candidates who might be considered to replace them?' she said, looking around the table.

'If I might be allowed to make a suggestion,' said the admiral. Everyone turned towards the old salt. 'Barrington's is a West Country firm with long-standing local connections. Our chairman is a Barrington, so perhaps the time has come to look to the next generation, and invite Sebastian Clifton to join the board, allowing us to continue the family tradition.'

'But he's only twenty-four!' protested Emma.

'That's not much younger than our beloved Queen when she ascended the throne,' the admiral reminded her.

'Cedric Hardcastle, who's a shrewd old buzzard, considered Sebastian good enough to be his personal assistant at Farthings Bank,' interjected Bob Bingham, winking at Emma. 'And I'm informed that he's recently been promoted to second-in-command of the bank's property division.'

'And I can tell you in confidence,' said Giles, 'that when I joined the government, I didn't hesitate to put Sebastian in charge of the family's share portfolio.'

'Then all that's left for me to do,' said the admiral, 'is propose that Sebastian Clifton be invited to join the board of Barrington's Shipping.'

'I'd be delighted to second that,' said Bingham.

'I confess that I'm embarrassed,' said Emma.

'That will be a first,' said Giles, which helped lighten the mood.

'Shall I call for a vote, chairman?' asked Webster. Emma nodded, and sat back in her chair. 'Admiral Summers has proposed,' continued the company secretary, 'and Mr Bingham has seconded, that Mr Sebastian Clifton be invited to join the board of Barrington's.' He paused for a moment before asking, 'Those in favour?' Every hand rose except Emma's and Giles's. 'Those against?' No hands were raised. The round of applause that followed made Emma feel very proud.

'I therefore declare that Mr Sebastian Clifton has

been elected as a member of the Board of Barrington's.'

'Let's pray there will be a board for Seb to join,' Emma whispered to her brother once the company secretary had declared the meeting closed.

◄O►

'I've always considered he was up there with Lincoln and Jefferson.'

A middle-aged man, dressed in an open-necked shirt and sports jacket, looked up but didn't close his book. The few strands of wispy fair hair that were still in evidence had been carefully combed in an attempt to hide his premature baldness. A walking stick was propped against his chair.

'I apologize,' said Giles. 'I didn't mean to interrupt you.'

'No problem,' said the man in an unmistakable southern drawl, but he still didn't close his book. 'In fact I'm always embarrassed,' he added, 'by how little we know of your country's history, while you seem to be so well informed about ours.'

'That's because we no longer rule half the world,' said Giles, 'and you look as if you are just about to. Mind you, I wonder if a man in a wheelchair could be elected as President in the second half of the twentieth century,' he added, glancing down at the man's book.

'I doubt it,' said the American with a sigh. 'Kennedy beat Nixon because of a TV debate. If you'd heard it on the radio, you would have concluded that Nixon won.'

'Nobody can see you sweat on the radio.'

The American raised an eyebrow. 'How come you're so well informed about American politics?'

'I'm a Member of Parliament. And you?'

'I'm a state representative from Baton Rouge.'

'And as you can't be a day over forty, I presume you have your sights on Washington.'

Rankin smiled, but revealed nothing. 'My turn to ask you a question. What's my wife's name?'

Giles knew when he was beaten. 'Rosemary,' he said.

'So now we've established that this meeting wasn't a coincidence, Sir Giles, how can I help you?'

'I need to talk to you about last night.'

'I'm not surprised, as I have no doubt you're among the handful of people on board who knows what really happened in the early hours of this morning.'

Giles looked around. Satisfied no one could overhear them, he said, 'The ship was the target of a terrorist attack, but fortunately we managed to—'

The American waved a hand dismissively. 'I don't need to know the details. Just tell me how I can help.'

'Try to convince your fellow countrymen on board that the Home Fleet were really out there. If you can manage that, I know someone who'd be eternally grateful.'

'Your sister?'

Giles nodded, no longer surprised.

'I realized there had to be a serious problem when I saw her earlier, sitting on the upper deck looking as if she didn't have a care in the world. Not the action of a confident chairman who I have a feeling isn't all that interested in sunbathing.'

'Mea culpa. But we're up against—'

'As I said, spare me the details. Like him,' he said, pointing to the photo on the cover of his book, 'I'm not interested in tomorrow's headlines. I'm in politics for the long game, so I'll do as you ask. However, Sir Giles, that means you owe me one. And you can be sure there'll come a time when I call in my marker,' he added before returning to *A Life of Roosevelt*.

◄o►

'Have we docked already?' asked Sebastian as he and Samantha joined his parents for breakfast.

'Over an hour ago,' said Emma. 'Most of the passengers have already gone ashore.'

'And as it's your first visit to New York,' said Sam as Seb sat down beside her, 'and we only have thirty-six hours before we sail back to England, we haven't a moment to waste.'

'Why will the ship only be in port for thirty-six hours?' Seb asked.

'You can only make money when you're on the move, and besides, the docking fees are horrendous.'

'Do you remember your first trip to New York, Mr Clifton?' asked Samantha.

'I most certainly do,' said Harry with feeling. 'I was arrested for a murder I didn't commit, and spent the next six months in an American prison.'

'Oh, I'm sorry,' said Samantha, recalling the story Seb had once told her. 'It was tactless of me to remind you of such a terrible experience.'

'Don't give it a second thought,' said Harry. 'Just make sure Seb isn't arrested on this visit, because I don't want that to become another family tradition.'

'Not a chance,' said Samantha. 'I've already planned visits to the Metropolitan, Central Park, Sardi's and the Frick.'

'Jessica's favourite museum,' said Emma.

'Although she never got to visit it,' said Seb.

'Not a day goes by when I don't miss her,' said Emma.

'And I only wish I had known her better,' said Sam.

'I took for granted,' said Seb, 'that I would die before my younger sister.' A long silence followed, before Seb, clearly wanting to change the subject, asked, 'So we won't be visiting any nightclubs?'

'No time for such frivolity,' said Samantha. 'In any case, my father's got us a couple of tickets for the theatre.'

'What are you going to see?' asked Emma.

'*Hello, Dolly!*'

'And that's not frivolous?' said Harry.

'Dad considers Wagner's Ring Cycle a tad too trendy,' explained Seb before asking, 'Where's Uncle Giles?'

'He was among the first to leave the ship,' said Emma, as a waiter poured her a second cup of coffee. 'Our ambassador whisked him off to the United Nations so they could go over his speech before the afternoon session.'

'Perhaps we should try and fit the UN in as well?' suggested Sam.

'I don't think so,' replied Seb. 'The last time I attended one of my uncle's speeches, he had a heart attack shortly afterwards and failed to become the leader of the Labour Party.'

'That's something you haven't mentioned before!'

'There's still a lot you don't know about our family,' Seb admitted.

'Which reminds me,' said Harry. 'I haven't had the chance to congratulate you on being elected to the board.'

'Thank you, Dad. And now that I've read the minutes of the last meeting, I can't wait' – Seb looked up to see an anxious look on his mother's face – 'to meet my fellow board members, especially the admiral.'

'A one-off,' said Emma, although she was still wondering if the next board meeting would be her last, because if the truth came out she'd be left with no choice but to resign. However, as the memory of that first morning at sea began to fade, she relaxed, and she was feeling a little more confident now that the *Buckingham* had docked in New York. She glanced out of the window. As far as she could see, there were no press hounds hovering at the bottom of the gangway, barking and baying while flashbulbs popped. Perhaps they were more interested in the result of the presidential election. But she wouldn't breathe a sigh of relief until the *Buckingham* had set sail on its return journey to Avonmouth.

'So how do you plan to spend your day, Dad?' asked Seb, breaking into his mother's reverie.

'I'm having lunch with my publisher, Harold Guinzburg. No doubt I'll find out what he has planned for my latest book, and what he thought of it.'

'Any hope of an early copy for my mom?' said Samantha. 'She's such a fan.'

'Of course,' said Harry.

'That will be nine dollars ninety-nine cents,' said Seb, holding out his hand. Samantha placed a hot boiled egg in it. 'And what about you, Mum? Any plans for painting the hull?'

'Don't encourage her,' said Harry, not laughing.

'I'll be the last off the ship and the first back on board. Although I do intend to visit my cousin Alistair and apologize for not attending Great-aunt Phyllis's funeral.'

'Seb was in hospital at the time,' Harry reminded her.

'So where are we going to start?' demanded Seb as he folded his napkin.

Sam looked out of the window to check the weather.

'We'll take a cab to Central Park and walk the loop before visiting the Met.'

'Then we'd better get going,' said Seb as he rose from the table. 'Have a good day, revered parents.'

Emma smiled as the two of them left the dining room, hand in hand. 'I wish I'd known they were sleeping together.'

'Emma, it's the second half of the twentieth century and, let's face it, we are hardly in a position to—'

'No, I wasn't moralizing,' said Emma. 'It's just that I could have sold the extra cabin.'

4

'IT WAS GOOD OF YOU to fly back at such short notice, colonel,' said Sir Alan Redmayne, as if he'd had any choice.

The SAS commander had been handed a telegram the moment he stepped off the *Buckingham* in New York. A car had whisked him to JFK, where he boarded the first flight back to London. Another car and driver were waiting for him at the bottom of the aircraft steps at Heathrow.

'The cabinet secretary thought you would want to see this morning's papers,' was all the driver said before setting off for Whitehall.

IN YOUR HEART YOU KNEW HE'D LOSE was the headline in the *Telegraph*. The colonel turned the pages slowly, but there was no mention of the *Buckingham*, or any article filed under the name of Derek Hart, because if there had been, despite Lyndon Johnson's landslide election victory over Barry Goldwater, it would surely have led the front page.

The *Buckingham* did make the centre pages of the *Daily Express*, with a glowing report from the paper's travel correspondent, extolling the pleasures of crossing the Atlantic on the latest luxury liner. The *Daily Mail* had pictures of their twelve lucky readers posing in front of the Statue of Liberty. Another twelve free tickets offered for some future date ensured that there was no reference to any inconvenience caused by the Home Fleet.

One hour later, having had no change of clothes or a chance to shave, Colonel Scott-Hopkins was sitting opposite the cabinet secretary in his office at No.10 Downing Street.

The colonel began with a detailed debrief before answering Sir Alan's questions.

'Well, at least some good came out of this,' said Sir Alan, taking a leather attaché case from under his desk and placing it on top. 'Thanks to the diligence of your SAS colleagues, we located an IRA warehouse in Battersea. We also recovered over twenty-three thousand pounds in cash from the boot of the taxi that took Martinez to Heathrow. I suspect that Kevin "four fingers" Rafferty will soon be known as "three fingers" if he can't explain to his area commander what happened to the money.'

'And Martinez? Where is he now?'

'Our ambassador in Buenos Aires assures me that he's frequenting his usual haunts. I don't think we'll be seeing him or his sons at Wimbledon or Ascot again.'

'And Doherty and his compatriots?'

'On their way back to Northern Ireland, not on a luxury liner this time, but on a Royal Navy ship. Once they dock in Belfast, they'll be transported straight to the nearest prison.'

'On what charge?'

'That hasn't been decided yet,' said Sir Alan.

'Mrs Clifton warned me that a journalist from the

Telegraph had been sniffing around, asking far too many questions.'

'Derek Hart. The damn man ignored the IMF loan story that Giles fed him, went ahead and filed his copy on the Home Fleet incident the moment he set foot in New York. However, there were so many ifs and buts in the piece it wasn't difficult to convince the editor to spike it, not least because he was far more interested in finding out how Leonid Brezhnev, an old school hard-liner, managed to replace Khrushchev in a surprise coup.'

'And how did he?' asked the colonel.

'I suggest you read tomorrow's *Telegraph*.'

'And Hart?'

'I'm told he's on his way to Johannesburg to try to get an interview with a terrorist called Nelson Mandela, which might prove difficult, as the man's been in prison for more than two years, and no other journalist has been allowed anywhere near him.'

'Does that mean my team can be stood down from protecting the Clifton family?'

'Not yet,' said Sir Alan. 'The IRA will almost certainly lose interest in the Barrington and Clifton families now Don Pedro Martinez is no longer around to pay the bills. However, I still need to convince Harry Clifton to assist me in another matter.' The colonel raised an eyebrow, but the cabinet secretary simply rose and shook hands with the SAS commanding officer. 'I'll be in touch,' was all he said.

—◆—

'Have you made up your mind?' asked Seb as they strolled past the Boathouse Café on the east side of Central Park.

'Yes,' said Samantha, letting go of his hand. Seb turned to face her and waited anxiously. 'I've already written to King's College and told them I'd like to take up their offer to do my PhD at London University.'

Seb leapt in the air with undisguised delight and screamed 'Great balls of fire!' at the top of his voice. No one gave them a second look, but then they were in New York. 'Does that mean you'll move in with me once I find a new flat? We could even choose it together,' he added before she could reply.

'Are you sure that's what you really want?' asked Samantha, quietly.

'I couldn't be surer,' said Seb, taking her in his arms. 'And as you'll be based in the Strand, while I'm working in the City, perhaps we should look for a place somewhere near, like Islington?'

'Are you sure?' Sam repeated.

'As sure as I am that Bristol City will never win the Cup.'

'Who are Bristol City?'

'We don't know each other well enough for me to burden you with their problems,' said Seb as they left the park. 'Perhaps given time, a lot of time, I'll tell you about eleven hopeless men who regularly ruin Saturday afternoons for me,' he added as they reached Fifth Avenue.

◄○►

When Harry walked into the offices of the Viking Press, a young woman he recognized was waiting in reception.

'Good morning, Mr Clifton,' said Harold Guinzburg's secretary, stepping forward to greet him. He couldn't help wondering how many authors received this sort of treatment. 'Mr Guinzburg is looking forward to seeing you.'

'Thank you, Kirsty,' said Harry. She led him through to the publisher's oak-panelled office, adorned with photographs of past and present authors: Hemingway, Shaw, Fitzgerald and Faulkner. He wondered if you had to die before your picture could be added to the Guinzburg collection.

Despite being nearly seventy, Guinzburg leapt up from behind his desk the moment Harry entered the room. Harry had to smile. Dressed in a three-piece suit and wearing a half-hunter pocket watch with a gold chain, Guinzburg looked more English than the English.

'So how's my favourite author?'

Harry laughed as they shook hands. 'And how many times a week do you greet authors with those words?' he asked as he sank down in the high, buttoned-back leather chair facing his publisher.

'A week?' said Guinzburg. 'At least three times a day, sometimes more – especially when I can't remember their names.' Harry smiled. 'However, I can prove it's true in your case, because after reading *William Warwick and the Defrocked Vicar*, I've decided the first print run will be eighty thousand copies.'

Harry opened his mouth, but didn't speak. His last William Warwick novel had sold 72,000 copies so he was well aware of the commitment his publisher was making.

'Let's hope there won't be too many returns.'

'The advance orders rather suggest that eighty thousand won't be enough. But forgive me,' Guinzburg said, 'first tell me, how is Emma? And was the maiden voyage a triumph? I couldn't find a mention of it, despite scouring the *New York Times* this morning.'

'Emma couldn't be better, and sends her love. At this moment, I wouldn't be surprised if she's buffing up the brasswork on the bridge. As for the maiden voyage, I have a feeling she'll be quite relieved there's no mention of it in the *New York Times* – although the whole experience may have given me an idea for my next novel.'

'I'm all ears.'

'Not a hope,' replied Harry. 'You'll just have to be patient, which I'm well aware is not your strongest suit.'

'Then let's hope your new responsibilities won't cut into your writing schedule. Many congratulations.'

'Thank you. Though I only allowed my name to go forward as president of English PEN for one reason.'

Guinzburg raised an eyebrow.

'I want a Russian called Anatoly Babakov to be released from prison immediately.'

'Why do you feel so strongly about Babakov?' asked Guinzburg.

'If you'd been locked up in prison for a crime you hadn't committed, Harold, believe me, you'd feel strongly. And don't forget, I was in an American jail, which frankly is a Holiday Inn compared to a gulag in Siberia.'

'I can't even remember what Babakov was meant to have done.'

'He wrote a book.'

'That's a crime in Russia?'

'It is if you decide to tell the truth about your employer, especially if your employer was Josef Stalin.'

'*Uncle Joe*, I remember,' said Guinzburg, 'but the book was never published.'

'It was published but Babakov was arrested long before a copy reached the bookshelves, and after a show trial he was sentenced to twenty years in prison, with no right of appeal.'

'Which only makes one wonder what can be in that

book to make the Soviets so determined that no one should ever get to read it.'

'I've no idea,' said Harry. 'But I do know that every copy of *Uncle Joe* was removed from the bookshelves within hours of publication. The publisher was shut down, Babakov was arrested, and he hasn't been seen since his trial. If there's a copy out there I intend to find it when I go to the international book conference in Moscow in May.'

'If you do lay your hands on a copy, I'd love to have it translated and publish it over here, because I can guarantee that not only would it be a runaway bestseller but also it would finally expose Stalin as a man every bit as evil as Hitler. Mind you, Russia's a pretty big haystack in which to be searching for that particular needle.'

'True, but I'm determined to find out what Babakov has to say. Don't forget, he was Stalin's personal interpreter for thirteen years, so few people would have had a better insight into the regime – although even he didn't anticipate how the KGB would react when he decided to publish his version of what he witnessed first-hand.'

'And now that Stalin's old allies have removed Khrushchev and are back in power, no doubt some of them have things they'd prefer to keep hidden.'

'Like the truth about Stalin's death,' said Harry.

'I've never seen you so worked up about anything,' said Guinzburg. 'But it might not be wise for you to poke a stick at the big bear. The new hardline regime there seems to have little regard for human rights, whichever country you come from.'

'What's the point of being president of PEN if I can't express my views?'

The carriage clock on the bookshelf behind Guinzburg's desk struck twelve.

'Why don't we go and have lunch at my club, and we can discuss less contentious matters, like what Sebastian's been up to.'

'I think he's about to propose to an American girl.'

'I always knew that boy was smart,' said Guinzburg.

◄o►

While Samantha and Seb were admiring the shop windows on Fifth Avenue, and Harry was enjoying a rib-eye steak at the Harvard Club with his publisher, a yellow cab came to a halt outside a smart brownstone on 64th and Park.

Emma stepped out, carrying a shoebox with 'Crockett & Jones' emblazoned on the lid. Inside was a pair of size nine, made-to-measure black brogues, which she knew would fit her cousin Alistair perfectly, because he always had his shoes made in Jermyn Street.

As Emma looked up at the shiny brass knocker on the front door, she recalled the first time she had climbed those steps. A young woman, barely out of her teens, she'd been shaking like a leaf and had wanted to run away. But she'd spent all her money to get to America, and didn't know who else to turn to in New York if she was to find Harry, who was locked up in an American prison for a murder he hadn't committed. Once she'd met Great-aunt Phyllis, Emma didn't return to England for over a year – until she found out Harry was no longer in America.

This time she climbed the steps more confidently, rapped firmly with the brass knocker, stood back and waited. She hadn't made an appointment to see her cousin because she had no doubt he'd be in residence. Although he'd recently retired as the senior partner of Simpson, Albion & Stuart, he was not a country animal, even at weekends. Alistair was quintessentially a New Yorker. He'd been born on 64th and Park, and that, undoubtedly, was where he would die.

When the door opened a few moments later, Emma was surprised to see a man she immediately recognized, although it must have been more than twenty years since she had last seen him. He was dressed in a black morning coat, striped trousers, white shirt and grey tie. Some things never change.

'How nice to see you, Mrs Clifton,' he said as if she dropped by every day.

Emma felt embarrassed as she wrestled to recall his name, knowing that Harry would never have forgotten it. 'And it's so nice to see you,' she ventured. 'I was rather hoping to catch up with my cousin Alistair, if he's at home.'

'I fear not, madam,' said the butler. 'Mr Stuart is attending the funeral of Mr Benjamin Rutledge, a former partner of the firm, and isn't expected back from Connecticut until tomorrow evening.'

Emma couldn't hide her disappointment.

'Perhaps you'd care to come inside and I could make you a cup of tea – Earl Grey, if I remember correctly?'

'That's very kind of you,' said Emma, 'but I ought to be getting back to the ship.'

'Of course. I do hope the *Buckingham*'s maiden voyage was a success?'

'Better than I might have hoped for,' she admitted. 'Would you be kind enough to pass on my best wishes to Alistair, and say how sorry I was to miss him?'

'I'd be delighted to do so, Mrs Clifton.' The butler gave a slight bow before closing the door.

Emma made her way back down the steps and began searching for a cab, when she suddenly realized she was still clutching the shoebox. Feeling embarrassed, she climbed the steps a second time and rapped the door with the brass knocker a little more tentatively.

Moments later the door opened a second time and the butler reappeared. 'Madam?' he said, giving her the same warm smile.

'I'm so sorry, but I quite forgot to give you this gift for Alistair.'

'How thoughtful of you to remember Mr Stuart's favourite shoe shop,' he said as Emma handed over the box. 'I know he'll appreciate your kindness.'

Emma stood there, still helplessly trying to recall his name.

'I do hope, Mrs Clifton, that the return voyage to Avonmouth will be equally successful.'

Once again he bowed and closed the door quietly behind him.

'Thank you, Parker,' she said.

5

ONCE BOB BINGHAM had finished dressing, he checked himself in the long mirror inside the wardrobe door. His double-breasted, wide-lapelled dinner jacket was unlikely to come back into fashion in the near future, as his wife regularly reminded him. He'd pointed out to her that the suit had been good enough for his father when he was chairman of Bingham's Fish Paste, and therefore should be good enough for him.

Priscilla didn't agree, but then they hadn't agreed on much lately. Bob still blamed her close friend, Lady Virginia Fenwick, for Jessica Clifton's untimely death, and the fact that their son Clive – who had been engaged to Jessica at the time – hadn't been back to Mablethorpe Hall since that fateful day. His wife was naïve and over-awed when it came to Virginia, but he still lived in the hope that Priscilla would finally come to her senses and see the damned woman for what she was, which would allow them to once again come together as a family. But that, he feared, would not be for some time, and in any case Bob had more immediate problems on his mind. Tonight, they would be on public display, as guests at the chairman's table. He wasn't at all confident that Priscilla would be able to remain on her best behaviour for more than a few minutes. He just hoped they'd get back to their cabin unscathed.

Bob admired Emma Clifton, 'the Boadicea of Bristol' as she was known by friend and foe alike. He suspected that if she had been aware of the nickname, she would have worn it as a badge of honour.

Emma had slipped a *pour mémoire* under their cabin door earlier that day, suggesting they meet in the Queen's Lounge around 7.30 p.m., before going into dinner. Bob checked his watch. It was already ten to eight, and there was still no sign of his wife, although he could hear the sound of running water coming from the bathroom. He began to pace around the cabin, barely able to hide his irritation.

Bob was well aware that Lady Virginia had brought a libel suit against the chairman, not something he was likely to forget as he was sitting just behind her when the exchange took place. During question time at this year's AGM, Lady Virginia had asked from the floor if it was true that one of the directors of Barrington's had sold all his shares with the intention of bringing down the company. She was of course referring to Cedric Hardcastle's little ploy to save the company from a hostile takeover by Don Pedro Martinez.

Emma had responded robustly, reminding Lady Virginia that it was Major Fisher, her representative on the board, who had sold her shares and then bought them back a fortnight later in order to damage the company's reputation, while making a handsome profit for his client.

'You'll be hearing from my solicitor,' was all Virginia had to say on the subject, and a week later Emma did. Bob wasn't in any doubt which camp his wife would be supporting if the action ever came to court. Were Priscilla to pick up any useful ammunition during dinner that might assist her friend's cause, he was sure it would be passed on to Virginia's legal team within moments of them stepping ashore in Avonmouth. And both sides were well aware that if Emma were to lose the case, it wouldn't be simply her reputation that would be in tatters, but she would also undoubtedly have to resign as chairman of Barrington's.

He hadn't told Priscilla anything about the IRA or what had been discussed during the emergency board meeting on that first morning of the voyage, other than to repeat the story about the Home Fleet, and although she clearly didn't believe him, Priscilla learned nothing other than that Sebastian had been appointed to the board.

After a day's shopping in New York which would cost Bob several crates of fish paste, she didn't mention it again. However, Bob was afraid she might raise it with Emma over dinner, and if she did, he would have to deftly change the subject. Thank God Lady Virginia hadn't carried out her threat to join them on the voyage, because if she had, she wouldn't have rested until she'd found out exactly what had happened in the early hours of that first night.

Priscilla eventually emerged from the bathroom, but not until ten past eight.

◄○►

'Perhaps we should go through to dinner,' Emma suggested.

'But aren't the Binghams meant to be joining us?' said Harry.

54

'Yes,' said Emma, checking her watch. 'More than half an hour ago.'

'Don't rise, darling,' said Harry firmly. 'You're the chairman of the company, and you mustn't let Priscilla see that she's annoyed you, because that's exactly what she's hoping for.' Emma was about to protest when he added, 'And be sure you don't say anything over dinner that Virginia could use in court, because there's no doubt which side Priscilla Bingham is on.'

With all the other problems Emma had faced during the past week, she'd put aside the possible court case, and as she hadn't heard from Virginia's solicitors for several months, she'd even begun to wonder if she'd quietly dropped the action. The problem was, Virginia didn't do anything quietly.

Emma was about to place her order with the head waiter when Harry stood up.

'I'm so sorry to have kept you waiting,' said Priscilla, 'but I lost all track of time.'

'Not a problem,' said Harry as he pulled back her chair and waited until she was comfortably seated.

'Perhaps we should order,' said Emma, clearly wishing to remind her guest how long they had been kept waiting.

Priscilla took her time as she turned the pages of the leather-bound menu, and changed her mind several times before she finally made her choice. Once the waiter had taken her order, Harry asked her if she'd enjoyed her day in New York.

'Oh yes, there are so many wonderful shops on Fifth Avenue that have so much more to offer than London, although I did find the whole experience quite exhausting. In fact, when I got back to the ship, I simply collapsed on the bed and fell asleep. And you, Mr Clifton, did you manage to do any shopping?'

'No, I had an appointment with my publishers, while Emma went in search of a long-lost cousin.'

'Of course, I'd quite forgotten you're the one who writes novels. I just don't find the time to read books,' said Priscilla as a bowl of piping hot tomato soup was placed in front of her. 'I didn't order soup,' she said, looking up at the waiter. 'I asked for the smoked salmon.'

'I'm sorry, madam,' said the waiter, who removed the soup. While he was still in earshot, Priscilla said, 'I suppose it must be quite difficult to recruit experienced staff for a cruise ship.'

'I hope you won't mind if we start,' said Emma as she picked up her soup spoon.

'Did you catch up with your cousin?' asked Bob.

'Unfortunately not. He was visiting Connecticut, so I joined Harry later, and we were lucky enough to get a couple of tickets for an afternoon concert at Lincoln Center.'

'Who was performing?' asked Bob as a plate of smoked salmon was placed in front of Priscilla.

'Leonard Bernstein, who was conducting his *Candide* overture, before he played a Mozart piano concerto.'

'I just don't know how you find the time,' said Priscilla between mouthfuls.

Emma was about to say she didn't spend her life shopping, but looked up to see Harry frowning at her.

'I once saw Bernstein conducting the LSO at the Royal Festival Hall,' said Bob. 'Brahms. Quite magnificent.'

'And did you accompany Priscilla on her exhausting shopping trip up and down Fifth Avenue?' asked Emma.

'No, I checked out the lower East Side, to see if

there was any point in trying to break into the American market.'

'And your conclusion?' asked Harry.

'The Americans aren't quite ready for Bingham's fish paste.'

'So which countries are ready?' asked Harry.

'Only Russia and India, if the truth be known. And they come with their own problems.'

'Like what?' asked Emma, sounding genuinely interested.

'The Russians don't like paying their bills, and the Indians often can't.'

'Perhaps you have a one-product problem?' Emma suggested.

'I've thought about diversifying, but—'

'Can we possibly talk about something other than fish paste,' said Priscilla. 'After all, we are meant to be on holiday.'

'Of course,' said Harry. 'How is Clive?' he asked, regretting his words immediately.

'He's just fine, thank you,' said Bob, jumping in quickly. 'And you must both be so proud of Sebastian being invited to join the board.'

Emma smiled.

'Well, that's hardly a surprise,' said Priscilla. 'Let's face it, if your mother is the chairman of the company, and your family owns a majority of the stock, frankly you could appoint a cocker spaniel to the board and the rest of the directors would wag their tails.'

Harry thought Emma was about to explode, but luckily her mouth was full, so a long silence followed.

'Is that rare?' Priscilla demanded as a steak was placed in front of her.

The waiter checked her order. 'No, madam, it's medium.'

'I ordered rare. I couldn't have made it clearer. Take it away and try again.'

The waiter deftly removed the plate without comment, as Priscilla turned to Harry. 'Can you make a living as a writer?'

'It's tough,' admitted Harry, 'not least because there are so many excellent authors out there. However—'

'Still, you married a rich woman, so it really doesn't matter all that much, does it?'

This silenced Harry, but not Emma. 'Well, at last we've discovered something we have in common, Priscilla.'

'I agree,' said Priscilla, not missing a beat, 'but then I'm old-fashioned, and was brought up to believe it's the natural order of things for a man to take care of a woman. It somehow doesn't seem right the other way round.' She took a sip of wine, and Emma was about to respond when she added with a warm smile, 'I think you'll find the wine is corked.'

'I thought it was excellent,' said Bob.

'Dear Robert still doesn't know the difference between a claret and a burgundy. Whenever we throw a dinner party, it's always left to me to select the wine. Waiter!' she said, turning to the sommelier. 'We'll need another bottle of the Merlot.'

'Yes of course, madam.'

'I don't suppose you get to the north of England much,' said Bob.

'Not that often,' said Emma. 'But a branch of my family hails from the Highlands.'

'Mine too,' said Priscilla. 'I was born a Campbell.'

'I think you'll find that's the Lowlands,' said Emma, as Harry kicked her under the table.

'I'm sure you're right, as always,' said Priscilla. 'So I know you won't mind me asking you a personal question.' Bob put down his knife and fork and looked anxiously across at his wife. 'What really happened on the first night of the voyage? Because I know the Home Fleet was nowhere to be seen.'

'How can you possibly know that, when you were fast asleep at the time?' said Bob.

'So what do you think happened, Priscilla?' asked Emma, reverting to a tactic her brother often used when he didn't want to answer a question.

'Some passengers are saying that one of the turbines exploded.'

'The engine room is open for inspection by the passengers at any time,' said Emma. 'In fact, I believe there was a well-attended guided tour this morning.'

'I also heard that a bomb exploded in your cabin,' said Priscilla, undaunted.

'You are most welcome to visit our cabin at any time so you can correct the ill-informed rumour-monger who suggested that.'

'And someone else told me,' said Priscilla, ploughing on, 'that a group of Irish terrorists boarded the ship at around midnight—'

'Only to find we were fully booked, and as there wasn't a cabin available, they were made to walk the plank and swim all the way back to Belfast?'

'And did you hear the one about some Martians flying in from outer space and landing inside one of the funnels?' said Harry, as the waiter reappeared with a rare steak.

Priscilla gave it no more than a glance, before she rose from her place. 'You're all hiding something,' she said, dropping her napkin on the table, 'and I intend to find out what it is before we reach Avonmouth.'

The three of them watched as she glided serenely across the floor and out of the dining room.

'I apologize,' said Bob. 'That turned out even worse than I feared.'

'Don't worry about it,' said Harry. 'My wife snores.'

'I do not,' said Emma, as the two men burst out laughing.

'I'd give half my fortune to have the relationship you two enjoy.'

'I'll take it,' said Harry. This time it was Emma's turn to kick her husband under the table.

'Well, I'm grateful for one thing, Bob,' said Emma, reverting to her chairman's voice. 'Your wife clearly has no idea what really happened on our first night at sea. But if she ever found out . . .'

━◦━

'I'd like to open this meeting by welcoming my son Sebastian Clifton on to the board.'

Hear, hears echoed around the ballroom.

'While being inordinately proud of his achievement at such a young age, I feel I should warn Mr Clifton that the rest of the board will be observing his contributions with considerable interest.'

'Thank you, chairman,' said Sebastian, 'for both your warm welcome and your helpful advice.' Seb's words caused several members of the board to smile. His mother's confidence, with his father's charm.

'Moving on,' said the chairman, 'allow me to bring you

up to date on what has become known as the Home Fleet incident. Although we cannot yet afford to relax, it would appear that our worst fears have not been realized. Nothing of any real significance found its way into the press on either side of the Atlantic, not least, I'm told, because of a little assistance from Number Ten. The three Irishmen who were arrested in the early hours of our first night at sea are no longer on board. Once we'd docked and all the passengers had disembarked, they were discreetly transferred to a Royal Navy frigate, which is now on its way to Belfast.

'The damaged propeller, although not back to its full capacity, still has a rev count of around sixty per cent, and will be replaced once we arrive back in Avonmouth. Our maintenance team worked day and night on the damaged hull while we were docked in New York and have done a first-class job. Only a seasoned mariner would be able to spot any sign of repair. Further work on the hull will also be carried out while we're in Avonmouth. I anticipate that by the time the *Buckingham* sets out on its second voyage to New York in eight days' time, no one would know we ever had a problem. However, I think it would be unwise for any of us to discuss the incident outside the boardroom, and should you be questioned on the subject, just stick to the official Home Fleet line.'

'Will we be making a claim on our insurance policy?' asked Knowles.

'No,' said Emma firmly, 'because if we did, it would undoubtedly throw up a lot of questions I don't want to answer.'

'Understood, chairman,' said Dobbs. 'But how much has the Home Fleet incident cost us?'

'I don't yet have an accurate figure to present to the

board, but I'm told it could be as much as seven thousand pounds.'

'That would be a small price to pay, given the circumstances,' chipped in Bingham.

'I agree. However, no reference to the Home Fleet incident needs to be recorded in the minutes of this board or disclosed to our shareholders.'

'Chairman,' said the company secretary, 'I'll have to make some reference to what happened.'

'Then stick to the Home Fleet explanation, Mr Webster, and don't circulate anything without my approval.'

'If you say so, chairman.'

'Let's move on to some more positive news.' Emma turned a page of her file. 'The *Buckingham* has a one hundred per cent occupancy for the journey back to Avonmouth, and we already have a seventy-two per cent take-up for the second voyage to New York.'

'That is good news,' said Bingham. 'However, we mustn't forget the 184 free cabin spaces we have offered as compensation that are sure to be taken up at some time in the future.'

'At some time in the future is what matters, Mr Bingham. If they are evenly distributed over the next couple of years, they'll have little effect on our cash flow.'

'But I'm afraid there's something else that might well affect our cash flow. And what makes it worse, the problem is not of our making.'

'What are you referring to, Mr Anscott?' asked Emma.

'I had a very interesting chat with your brother on the way out, and found him fairly sanguine about the consequences of the country having to borrow one and a half billion pounds from the IMF in order to stop a run on the pound. He also mentioned the possibility of the government imposing a seventy per cent corporation tax on all companies, as well as ninety per cent income tax on anyone earning over thirty thousand a year.'

'Good God,' said the admiral. 'Will I be able to afford my own funeral?'

'And the chancellor's latest idea,' continued Anscott, 'which I find almost inconceivable, is that no businessman or holiday-maker will be allowed to leave the country with more than fifty pounds cash in their possession.'

'That won't exactly tempt people to travel abroad,' said Dobbs with some feeling.

'I think I may have found a way around that,' said Sebastian.

The rest of the board turned towards the newest recruit.

'I've been carrying out a little research into what our rivals are up to, and it seems that the owners of the SS *New York* and the SS *France* have come up with a solution to their tax problems.' Seb had caught the attention of the board. 'The SS *New York* is no longer registered as being owned by an American company, despite the fact that its headquarters are still in Manhattan, along with the vast majority of its employees. For tax purposes, the company is registered in Panama. In fact, if you look carefully at this picture,' Seb placed a large photograph of the SS *New York* in the centre of the table, 'you will see a small Panamanian flag flying from the stern, despite the fact that the Stars and Stripes remain emblazoned on everything on board, from the plates in the dining rooms to the carpets in the staterooms.'

'And are the French doing the same thing?' asked Knowles.

'They most certainly are, but with a subtle Gallic

difference. They're flying an Algerian flag from the stern of the SS *France*, which I suspect is no more than a political sop.' Another photo, this time of the great French liner, was passed around Seb's colleagues.

'Is this legal?' asked Dobbs.

'There's not a damn thing either government can do about it,' said Seb. 'Both ships are at sea for more than three hundred days a year, and as far as the passengers can tell, everything is exactly the same as it's always been.'

'I don't like the sound of it,' said the admiral. 'It doesn't seem right to me.'

'Our first duty must be to the shareholders,' Bob reminded his colleagues, 'so can I suggest that Clifton presents a paper on the subject, so we can discuss it in greater detail at the next board meeting?'

'Good idea,' said Dobbs.

'I'm not against the idea,' said Emma, 'but our finance director has come up with an alternative solution that some of you might find more attractive.' Emma nodded in the direction of Michael Carrick.

'Thank you, chairman. It's quite simple really. If we were to go ahead with building a second ship, and take advantage of our repeat order option with Harland and Wolff within the specified contract period, we would avoid paying any corporation tax for the next four years.'

'There must be a catch,' said Knowles.

'Apparently not,' said Emma. 'Any company can claim tax relief on a capital project, as long as it keeps to the price agreed in the original contract.'

'Why would the government agree to that, when their other proposed measures are so draconian?' asked Maynard.

'Because it helps to keep the unemployment figures

down,' said Seb. 'Which the Labour Party promised to do in their last manifesto.'

'Then I favour that solution,' said Dobbs. 'But how much time is there before we have to decide whether or not to take up Harland and Wolff's offer?'

'Just over five months,' said Carrick.

'More than enough time to come to a decision,' said Maynard.

'But that doesn't solve the fifty-pounds restriction on our passengers,' said Anscott.

Seb couldn't resist a smile. 'Uncle Giles pointed out to me that there's nothing to stop a passenger cashing a cheque while on board.'

'But we don't have any banking facilities on the *Buckingham*,' Dobbs reminded him.

'Farthings would be only too happy to open an on-board branch,' said Seb.

'Then I suggest,' said Anscott, 'that such a proposal also be included in Mr Clifton's report, and any recommendations should be circulated to all board members before the next meeting.'

'Agreed,' said Emma. 'So all we have to decide now is when that meeting will be.'

As usual, some considerable time was spent selecting a date that was convenient for all the board members.

'And let us hope,' said Emma, 'that by the time we next meet, the Home Fleet incident will be nothing more than folklore. Any other business?' she asked, looking around the table.

'Yes, chairman,' said Knowles. 'You asked us to suggest possible candidates for the other vacant position on the board.'

'Who do you have in mind?'

'Desmond Mellor.'

'The man who founded the Bristol Bus company?'

'The same, but he sold out to National Buses last year. Made a handsome profit, and now finds himself with time on his hands.'

'And considerable knowledge of the transport business,' chipped in Anscott, revealing that he and Knowles were working in tandem.

'Then why don't I invite Mr Mellor to come in and see me some time next week,' said Emma, before either man could put it to a vote.

Knowles reluctantly agreed.

When the meeting broke up, Emma was delighted to see how many directors went over to Sebastian and welcomed him to the board. So much so, that it was some time before she was able to have a private word with her son.

'Your plan worked perfectly,' she whispered.

'Yes, but it was pretty obvious that your idea was more palatable to the majority of the board than mine. But I'm still not convinced, Mother, that we should risk such a large capital outlay on building another ship. If the financial outlook for Britain is as bad as Uncle Giles is suggesting, we could be stuck with two turkeys next Christmas. And if that's the case, it will be the board of Barrington's who are stuffed.'

6

'HOW KIND OF YOU to find the time to see me, Mr Clifton,' said the cabinet secretary, ushering Harry to a seat at the small oval table in the centre of the room, 'especially remembering how busy you are.'

Harry would have laughed if he hadn't been sitting in No.10 Downing Street opposite one of the busiest men in the country. A secretary appeared and placed a cup of tea in front of him, as if he were a regular at his local café.

'I hope your wife and son are well?'

'They are, thank you, Sir Alan.' Harry would have enquired about the cabinet secretary's family, but he had no idea if he even had one. He decided to cut the small talk. 'I presume it was Martinez who was behind the bombing?' he ventured, after taking a sip of his tea.

'It was indeed, but as he's now back in Buenos Aires, and all too aware that if he or either of his sons ever set foot in England they'll be arrested immediately, I don't think he'll be troubling you again.'

'And his Irish friends?'

'They were never his friends. They were only interested in his money, and as soon as that dried up, they were quite prepared to dispose of him. But as their ring leader and two of his associates are now safely behind bars, I can't imagine we'll be hearing from them for some considerable time.'

'Did you find out if there were any other IRA operatives on board the ship?'

'Two. But they haven't been seen since. Intelligence reports that they're holed up somewhere in New York, and aren't expected to return to Belfast for the foreseeable future.'

'I'm grateful, Sir Alan,' said Harry, assuming the meeting was over. The cabinet secretary nodded, but just as Harry was about to rise, he said, 'I must confess, Mr Clifton, that wasn't the only reason I wanted to see you.'

Harry sat back down and began to concentrate. If this man wanted something, he'd better be wide awake.

'Your brother-in-law once told me something that I found difficult to believe. Perhaps you'd be kind enough to indulge me, so I can see if he was exaggerating.'

'Politicians do have a tendency to do that.'

Sir Alan didn't reply but simply opened a file in front of him, extracted a single sheet of paper, slid it across the table, and said, 'Would you be kind enough to read that through slowly?'

Harry looked at a memo that was about three hundred words in length, containing several place names and details of troop movements in the Home Counties, with the ranks of all the senior officers involved. He read the seven paragraphs as instructed, and when he'd finished, he looked up and nodded. The cabinet secretary retrieved the piece of paper and replaced it on the table with a lined pad and a biro.

'Would you now be kind enough to write out what you've just read?'

Harry decided to play the game. He picked up the biro and began writing. When he'd finished, he passed the pad to the cabinet secretary, who compared it with the original.

'So it's true,' he said a few moments later. 'You are one of those rare people with a photographic memory. Though you made one mistake.'

'Godalming and not Godmanchester?' said Harry. 'Just wanted to make sure you were paying attention.'

A man who was not easily impressed was impressed.

'So are you hoping to recruit me for your pub quiz team?' asked Harry.

Sir Alan didn't smile. 'No, I'm afraid it's a little more serious than that, Mr Clifton. In May you'll be travelling to Moscow as the President of English PEN. Our ambassador there, Sir Humphrey Trevelyan, has come into possession of a document that is so sensitive he can't even risk sending it in the diplomatic pouch.'

'Can I ask its contents?'

'It's a comprehensive list of the name and location of every Russian spy operating in the UK. Sir Humphrey hasn't even shown it to his deputy. If you could bring it back in your head, we would be able to dismantle the entire Soviet spy network in this country, and as no documents would be involved you wouldn't be in any danger.'

'I'd be quite willing to do that,' said Harry without hesitation. 'But I will expect something in return.'

'I'll do anything within my power.'

'I want the foreign secretary to make an official protest about the imprisonment of Anatoly Babakov.'

'Stalin's interpreter? Didn't he write a book that was banned – what was it called . . .'

'*Uncle Joe*,' said Harry.

'Ah yes, of course. Well, I'll do what I can, but I can't guarantee anything.'

'And he must also make an official statement to all national and foreign press agencies the day before I fly to Russia.'

'I can't promise you that, but be assured I'll recommend that the foreign secretary supports your campaign to have Mr Babakov released.'

'I'm sure you will, Sir Alan. But if you are unable to assist me with Babakov's plight,' he paused, 'you can bugger off and find someone else to be your messenger boy.'

Harry's words had exactly the effect he had hoped for. The cabinet secretary was speechless.

◄○►

Emma looked up as her secretary entered the office, accompanied by a man she knew as soon as they shook hands she wasn't going to like. She ushered Mr Mellor towards two comfortable chairs by the fireplace.

'It's very nice to meet you at last, Mrs Clifton,' he said. 'I've heard, and read, so much about you over the years.'

'And I've recently been reading a great deal about you, Mr Mellor,' said Emma as she sat down and took a closer look at the man seated opposite her. She knew from a recent profile in the *Financial Times* that Desmond Mellor had left school at sixteen and begun his working life as a booking clerk at Cooks Travel. By the age of twenty-three, he'd started up his own company, which he'd recently sold for close to £2 million, having had several well-chronicled scrapes along the way. But Emma accepted that that would be true of most successful entrepreneurs. She had been prepared for his charm, but was surprised to find that he looked far younger than his forty-eight years. He was clearly fit, with no surplus pounds that needed to be shed, and she had to agree with her secretary that he was a good-looking man, even if his dress sense hadn't quite kept pace with his financial success.

'Not all bad, I hope,' he said with a self-deprecating laugh.

'Well, if your recent takeover battle is anything to go by, Mr Mellor, you certainly don't believe in taking prisoners.'

'It's tough out there at the moment, Mrs Clifton, as I'm sure you're finding, so sometimes you have to cover your backside, if you'll excuse the expression.'

Emma wondered if she could come up with an excuse to cut the meeting short, despite the fact that she had instructed her secretary that she was not to be disturbed for at least thirty minutes.

'I've been following your husband's activities on behalf of Babakov,' said Mellor. 'Seems he might also have to cover his backside,' he added with a grin.

'Harry feels passionately about Mr Babakov's plight.'

'As I'm sure we all do. But I have to ask, is it worth the candle? Those Russians don't seem to give a damn about human rights.'

'That won't stop Harry fighting for something he believes in.'

'Is he away often?'

'Not that much,' Emma said, trying not to show she'd been taken by surprise by the sudden change of subject. 'The occasional book tour or conference. But when you chair a public company, that can sometimes be a blessing in disguise.'

'I know just how you feel,' said Mellor, leaning forward. 'My wife prefers to live in the country, which is why I stay in Bristol during the week.'

'Do you have any children?' asked Emma.

'One girl by my first marriage. She's a secretary in London. And another by my second.'

'And how old is she?'

'Kelly is four, and, of course, I know your son Sebastian has recently joined the board of Barrington's.'

Emma smiled. 'Then perhaps I can ask, Mr Mellor, why you want to join us on the board?'

'Des, please. All my friends call me Des. As you know, my experience is mainly in the travel business, although since I sold the company, I've started dabbling in the odd property deal. But as I still find myself with time on my hands, I thought it might be fun to work under a woman chairman.'

Emma ignored this. 'If you were to become a member of the board, what would be your attitude to a hostile takeover bid?'

'To begin with, I'd pretend I wasn't interested and see how much I could milk them for. The secret is to be patient.'

'There wouldn't be any circumstances under which you'd consider holding on to the company?'

'Not if the price was right.'

'But when National Buses took over your company, weren't you worried about what might happen to your staff?'

'If they were half awake they must have seen it coming for years, and in any case I wasn't going to get another chance like that.'

'But if the *FT* is to be believed, within a month of the takeover, half your staff, some of whom had been with you for over twenty years, were made redundant.'

'With a six-month salary bonus. And a number of them had no difficulty finding employment elsewhere, one or two at Barrington's.'

'But within another month, National Buses had dropped your name from the company masthead and, with it, the reputation you'd built over many years.'

'You dropped your name when you married Harry Clifton,' said Des, 'but it didn't stop you becoming chairman of Barrington's.'

'I wasn't given a choice, and I suspect even that may change in the future.'

'Let's face it, when it comes to the bottom line, you can't afford to be sentimental.'

'It's not difficult to see how you've become such a successful businessman, Des, and why, for the right firm, you'd make an ideal director.'

'I'm glad you feel that way.'

'But I still need to speak to my colleagues just in case they don't agree with me. When I have, I'll be back in touch.'

'I look forward to that, Emma.'

7

SEBASTIAN ARRIVED outside the American Embassy in Grosvenor Square just before nine o'clock the following day for his appointment with the *chef de mission*.

After he'd reported to the front desk, a marine sergeant accompanied him to the second floor and knocked on a door at the end of the corridor. Seb was surprised when the door was opened by Mr Sullivan.

'Good to see you, Seb. Come on in.'

Seb entered a room that overlooked Grosvenor Gardens, but he didn't take in the view.

'Would you like some coffee?'

'No, thank you, sir,' said Seb, who was far too nervous to think about anything other than his opening line.

'So what can I do for you?' asked the *chef de mission* as he took a seat behind his desk.

Seb remained standing.

'I'd like your permission, sir, to ask for your daughter's hand in marriage.'

'How wonderfully old-fashioned,' said Mr Sullivan. 'I'm touched that you took the trouble to ask, Seb, and if that's what Samantha wants, it's fine by me.'

'I don't know what she wants,' admitted Seb, 'because I haven't asked her yet.'

'Then good luck, because I can tell you, nothing would please her mother and me more.'

'That's a relief,' said Seb.

'Have you told your parents yet?'

'Last night, sir.'

'And how do they feel about it?'

'Mother couldn't be more pleased, but my father said that if Sam's got any sense, she'll turn me down.'

Sullivan smiled. 'But if she does say yes, can you keep her in a style she isn't accustomed to? Because as you know, she hopes to be an academic, and they are not overpaid.'

'I'm working on it, sir. I've just been promoted at the bank, and am now number two in the property division. And as I think you know I've recently joined the board of Barrington's.'

'That all sounds pretty promising, Seb, and frankly, Marion was wondering what took you so long.'

'Does that mean I have your blessing?'

'It most certainly does. But never forget that Samantha sets standards, like your mother, that the rest of us normal mortals find hard to live with, unless, like your father, they're guided by the same moral compass. Now that we've got that out of the way, would you like to sit down?'

◄○►

When Sebastian returned to the City later that morning, he found a note on his desk from Adrian Sloane, asking him to report to his office the moment he got back.

Sebastian frowned. The one blip on his radar screen

during the past few months had been his immediate boss. He'd never been able to please Sloane from the moment Cedric Hardcastle had appointed him as his deputy in the property division. Sloane always managed to leave the impression that he was efficient at his job, and, to be fair, the division's month-on-month revenues and profits were continually impressive. However, for some reason he didn't seem to trust Seb, and made no attempt to confide in him – in fact, he went out of his way to keep him out of the loop. Seb also knew from one of his colleagues that whenever his name came up in discussions, Sloane didn't hesitate to undermine him.

Seb had considered mentioning the problem to Cedric, but his mother had counselled against it, saying Sloane was bound to find out, which would only make him more antagonistic.

'In any case,' Emma had added, 'you should learn to stand on your own two feet, and not expect Cedric to wet-nurse you every time you come up against a problem.'

'That's all very well,' said Seb, 'but what else can I be expected to do?'

'Just get on with your job, and do it well,' said Emma. 'Because that's all Cedric will care about.'

'That's exactly what I am doing,' insisted Seb. 'So why is Sloane treating me this way?'

'I can explain that in one word,' said Emma. 'Envy. And you'd better get used to it if you're hoping to climb further up the corporate ladder.'

'But I never had that problem when I worked for Mr Hardcastle.'

'Of course you didn't, because Cedric never saw you as a threat.'

'Sloane thinks I'm a threat?'

'Yes. He assumes you're after his job, and that only makes him more secretive, insecure, paranoid, call it what you will. But to use one of Des Mellor's favourite expressions, just be sure you cover your backside.'

◄○►

When Seb reported to Sloane, his boss came straight to the point, and didn't seem to mind that his secretary was listening to every word.

'As you weren't at your desk when I came in this morning, I assume you must have been visiting a client.'

'No, I was at the American Embassy dealing with a personal matter.'

This silenced Sloane for a moment. 'Well, in future, when you're dealing with personal matters, do it in your own time, and not the company's. We're running a bank, not a social club.'

Seb gritted his teeth. 'I'll remember that in future, Adrian.'

'I'd prefer to be called Mr Sloane, during working hours.'

'Anything else . . . Mr Sloane?' asked Seb.

'No, not for the moment, but I expect to see your monthly report on my desk by close of business this evening.'

Seb returned to his office, relieved to be a step ahead of Sloane, as he'd already prepared his monthly report over the weekend. His figures were up again, for the tenth month in a row, although it had recently become clear to him that Sloane was adding his own results in with Seb's, and taking the credit. If Sloane hoped that his tactics would eventually grind Seb down, even force him to resign, he needn't hold his breath. As long as Cedric was chairman of the bank, Seb knew his position was secure, and while he continued to deliver, he need have no fear of Sloane, because the chairman was well capable of reading between the lines.

At one o'clock, Seb grabbed a ham sandwich from a nearby café and ate it on the move, not something his mother would have approved of – at your desk if you have to, but not on the move.

As he searched for a taxi, he thought about some of the lessons he'd learnt from Cedric when it came to closing a deal, some basic, some more subtle, but most of it good old-fashioned common sense.

'Know how much you can afford, never overstretch yourself, and try to remember that the other side are also hoping to make a profit. And build good contacts because they'll be your lifeline during bad times, as only one thing is certain in banking – you will experience bad times. And by the way,' he'd added, 'never buy retail.'

'Who taught you that?' Seb had asked.

'Jack Benny.'

Armed with sound advice from both Cedric Hardcastle and Jack Benny, Seb went in search of an engagement ring. The contact had been suggested by his old school chum, Victor Kaufman, who now worked on the foreign exchange desk at his father's bank, just a few blocks away from Farthings. He'd advised Seb to visit a Mr Alan Gard in Hatton Garden.

'He'll supply you with a larger stone, at half the price of any jeweller on the high street.'

Seb was eating on the move and taking a taxi because he knew he had to be back at his desk within the hour if he didn't want to fall foul of Adrian Sloane yet again. It pulled up outside a green door that Seb would have passed without noticing if the number 47 hadn't been painted neatly on it. There was nothing to hint of the treasures that lay within. Seb realized that he must be dealing with a private and cautious man.

He pressed the bell, and a moment later a Dickensian figure wearing a skull cap and with long black ringlets greeted him. When Seb said he was a friend of Victor Kaufman, he was quickly ushered through to Mr Gard's inner sanctum.

A wiry man, no taller than five feet, and dressed casually in an open-necked shirt and well-worn jeans, rose from behind his desk and gave his potential customer a warm smile. When he heard the name Kaufman, the smile broadened and he rubbed his hands together as if he was about to roll some dice.

'If you're a friend of Saul Kaufman, you're probably expecting to get the Koh-I-Noor for five pounds.'

'Four,' said Seb.

'And you're not even Jewish.'

'No,' said Seb, 'but I was trained by a Yorkshireman.'

'That explains everything. So how can I help you, young man?'

'I'm looking for an engagement ring.'

'And who's the lucky girl?'

'An American, called Sam.'

'Then we'll have to find Sam something special, won't we?' Mr Gard opened his desk drawer, took out a vast key ring and selected a single key from the bunch. He walked across to a large safe embedded in the wall, unlocked the heavy door and opened it to reveal a dozen neatly stacked trays. After hesitating for a moment, he selected the third tray from the bottom, pulled it out and placed the contents on his desk.

Several small diamonds winked up at Seb. He studied them for a few moments before shaking his head gravely. The gemmologist made no comment. He returned the tray to the safe and extracted the one above.

Seb took a little more time considering the slightly larger stones that shone up at him, but once again rejected them.

'Are you sure you can afford this girl?' asked the jeweller, as he removed the third tray from the top.

Seb's eyes lit up the moment he saw a sapphire surrounded by a cluster of tiny diamonds that rested in the centre of the black velvet cloth.

'That one,' he said without hesitation.

Gard picked up a loupe from his desk and studied the ring more closely. 'This beautiful sapphire came from Ceylon, and is one point five carats. The cluster of eight diamonds are all point zero five of a carat, and were recently purchased from India.'

'How much?'

Gard didn't reply for some time. 'I have a feeling you're going to be a long-term customer,' he finally said, 'so I'm tempted to let you have this magnificent ring at an introductory price. Shall we say one hundred pounds?'

'You can say anything you like, but I don't have a hundred pounds.'

'Look upon it as an investment.'

'For whom?'

'I'll tell you what I'll do,' said Gard, returning to his desk and opening a large ledger. He turned over several pages, then ran a forefinger down a list of figures. 'To show how confident I am that you'll be a future customer, I'll let you have the ring for the price I paid for it. Sixty pounds.'

'We'll have to go back to the bottom shelf,' said Seb reluctantly.

Gard threw his arms in the air. 'How can a poor man hope to make a profit when he has to bargain with someone as sharp as you? My lowest possible offer is,' he paused, 'fifty pounds.'

'But I only have about thirty pounds in my bank account.'

Gard considered this for a few moments. 'Then let us agree on a ten-pound deposit and five pounds a month for one year.'

'But that takes it back up to seventy pounds!'

'Eleven months.'

'Ten.'

'You have a deal, young man. The first of many, I hope,' he added, as he shook Seb's hand.

Seb wrote out a cheque for ten pounds, while Mr Gard selected a small red leather box in which to place the ring.

'Pleasure to do business with you, Mr Clifton.'

'One question, Mr Gard. When do I get to see the top shelf?'

'Not until you're chairman of the bank.'

8

ON THE DAY BEFORE Harry flew to Moscow, Michael Stewart, the British foreign secretary, summoned the Russian ambassador to his office in Whitehall and, on behalf of Her Majesty's Government, protested in the strongest possible terms about the disgraceful treatment of Anatoly Babakov. He went as far as to suggest that Babakov be released from prison, and the ban on his book lifted immediately.

Mr Stewart's subsequent statement to the press made the front pages of every broadsheet in the country, with supportive leaders in *The Times* and the *Guardian*, both of which mentioned the campaign mounted by the popular author, Harry Clifton.

During Prime Minister's Questions that afternoon, Alec Douglas-Home, the leader of the opposition, voiced his concern for Babakov's plight, and called upon the PM to boycott the bilateral talks that were due to take place with the Soviet leader, Leonid Brezhnev, in Leningrad later that month.

The following day, profiles of Babakov, along with photos of his wife Yelena, appeared in several of the papers. The *Daily Mirror* described his book as a time bomb that, if published, would blow the Soviet regime apart. Harry did wonder how they could possibly know that when they couldn't have read the book. But he felt that Sir Alan couldn't have done any more to assist him and was determined to keep his side of the bargain.

On the night flight to Moscow, Harry went over his conference speech again and again, and by the time the BOAC plane touched down at Sheremetyevo airport, he felt confident that his campaign was gathering momentum and that he would deliver a speech Giles would be proud of.

It took him over an hour to get through customs, not least because his suitcase was unpacked by them, and then re-packed by him, twice. Clearly he was not a welcome guest. When he was finally released, he and several of his fellow delegates were herded on to an old school bus which trundled into the city centre, arriving outside the Majestic Hotel some fifty minutes later. Harry was exhausted.

The receptionist assured him that as the leader of the British delegation, he had been allocated one of the hotel's finest rooms. She handed him his key and, as the lift had broken down and there were no porters available, Harry dragged his suitcase up to the seventh floor. He unlocked the door to enter one of the hotel's finest rooms.

The sparsely furnished box brought back memories of his schooldays at St Bede's. A bed with a thin, lumpy mattress, and a table scarred by cigarette burns and stained with beer glass circles passed as furniture. In the corner was a washbasin with a tap that produced a trickle of cold water, whether it was turned on or off. If he wanted a bath, a notice informed him that the bathroom was at the far end of the corridor: *Remember to bring your towel, and you must not stay in the bath for more than ten minutes, or leave the tap running.* It was so reminiscent of his old school that if there'd been a knock on the door, Harry wouldn't have been surprised to see Matron appear to check his fingernails.

As there was no mini-bar, or even the suggestion of a shortbread biscuit, Harry went back downstairs to join his colleagues for supper. After a one-course, self-service meal, he began to realize why Bingham's fish paste was considered a luxury in the Soviet Union.

He decided on an early night, not least because the first day's programme revealed that he would be addressing the conference as the keynote speaker at eleven the following morning.

He may have gone to bed, but it was some hours before he could get to sleep, and not just because of the lumpy mattress, the paper-thin blanket or the garish neon lights that invaded every corner of his room through nylon curtains that didn't quite meet. By the time he finally fell asleep, it was eleven o'clock in Bristol, two in the morning in Moscow.

Harry rose early the following morning and decided to take a stroll around Red Square. It was impossible to miss Lenin's mausoleum, which dominated the square and served as a constant reminder of the founder of the Soviet state. The Kremlin was guarded by a massive bronze cannon, another symbol of victory over another enemy. Even wearing the overcoat insisted on by Emma, with the collar turned up, Harry's ears and nose had quickly turned red with the cold. He now understood why the Russians wore those magnificent fur hats, accompanied by scarves and long coats. Locals passed him on their way to work but few of them gave him a second look, despite the fact that he was continually slapping himself.

When Harry returned to the hotel, rather earlier than planned, the concierge handed him a message. Pierre Bouchard, the conference chairman, hoped he would be able to join him for breakfast in the dining room.

'I've allocated you the eleven o'clock slot this morning,' said Bouchard, having already given up on some scrambled egg that could never have seen a chicken. 'It's always the best attended of the conference meetings. I will open proceedings at ten thirty, when I'll welcome the delegates from seventy-two countries. A record number,' he added with Gallic panache. 'You'll know I've come to the end of my speech when I remind the delegates that there's one thing the Russians do better than anyone else on earth.' Harry raised an eyebrow. 'The ballet. And we're all lucky enough to be attending *Swan Lake* at the Bolshoi this evening. After I mention that to the delegates, I will invite you on to the stage to deliver the opening speech.'

'I'm flattered,' said Harry, 'and better be on my toes.'

'You shouldn't be,' said Bouchard. 'The committee were unanimous in their choice of you as the keynote speaker. We all admire the campaign you've been masterminding on behalf of Anatoly Babakov. The international press are showing considerable interest, and it will amuse you to know that the KGB asked me if they could see an advance copy of your speech.'

Bouchard's words caused Harry a moment of anxiety. Until then, he hadn't realized how widely his campaign had been followed abroad, and how much was expected of him. He looked at his watch, hoping there was still time to go over his speech once again, drained his coffee, apologized to Bouchard and headed quickly back up to his room. It was a relief to find the lift was now working. He didn't need reminding that he might never have another opportunity like this to promote Babakov's cause, and certainly not in Russia's back yard.

He almost ran into his room and pulled open the drawer of the small side table where he'd left his speech. It was no longer there. After searching the room, he realized that the KGB were now in possession of the advance copy they'd been so keen to get their hands on.

He checked his watch again. Forty minutes before the conference opened, when he would be expected to deliver a speech he'd spent the last month working on, but no longer had a copy of.

When ten chimes rang out in Red Square, Harry was shaking like a schoolboy who had an appointment with his headmaster to discuss an essay that existed only in his head. He'd been left with no choice but to test out just how good his memory was.

He walked slowly back downstairs, aware how an actor must feel moments before the curtain is due to rise, and joined a stream of delegates making their way to the conference centre. On entering the ballroom, all he wanted to do was go straight back to his room and lock himself in. Bookshelves of chattering authors were even more intimidating than advancing Germans.

Several delegates were searching for seats in a room that was already packed. But as instructed by Bouchard, Harry made his way to the front and took his place at the end of the second row. As he glanced around the vast hall, his eyes settled on a group of expressionless, heavily built men wearing long black coats, standing with their backs against the wall, evenly spaced around the room. They had one other thing in common: none of them looked as if they'd ever read a book in their lives.

Bouchard was coming to the end of his opening address when he caught Harry's eye and gave him a warm smile.

'And now for the moment you've all been waiting for,' he said. 'An address by our distinguished colleague from England, the writer of nine highly successful crime novels featuring Detective Sergeant William Warwick. I only wish that my own French counterpart, Inspector Benoît, was half as popular. Perhaps we are about to find out why?'

After the laughter had died down, Bouchard continued: 'It is my honour to invite Harry Clifton, the President of English PEN, to address the conference.'

Harry made his way slowly up to the platform, surprised by the flashing bulbs of so many photographers surrounding the stage, while at the same time his every step was dogged by a stalking television crew.

He shook hands with Bouchard before taking his place behind the lectern. He took a deep breath and looked up to face the firing squad.

'Mr President,' he began, 'allow me to start by thanking you for your kind words, but I should warn you that I will not be speaking today about either Detective Sergeant William Warwick, or Inspector Benoît, but about a man who is not a fictional character, but flesh and blood, like every one of us in this room. A man who is unable to attend this conference today, because he is locked up far away in the Siberian gulag. His crime? Writing a book. I am of course referring to that martyr, and I use the word advisedly, Anatoly Babakov.'

Even Harry was surprised by the outburst of applause

that followed. Book conferences are usually sparsely attended by thoughtful academics, who manage a polite round of applause once the speaker has sat down. But at least the interruption allowed him a few moments to gather his thoughts.

'How many of us in this room have read books about Hitler, Churchill or Roosevelt? Three of the four leaders who determined the outcome of the Second World War. But until recently the only inside account about Josef Stalin to come out of the Soviet Union was an official pamphlet censored by a committee of KGB officials. As you all know, the man who translated that book into English was so disillusioned with it that he decided to write his own unauthorized biography, which would surely have given us a different perspective of the man we all know as Uncle Joe. But no sooner was the book published than every copy of it was destroyed, its publisher shut down and, following a show trial, the author disappeared off the face of the earth. I'm not talking about Hitler's Germany, but present-day Russia.

'One or two of you may be curious to know what Anatoly Babakov could possibly have written that caused the authorities to act in such a tyrannical manner – myself included. After all, the Soviets never stop trumpeting the glories of their utopian state, which they assure us is not only a model for the rest of the world, but one which, in time, we will have no choice but to copy. If that is the case, Mr President, why can't we read a contrary view and make up our own minds? Don't let's forget that *Uncle Joe* was written by a man who stood one pace behind Stalin for thirteen years, a confidant of his innermost thoughts, a witness to how he conducted his day-to-day life. But when Babakov decided to write his own version of those events, no one, including the Soviet people, was allowed to share his thoughts. I wonder why?

'You won't find a copy of *Uncle Joe* in any bookshop in England, America, Australia, Africa or South America, and you certainly won't find one in the Soviet Union. Perhaps it's appallingly written, boring, without merit and unworthy of our time, but at least let us be the judge of that.'

Another wave of applause swept through the room. Harry had to suppress a smile when he noticed that the men in long black coats kept their hands firmly in their pockets, and their expressions didn't change when the interpreter translated his words.

He waited for the applause to die down before he began his peroration. 'Attending this conference today are historians, biographers, scientists and even a few novelists, all of whom take for granted their latest work will be published, however critical they are of their governments, their leaders, even their political system. Why? Because you come from countries that can handle criticism, satire, mockery, even derision, and whose citizens can be entrusted to make up their own minds as to a book's merit. Authors from the Soviet Union are published only if the State approves of what they have to say. How many of you in this room would be languishing in jail if you had been born in Russia?

'I say to the leaders of this great country, why not allow your people the same privileges we in the West take for granted? You can start by releasing Anatoly Babakov and allowing his book to be published. That is, if you have nothing to fear from the torch of freedom. I will not rest until I can buy a copy of *Uncle Joe* at Hatchards on Piccadilly, Doubleday on Fifth Avenue, Dymocks in Sydney, and George's bookshop in Park Street, Bristol. But most of all, I'd like to see a copy on the shelves of the Lenin Library in Vozdvizhenka Street, a few hundred yards from this hall.'

Although the applause was deafening, Harry just clung to the lectern, because he hadn't yet delivered his final paragraph. He waited for complete silence before he looked up and added, 'Mr President, on behalf of the British delegation, it is my privilege to invite Mr Anatoly Babakov to be the keynote speaker at our international conference in London next year.'

Everyone in the room who wasn't wearing a long black coat rose to their feet to give Harry a standing ovation. A senior KGB official who was seated in a box at the back of the room turned to his superior and said, 'Word for word. He must have had a spare copy of the speech that we didn't know about.'

—◇—

'Mr Knowles on line one, chairman.'

Emma pressed a button on her phone. 'Good afternoon, Jim.'

'Good afternoon, Emma. I thought I'd give you a call because Desmond Mellor tells me he had a meeting with you, and he felt it went quite well.'

'I'm sure he did,' said Emma, 'and I have to admit I was impressed with Mr Mellor. Unquestionably a capable businessman, with a great deal of experience in his field.'

'I agree,' said Knowles. 'So can I assume you'll be recommending he joins us on the board?'

'No, Jim, you cannot. Mr Mellor has many admirable qualities, but in my opinion he has one overriding flaw.'

'And what might that be?'

'He's only interested in one person, himself. The word "loyalty" is anathema to him. When I sat and listened to Mr Mellor, he reminded me of my father, and I only want people on the board who remind me of my grandfather.'

'That puts me in a very awkward position.'

'Why would that be, Jim?'

'I recommended Mellor to the board in the first place, and your decision rather undermines my position.'

'I'm sorry to hear you feel that way, Jim.' Emma paused before adding, 'Of course I would understand if you felt you had to resign.'

◄о►

Harry spent the rest of the day shaking hands with people he'd never met before, several of whom promised to promote Babakov's cause in their own countries. Glad-handing was something Giles, as a politician, did quite naturally, while Harry found it exhausting. However, he was pleased that he had walked the streets of Bristol with his brother-in-law during past election campaigns because it wasn't until now that he realized just how much he'd picked up from him.

By the time he climbed on the bus for the conference delegates' visit to the Bolshoi Theatre, he was so tired he feared he might fall asleep during the performance. But from the moment the curtain rose he was on the edge of his seat, exhilarated by the artistic movement of the dancers, their skill, their grace and their energy, making it impossible for him to take his eyes off the stage. When the curtain finally fell he was in no doubt that this was one field in which the Soviet Union really did lead the world.

When he returned to his hotel, the receptionist

handed him a note confirming that an embassy car would pick him up at ten to eight the following morning, so he could join the ambassador for breakfast. That would give him more than enough time to catch his twelve o'clock flight back to London.

Two men sat silently in a corner of the lobby, observing his every move. Harry knew they would have read the message from the ambassador long before he had. He picked up his key, gave them a broad smile and wished them goodnight before taking the lift to the seventh floor.

Once he'd undressed, Harry collapsed on to the bed and quickly fell into a deep sleep.

9

'NOT A GOOD MOVE, Mama.'

'Why not?' said Emma. 'Jim Knowles has never been supportive, and frankly I'll be glad to be rid of him.'

'Remember what Lyndon Johnson said about J. Edgar Hoover? I'd rather have him inside the tent pissing out than outside pissing in.'

'One sometimes wonders why your father and I spent so much money having you educated. But what harm can Knowles possibly do?'

'He has a piece of information that could bring the company down.'

'He wouldn't dare to make the Home Fleet incident public. If he did, he'd never get another job in the City.'

'He doesn't have to make it public. All he has to do is have a quiet lunch at his club with Alex Fisher, and Lady Virginia will know every detail of what really happened that night half an hour later. And you can be sure she'll save the most sensational bits for the witness box, because it will not only bring you down, but the company with it. No, I'm afraid you're going to have to eat a slice of humble pie, Mother, if you don't want to spend every day wondering when the bomb will finally drop.'

'But Knowles has already made it clear that if Mellor isn't made a director, he'll resign from the board.'

'Then Mr Mellor will have to be offered a place on the board.'

'Over my dead body.'

'Your words, Mother, not mine.'

―◇―

Tap, tap, tap. Harry's eyes blinked open. Tap, tap, tap. Was someone knocking on the door, or was it just noise coming from outside? Tap, tap, tap. It was definitely the door. He wanted to ignore it, but it had a persistence that suggested it wasn't going away. Tap, tap, tap. He reluctantly placed his feet on the cold linoleum floor, pulled on his dressing gown and shuffled across to the door.

If Harry was surprised when he opened the door, he tried not to show it.

'Hello, Harry,' said a sultry voice.

Harry stared in disbelief at the girl he'd fallen in love with twenty years ago. A carbon-copy of Emma in her early twenties stood in front of him wearing a sable coat and, he suspected, nothing much else. She held a cigarette in one hand and a bottle of champagne in the other. Clever Russians, Harry thought.

'My name is Alina,' she purred as she touched his arm. 'I've been looking forward to meeting you.'

'I think you've got the wrong room,' said Harry.

'No, I don't think so,' said Alina. She tried to slip past him, but Harry remained lodged in the doorway, blocking her path.

'I'm your reward, Harry, for making such a brilliant speech. I promised the President that I'd give you a night you will never forget.'

'You've already achieved that,' said Harry, wondering which President Alina worked for.

'Surely there's something I can do for you, Harry?'

'Nothing I can think of, but please thank your masters and let them know I'm just not interested.' Alina looked disappointed.

'Boys, perhaps?'

'No, thank you.'

'Money?' she suggested.

'How kind, but I have enough already.'

'Is there nothing I can tempt you with?'

'Well,' said Harry, 'now you mention it, there is something I've always wanted, and if your masters can deliver it, I'm their man.'

'And what might that be, Harry?' she said, sounding hopeful for the first time.

'The Nobel Prize for literature.'

Alina looked puzzled, and Harry couldn't resist leaning forward and kissing her on both cheeks as if she was a favourite aunt. He quietly closed the door and crept back into bed. 'Damn the woman,' he said, quite unable to sleep.

◄○►

'There's a Mr Vaughan on the line, Mr Clifton,' said the girl on the switchboard. 'Says he needs to speak to Mr Sloane urgently, but he's away at a conference in York and isn't expected back until Friday.'

'Put the call through to his secretary and ask her to deal with it.'

'Sarah's not answering her phone, Mr Clifton. I don't think she's back from lunch yet.'

'OK, put him through,' said Seb reluctantly. 'Good morning, Mr Vaughan, how can I help you?'

'I'm the senior partner of Savills estate agents,' said Vaughan, 'and I need to speak to Mr Sloane urgently.'

'Can it wait until Friday?'

'No. I now have two other offers on the table for Shifnal Farm in Shropshire, and as bidding closes on Friday I need to know if Mr Sloane is still interested.'

'Perhaps you could give me the details, Mr Vaughan,' said Seb, picking up a pen, 'and I'll look into it immediately.'

'Could you let Mr Sloane know that Mr Collingwood is happy to accept his offer of one point six million, which means I'll need a deposit of £160,000 by five o'clock on Friday if he still hopes to secure the deal.'

'One point six million,' repeated Seb, not sure he'd heard the figure correctly.

'Yes, that of course includes the thousand acres as well as the house.'

'Of course,' said Seb. 'I'll let Mr Sloane know the moment he calls in.' Seb put down the phone. The amount was larger than any deal he'd ever been involved in for a London property, let alone a farm in Shropshire, so he decided to double-check with Sloane's secretary. He walked across the corridor to her office to find Sarah hanging up her coat.

'Good afternoon, Mr Clifton, how can I help?'

'I need to see the Collingwood file, Sarah, so I can brief Mr Sloane when he calls in.'

Sarah looked puzzled. 'I'm not familiar with that particular client, but just let me check.'

She pulled open a filing cabinet marked A to H and quickly flicked through the Cs. 'He's not one of Mr

Sloane's clients,' she said. 'There must be some mistake.'

'Try looking under Shifnal Farm,' said Seb.

Sarah turned her attention to the S–Z file, but once again shook her head.

'Must be my mistake,' said Seb. 'Perhaps it would be better if you didn't mention it to Mr Sloane,' he added as she closed the filing cabinet. He walked slowly back to his office, closed the door and thought about his conversation with Mr Vaughan for some time before he picked up the phone and dialled directory enquiries.

When a voice eventually answered, Seb asked for a Mr Collingwood at Shifnal Farm in Shropshire. It was a few moments before the operator came back on the line.

'I have a Mr D. Collingwood, Shifnal Farm, Shifnal?'

'That must be him. Can you give me his number?'

'I'm afraid not, sir. He's ex-directory.'

'But this is an emergency.'

'It may well be, sir, but I'm not allowed to give out ex-directory numbers under any circumstances.' The phone went dead.

Seb hesitated for a moment before he picked up the phone again and dialled an internal number.

'Chairman's office,' said a familiar voice.

'Rachel, I need fifteen minutes with the boss.'

'Five forty-five, but no more than fifteen minutes, because he has a meeting with the deputy chairman at six and Mr Buchanan is never late.'

◄○►

The embassy Rolls-Royce, Union Jacks fluttering on both wings, was waiting outside the Majestic Hotel long before Harry appeared in the lobby at ten to eight that morning. The same two men were slumped in the corner, pretending not to notice him. Did they ever sleep, Harry wondered.

After Harry had checked out, he couldn't resist giving his guards a little farewell bow before he left the hotel, Majestic in nothing but name. A chauffeur opened the back door of the Rolls to allow Harry to step inside. He leant back and began to think about the other reason he'd come to Moscow.

The car made its way through the rain-swept streets of the capital, passing St Basil's Cathedral, a building of rare beauty, nestled at the south end of Red Square. The car crossed the Moskova, turned left, and a few moments later the gates of the British Embassy opened, splitting the royal crest in two. The chauffeur drove into the compound and came to a halt outside the front door. Harry was impressed. A palatial residence, worthy of a tsar, towered over him, reminding visitors of Britain's past empire, rather than its reduced status in the post-war world.

The next surprise came when he saw the ambassador standing on the Embassy steps waiting to greet him.

'Good morning, Mr Clifton,' said Sir Humphrey Trevelyan as Harry stepped out of the car.

'Good morning, your excellency,' said Harry as the two men shook hands – which was appropriate, as they were about to close a deal.

The ambassador led him into a vast circular hall that boasted a life-size statue of Queen Victoria, as well as a full-length portrait of her great-great-granddaughter.

'You won't have read *The Times* this morning,' said Trevelyan, 'but I can tell you that your speech to the PEN conference seems to have had the desired effect.'

'Let's hope so,' said Harry. 'But I'll only be convinced when Babakov is released.'

'That might take a little longer,' warned the ambassador. 'The Soviets are not known for rushing into anything, especially if it wasn't their idea in the first place. It might be wise to prepare yourself for the long game. Don't be disheartened, though, because I can tell you the Politburo has been surprised by the support you've received from the international community. However, the other side of that coin is that you're now considered . . . persona non grata.'

He led his guest down a marble corridor, dominated by portraits of British monarchs who had not suffered the same fate as their Russian relatives. A floor-to-ceiling double door was pulled open by two servants, although the ambassador was still several paces away. He walked straight into his study, took his place behind a large uncluttered desk and waved Harry into the seat opposite him.

'I have given instructions that we are not to be disturbed,' said Trevelyan as he selected a key from a chain and unlocked his desk drawer.

He pulled out a file and extracted a single sheet of paper which he handed to Harry. 'Take your time, Mr Clifton. You are not under the same restrictions that Sir Alan imposed on you.'

Harry began to study a random list of names, addresses and telephone numbers that seemed to have no sequence or logic to them. After he'd gone over it a second time, he said, 'I think I have it, sir.'

The incredulous look on the ambassador's face suggested that he wasn't convinced. 'Well, let's be sure, shall we?' He retrieved the list and replaced it with a couple of sheets of Embassy notepaper and a fountain pen.

Harry took a deep breath and began to write out the

twelve names, nine addresses and twenty-one telephone numbers. Once he'd completed the task, he handed his effort back to the ambassador to be marked. Sir Humphrey slowly checked it against the original.

'You spelt Pengelly with one "l" instead of two.'

Harry frowned.

'Perhaps you'd be kind enough to repeat the exercise, Mr Clifton,' the ambassador said as he sat back, struck a match and set light to Harry's first effort.

Harry completed his second attempt far more quickly.

'Bravo,' said the ambassador, after double-checking it. 'I only wish you were a member of my staff. Now, as we can assume the Soviets will have read the note I left at your hotel, perhaps we shouldn't disappoint them.' He pressed a button under his desk and a few moments later the doors opened again and two members of staff dressed in white linen jackets and black trousers entered, pushing a trolley.

Over a breakfast of hot coffee, brown toast, Oxford marmalade and an egg that had been produced by a chicken, the two men chatted about everything from England's chances in the forthcoming Test series against the South Africans – Harry felt that England would win, the ambassador wasn't convinced; the abolition of hanging – Harry in favour, the ambassador against; Britain joining the Common Market – something they were able to agree on. They never once touched on the real reason they were having breakfast together.

When the trolley was removed and they were once again alone, Trevelyan said, 'Forgive me for being a bore, old chap, but would you be kind enough to carry out the exercise one more time?'

Harry returned to the ambassador's desk and wrote out the list for a third time.

'Remarkable. I now understand why Sir Alan chose you.' Trevelyan led his guest out of the room. 'My car will take you to the airport, and although you may think you have more than enough time, I have a feeling the customs officials will assume I have given you something to take back to England and you will therefore be subject to a lengthy search. They are right, of course, but fortunately it's not something they can get their hands on. So all that is left for me to do, Mr Clifton, is to thank you, and suggest that you do not write out the list until the wheels of the aircraft have left the tarmac. You might even feel it advisable to wait until you are no longer in Soviet airspace. After all, there's bound to be someone on board watching your every move.'

Sir Humphrey accompanied his guest to the front door and they shook hands for a second time before Harry climbed into the back of the Rolls-Royce. The ambassador remained on the top step until the car was out of sight.

The chauffeur dropped Harry outside Sheremetyevo airport, two hours before his flight was due to take off. The ambassador turned out to be correct, because Harry spent the next hour in customs, where they checked, and double-checked, everything in his suitcase, before unstitching the lining of his jacket and overcoat.

After they had failed to find anything, he was taken to a small room and asked to remove his clothes. When their efforts failed yet again, a doctor appeared, and searched in places Harry hadn't even considered before, but certainly wouldn't be describing in graphic detail in his next book.

An hour later, his case was reluctantly given a chalk

cross to show it had been cleared, but it never did turn up in London. He decided not to protest, even though the guards at customs also failed to return his overcoat, a Christmas present from Emma. He would have to buy an identical one from Ede & Ravenscroft before he drove back to Bristol as he didn't want his wife to find out the real reason Sir Alan had wanted to see him.

When Harry finally boarded the plane, he was delighted to find he'd been upgraded to first class, as he had been on the last occasion he'd worked for the cabinet secretary. Equally pleasing, no one had been allocated the seat beside him. Sir Alan didn't leave anything to chance.

He waited until he had been in the air for over an hour before asking a steward for a couple of sheets of BOAC writing paper. But when they arrived, he changed his mind. Two men seated across the aisle from him had glanced in his direction once too often.

He adjusted his seatback, closed his eyes and went over the list in his mind again and again. By the time the plane touched down at Heathrow, he was mentally and physically exhausted. He was only glad being a spy wasn't his full-time job.

Harry was the first to disembark from the aircraft, and he wasn't surprised to see Sir Alan waiting on the tarmac at the bottom of the steps. He joined him in the back of a car that made its way quickly out of the airport without being bothered by a customs officer.

Other than, 'Good morning, Clifton,' the cabinet secretary didn't say a word before he passed over the inevitable pad and pen.

Harry wrote out the twelve names, nine addresses and twenty-one telephone numbers that had been lodged in his mind for several hours. He double-checked the list before handing it to Sir Alan.

'I am most grateful,' he said. 'And I thought you'd be pleased to hear that I've added a couple of paragraphs to the speech the foreign secretary will be making at the UN next week, which I hope will assist Mr Babakov's cause. By the way, did you spot my two minders sitting across the aisle from you in first class? I put them there to protect you, just in case you had any trouble.'

◄o►

'There's no deal for one point six million in the offing that I'm aware of,' said Cedric, 'and it's hardly likely to be something I'd forget. I'm bound to wonder what Sloane's up to.'

'I've no idea,' said Sebastian, 'but I'm sure there's a simple explanation.'

'And you say he won't be back until Friday?'

'That's right. He's at a conference in York.'

'So that gives us a couple of days to look into it. You're probably right, and there's a simple explanation. But one point six million,' he repeated. 'And Mr Collingwood has accepted his offer?'

'That's what Mr Vaughan of Savills said.'

'Ralph Vaughan is old school and doesn't make that kind of mistake.' Cedric remained silent for a few moments before adding, 'You'd better go up to Shifnal first thing in the morning and start digging around. Begin at the local pub. The publican always knows everything that's going on in his village, and one point six million would have all the gossips chattering. After you've spoken to him, check the local estate agents, but make sure you don't go anywhere near Collingwood. If you do, Sloane is certain to hear about it and will assume you're trying to undermine him. I think we'd better keep this between ourselves in case it turns out to be totally innocent. When you get back to London, come straight round to Cadogan Place and you can brief me over dinner.'

Seb decided that this wasn't the time to tell Cedric that he'd booked a table at the Mirabelle for dinner tomorrow night with Samantha. The clock on the mantelpiece struck six, so he knew the deputy chairman Ross Buchanan would be waiting outside. He rose to leave.

'Well done, Seb,' said Cedric. 'Let's hope there is a simple explanation. But in any case, thank you for keeping me briefed.'

Seb nodded. When he reached the door he turned back to say goodnight, to see Cedric swallowing a pill. He pretended not to notice, as he closed the door behind him.

10

SEB WAS UP, dressed and had left the house before Sam woke the following morning.

Cedric Hardcastle never travelled first class, but he always allowed his senior management to do so when it was a long journey. Although Seb picked up a copy of the *Financial Times* at Euston, he barely glanced at the headlines during the three-hour journey to Shropshire. His mind was preoccupied with how best to use his time once he arrived in Shifnal.

The train pulled into Shrewsbury station just after eleven thirty, and Seb didn't hesitate to take a taxi on to Shifnal rather than wait for the connecting train because on this occasion time was money. He waited until they had left the county town behind them, before he fired his first question at the driver. 'Which is the best pub in Shifnal?'

'Depends what you're looking for, good grub or the best ale in the county.'

'I always think you can judge a pub by its landlord.'

'Then it has to be the Shifnal Arms, owned by Fred and Sheila Ramsey. They don't just run the pub, but the village as well. He's president of the local cricket club, and used to open the bowling for the village. Even played for the county on a couple of occasions. And she sits on the parish council. But be warned, the food's lousy.'

'Then it's the Shifnal Arms,' said Seb. He sat back and began to go over his strategy, aware that he didn't need Sloane to discover why he wasn't in the office.

The taxi drew up outside the Shifnal Arms a few minutes after twelve. Seb would have given the driver a larger tip, but he didn't want to be remembered.

He strolled into the pub trying to look casual, which wasn't easy when you're the first customer of the day, and took a close look at the man standing behind the bar. Although he must have been over forty, and his cheeks and nose revealed that he enjoyed the product he sold, while his paunch suggested he preferred pork pies to fine dining, it was not hard to believe this giant of a man had once opened the bowling for Shifnal.

'Afternoon,' said the landlord. 'What can I get you?'

'A half of your local beer will suit me fine,' said Seb, who didn't usually drink during working hours, but today it was part of the job. The publican drew half a pint of Wrekin IPA and placed it on the bar. 'That'll be one shilling and sixpence.' Half the price Seb would have had to pay in London. He took a sip. 'Not bad,' he said, before bowling his first long hop. 'It's not a West Country brew, but it's not half bad.'

'So you're not from around these parts?' said the publican.

'No, I'm a Gloucestershire lad, born and bred,' Seb told him before taking another sip.

'So what brings you to Shifnal?'

'My firm is opening a branch in Shrewsbury, and my

wife won't agree to the move unless I can find a house in the country.'

'You don't play cricket by any chance?'

'I open the batting for the Somerset Stragglers. Another reason why I'm not that keen on moving.'

'We've got a decent enough eleven, but we're always on the lookout for fresh talent.'

Seb pointed to a photograph behind the bar. 'Is that you holding up the cup?'

'It is. 1951. When I was about fifteen years younger and some fifteen pounds lighter. We won the county cup that year, for the first and, I'm sorry to say, last time. Although we did reach the semi-finals last year.'

Time for another slow long hop. 'If I was thinking of buying a house in the area, who would you suggest I deal with?'

'There's only one half-decent estate agent in town. Charlie Watkins, my wicket keeper. You'll find his place on the High Street, can't miss it.'

'Then I'll go and have a chat with Mr Watkins, and come back for a bite of lunch.'

'Dish of the day is steak and kidney pie,' said the publican, patting his stomach.

'I'll see you later,' said Seb after he'd downed his drink.

It wasn't difficult to find the High Street, or to spot Watkins Estate Agency with its gaudy sign flapping in the breeze. Seb took some time studying the properties for sale in the window. The prices seemed to range from seven hundred pounds to twelve thousand, so how was it possible for anything in the area to be worth one point six million?

He opened the front door to the sound of a jangling

bell and as he stepped inside a young man looked up from behind his desk.

'Is Mr Watkins around?' asked Seb.

'He's with a customer at the moment, but he shouldn't be long,' he added as a door behind him opened and two men walked out.

'I'll have the paperwork completed by Monday at the latest, so if you could arrange for the deposit to be lodged with your solicitor, that should help move things along,' the elder of the two men said as he opened the door for his customer.

'This gentleman's waiting to see you, Mr Watkins,' said the young man behind the desk.

'Good morning,' said Watkins, thrusting out his hand. 'Come into my office.' He opened the door and ushered his potential client through.

Seb walked into a small room that boasted a partner's desk and three chairs. On the walls were photographs of past triumphs, every one marked with a red sticker declaring *SOLD*. Seb's eyes settled on a large property with several acres. He needed Watkins to quickly work out which end of the market he was interested in. A warm smile appeared on the estate agent's face.

'Is that the type of property you're looking for?'

'I was hoping to find a large country house with several acres of farmland attached,' Seb said as he took the seat opposite Watkins.

'I'm afraid that sort of thing doesn't come on the market very often. But I have one or two properties that might interest you.' He leant back, pulled open the drawer of the only filing cabinet and extracted three folders. 'But I have to warn you, sir, that the price of farm land has rocketed since the government decided to allow tax relief for anyone investing in agricultural land.' Seb didn't comment as Watkins opened the first folder.

'Asgarth Farm is situated on the Welsh border, seven hundred acres, mainly arable, and a magnificent Victorian mansion . . . in need of a little repair,' he added reluctantly.

'And the price?'

'Three hundred and twenty thousand,' said Watkins, passing over the brochure before quickly adding, 'or near offer.'

Seb shook his head. 'I was hoping for something with at least a thousand acres.'

Watkins's eyes lit up as if he'd won the pools. 'There is one exceptional property that's recently come on the market, but I'm only a sub-agent, and unfortunately bids have to be in by five this Friday.'

'If it's the right property, that wouldn't put me off.'

Watkins opened his desk drawer and, for the first time, offered a customer Shifnal Farm.

'This looks more interesting,' said Seb as he turned the pages of the brochure. 'How much are they asking?'

The estate agent hesitated, almost as if he didn't want to reveal the figure. Seb waited patiently.

'I know there's a bid in with Savills for one point six million,' said Watkins. His turn to wait patiently, expecting the client to reject it out of hand.

'Perhaps I could study the details over lunch and then come back this afternoon and discuss it with you?'

'In the meantime, shall I make arrangements for you to see over the property?'

That was the last thing Seb wanted, so he quickly replied, 'I'll make that decision once I've had a chance to check the details.'

'Time is against us, sir.'

True enough, thought Seb. 'I'll let you know my decision when I come back this afternoon,' he repeated a little more firmly.

'Yes, of course, sir,' said Watkins as he leapt up, accompanied him to the door and, after shaking hands once again, said, 'I look forward to seeing you later.'

Seb stepped out on to the High Street and made his way quickly back to the pub. Mr Ramsey was standing behind the bar polishing a glass when Seb sat on the stool in front of him.

'Any luck?'

'Possibly,' said Seb, placing the glossy brochure on the counter so the landlord couldn't miss it. 'Another half, please, and won't you join me?'

'Thank you, sir. Will you be having lunch?'

'I'll have the steak and kidney pie,' said Seb, studying the menu chalked up on a blackboard behind the bar.

Ramsey didn't take his eyes off the brochure, even as he drew the customer's half pint.

'I can tell you a thing or two about that property,' he said as his wife came out of the kitchen.

'Seems a bit overpriced to me,' said Seb, bowling his third long hop.

'I should say so,' said Ramsey. 'Only five year back it were on the market at three hundred thousand, and even at that price, young Mr Collingwood couldn't shift it.'

'The new tax incentives could be the reason,' suggested Seb.

'That wouldn't explain the price I'm hearing.'

'Perhaps the owner's been granted planning permission to build on the land. Housing, or one of those new industrial estates the government are so keen on.'

'Not on your nelly,' said Mrs Ramsey as she joined them. 'The parish council may not have any power, but that lot at County Hall still have to keep us informed if they want to build anything, from a letterbox to a multi-storey car park. It's been our right since Magna Carta to be allowed to lodge an objection and hold up proceedings for ninety days. Not that they take much notice after that.'

'Then there has to be oil, gold or the lost treasure of the Pharaohs buried under the land,' said Seb, trying to make light of it.

'I've heard wilder suggestions than that,' said Ramsey. 'A hoard of Roman coins worth millions, buried treasure. But my favourite is that Collingwood was one of them train robbers, and Shifnal Farm is where they buried the loot.'

'And don't forget,' said Mrs Ramsey, reappearing with a steak and kidney pie, 'Mr Swann says he knows exactly why the price has rocketed, but he won't tell anyone unless they make a substantial donation to his school theatre appeal.'

'Mr Swann?' said Seb as he picked up his knife and fork.

'Used to be headmaster of the local grammar school, retired some years back and now devotes his time to raising money for the school theatre. Bit obsessed with the idea if you ask me.'

'Do you think we can beat the South Africans?' asked Seb, having gained the information he needed and now wanting to move on.

'M.J.K. Smith will have his hands full with that lot,' said the barman, 'but if you ask me . . .'

Seb sipped his beer, while selecting carefully which

parts of the steak and kidney pie he could safely eat. He settled on the burnt crust, as he continued to listen to the landlord's views on everything from the Beatles being awarded the MBE (Harold Wilson after the young vote), to the possibility of the Americans landing a man on the moon (What's the point?).

When a rowdy group of customers entered the pub and Ramsey became distracted, Seb left half a crown on the bar and slipped out. Once he was back on the street, he asked a woman clutching the hand of a young boy where the grammar school was.

'About half a mile up the road,' she said. 'You can't miss it.'

It felt more like a mile, but he certainly couldn't miss the vast, red-brick Victorian edifice, which John Betjeman would have admired.

Seb didn't even have to pass through the school gates before he spotted what he was looking for. A prominent notice announced an appeal for £10,000 to build a new theatre for the school. Next to it was a large drawing of a thermometer, but Seb observed that the red line only reached £1,766. *To learn more about the project, please contact Mr Maurice Swann MA (Oxon) on Shifnal 2613.*

Seb wrote down two numbers in his diary, 8234 and 2613, then turned and headed back towards the High Street. In the distance he spotted a red telephone box, and he was pleased to see it wasn't occupied. He stepped inside and rehearsed his lines for a few moments, before checking the number in his diary. He dialled 2613, pressed four pennies into the slot, and waited for some time before an elderly voice answered.

'Maurice Swann.'

'Good afternoon, Mr Swann. My name is Clifton. I'm

the head of corporate donations for Farthings Bank, and we are considering making a donation to your theatre appeal. I wonder if it might be possible for us to meet. I would of course be quite happy to come and see you.'

'No, I'd prefer to meet at the school,' said Swann eagerly. 'Then I can show you what we have planned.'

'That's fine,' said Seb, 'but unfortunately I'm only in Shifnal for the day, and will be returning to London this evening.'

'Then I'll come over immediately. Why don't I see you outside the school gates in ten minutes?'

'I look forward to meeting you,' said Seb. He put the phone down and quickly retraced his steps back to the grammar school. He didn't have to wait long before he spotted a frail-looking gentleman walking slowly towards him with the aid of a stick.

After Seb had introduced himself, Swann said, 'As you have such a short time, Mr Clifton, why don't I take you straight through to the Memorial Hall, where I can show you the architect's plans for the new theatre and answer any questions you might have.'

Seb followed the old man through the school gates, across the yard and into the hall, while listening to him talk about the importance of young people having their own theatre and what a difference it would make to the local community.

Seb took his time studying the detailed architect's drawings that were pinned to the wall, while Swann continued to enthuse about the project.

'As you can see, Mr Clifton, although we will have a proscenium arch, there would still be enough room backstage to store props, while the actors standing in the wings won't be cramped, and if I raise the full amount the boys and girls will be able to have separate dressing rooms.' He stood back. 'My life's dream,' he admitted, 'which I hope to see completed before I die. But may I ask why your bank would be interested in a small project in Shifnal?'

'We are currently buying land in the area on behalf of clients who are interested in taking advantage of the government's latest tax incentives. We realize that's not likely to be popular in the village, so we've decided to support some local projects.'

'Would one of those pieces of land be Shifnal Farm?'

Seb was taken by surprise by Swann's question, and it was some time before he managed, 'No, we looked at Mr Collingwood's property and on balance decided it was overpriced.'

'How many children do you think I've taught in my lifetime, Mr Clifton?'

'I've no idea,' said Seb, puzzled by the question.

'Just over three thousand, so I know when someone is trying to get away with only telling me half the story.'

'I'm not sure I understand, sir.'

'You understand all too well, Mr Clifton. The truth is, you're on a fishing trip, and you have absolutely no interest in my theatre. What you really want to know is why someone is willing to pay one point six million pounds for Shifnal Farm, when no one else has bid anywhere near that amount. Am I right?'

'Yes,' admitted Seb. 'And if I knew the answer to that question, I'm sure my bank would be willing to make a substantial donation towards your new theatre.'

'When you're an old man, Mr Clifton, and you will be one day, you'll find you have a bit of time on your hands, especially if you've led an active and worthwhile life. So when someone bid far too much for Shifnal Farm, my curiosity got the better of me, and I decided to spend some of my spare time trying to find out why. I began, like any good detective, by looking for clues, and I can tell you that after six months of diligent research, following up even the most unlikely leads, I now know exactly why someone is willing to pay way over the asking price for Shifnal Farm.'

Seb could feel his heart thumping.

'And if you want to know what it is that I've found out, you won't just make a substantial donation to the school theatre, you'll finance the entire project.'

'But what if you're wrong?'

'That's a risk you're going to have to take, Mr Clifton, because there's only a couple of days before the bidding closes.'

'Then you must also be willing to take the risk,' said Seb, 'because I'm not going to fork out over eight thousand pounds unless, and until, you're proved right.'

'Before I agree to that, it's my turn to ask you a question.'

'Of course,' said Seb.

'Are you, by any chance, related to Harry Clifton, the author?'

'Yes, he's my father.'

'I thought I saw a resemblance. Although I've never read any of his books, I've followed his campaign for Anatoly Babakov with great interest, and if Harry Clifton is your father, that's good enough for me.'

'Thank you, sir,' said Seb.

'Now, sit down, young man, because time is against us.'

Seb perched on the edge of the stage, while Swann took him slowly through the meticulous research he'd carried out during the past six months, that had led him to only one conclusion. A conclusion Seb couldn't find fault with. He jumped down from the stage.

'May I ask you one more question before I leave, sir?'

'Of course, young man.'

'Why didn't you tell Collingwood what you'd discovered? After all, he couldn't have lost a penny if he didn't have to pay up until you were proved right.'

'I taught Dan Collingwood when he was at the grammar school,' said Swann. 'Even as a boy he was greedy and stupid, and he hasn't improved much since. But he wasn't interested in what I might have to tell him, just fobbed me off with a five-pound donation and wished me luck.'

'So you haven't told this to anyone else?' said Seb, trying not to sound anxious.

The old man hesitated for a moment. 'I did tell one other person,' he admitted, 'but I haven't heard from him since.'

Seb didn't need to ask his name.

◄○►

Sebastian knocked on the door of 37 Cadogan Place just after eight o'clock. Cedric answered the summons and, without a word, led his young protégé through to the drawing room. Seb's eyes immediately settled on a Hockney landscape hanging above the fireplace, before he admired the Henry Moore maquette on the sideboard. Seb didn't doubt that if Picasso had been born in Yorkshire his work would also be part of Cedric's collection.

'Would you care to join me for a glass of wine?' asked Cedric. 'Châteauneuf-du-Pape 1959, which from the expression on your face I have a feeling you may have earned.'

'Thank you, sir,' said Seb as he sank into the nearest chair. Cedric handed him a glass and took the seat opposite him.

'When you've caught your breath, take me through the day, slowly.'

Seb took a sip. Not a vintage Mr Ramsey would be serving at the Shifnal Arms that evening.

When Seb came to the end of his tale twenty minutes later, Cedric remarked, 'Swann sounds to me like a shrewd old cove. I have a feeling I'd like him. But what did you learn from the encounter?' A question he had frequently posed when Seb had been his personal assistant.

'Just because a man is physically frail, doesn't mean his mind isn't still sharp.'

'Good. Anything else?'

'The importance of reputation.'

'Your father's, in this case,' Cedric reminded him. 'If you get nothing else out of today, Seb, that lesson alone will have made your journey to Shifnal worthwhile. However, now I have to face the fact that one of my most senior members of staff may be dealing behind my back.' He took a sip of wine before he continued. 'It is possible, of course, that Sloane will have a simple explanation, but somehow I doubt it.'

Seb suppressed a smile. 'But shouldn't we do something about the deal, now we know what the government has in mind?'

'All in good time. First I'll need to have a word with Ralph Vaughan, because he's not going to be pleased when I withdraw the bank's offer, and he'll be even more angry when I tell him the reason why.'

'But won't he simply accept one of the lower offers?'

'Not if he thinks there's still a chance he might get a higher price if he hangs on for a few more days.'

'And Mr Swann?'

'I'm tempted to give him the £8,234 whatever happens. I think he's earned it.' Cedric took another sip of wine before he added, 'But there's nothing else we can do tonight, Seb, I suggest you go home. In fact, as all hell is going to break loose tomorrow, perhaps it might be wise for you to take the day off and stay as far away from the office as possible. But report to me first thing on Monday morning, as I have a feeling you could be on your way back to Shropshire.'

As they left the room and walked down the corridor towards the front door, Cedric said, 'I hope you didn't have anything planned for this evening?'

Nothing special, thought Seb. I was just going to take Samantha out to dinner and ask her to marry me.

11

ONCE SEBASTIAN realized that he wouldn't be expected back at the office before Monday morning, he began to plan a surprise weekend for Samantha. He spent the morning booking trains, planes, hotels and even checked the opening times of the Rijksmuseum. He wanted the weekend in Amsterdam to be perfect, so when they emerged from customs, he ignored the signs for buses and trains and headed straight for the taxi rank.

'Cedric must have been pleased when you discovered what Sloane was up to,' said Sam as the cab joined the traffic making its way out of the airport. 'What do you think will happen next?'

'I expect Sloane will be sacked around five o'clock this afternoon.'

'Why five this afternoon?'

'That's when he was hoping to close the Shifnal Farm deal.'

'There's almost an element of Greek tragedy about that,' said Sam. 'So, with a bit of luck, Sloane will be gone by the time you turn up for work on Monday.'

'Almost certainly, because Cedric asked me to report to him first thing.'

'Do you think you'll get Sloane's job?' asked Sam as the cab headed on to the motorway.

'Possibly. But it's only likely to be a temporary appointment while Cedric looks for someone more experienced.'

'But if you managed to pull off the Shifnal deal, he might not bother to look for someone else.'

'That's also a possibility, and I wouldn't be surprised to find I was on a train back to Shrewsbury on Monday. Did he go left around that roundabout?'

'No, right,' said Sam, laughing. 'Don't forget we're on the continent.' She turned to Seb, who was clinging on to the front seat, and placed a hand on his leg. 'I'm so sorry,' she said. 'I sometimes forget about that dreadful accident.'

'I'm fine,' said Seb.

'I like the sound of Mr Swann. Perhaps it would be wise to keep him on your side.'

'Cedric agrees with you. And if we pull off the deal, we'll probably end up having to build his school a concert hall,' Seb added as they entered the outskirts of the city.

'I assume we're staying at the Amstel?' said Sam as the deluxe five-star hotel overlooking the Amstel river loomed up in front of them.

'Not this time, that will have to wait until I'm chairman of the bank. But until then, it's the Pension De Kanaal, a well-known one-star guest house frequented by the up-and-coming.'

Sam smiled as the taxi drew up outside a little guest house wedged between a greengrocer and an Indonesian restaurant. 'Far better than the Amstel,' she declared as they walked into the cramped lobby. Once they'd checked in, Seb lugged their bags up to the top floor, as the pension didn't have a lift or a porter. He unlocked the door of their room and switched on the light.

'Palatial,' Sam declared.

Seb couldn't believe how small the room was. There was only just enough space for them to stand on each side of the double bed. 'I'm so sorry,' he said. 'I wanted this weekend to be just perfect.'

Sam took him in her arms. 'You are a silly thing at times. This *is* perfect. I prefer being up-and-coming. Gives us something to look forward to.'

Seb fell back on the bed. 'I know what I'm looking forward to.'

'A visit to the Rijksmuseum?' suggested Sam.

–◦–

'You wanted to see me?' said Sloane as he marched into the chairman's office. He didn't wait to be offered a seat.

Cedric looked up at the head of his property division, but didn't smile. 'I've just finished reading your monthly report.'

'Up two point two per cent on last month,' Sloane reminded him.

'Very impressive. But I wonder if you might have done even better if . . .'

'If what, chairman?' said Sloane abruptly.

'If Shifnal Farm had also been included in your report,' said Cedric, picking up a brochure from his desk.

'Shifnal Farm? Are you sure that's one of my properties, and not Clifton's?' said Sloane, nervously touching the knot of his tie.

'I'm absolutely certain it's one of your properties, Sloane. What I can't be sure about is whether it's one of the bank's.'

'What are you getting at?' said Sloane, suddenly on the defensive.

'When I called Ralph Vaughan, the senior partner of Savills, a few moments ago, he confirmed that you'd put in a bid of one point six million pounds for the property, with the bank acting as guarantor.'

Sloane shifted uneasily in his chair. 'You're quite right, chairman, but as the deal hasn't finally been closed, you won't have all the details until I send you next month's report.'

'One of the details that will take some explaining is why the account is registered to a client in Zurich.'

'Ah, yes,' said Sloane. 'Now I remember. You're quite right, we were acting for a Swiss client who prefers anonymity, but the bank charges three per cent commission on every deal we carry out for that particular customer.'

'And it didn't take a great deal of research,' said Cedric, patting a pile of papers on the desk in front of him, 'to discover that that particular client has conducted another six transactions during the past year, and made himself a handsome profit.'

'But isn't that what my department is supposed to do?' protested Sloane. 'Make profits for our clients, while at the same time earning the bank a handsome commission?'

'It is indeed,' said Cedric, trying to remain calm. 'It's just a pity the Swiss client's account is in your name.'

'How can you possibly know that,' blurted out Sloane, 'when client accounts in Switzerland are not named but numbered?'

'I didn't. But you've just confirmed my worst fears, so your number is up.'

Sloane leapt from his chair. 'I've made a twenty-three per cent profit for the bank over the past ten months.'

'And if my calculations are correct,' came back Cedric, 'you've made another forty-one per cent for yourself during the same period. And I have a feeling Shifnal Farm was going to be your biggest payday yet.'

Sloane collapsed back in his chair, a look of desperation on his face. 'But . . .'

'I'm sorry to be the bearer of bad news,' continued Cedric, 'but this is one deal you're not going to pull off for your Swiss client, because I called Mr Vaughan at Savills a few minutes ago and withdrew our bid for Shifnal Farm.'

'But we could have made a massive profit on that deal,' said Sloane, now staring defiantly at the chairman. 'Possibly as much as a million pounds.'

'I don't think you mean *we*,' said Cedric, 'I think you mean *you*. Although it was the bank's money you were putting up as collateral, not your own.'

'But you only know half the facts.'

'I can assure you, Sloane, that thanks to Mr Swann, I know all the facts.'

Sloane rose slowly from his seat.

'You are a stupid old man,' he said, spitting out the words. 'You're out of touch, and you don't begin to understand modern banking. The sooner you make way for a younger man, the better.'

'No doubt in time I will,' said Cedric, as he stood up to face his adversary, 'but of one thing I'm certain, that young man is no longer going to be you.'

'You'll live to regret this,' said Sloane, leaning across the desk and eyeballing the chairman.

'Don't waste your time threatening me, Sloane. Far bigger men than you have tried and failed,' said Cedric, his voice rising with every word. 'There's only one thing left for you to do, and that's make sure you've cleared your desk and are off the premises within thirty minutes, because if you're not, I'll personally put your belongings out on the pavement for every passer-by to see.'

'You'll be hearing from my lawyers,' shouted Sloane, as he turned to leave.

'I don't think so, unless you plan to spend the next few years in prison, because I can assure you, once this stupid old man has reported your behaviour to the ethics committee of the Bank of England, you'll never work in the City again.'

Sloane turned back, his face as white as a sheet and, like a gambler with only one chip left, spun the wheel for the last time. 'But I could still make the bank a fortune, if you'll only—'

'Twenty-nine minutes,' shouted Cedric, trying to control his temper, as he lurched forward and grabbed the edge of his desk.

Sloane didn't move as the chairman pulled open a drawer and took out a small bottle of pills. He fumbled with the safety cap, but lost his grip and dropped the bottle on to his desk. They both watched as it rolled on to the floor. Cedric attempted to fill a glass with water, but he no longer had the strength to pick up the jug.

'I need your help,' he slurred, looking up at Sloane, who just stood there, watching him carefully.

Cedric stumbled, took a pace backwards and fell heavily on the floor, gasping for breath. Sloane walked slowly around the desk, his eyes never leaving the chairman as he lay on the floor fighting for his life. He picked up the bottle and unscrewed the cap. Cedric stared up at him as he shook the pills on to the floor, just out of his

reach. He then wiped the empty bottle with a handkerchief from his top pocket and placed it in the chairman's
hand.

Sloane leant over and listened carefully, to find that
the chairman was no longer breathing quite so heavily.
Cedric tried to raise his head, but he could only watch
helplessly as Sloane gathered up all the papers on his desk
that he'd been working on for the past twenty-four hours.
Sloane turned and walked slowly away, without once looking back, avoiding those eyes that were burning into him.

He opened the door and looked out into the corridor.
No one in sight. He closed the door quietly behind him
and went in search of the chairman's secretary. Her hat
and coat were no longer on the stand, so he assumed
she must have left for the weekend. He tried to remain
calm as he walked down the corridor, but beads of sweat
were pouring off his forehead and he could feel his heart
pounding.

He stood for a moment and listened, like a blood-
hound sniffing for danger. He decided to throw the dice
once again.

'Anyone around?' he shouted.

His voice echoed through the high-ceilinged corridor
as if it were a concert hall, but there was no response. He
checked the executive offices one by one, but they were
all locked. No one on the top floor, other than Cedric,
would still be in the office at six o'clock on a Friday
evening. Sloane knew there would still be junior staff in
the building who wouldn't think of leaving before their
bosses, but none of them would consider disturbing the
chairman, and the cleaners wouldn't be returning until
five o'clock on Monday morning. That only left Stanley,

the night porter, who would never budge from his comfortable chair at the front desk unless the building was on fire.

Sloane took the lift to the ground floor and, as he crossed the lobby, he noticed that Stanley was dozing quietly. He didn't disturb him.

◄○►

'The Rijksmuseum,' said Sam as they entered the Dutch national gallery, 'houses one of the finest collections on earth. The Rembrandts are show-stoppers but the Vermeers, De Wittes and Steens are also among the finest examples of the Dutch masters you'll ever see.'

Hand in hand they made their way slowly around the grand gallery, Sam often stopping to point out a character, or a feature of a particular work, without ever once referring to her guidebook. Whenever heads turned, and they often did, Seb wanted to shout, 'And she's bright, too!'

At the far end of the gallery stood a small crowd, admiring a single work.

'*The Night Watch*,' said Sam, 'is a masterpiece, and probably Rembrandt's best-known work. Although sadly we'll never know what the original looked like because the city council later trimmed the painting to fit between two columns in the town hall.'

'They should have knocked down the columns,' said Seb, unable to take his eyes off the group of figures surrounding a finely dressed man carrying a lantern.

'Pity you weren't on the town council,' said Sam as they walked into the next room. 'And here's a painting that will feature in my PhD thesis,' she continued as they stopped in front of a large canvas. 'It's hard to believe that Rubens completed the work in a weekend, because he had to attend the signing of a peace treaty between the English and Spanish on the following Monday. Most people are quite unaware that he was a diplomat as well as an artist,' she said before moving on.

Seb felt he ought to be taking notes, but his mind was on other things.

'This is one of my favourites,' said Sam, stopping in front of *The Arnolfini Wedding*.

'I've seen that somewhere else,' said Seb.

'Ah, so you do listen to me occasionally. You saw it when we visited the National Gallery last year.'

'So what's it doing here?'

'It's probably on loan,' said Sam. 'But only for another month,' she added after taking a closer look at the label on the wall beside the portrait. 'But more important, do you remember what I told you about it at the time?'

'Yes, it's the wedding of a wealthy merchant, and Van Eyck must have been commissioned to record the event.'

'Not bad,' said Sam. 'So really Van Eyck was just doing the job of a modern-day wedding photographer.'

Seb was about to say something, but she added, 'Look at the texture of the bride's dress, and the fur on the lapels on the groom's coat – you can almost feel it.'

'The bride looks heavily pregnant to me.'

'How observant of you, Seb. But any wealthy man at the time had to be sure that the woman he'd chosen to be his wife was capable of producing an heir to inherit his fortune.'

'What a practical lot those Dutch were,' said Seb. 'But what if you weren't rich?'

'The lower classes were expected to behave more properly.'

Seb fell on one knee in front of the painting, looked up

at Sam and said, 'Samantha Ethel Sullivan, I adore you, and always will, and more than anything on earth I want you to be my wife.'

Sam blushed and, bending down, whispered, 'Get up, you idiot. Everyone's staring at us.'

'Not until you've answered my question.'

A small group of visitors had stopped looking at the paintings and were waiting for her reply.

'Of course I'll marry you,' she said. 'I've loved you since the day you got me arrested.' Several of the on-lookers, looking rather puzzled, tried to translate her words.

Seb stood up, took out a small red leather box from his jacket pocket and presented it to her. When Sam opened the box and saw the exquisite blue sapphire surrounded by a cluster of little diamonds, she was for once lost for words.

Seb took out the ring and placed it on the third finger of her left hand. When he leant forward to kiss his fiancée, he was greeted with a round of applause. As they walked away, hand in hand, Samantha glanced back at the painting and wondered if she ought to tell him.

12

'MAY I ASK what time you left the office on Friday evening, sir?'

'It must have been around six o'clock, inspector,' said Sloane.

'And what time was your appointment with Mr Hard-castle?'

'Five. We always met at five on the last Friday of the month, to go over my department's figures.'

'And when you left him, did he seem in good spirits?'

'Never better,' said Sloane. 'My monthly results were up by two point two per cent, and I was able to tell him the details of a new project I'd been working on that he became very excited about.'

'It's just that the pathologist has put the time of death at around six o'clock on Friday evening, so you must have been the last person to see him alive.'

'If that's the case, I only wish our meeting had lasted a little longer,' said Sloane.

'Quite so. Did Mr Hardcastle take any pills while you were with him?'

'No. And although we all knew Cedric had a heart

problem, he made a point of not taking his medication in front of members of staff.'

'It seems odd that his pills were scattered randomly over the floor of his office while the empty bottle was in his hand. Why wasn't he able to get hold of at least one of the pills?'

Sloane said nothing.

'And Stanley Davis, the night porter, told me that you phoned in on Saturday morning to check if a package had arrived for you.'

'Yes, I did. I needed a particular document for a meeting that was scheduled for Monday morning.'

'And did it arrive?'

'Yes, but not until this morning.'

'Mr Davis tells me he's never known you to telephone on a Saturday morning before.'

Sloane didn't rise to the bait.

'The pathologist has issued a death certificate concluding that Mr Hardcastle died of a heart attack, which I have no doubt the coroner will confirm at the inquest.' Still Sloane said nothing. 'Can I assume that you'll be around for the next few days, Mr Sloane, should I have any more questions?'

'Yes, you can, although I was planning to travel up to Huddersfield tomorrow to pay my respects to Mr Hardcastle's widow, and to see if there's anything I can do to help with the funeral arrangements.'

'How very thoughtful of you. Well, I only have one or two more people to interview, Mr Sloane, and then I'll be on my way.'

Sloane waited for the inspector to leave his office and close the door behind him before he picked up the phone.

'I need those documents ready for signature by close of business today.'

'I've got a team working on them right now, sir.'

Sloane's second call was to Ralph Vaughan at Savills, who passed on his condolences, but didn't go into the details of his conversation with Cedric Hardcastle on Friday afternoon.

'And like you,' said Sloane, 'our thoughts are with Cedric and his family at this time. But the last thing he said to me on Friday evening was to be sure we closed the Shifnal Farm deal.'

'But surely you know he withdrew the bank's offer on Friday afternoon, which was embarrassing, to say the least.'

'That was before I was able to brief him on the full details, and I know he had intended to call you first thing this morning.'

'If that's the case, I'm willing to extend the deadline for one more week, but no more,' emphasized Vaughan.

'That's good of you, Ralph. And be assured the deposit of a hundred and sixty thousand will be with you later today, and we'll just have to wait and see if anyone outbids me.'

'I can't imagine anyone will,' said Vaughan. 'But I must ask if you have the authority to make an offer of one point six million on behalf of the bank.'

'It's no more than my duty to see that Cedric's final wishes are carried out,' said Sloane, before putting down the phone.

Sloane's third and fourth calls were to two of the bank's major shareholders, who said they would back him, but only if Mrs Hardcastle went along with his proposal.

'I'll have the documents on your desk ready for

signature by close of business tomorrow,' he assured them.

Sloane's fifth call was to the Bank of Zurich in Switzerland.

◄o►

Seb phoned his mother from the office that morning and told her the news.

'I'm so sorry,' said Emma. 'I know how much you admired Cedric.'

'I can't help thinking that my days at Farthings are numbered, especially if Adrian Sloane takes Cedric's place.'

'Just keep your head down, and remember it's quite hard to sack someone who's doing a good job.'

'You clearly haven't met Sloane. He would have sacked Wellington on the morning of Waterloo if it would have guaranteed he became a general.'

'Don't forget that Ross Buchanan is still the deputy chairman, and the most likely candidate to replace Cedric.'

'I hope you're right,' said Seb.

'I'm sure Cedric kept Ross well briefed on Sloane's activities. And please let me know when and where the funeral will take place, as your father and I will want to attend.'

◄o►

'I'm so sorry to trouble you at a time like this, Mrs Hardcastle, but we both know that Cedric would have expected nothing less of me.'

Beryl Hardcastle drew her woollen shawl tightly around her and shrank back, almost disappearing into the large leather armchair.

'What do you need me to do?' she whispered.

'Nothing too demanding,' said Sloane. 'Just a couple of documents that need to be signed, and then I know the Reverend Johnson is waiting to take you through the order of service. His only concern is that the church won't be large enough to accommodate the local community as well as all Cedric's friends and colleagues who will be travelling up from London on Thursday.'

'He wouldn't have wanted them to miss a day's work for his sake,' said Beryl.

'I didn't have the heart to stop them.'

'That's very considerate of you.'

'It's no more than he deserves,' said Sloane. 'But there is still one small matter that needs to be dealt with.' He extracted three thick documents from his briefcase. 'I just need your signature, so the bank can carry on with its day-to-day business.'

'Can it wait until this afternoon?' asked Beryl. 'My son Arnold is on his way up from London. As you probably know, he's a QC, and he usually advises me on any matters concerning the bank.'

'I fear not,' said Sloane. 'I'll have to take the two o'clock train back to London if I'm to keep all the appointments Mr Hardcastle had scheduled. If it would help, I'll happily send copies of the documents round to Arnold's chambers as soon as I get back to the bank.' He took her by the hand. 'I just need three signatures, Mrs Hardcastle. But by all means read through the documents if you are in any doubt.'

'I suppose it will be all right,' Beryl said, taking the pen Sloane handed to her and making no attempt to read the densely typed small print. Sloane left the room and asked the vicar to join them. He then knelt down beside Mrs Hardcastle, turned to the last page of the first document and placed a finger on the dotted line. Beryl signed all three documents in the presence of the Reverend Johnson, who innocently witnessed her signature.

'I look forward to seeing you again on Thursday,' said Sloane, getting up off his knees, 'when we will recall with admiration and gratitude all that Cedric achieved in his remarkable life.'

He left the old lady with the vicar.

◄○►

'Mr Clifton, can you tell me where you were at five o'clock on Friday evening?'

'I was in Amsterdam with my girlfriend, Samantha, visiting the Rijksmuseum.'

'When did you last see Mr Cedric Hardcastle?'

'I went to his home in Cadogan Place just after eight on Thursday evening, having returned from Shifnal in Shropshire.'

'May I ask why Mr Hardcastle wanted you to visit him outside working hours, when you could have seen him at the office the following morning?'

Sebastian spent a little time considering his response, well aware that all he needed to say was that it was a private matter concerning the bank, and the inspector would have to move on.

'I was checking on a deal, where the chairman had reason to believe that a senior member of staff had been working behind his back.'

'And did you discover that the person concerned was working behind Mr Hardcastle's back?'

'Yes, I did.'

'Was that senior member of staff Mr Adrian Sloane, by any chance?'

Seb remained silent.

'What was Mr Hardcastle's attitude, after you told him what you'd found out?'

'He warned me that he intended to sack the person concerned the following day, and advised me to be as far away from the office as possible when he did so.'

'Because he was going to sack your boss?'

'Which is why I was in Amsterdam on Friday evening,' said Seb, ignoring the question. 'Which I now regret.'

'Why?'

'Because if I'd gone to the office that day, I just might have been able to save Mr Hardcastle.'

'Do you believe Mr Sloane would have saved him, faced with the same circumstances?'

'My father always says that a policeman should never ask a hypothetical question.'

'Not all of us can solve every crime quite as easily as Inspector Warwick.'

'Do you think Sloane murdered Mr Hardcastle?' asked Seb.

'No, I don't,' said the inspector. 'Although it's just possible that he could have saved his life. But even Inspector Warwick would find that hard to prove.'

◄○►

The Rt Rev. Ashley Tadworth, Bishop of Huddersfield, climbed the half-dozen steps and took his place in the pulpit during the last verse of 'Abide With Me'.

He looked down at the packed congregation and waited until everyone was settled. Some, who hadn't been able to find a seat, were standing in the aisles, while others, who'd arrived late, were crammed together at the back of the church. It was a mark of the man.

'Funerals are, naturally, sad events,' began the bishop. 'Even more so when the departed has achieved little more than leading a blameless life, which can make delivering their eulogy a difficult task. That was not my problem when I prepared my address on the life, the exemplary life, of Cedric Arthur Hardcastle.

'If you were to liken Cedric's life to a bank statement, he left this world with every account in credit. Where do I begin, to tell you the unlikely tale of this remarkable Yorkshireman?

'Cedric left school at the age of fifteen and joined his father at Farthings Bank. He always called his father "sir", both at work and at home. In fact, his father retired just in time not to have to call his son "sir".'

A little laughter broke out among the congregation.

'Cedric began his working life as a junior trainee. Two years later he became a teller, even before he was old enough to open a bank account. From there he progressed to under-manager, branch manager, and later, area controller, before becoming the youngest director in the bank's history. And frankly no one was surprised when he became chairman of the bank at the age of forty-two, a position he held for the past twenty-three years, during which time he took Farthings from being a local bank in a small town in Yorkshire to one of the most respected financial institutions in the City of London.

'But something that would not have changed, even if Cedric had become chairman of the Bank of England, was his constant refrain that if you take care of the pennies, the pounds will take care of themselves.'

'Do you think we've got away with it?' asked Sloane nervously.

'If, by that, you're asking if everything you've done in the past four days is legal and above board, the answer is yes.'

'Do we have a quorum?'

'We do,' said Malcolm Atkins, the bank's chief legal advisor. 'The managing director, the company secretary and six non-executive directors are waiting for you in the boardroom. Mind you,' he added, 'I'd be fascinated to know what you said to them when they suggested that perhaps they ought to be attending a funeral in Huddersfield today rather than a board meeting in London.'

'I told them quite simply that the choice was theirs. They could vote for a place in this world or the next.'

Atkins smiled and checked his watch. 'We should join them. It's almost ten.'

The two men left Sloane's office and walked silently down the thickly carpeted corridor. When Sloane entered the boardroom, everyone stood, just as they'd always done for the late chairman.

'Gentlemen,' said the company secretary once they had all settled. 'This extraordinary meeting has been called for one purpose, namely . . .'

◄o►

'Whenever we think of Cedric Hardcastle,' continued the bishop, 'we should remember one thing above all. He was quintessentially a Yorkshireman. If the second coming had taken place at Headingley during the tea interval of a Roses match, he would not have been surprised. It was Cedric's unswerving belief that Yorkshire was a country, not a county. In fact, he considered Farthings Bank to have become international not when he opened a branch in Hong Kong but when he opened one in Manchester.'

He waited for the laughter to die down before he continued.

'Cedric was not a vain man, but that didn't stop him being a proud one. Proud of the bank he served every day, and even prouder of how many customers and staff had prospered under his guidance and leadership. So many of you in this congregation today, from the most junior trainee to the president of Sony International, have been beneficiaries of his wisdom and foresight. But what he will most be remembered for is his unquestionable reputation – for honesty, integrity and decency. Standards he took for granted when dealing with his fellow men. He considered a good deal was one in which both sides made a profit, and would be happy to raise their hats to each other whenever they passed in the street.'

◄○►

'The one item on today's agenda,' continued the company secretary, 'is for the board to elect a new chairman, following the tragic death of Cedric Hardcastle. Only one name has been proposed, that of Mr Adrian Sloane, the head of our highly profitable property division. Mr Sloane has already obtained the legal backing of sixty-six per cent of our shareholders, but he felt his appointment should also be ratified by the board.'

Malcolm Atkins came in on cue. 'It is my pleasure to propose that Adrian Sloane be the next chairman of Farthings Bank, as I feel that is what Cedric would have wanted.'

'I'm delighted to second that motion,' said Desmond Mellor, a recently appointed non-executive director.

'Those in favour?' said the company secretary. Eight hands shot up. 'I declare the motion carried unanimously.'

Sloane rose slowly to his feet. 'Gentlemen. Allow me to begin by thanking you for the confidence you have shown by electing me as the next chairman of Farthings. Cedric Hardcastle's shoes are not easy ones to step into. I replace a man who left us in tragic circumstances. A man we all assumed would be with us for many years to come. A man I could not have admired more. A man I considered not only a colleague, but a friend, which makes me all the more proud to pick up his baton and carry it on the next leg of the bank's race. I respectfully suggest that we all rise, and bow our heads in memory of a great man.'

◄○►

'But ultimately,' continued the bishop, 'Cedric Hardcastle will best be remembered as a family man. He loved Beryl from the day she gave him an extra third of a pint when she was the milk monitor at their primary school in Huddersfield, and he could not have been more proud when their only son, Arnold, became a QC. Although he could never understand why the lad had chosen Oxford, and not Leeds, to complete his education.

'Allow me to end by summing up my feelings for one of my oldest and dearest friends with the words from the epitaph on Sir Thomas Fairfax by the Duke of Buckingham:

He never knew what envy was, nor hate;
His soul was filled with worth and honesty,
And with another thing besides, quite out of date,
Called modesty.'

◄○►

Malcolm Atkins raised a glass of champagne.

'To the new chairman of Farthings,' he toasted, as Sloane sat in the chair behind Cedric's desk for the first time. 'So, what will be your first executive action?'

'Make sure we close the Shifnal deal before anyone else works out why it's so cheap at one point six million.'

'And your second?' asked Mellor.

'Sack Sebastian Clifton,' he spat out, 'along with anyone else who was close to Hardcastle and went along with his outdated philosophy. This bank is about to join the real world, where profits, not people, will be its only mantra. And if any customers threaten to move their account, let them, especially if they're from Yorkshire. From now on, the bank's motto will be, *If you've only got pennies, don't bother to bank with us.*'

◄o►

Sebastian bowed his head as the pallbearers lowered the coffin into the grave so no one would see his tears. Ross Buchanan didn't attempt to hide his feelings. Emma and Harry held hands. They had all lost a good and wise friend.

As they walked slowly away from the graveside, Arnold Hardcastle and his mother joined them.

'Why wasn't Adrian Sloane here?' asked Ross. 'Not to mention half a dozen other directors?'

'Father wouldn't have missed Sloane,' said Arnold. 'He was just about to sack him before he died.'

'He told you that?' said Ross.

'Yes. He rang me early on Friday morning to find out what the legal position was if the head of a department was caught using the bank's money to carry out private deals.'

'Did he say which head of department?' asked Ross.

'He didn't need to.'

'Did you say six directors?' interrupted Emma.

'Yes,' said Ross. 'Why's that important?'

'It constitutes a quorum. If Cedric were still alive, he would have spotted what Sloane was up to.'

'Oh my God. Now I realize why he needed me to sign those documents,' said Beryl. 'Cedric will never forgive me.'

'Like you, I'm appalled, Mother, but don't worry, you still own fifty-one per cent of the bank.'

'Can someone kindly explain in simple English,' asked Harry, 'what you're all talking about?'

'Adrian Sloane has just appointed himself as the new chairman of Farthings,' said Sebastian. 'Where's the nearest phone?'

13

SEBASTIAN CHECKED his watch. Just enough time to make one call. He was relieved to find the only phone box within sight was empty, and wasn't out of order. He dialled a number he knew by heart.

'Victor Kaufman.'

'Vic, it's Seb.'

'Seb, hi. You sound as if you're phoning from the other side of the world.'

'Not quite. I'm at Huddersfield station. I've just been to Cedric Hardcastle's funeral.'

'I read his obituary in today's *FT*. That was one hell of a man you were working for.'

'You don't know the half of it. Which is why I'm calling. I need to see your father urgently.'

'Just give his secretary a call, and I'll make sure she fixes an appointment.'

'What I want to discuss can't wait. I need to see him this evening, tomorrow morning at the latest.'

'Am I sensing a big deal?'

'The biggest ever to cross my desk.'

'Then I'll speak to him immediately. When will you be back in London?'

'My train's due to arrive at Euston at ten past four.'

'Give me a call from the station and I'll—'

A shrill whistle blew and Seb turned to see a green flag waving. He dropped the phone, ran out on to the platform, and jumped on to the moving train.

He took a seat at the rear of the carriage and, once he'd got his breath back, he thought about how he'd first met Vic at St Bede's, when he'd shared a study with him and Bruno Martinez, and they had become his two closest friends; one the son of an immigrant Jew, and the other the son of an Argentinian arms dealer. Over the years they'd become inseparable. That friendship grew even closer when Seb had ended up with a black eye for defending his Jewish friend, not that he had been altogether sure what a Jew was. Like a blind man, unaware of race or religion, he quickly discovered that prejudice was often taught at the breakfast table.

He turned his attention to the sage advice his mother had given him just before she and Dad had driven back to Bristol after the funeral. He knew she was right.

Seb took his time writing a first draft, then a second. By the time the train pulled into Euston, he'd completed a final draft which he hoped would meet with both his mother's and Cedric's approval.

◄◊►

Sloane immediately recognized the handwriting. He tore open the envelope and pulled out a letter, becoming angrier with each word he read.

> *Dear Mr Sloane,*
>
> *I cannot believe that even you could stoop so low as to hold a board meeting on the day of Cedric*

Hardcastle's funeral, with the sole purpose of appointing yourself chairman. Unlike me, Cedric would probably not have been surprised by your duplicity.

You may think you've got away with it, but I can assure you, you haven't, because I will not rest until you are exposed for the fraud you are, as we both know you are the last person Cedric would have wanted to succeed him.

After reading this letter, you won't be surprised to learn that I no longer want to work for an amoral charlatan like you.

S. Clifton

Sloane leapt out of his chair, unable to control his temper. He charged into his secretary's office and shouted, 'Is he still in the building?'

'Who?' asked Rachel innocently.

'Clifton, who else?'

'I haven't seen him since he handed me a letter and asked me to put it on your desk.'

Sloane marched out of his office and down the corridor, still hoping to find Clifton at his desk so he could publicly sack him.

'Where's Clifton?' he demanded as he strode into Sebastian's room. Bobby Rushton, Seb's young assistant, looked up at the new chairman, and was so petrified he couldn't get any words out. 'Are you deaf?' said Sloane. 'Didn't you hear what I said? Where's Clifton?'

'He packed his things and left a few minutes ago,' said Rushton. 'He told us all that he'd resigned and wouldn't be back.'

'Only minutes before he would have been sacked,'

said Sloane. Looking down at the young man, he added, 'And you can join him. Make sure you're off the premises within the hour, and be certain you leave nothing in this room that even hints that Clifton ever existed.'

Sloane stormed back to his office and sat down at his desk. Five more envelopes, all marked *Personal*, were waiting to be opened.

—◦—

'I only met Cedric Hardcastle on half a dozen occasions, mostly social,' said Saul Kaufman. 'We never did any business, but I'd have liked to, because he was one of the few men in the City who still believed a handshake closed a deal, not a contract.'

'Even a contract won't necessarily close a deal with the new chairman,' said Seb.

'I've never met Adrian Sloane, I only know him by reputation. Is he the reason you wanted to see me so urgently?'

'Yes, sir,' said Seb. 'I was looking into a major deal involving Sloane when the chairman had his heart attack.'

'Then take me through the deal slowly, and don't leave out any details.'

Seb began by telling Mr Kaufman how he'd taken a phone call from Ralph Vaughan of Savills that had alerted him to what Sloane was up to. And how the following morning, on Cedric's instructions, he'd travelled up to Shifnal, and how the day had ended with him meeting Mr Swann and discovering why Sloane was willing to pay way over the odds for a thousand-acre farm in Shropshire.

When Seb came to the end of his story, an enigmatic smile appeared on Kaufman's face.

'Could it be possible that Mr Swann has stumbled

across something we all missed? We'll find out soon enough, because the government is expected to announce its findings in the next few weeks.'

'But we haven't got weeks, only a couple of days. Don't forget, closing bids have to be in by five o'clock tomorrow.'

'So you want me to outbid Sloane, on the possibility that Mr Swann has worked out what the government has planned?'

'Cedric was willing to take that risk.'

'And, unlike Sloane, Cedric Hardcastle had the reputation of being a cautious man.' Kaufman placed his hands together as if in prayer, and when his prayer was answered, he said, 'I'll need to make a few phone calls before I come to a final decision, so come back to my office at 4.40 tomorrow afternoon. If I'm convinced, we'll take it from there.'

'But by then it will be too late.'

'I don't think so,' said Kaufman.

◄◉►

When Seb left the bank he was in a daze, and not at all convinced that Kaufman would go ahead with the deal. But he had nowhere else to turn.

He hurried home. He wanted to share everything that had happened since he'd left the flat that morning with Samantha. She always saw things from a different angle, often coming out of left field, to use one of her favourite American expressions.

While Sam prepared supper, Seb told her who'd attended the funeral that morning and, more important, who hadn't, and what Sloane and his cronies had been up to while he was in Huddersfield . . . and why he was now looking for a job.

When he finally stopped pacing around the kitchen and sat down, Sam said, 'But you've always known Sloane was a crook, so it shouldn't have come as a surprise that he'd call a board meeting when everyone who would have opposed him was out of town. I bet your mother would have worked that one out.'

'She did, but by then it was too late. But I still think we can beat Sloane at his own game.'

'Not at his own game,' said Sam. 'Try to think what Cedric would have done in the circumstances, not Sloane.'

'But if I'm ever going to beat him, I'll have to think like him.'

'Possibly, but that doesn't mean you have to act like him.'

'Shifnal Farm is a once-in-a-lifetime opportunity.'

'That's not a good enough reason to crawl around in the same gutter as Sloane.'

'But, Sam, I might never get another chance like this again.'

'Of course you will, Seb. Think long term, and you'll understand the difference between Adrian Sloane and Cedric Hardcastle. Because I'm absolutely sure of one thing, very few people will be attending Sloane's funeral.'

◄○►

Friday turned out to be the longest day of Sebastian's life. He'd hardly slept the previous night as he tried to work out what Kaufman was up to.

When Sam left to attend a lecture at King's, he pottered around the flat, pretended to read a morning paper, spent an inordinate amount of time washing up the few breakfast dishes, even went for a run in the park, but by the time he got back, it was still only just after eleven.

He took a shower, shaved and opened a tin of baked beans. He continually glanced at his watch, but the second hand still only circled the dial every sixty seconds.

After what passed for a fork lunch, he went upstairs to the bedroom, took his smartest suit out of the wardrobe and put on a freshly ironed white shirt and his old school tie. He finally polished a pair of shoes until a sergeant major would have been proud of them.

At four o'clock he was standing at the bus stop waiting for the number 4 to take him into the City. He jumped off at St Paul's and, although he walked slowly, he was standing outside Kaufman's bank on Cheapside by 4.25. There was nothing for it but to stroll around the block. As he walked past so many familiar City institutions, he was reminded just how much he enjoyed working in the Square Mile. He tried not to think about being un-employed for any length of time.

At 4.38, Seb marched into the bank and said to the receptionist, 'I have an appointment with Mr Kaufman.'

'Which Mr Kaufman?' she asked, giving him a warm smile.

'The chairman.'

'Thank you, sir. If you'd like to take a seat, I'll let him know you're here.'

Seb paced around the lobby watching another second hand make a larger circle around a larger clock but with exactly the same result. His thoughts were interrupted by a tap on his shoulder and the words, 'The chairman is waiting for us in his office. I'll take you up.'

Seb was impressed that Vic hadn't said 'Dad'. He could feel the palms of his hands sweating, and as the lift trundled slowly up to the top floor he rubbed them on his trousers. When they entered the chairman's office, they found Mr Kaufman on the phone.

'I need to speak to a colleague before I can make that decision, Mr Sloane. I'll call you back around five.' Seb looked horrified, but Kaufman put a finger to his lips. 'If that's convenient.'

━◅◦▻━

Sloane put the receiver down, picked it up again immediately and without going through to his secretary dialled a number.

'Ralph, it's Adrian Sloane.'

'I thought it might be,' said Vaughan, checking his watch. 'You'll be pleased to hear that no one has called about Shifnal Farm all day. So with just fifteen minutes to go, I think it's safe to assume the property is yours. I'll give you a call just after five, so we can discuss how you want to deal with the paperwork.'

'That's fine by me,' said Sloane, 'but don't be surprised if my line's engaged when you call, because I'm currently involved in a deal that's even bigger than Shifnal Farm.'

'But if someone was to make a bid between now and five—'

'That isn't going to happen,' said Sloane. 'Just make sure you send the contract round to Farthings first thing on Monday morning. There'll be a cheque waiting for you.'

━◅◦▻━

'It's ten to five,' said Vic.

'Patience, child,' said the old man. 'There is only one thing that matters when you're trying to close a deal.

Timing.' He leant back and closed his eyes, although he was wide awake. He had told his secretary that under no circumstances was he to be disturbed between ten to five and ten past. Neither Vic nor Seb said another word.

Suddenly Saul's eyes opened and he sat bolt upright. He checked that the two phones on his desk were placed exactly where he wanted them. At six minutes to five, he leant forward and picked up the black phone. He dialled the number of an estate agent in Mayfair, and asked to speak to the senior partner.

'Mr Kaufman, this is an unexpected pleasure,' said Vaughan. 'How can I help you?'

'You can start by telling me the time, Mr Vaughan.'

'I make it five to five,' said a puzzled voice. 'Why do you ask?'

'Because I wanted to be sure that you're still open for bids on Shifnal Farm in Shropshire.'

'We most certainly are. But I must warn you that we already have an offer of one point six million pounds from another bank.'

'Then I bid one million, six hundred and ten thousand.'

'Thank you, sir,' said Vaughan.

'And what time do you make it now?'

'Three minutes to five.'

'Please hold on, Mr Vaughan, there's someone on the other line. I'll only be a moment.' Kaufman placed the black receiver on his desk, picked up the red one and dialled a number.

After three rings a voice said, 'Adrian Sloane.'

'Mr Sloane, I'm calling back about the Nigerian oil bonds your bank is offering to selected investors. As I said earlier, it sounds a most exciting opportunity. What is the maximum amount that you'll allow any one institution to invest?'

'Two million pounds, Mr Kaufman. I'd offer you more, but the majority of the shares have already been taken up.'

'Can you just hold on while I consult one of my colleagues?'

'Of course, Mr Kaufman.'

Saul placed the red phone back on his desk and picked up the black one. 'I'm sorry to have kept you waiting, Mr Vaughan, but I must ask you once again, what time do you make it?'

'One minute to five.'

'Excellent. Would you now be kind enough to open your office door?'

Kaufman put the black receiver back down on his desk and picked up the red one. 'My colleague is asking, if we were to invest the full two million, would that entitle us to a place on the board of the new company?'

'Most certainly,' said Sloane. 'In fact, I could offer you two places, as you would own ten per cent of the stock.'

'Allow me to consult my colleague again.' The red phone was placed back on the desk, and Kaufman picked up the black one.

'What did you find when you opened the door, Mr Vaughan?'

'A messenger handed me an envelope containing a banker's draft for one hundred and sixty-one thousand pounds.'

'The ten per cent required to close the transaction. What time do you make it now, Mr Vaughan?'

'Two minutes past five.'

'Then the deal is closed. And as long as I pay the

remaining ninety per cent within thirty days, Shifnal Farm is mine.'

'It most certainly is,' said Vaughan, unwilling to admit how much he was looking forward to telling Sloane that he'd lost the deal.

'Have a good weekend,' said Kaufman as he placed the black phone back on its cradle and returned to the red one.

'Mr Sloane, I want to invest two million pounds in this most exciting project.' Kaufman wished he could see the look on Sloane's face. 'But unfortunately I couldn't get my colleagues to agree with me, so sadly I'll have to withdraw my offer. As you assured me the majority of the shares have already been taken up, I don't suppose that will cause you too much of a problem.'

14

SEBASTIAN DIDN'T TELL Samantha the tactics Mr Kaufman had resorted to in order to close the Shifnal Farm deal, because he knew she wouldn't approve, even though it was Sloane who'd lost out. What he did tell her was that Kaufman had offered him a job.

'But I thought his bank didn't have a property division.'

'It does now,' said Seb. 'He's asked me to set up my own department. Small transactions to begin with, but with a view to expanding, if I prove myself.'

'That's wonderful news,' said Sam, giving him a hug.

'And it shouldn't be too difficult to pick up good staff, since Sloane's sacked my entire team, not to mention several others who've resigned, including Rachel.'

'Rachel?'

'She used to be Cedric's secretary, but she only lasted a week under the new regime. I've asked her to join me. We start on Monday with a clean sheet. Well, not exactly a clean sheet, because Sloane sacked my assistant, and ordered him to remove everything from the office that even hinted of me, so he gathered up all the files I was working on, walked across to Cheapside and handed them to me.'

'Is that legal?'

'Who gives a damn, when Sloane's never going to find out?'

'Farthings Bank is not just Adrian Sloane, and you still have an obligation to it.'

'After the way Sloane treated me?'

'No, after the way Cedric treated you.'

'But that doesn't apply to Shifnal Farm, because Sloane was working behind Cedric's back on that deal.'

'And now you're working behind his.'

'You bet I am, if it's going to make it possible for us to buy a flat in Chelsea.'

'We shouldn't be thinking about buying anything until you've paid off all your debts.'

'Mr Kaufman has promised me a forty-thousand-pound bonus when the government makes its announcement, so I won't have any debts then.'

'*If* the government makes an announcement,' said Sam. 'Don't start spending the money before you've got it. And even if you do pull the deal off, you'll still owe Mr Swann over eight thousand pounds, so perhaps we ought not to be thinking about moving quite yet.'

That was something else Seb decided he wasn't going to tell Sam about.

◄○►

Seb spent the next few weeks working hours that would have impressed even Cedric and, with the help of Rachel and his old team from Farthings, they were up and running far more quickly than Mr Kaufman would have thought possible.

Seb wasn't satisfied with just being reunited with his old customers, but like a marauding pirate he began to plunder several of Farthings' other clients, convincing himself that it was no more than Sloane deserved.

It was about three months after he'd begun working at Kaufman's that the chairman called him into his office.

'Did you read the *Financial Times* this morning?' he said, even before Seb had closed the door.

'Only the front page and the property section. Why?'

'Because we're about to find out if Mr Swann's prediction is correct.' Seb didn't interrupt Kaufman's flow. 'It seems the transport minister will be making a statement in the House at three o'clock this afternoon. Perhaps you and Victor should go along and hear what he has to say, then call and let me know if I've made or lost a fortune.'

As soon as Seb returned to his office, he called Uncle Giles at the Commons and asked if he could arrange a couple of tickets for the Strangers' Gallery that afternoon, so he and a friend could hear the statement by the minister of transport.

'I'll leave them in Central Lobby,' said Giles.

After he'd put the phone down, Giles studied the order paper, and wondered why Sebastian would be interested in a decision that would only affect a handful of people living in Shropshire.

◀◦▶

Seb and Vic were seated in the fourth row of the Strangers' Gallery long before the minister rose to deliver his statement. Uncle Giles smiled up at them from the government benches, still puzzled as to what would be in the statement that could possibly be of any interest to his nephew.

The two young bankers were sitting on the edge of the green leather bench when the Speaker called for the Secretary of State for Transport to deliver his statement to the House.

'Mr Speaker,' the minister began, as he gripped the dispatch box, 'I rise to inform the House which route has been selected by my department for the proposed motorway extension that will run through the county of Shropshire.'

If the word *SILENCE* hadn't been displayed in bold on the wood-panelled walls, Seb would have leapt in the air when the minister referred to the outskirts of Shifnal, including Shifnal Farm, as a section of the route for the proposed new motorway.

Once the minister had dealt with several questions from local members, he resumed his place on the front bench to allow a debate on foreign affairs to begin.

Seb and Vic had no interest in whether the government intended to impose economic sanctions on South Africa, so they slipped quietly out of the Strangers' Gallery, made their way downstairs to the central lobby and out on to Parliament Square. That's when Seb leapt in the air and screamed, 'We did it!'

--◦--

Samantha was reading the *Guardian* when a sleepy Sebastian appeared for breakfast the following morning.

'Where were you last night?' she asked. 'I didn't even hear you come in.'

'Vic and I were out celebrating. Sorry, I should have called to let you know.'

'Celebrating what?' asked Sam, but Seb didn't answer as he helped himself to a bowl of cornflakes.

'Could it possibly be that Mr Swann worked out that the new motorway would go straight through the middle of Shifnal Farm and, to quote the *Guardian*,' said Sam, looking down at the article in front of her, 'make a small fortune for a handful of speculators?' She handed the newspaper to Seb, who only glanced at the headline.

'You have to understand,' said Seb between mouthfuls, 'this means we'll now have enough money to buy a house in Chelsea.'

'But will there be enough money left over for Mr Swann to build his theatre in Shifnal?'

'That depends . . .'

'On what? You gave him your word that if the information he supplied turned out to be correct, you would pay him the £8,234 he needed to complete his theatre.'

'But I only earn four thousand a year,' protested Seb.

'And you're about to be given a bonus of forty thousand.'

'On which I'll have to pay capital gains tax.'

'Not on a charitable donation, you won't.'

'But there was nothing in writing.'

'Seb, did you hear what you just said?'

'In any case,' added Seb quickly, 'it's Mr Kaufman who will make the small fortune, not me.'

'And it was Mr Kaufman who took the risk in the first place, and could have *lost* a small fortune. Whereas you had nothing to lose, and everything to gain.'

'You don't understand—' began Seb.

'I understand only too well,' said Sam as Seb pushed his bowl aside and got up from the table.

'I ought to be going,' he said. 'I'm already late, and I've got a lot to do today.'

'Like deciding how to spend the money Mr Swann has made for you?'

He leant down to kiss her, but she turned away.

'The truth is, you never had any intention of paying Mr Swann, did you?'

Seb made no attempt to answer her question as he turned and walked quickly towards the door.

'Can't you see that if you don't pay Mr Swann, you'll be just as bad as Adrian Sloane?' said Sam with feeling.

Seb didn't reply as he picked up his briefcase and hurried out of the flat without saying goodbye. Once he was safely out on the street, he hailed a taxi. As it made its way along City Road he began to wonder how long it would be before, like Saul Kaufman, he had his own car and driver. But his mind kept returning to Sam and her words: 'you'll be just as bad as Adrian Sloane'.

He would book a table for two at the Mirabelle tonight, when they would talk about anything but banking. During his lunch break he would visit Mr Gard in Hatton Garden and buy that marcasite brooch. Then surely Sam would begin to appreciate the advantages of being engaged to Sebastian Clifton.

◄○►

'Your usual table, Mr Kaufman?'

Seb wondered how long it would be before the head waiter would say to him, 'Your usual table, Mr Clifton?'

Over lunch in the Grill Room, he told the chairman he'd already spotted one or two other properties whose sellers seemed unaware of their true value.

After a lunch at which he'd drunk a little too much, he took a taxi to Hatton Garden. Mr Gard opened the safe and pulled out the third tray from the top. Seb was delighted to see it was still there: a Victorian marcasite brooch surrounded by diamonds that he was sure Sam would find irresistible.

In the taxi on his way back to Islington, he felt confident that over dinner at the Mirabelle, he could bring her round to his way of thinking.

When he put the key in the lock, his first thought was, we won't be living here much longer, but when he opened the door, he was puzzled to find that all the lights were out. Could Sam be attending an evening lecture? The moment he switched on the light, he sensed that something was wrong. Something was missing, but what? He sobered up instantly when he realized that several personal objects, including the photograph of the two of them in Central Park, one of Jessica's drawings and Sam's print of *The Night Watch*, were nowhere to be seen. He rushed through to their bedroom and flung open the cupboards on Sam's side of the bed. Empty. He looked under the bed, to find her suitcases were no longer there.

'No, no,' he screamed as he ran out of the bedroom and into the kitchen, where he saw the envelope. It was propped up against a small red leather box and addressed to Sebastian. He tore it open and pulled out a letter that was written in her strong, bold hand.

Dearest Seb,

This is the most difficult letter I've ever had to write in my life, because you were my life. But I fear the man who came to Agnew's Gallery willing to spend every penny he possessed to buy one of his sister's drawings is not the same man I had breakfast with this morning.

The man who was so proud to work alongside Cedric Hardcastle and despised everything Adrian Sloane stood for is not the same man who now feels he has no obligation to Mr Swann, the one person who made it possible for him to receive such a handsome bonus. Have you forgotten Mr Swann's words, 'If Harry Clifton is your father, that's good enough for me'?

If only Cedric were alive today, none of this would have happened, because you know he would have made sure you kept your side of the bargain and if you hadn't he would have kept it for you.

I have no doubt that your career will continue to go from strength to strength, and that you will be an outstanding success at everything you do. But that's not the kind of success I want to be a part of.

I fell in love with the son of Harry and Emma Clifton, the brother of Jessica Clifton, which is one of the many reasons I wanted to be the wife of Sebastian Clifton. But that man no longer exists. Despite everything, I will treasure our short time together for the rest of my life.

Samantha

Sebastian fell to his knees, the words of Sam's father ringing in his ears. 'Samantha sets standards, like your mother, that the rest of us normal mortals find hard to live with, unless, like your father, they're guided by the same moral compass.'

LADY VIRGINIA FENWICK

1966

15

'I'LL SEE IF HER LADYSHIP is at home,' said the butler.

What a ridiculous remark, thought Lady Virginia. Morton knows only too well that I'm at home. What he actually means is, I'll find out if her ladyship wants to talk to you.

'Who is it, Morton?' she asked as the butler entered the room.

'Mrs Priscilla Bingham, my lady.'

'Of course I'm at home to Mrs Bingham,' said Virginia, picking up the phone by her side. 'Priscilla, darling.'

'Virginia, darling.'

'It's been so long.'

'Far too long, and I've so much to tell you.'

'Why don't you pop up and spend a few days in London? It will be just like old times. We can go shopping, catch a show, try out one or two new restaurants, and even visit Annabel's, where one just has to be seen, darling.'

'Sounds terrific. I'll check my diary and ring you back.'

Virginia put down the phone and thought about her friend. They hadn't seen much of each other since her last visit to Mablethorpe Hall, when Priscilla's husband Robert had behaved so badly. And worse, since then, Robert had gone over to the other side and joined the enemy. He not only sat on the board of Barrington Shipping but had played a part in ensuring that Major Fisher, Virginia's representative, had been summarily dismissed from the board. To make matters worse, he'd insisted that Priscilla accompany him on the *Buckingham*'s maiden voyage to New York, despite Virginia telling her that she had been refused a first-class cabin.

When Priscilla returned home a fortnight later, she told Virginia that something had gone badly wrong on the first night of the voyage, but Robert refused to confide in her. Virginia vowed to get to the bottom of it, but that would have to wait because for the moment it was not Emma Clifton she had in her sights, but Bob Bingham.

When Priscilla turned up at Virginia's flat a few days later, she recited a litany of disasters that had taken place during the voyage, including a dreadful dinner she'd had to endure with that frightful social climber, Emma Clifton. The food was inedible, the wine was corked and the staff might as well have come from Butlin's. However, Priscilla assured Virginia that on more than one occasion she had put Mrs Clifton firmly in her place.

'And did you find out what really happened on the first night?' asked Virginia.

'No, but I did hear Robert say to one of the other directors that if the truth ever got out, the chairman would have to resign and the company could even face bankruptcy. That would certainly help with your libel trial.'

Virginia hadn't told her friend that the case was on hold because her extremely expensive lawyers considered her chances of winning not much better than fifty-fifty, and her latest bank statement reminded her that she wasn't in a strong enough financial position to risk that. However, what she had planned for Bob Bingham was not fifty-fifty. He would end up having to part with at least half of his entire fortune, with a twist. And once she'd dealt with him, Virginia would then turn her attention to Emma Clifton and the Home Fleet incident. But if her plan for Bob Bingham was to succeed, she would once again have to enlist the services of Major Alex Fisher, someone who hated the Barrington family almost as much as she did.

Bob Bingham was not pleased when Priscilla announced she would be staying at their house in The Boltons for a few days so she could spend some time with Virginia. He sensed that that woman was up to something, and it wasn't too difficult to work out what she might have in mind.

The only good thing about Priscilla being away for a week was that it would give him a chance to invite Clive to join him for a few days at Mablethorpe Hall. Clive had recently been promoted and no longer relied on Bob to subsidize him. In fact, Jessica's tragic death may have been the reason he had become so fiercely independent. Bob had seen too little of his son since that dreadful night when Jessica Clifton had taken her own life, and it would never have happened if Priscilla hadn't invited that conniving woman to spend the weekend with them. It was only later that his wife admitted that Virginia had originally turned down the invitation, but had changed her mind when she heard that Jessica Clifton would be among the guests, and that Clive was planning to propose to her that weekend.

Bob tried to push that vile woman out of his mind as he wanted to concentrate on the minutes of Barrington's most recent board meeting. He agreed with young Sebastian – he must stop thinking of him in those terms – after all, he had already proved himself to be a capable director, and few of the board doubted that, in time, he would become the next chairman of the company. And if his new lifestyle was anything to go by, he was clearly doing well at Kaufman's, even if his father had hinted that his personal life was a mess.

Bob Bingham and Harry Clifton had become friends during the past few years, which had seemed unlikely, considering how little they had in common other than Jessica. Harry was a renaissance man, a man of letters, whose constant stand on behalf of Anatoly Babakov had captured the public's imagination. Bob, on the other hand, was a man of business, of balance sheets, who only ever read a book when he was on holiday. Perhaps it was simply the game of cricket that brought the two men together, except on those occasions when Gloucestershire played Yorkshire.

Bob turned his attention to a paper that was to be presented by Sebastian, setting out why he felt the company shouldn't be investing in a new luxury liner at the present time.

◄◦►

'Major Fisher,' intoned the butler before closing the door.

'Alex, it's good to see you again,' said Virginia as she poured him a double gin and tonic. 'I do hope things are going well for you.'

'Up and down like Tower Bridge,' said Alex as she passed him his drink, all too aware that Lady Virginia only ever invited him to visit her when she wanted something. Not that he could complain; he wasn't exactly flush since he'd lost his place on the board of Barrington's. Virginia wasted no time coming to the point.

'Do you recall our successful little sortie with Bob Bingham a couple of years ago?'

'Could I ever forget?' said Alex. 'Mind you, it's not something I'd ever want to repeat,' he added quickly.

'No, that wasn't what I had in mind. But I do need you to do a little digging for me. I'd like to know how much Bingham is worth. His company, his shareholdings, properties, particularly the properties, and any other source of income he may have that he wouldn't want the taxman to know about. Dig deep and spare no details, however insignificant they might seem.'

'And . . .'

'You'll be paid five pounds an hour plus expenses, and a bonus of twenty-five pounds if I'm satisfied with your work.'

Alex smiled. Virginia had never once in the past paid the promised bonus, and her idea of expenses was to travel third class and not stay overnight. But given his present circumstances, he wasn't able to scoff at five pounds an hour.

'When do you need my report?'

'In ten days' time, Alex. And then I may well have another job for you, nearer home.'

—◦—

Virginia had planned Priscilla Bingham's visit to London with military precision. Nothing was left to chance.

On the Monday, the two of them were driven to Epsom, where they joined Lord Malmsbury in his private box on the finishing line. Priscilla clearly enjoyed having a badge for the royal enclosure, where several men complimented her on her Hartnell outfit and 'Jackie Kennedy' pillbox hat. She hadn't received so much attention in years.

On Tuesday, following a light lunch at Simpson's, they dropped into a drinks reception at the Banqueting House before going on to a gala dinner at the Savoy in aid of the Red Cross, where Matt Monro serenaded the guests.

On Wednesday, it was the turn of the Queen's Club, where they watched a polo match between a Windsor team captained by the young Prince Charles, and a visiting Argentinian side, most of whom Priscilla couldn't take her eyes off. In the evening, they had house seats for *Funny Girl*, a new musical with its original Broadway star, Barbra Streisand, which had queues for returns that were the envy of every other West End theatre.

On Thursday, and heaven knows how Virginia fixed the tickets, they attended a royal garden party at Buckingham Palace, where Priscilla was presented to Princess Alexandra. In the evening, they dined with the Duke of Bridgwater and his eldest son, Bofie, who couldn't take his eyes off Priscilla. In fact, Virginia had to warn him that despite her encouragement, he just might be overdoing it.

On Friday, Priscilla was so exhausted she spent the morning in bed, and was only just up in time to keep an appointment with her hairdresser, before going on in the evening to Covent Garden to see a production of *Giselle*.

On Saturday morning, they attended trooping the colour, watching the ceremony from the Scottish Office overlooking Horse Guards. In the evening they had a quiet supper *à deux* at Virginia's flat. 'No one in London would dream of venturing out on a Saturday night,' she explained. 'The streets are full of foreigners and visiting football hooligans.' But then Virginia had always intended to use that night to sow the first seeds of doubt in her friend's mind.

'What a week,' said Priscilla as they sat down for supper. 'What fun, and to think that tomorrow I have to go back to Mablethorpe.'

'You don't have to go back,' said Virginia.

'But Robert is expecting me.'

'Is he? Frankly, would he even notice if you were to spend a few more days in London?'

Priscilla put down her knife and fork, clearly considering the proposition. In truth, Virginia didn't want her to remain in London a day longer, as she was exhausted and had nothing planned for the following week.

'Have you ever thought about leaving Robert?' asked Virginia as Morton refilled Priscilla's wine glass.

'Regularly. But how could I possibly survive without him?'

'Rather well, I suspect. After all, you have a lovely home in The Boltons, not to mention—'

'But it's not mine.'

'It could be,' said Virginia, warming to her task.

'What do you mean?'

'Did you read that article about Robert in the business section of the *Telegraph* a couple of weeks ago?'

'I never read the business section of any paper.'

'Well, it was most illuminating. It seems that Bingham's Fish Paste is valued at around fifteen million, with no debts and healthy cash reserves.'

'But if I left Robert, I wouldn't want anything to do with the company.'

'You wouldn't have to have anything to do with it. Mablethorpe Hall, The Boltons and your villa in the South of France, not to mention the three million sitting in the company's bank account, would still be less than fifty per cent of what he's worth. And fifty per cent is what you could expect after twenty-six years of marriage and a son you virtually brought up on your own because of all those hours your husband spent away from home, pursuing his career.'

'How do you know there's three million in the company's account?'

'It's listed for anyone to see at Companies House. £3,142,900 to be exact.'

'I had no idea.'

'Still, whatever you decide, my darling, I'll always be here to support you.'

◄○►

Even Virginia was surprised to receive a tearful call from Mablethorpe Hall on the following Friday.

'I'm so lonely,' Priscilla moaned, 'and there's just nothing for me to do up here.'

'Then why don't you come down to London and visit me for a few days, darling? Bofie Bridgwater was only asking me yesterday when you were expected back in town.'

When Priscilla turned up on Virginia's doorstep the following afternoon, the first thing she said was, 'Do you know a good divorce lawyer?'

'The best,' Virginia replied. 'After all, she's acted for me on two occasions.'

Twenty-two days later, Robert Bingham was served

with a divorce writ. But Major Fisher still didn't get his bonus.

━◅◦▻━

Everyone rose as Mrs Justice Havers entered the court-room. The judge took her place and peered down at the two warring parties. She had read both submissions care-fully and, after a thousand divorces, knew exactly what she was looking for.

'Mrs Everitt.'

Priscilla's counsel immediately rose from her place. 'My lady,' she said.

'I understand that a settlement has been reached between the two parties, and I wonder if you'd be kind enough to outline the terms for me.'

'Certainly, my lady. In this case I represent the plain-tiff, Mrs Priscilla Bingham, while my learned friend Mr Brooke represents the defendant, Mr Robert Bingham. My lady, Mrs Bingham has been married to the defendant for the past twenty-six years. During that time, she has been a faithful, loyal and dutiful wife. She bore a son, Clive, who, because of her husband's various business commitments, she had to raise virtually single-handed.'

'With the help of a nanny, a cook, a maid and a cleaner,' whispered Bob, which his counsel duly noted.

'Even during the school holidays, my lady, it was rare for Mr Bingham to spend more than a week with his wife and child, always wanting to get back to his factory in Grimsby. We are therefore proposing,' continued learned counsel, 'that Mrs Bingham should retain the family home in which she has lived for the past twenty-six years, along with the house in London, and the villa near Cap Ferrat in the South of France, where she and her son always spent the long summer vacation together. Mrs Bingham would also ask the court for the sum of three million pounds in order that she can maintain the three houses and continue to live in a style to which she has grown accustomed. I should point out, my lady, that this is far less than fifty per cent of Mr Bingham's considerable fortune.' Mrs Everitt sat down.

'And is Mr Bingham agreeable to these terms, Mr Brooke?'

Robert's solicitor rose slowly to his feet, tugged the lapels of his gown and said, 'Indeed, my lady. Mr Bingham will retain the family company, Bingham's Fish Paste, which was founded by his grandfather over a hundred years ago. He makes no other demands.'

'So be it,' said the judge, 'but before final settlement is agreed, I always like both parties to confirm they are satisfied with the division, so there can be no recriminations at some later date, or any suggestion that they didn't fully understand what had been proposed. Mr Bingham –' Robert's counsel nudged him and Bob jumped up. 'Are you satisfied with this division of your goods and chattels?'

'I am, my lady.'

'Thank you, Mr Bingham.' Turning her attention to the other side of the courtroom, the judge asked Mrs Bingham the same question.

Priscilla rose to her feet, smiled up at the judge and said, 'I am satisfied. Indeed, I am happy for my ex-husband to select whichever of the two packages he would prefer.'

'How very magnanimous of you,' declared the judge as consternation appeared on the faces of both counsel, who had been quite unprepared for this unrehearsed

intervention. Although it would surely make no difference to the outcome, counsel never likes to be taken by
surprise.

'Then I will put the question to Mr Bingham once
again,' said the judge. 'But as it deserves careful consid-
eration, I will allow Mr Bingham to consider his position
overnight. Court is adjourned until ten a.m. tomorrow.'

Bob was quickly on his feet. 'That's most kind of you,
my lady, but I have already made up—'

Bob's counsel pulled him back down, because Mrs
Justice Havers had already left the court.

If that was the first surprise of the day for Bob, the
second was to see Sebastian Clifton sitting quietly at the
back of the courtroom taking notes. He was even more
surprised when Seb asked if he was free to join him for
dinner.

'Well, I had planned to go back to Lincolnshire
tonight, but now that I have to make a short reappearance
in court tomorrow morning, I'd be delighted to take up
your offer.'

They both watched as Priscilla left the courtroom on
Virginia's arm. She was sobbing quietly.

'I could kill that woman,' said Bob, 'and happily serve
a life sentence.'

'I don't think that will be necessary,' said Seb. 'I think
I've come up with a far better solution for dealing with
Lady Virginia.'

◄◦►

At ten o'clock the following morning, everyone was back
in their places when Mrs Justice Havers entered the
courtroom. Once she had settled herself, she looked

down at the counsels' bench and said, 'Only one matter remains to be resolved, and that is which of the two packages Mr Bingham has settled on.'

Bob rose from his place. 'I would like to thank you, my lady, for giving me the opportunity to reflect on my decision overnight, because I have decided to choose the three properties along with the three million pounds. I'd like to thank my wife for her most magnanimous gesture, and to wish her every success with running the company.'

Uproar broke out in court. Apart from Bob Bingham, only two other people didn't look surprised: the judge and Sebastian Clifton.

16

'WHAT POSSESSED YOU to do something quite so stupid?' said Virginia.

'I just wanted Robert to know how fair I considered the settlement was.'

'Well, that backfired spectacularly.'

'But I never thought for a moment he'd let go of his beloved company.'

'And I'm not convinced he has,' said Virginia. 'Those two are up to something.'

'Those two?'

'Yes, I should have realized that Sebastian Clifton would have an ulterior motive for being in court. He may have taken me by surprise this time, but he won't get away with it again.'

'But he's only a child.'

'A child who is fast gaining a reputation in the City as a whizz-kid. And never forget, he's the son of Emma and Harry Clifton, so he's not to be trusted.'

'But what's in it for him?'

'I haven't worked that out yet, but you can be sure he's after something. However, we can still stop them both in their tracks if we move quickly.'

'But what can I do, now I'm penniless and homeless?'

'Pull yourself together, Priscilla. You own a company worth fifteen million pounds that only last year declared a profit of over a million.'

'But for how much longer, now Robert's no longer around to manage it?'

'You needn't worry about that. I know exactly the right person to take his place. He has considerable experience of man management, has served as the director of a public company and, more important, he's available at short notice.'

—◄○►—

Sebastian, Bob and Clive Bingham met in Seb's office later that morning to discuss what needed to be done next.

'The first part of our plan went smoothly enough,' said Seb. 'But it won't be long before Virginia works out what we're up to. So we're going to have to move quickly, very quickly, if we're to get all the pieces off the chessboard in time.'

'Then I'll have to drive up to Grimsby this afternoon,' said Bob.

'It can't be too soon,' said Seb, 'because you need to be back in London by tomorrow evening at the latest. I want everyone at Bingham's, from the management to the factory workers, and all of its customers up and down the country, to think the only reason you're visiting the factory is to say goodbye to the staff and wish them luck under the new management. Just before you leave, Clive will issue the press statement he's been working on.'

Clive opened his briefcase and took out two sheets of foolscap paper.

'The statement needs to be short, unequivocal and to the point,' he said, passing a copy to his father and Seb. 'I won't release it until I know Dad's on his way back to London, when I'll send a copy to the *Grimsby Evening Telegraph*. It's sure to make the front page. After that, I'll release it to every business correspondent in Fleet Street.'

Bob read through the statement slowly, and was impressed by what his son had come up with. However, he realized that a lot more needed to be done if the public, and not least Lady Virginia, were to believe he meant what he said.

'And once I'm back in London, what do I do then?'

'Fly to Nice, go straight to the house at Cap Ferrat and stay put,' said Seb.

'And after that?' asked Bob. 'I've never lasted more than a few days in the South of France before I was bored out of my mind and had to fly home.'

'Well, you're going to have to do a lot better than that,' said Clive, 'if you're going to convince the world how much you're enjoying early retirement, and that you have absolutely no interest in returning to Grimsby.'

'Mind you, most people won't find that too hard to believe,' said Seb.

'Retirement?' said Bob, ignoring Seb's comment. 'I'd die rather than retire. And as for enjoying myself, I wasn't built for leisure, so perhaps you can tell me, Seb, how I'm supposed to pass the time of day?'

'Perhaps the occasional round of golf, followed by a long lunch at one of the many Michelin-starred restaurants along the Riviera, topped off by a visit to one of Nice's more exotic nightclubs?'

'And where will I find a pint of Bateman's, and cod and chips served in newspaper?'

'I don't think you'll find too many fish and chip shops at Cap Ferrat,' admitted Seb.

'And there's not much demand for mushy peas on the Riviera,' added Clive.

The three of them burst out laughing.

'I feel sorry for your mother, Clive,' said Bob. 'She's about to discover just how close a friend Lady Virginia Fenwick really is.'

◄○►

'Well, at least this time, major, you'll be chairman of a company that doesn't have a board, or anyone else you have to answer to. You can start with a blank sheet of paper and set your own ground rules.'

'Possibly. But you will have noticed that the company's shares collapsed yesterday following Bingham's press statement.'

'What statement?' said Virginia.

Fisher picked up a copy of *The Times* from the coffee table and turned to the lead story in the business section. Virginia stared at a photograph of Bob shaking hands with some members of the factory staff following his farewell speech, then carefully read his statement: 'Of course I'm sad to be leaving the company my grandfather founded in 1857, especially after serving as its chairman for the past twenty-three years. But I have no fear for the future of Bingham's while it's in the capable hands of my former wife, Priscilla. I hope everyone will continue to support her, as they have always supported me. However, it's time for me to retire to my beautiful home in the South of France and enjoy a well-earned rest.'

'I don't believe a word of it,' said Virginia. 'So the sooner you get yourself off to Grimsby, the better, major.

It's going to take all your skills and experience as an army officer to keep those people in their place.'

—‹o›—

When Clive drove his father to Heathrow later that evening, he couldn't get a word out of him.

'What's the problem, Dad?' he asked eventually.

'Some of the staff were in tears when I left. People I've worked with for over twenty years. It took all my willpower not to roll up my sleeves and start loading the lorries.'

'I understand how you feel, Dad, but believe me, you've made the right decision.'

'I hope so,' said Bob, as they came to a halt outside the terminal.

'And don't forget, if you spot a photographer, just smile and look relaxed. We don't want the press thinking you're unhappy, because then Lady Virginia will work out exactly what we're up to.'

'I'll bet she already has.'

'Dad, we can beat her, as long as you don't lose your nerve.'

'Please make my imprisonment as short as possible,' he pleaded after he'd checked his one bag in and given his son a hug.

'I'll phone every day,' said Clive, 'and bring you up to date with everything that's going on at this end.'

'And keep an eye on your mother. It's going to come as a dreadful shock when she meets up with the real Virginia for the first time.'

—‹o›—

By the time the major stepped on to the platform at Grimsby station, he knew exactly what needed to be done.

His plan was foolproof, and his strategy honed to the finest detail.

He already knew a great deal about Robert Bingham and the way he had run the company from the research he'd carried out for Lady Virginia. And on this occasion she hadn't even tried to bargain with him. She had met all his demands: £20,000 a year plus expenses, including a suite of rooms at the Royal Hotel whenever he had to stay in Grimsby.

Fisher felt there wasn't a moment to lose and instructed the taxi driver to take him straight to the factory. During the journey he went over the speech he'd prepared, which wouldn't leave the workers in any doubt who was the boss. It shouldn't be too difficult to run a fish-paste factory. After all, he'd commanded a company in Tobruk with the Germans snapping at his heels.

The taxi dropped him outside the factory. A scruffy man wearing a peaked cap, open-necked shirt and greasy overalls peered at the major from the other side of the locked gates.

'What do you want?' he demanded.

'I'm Major Fisher, the new chairman of the company, so open up immediately, my good man.'

The man touched the peak of his cap and pulled the gate open.

'Where's the chairman's office?' demanded Fisher.

'Bob never had what you'd call an office, but management are at the top of those steps,' the man said, pointing to the other side of the yard.

The major marched across the yard, a little surprised by the lack of activity because he knew the factory employed over two hundred full-time workers, with another hundred part-time. He climbed the iron steps up to the first floor and pushed open the door to be greeted by a large open-plan office with a dozen desks, only two of which were occupied.

A young man leapt to his feet. 'You must be Major Fisher,' he said as if he'd been expecting him. 'I'm Dave Perry, the assistant manager. I was told to show you round the factory and answer any questions you might have.'

'I was rather hoping to have a meeting with the managing director so I could be brought up to speed as quickly as possible.'

'Ah, you haven't heard?'

'Heard what?'

'Mr Jopling handed in his notice yesterday. Told me that as he only had a couple of years before he retired, this might be a good time for someone else to fill his boots.'

'And are you that someone else?' asked Fisher.

'Not on your nelly,' said Perry. 'I've only been here a few months. And in any case, I don't fancy any more responsibility.'

'Then it will have to be Pollock, the works manager,' said Fisher. 'Where's he?'

'Mr Jopling sacked him yesterday, for insubordination. It was almost the last decision he made before he resigned. Mind you, Steve Pollock can't complain. He's been sent home on full pay until the union completes its investigations. No one doubts that he'll be reinstated. The only trouble is, the committee usually takes a couple of months before they come to a decision.'

'But he must have had a deputy?' said Fisher, unable to hide his frustration.

'Yes, Les Simkins. But he's on a time-and-motion

course at Hull Poly. Waste of time and not a lot of motion, if you ask me.'

Fisher strode across the room and looked down on to the factory floor. 'Why isn't the machinery working? Isn't this meant to be a twenty-four-hour non-stop operation?' he said, staring down at a dozen workers who were standing around, hands in pockets, idly chatting, while one of them rolled a cigarette.

'We usually work an eight-hour-shift system,' said Perry, 'but you need a statutory number of qualified workers before the machinery can be turned on – regulations, you understand – and unfortunately an unusually large number of the lads are on sick leave this week.' The phone on his desk began to ring. He picked it up and listened for a moment. 'I'm sorry to hear that, sir, but our new chairman has just arrived, so I'll pass you over to him.' Perry covered the mouthpiece and said, 'It's the harbour master, Captain Borwick. Seems to have a problem.'

'Good morning, Borwick, it's Major Fisher, the chairman of the company. How can I help?'

'Good morning, major. It's quite simple really, you've got three days' supply of cod piled up on my dockside, which I'd like picked up as soon as possible.'

'I'll get on to it straight away.'

'Thank you, major, because if it hasn't been removed by four o'clock I'll have no choice but to dump it back in the sea.' The phone went dead.

'Where are the lorries that pick up the morning catch?'

'The drivers hung around until midday, but as no one had the authority to give the order for them to go to the harbour, they packed up for the day and went home. You only missed them by a few minutes, major. They'll be back at six tomorrow morning. Bob was always here first thing. Liked to go down to the docks and supervise the loading himself. That way, he could be sure no one palmed him off with yesterday's catch.'

Fisher slumped into a chair and stared at a pile of unopened letters addressed to Mr Bingham. 'Do I have a secretary, by any chance?' he asked.

'Val. There's nothing she doesn't know about this place.'

Fisher managed a weak smile. 'So where is she?'

'On maternity leave, and not expected back for some months. But I know she put an ad in the *Grimsby Evening Telegraph* for a temp,' he added as a man who looked like a heavyweight boxer stomped into the room.

'Which one of you's in charge?' he demanded.

Perry pointed to the major.

'We need some help with the unloading, guv.'

'Unloading what?'

''Undred and forty-eight crates of fish paste jars. Same time every Tuesday. If you haven't got anyone to unload them, we'll have to take them back to Doncaster, and that'll cost you.'

'Perhaps you could give them a hand, Perry.'

'I'm management, major. The unions would down tools if I so much as looked at a crate.'

That was when Fisher realized that every one of them was singing from the same hymn sheet, and he wasn't the choir-master.

The major lasted for three days, during which time not one pot of Bingham's fish paste left the factory. On balance, he decided that doing battle with the Germans in North Africa was far easier than trying to work with a bunch of bolshie shop stewards on Humberside.

On Friday night, after the workers – all two hundred of them – had collected their wage packets and gone home, the curtain finally came down. The major checked out of the Humber Royal Hotel and took the last train back to London.

◄O►

'Bingham's shares have fallen another ten per cent,' said Seb.

'What's the spot price?' asked Bob.

Seb checked the ticker-tape machine in his office. 'Seven shillings and sixpence. No, seven shillings and fourpence.'

'But they were a pound only a week ago.'

'I know, but that was before the major beat a hasty retreat back to London.'

'Then it must be time for me to come back and sort the place out,' said Bob.

'Not quite yet. But be sure to have the number of a local travel agent handy.'

'So what am I expected to do in the meantime?' growled Bob.

'Canasta?'

◄O►

Virginia and Priscilla had barely been on speaking terms for the past week, and a chance remark over breakfast started a row that had been simmering for some time.

'Bofie Bridgwater was telling me last night that—'

'Bofie Bridgwater is a chinless wonder and a prize ass,' snapped Priscilla.

'Who just happens to have a title, and thousands of acres.'

'I'm not interested in his title, and before all this happened I had thousands of acres.'

'And you still would have,' said Virginia, 'if you hadn't made such a fool of yourself in court.'

'How was I to know Robert would be willing to let go of the company? I was simply trying to show how generous I thought he'd been, and now I don't even have a roof over my head.'

'Well, you can stay here for a little longer,' said Virginia, 'but perhaps it might be wise to start looking for a place of your own. After all, I can hardly be expected to go on subsidizing you for ever.'

'But you said I could always rely on your support.'

'I don't remember saying always,' said Virginia, as she dropped a slice of lemon in her tea.

Priscilla stood up, folded her napkin and placed it on the table. She left the room without another word, walked upstairs to the guest bedroom and began to pack.

◄○►

'Dad, you can catch the next plane home.'

'At last. But why now?'

'Mum's finally come to her senses. She walked out of Lady Virginia's flat about an hour ago.'

'What makes you think she won't walk back in again?'

'Because she was lugging three suitcases, and took a taxi to the Mulberry Hotel in Pimlico.'

'I'm on my way to the airport,' said Bob.

Clive put the phone down. 'Should I pick Dad up at Heathrow and drive him to the Mulberry?'

'I don't think so,' said Seb. 'You'll only get in the way. Wait until he calls you.'

◄○►

Clive joined his mother and father later that evening for a drink at the Savoy.

'So romantic,' said Priscilla, who was holding Bob's hand. 'Your father has booked the same suite where we spent the first night of our honeymoon.'

'But you'll be living in sin,' mocked Clive.

'Not for long,' said Priscilla. 'We're off to see Mrs Justice Havers in the morning. Our counsel seems to think she can sort things out.'

'I have a feeling her ladyship won't be all that surprised,' said Clive.

'When did you suddenly become so wise?' asked Bob.

'When you left me with no choice but to stand on my own two feet.'

◄○►

'There's a Mr Bingham on the phone for you,' said the switchboard operator.

'Bob, are you still in London?' asked Seb. 'There's something I need to discuss with you.'

'No, I'm back in Grimsby, re-employing most of my staff. They seem to have enjoyed their extended holiday about as much as I did.'

'I see the share price is up a couple of pence.'

'Yes, but it will be some time before everything's up and running smoothly again. Perhaps you ought to buy a few shares while the price is so low.'

'I've been buying them for the past month,' said Seb. 'I now own about four per cent of Bingham's Fish Paste.'

'If I had a board,' said Bob, 'I'd put you on it. However, I'm still in your debt, not least for your role as matchmaker. So why don't you send me a hefty bill for your professional services.'

'Now that we've vanquished Lady Virginia, I'd rather seek your advice on another problem I'm facing.'

'Virginia Fenwick won't be vanquished until she's six foot under. But how can I help?'

'I want to take over Farthings Bank and remove Adrian Sloane once and for all. But I can't hope to pull it off without your help.'

--◇--

'You can't win them all,' said Lady Virginia, 'but as Wellington reminded us after Waterloo, it's only the final battle that really matters.'

'And who's playing Napoleon on this particular battle-field?'

'None other than Emma Clifton.'

'And what will my role be?' asked Fisher.

'I need you to find out what really happened on the first night of the *Buckingham*'s maiden voyage because clearly the Home Fleet story was nothing more than a smoke screen. Priscilla Bingham overheard one of the directors telling her husband that if the truth ever got out, Emma Clifton would have to resign and the company might even go bankrupt. Nothing would suit me better because that would leave our precious chairman with no choice but to settle the action and pay my costs.'

Fisher remained silent for some time, before he said, 'There are a couple of directors on the board who've recently had a run-in with Mrs Clifton, and one of them has a tendency to drink a little too much, especially when he's not paying. Do we have anything to offer him in return, should he decide to resign?'

'A place on the board of Farthings Bank.'

'That would swing it, but what makes you think you can pull it off?'

'The chairman, Adrian Sloane, has every reason to loathe Sebastian Clifton, and will do anything to bring him down.'

'How do you know that?'

'It's amazing what you can pick up at dinner parties, especially when your host thinks women couldn't possibly begin to understand what goes on in the City.'

GILES BARRINGTON

1970

17

GILES HADN'T GIVEN a moment's thought to how he wanted to spend his fiftieth birthday, but Gwyneth had.

Whenever Giles thought about his marriage – and he thought about it a great deal – he still couldn't pinpoint when things had begun to go wrong. The tragic death of their son Walter at the age of three, and the realization that Gwyneth couldn't have another child, had turned her from a bright spirit who lit up everyone's lives, to a melancholy shadow, lost in her own world. Instead of the tragedy drawing them closer together, Giles found they were slowly drifting apart, not helped by a Member of Parliament's unsocial hours and then a minister's demanding schedule.

Giles had hoped that time would prove a healer, but in truth they began to live separate lives almost as if they weren't a couple, and he couldn't remember the last time they had made love. Despite this, he was determined to remain loyal to Gwyneth, as he didn't want a second divorce and still hoped they might be reconciled.

Whenever they were together in public, they attempted to hide the truth, hoping Giles's constituents, his colleagues, and even their family wouldn't realize their marriage was a sham. But whenever Giles saw Harry and Emma together, he envied them.

Giles had rather assumed that on his birthday he'd be on his way to, or on his way back from, representing Her Majesty's government in some foreign field. Gwyneth, however, was insisting that the milestone should be properly celebrated.

'What do you have in mind?' asked Giles.

'A dinner, just the family and a few close friends?'

'And where would it be held?'

'The House of Commons. We could book one of the private dining rooms.'

'That's the last place I want to be reminded that I'm fifty.'

'Do try and remember, Giles, for most of us who don't go to the Palace of Westminster every day, it's still something rather special.'

Giles knew when he was beaten, so invitations were sent out the following day, and when he looked around the dining room table three weeks later, it was clear that Gwyneth had been right because everyone seemed to be enjoying themselves.

Emma, who was seated on his right, and their sister Grace, on his left, were chatting to their respective neighbours. Giles used the time to think about his speech, jotting down a note or two on the back of his menu.

'I know we shouldn't talk business on an occasion like this,' said Emma to Ross Buchanan, 'but you know how much I value your advice.'

'And an old man,' said Ross, 'is always flattered by a young woman seeking his advice.'

'I'll be fifty next year,' Emma reminded him, 'and you are an old flatterer.'

'Who will be seventy next year,' said Ross. 'Perhaps by then it will be time to put me out to grass, so while I'm still sixty-nine, how can I help?'

'I'm having trouble with Desmond Mellor.'

'I never understood why you put him on the board in the first place.'

'*Force majeure*,' whispered Emma. 'But now he's pushing for deputy chairman.'

'Avoid it at all costs. He'll see it as nothing more than a stepping stone to the job he really wants.'

'All the more reason to hold on until I think Sebastian is ready to take my place.'

'Seb thinks he's ready to take your place right now,' said Ross. 'But if Mellor were to become your deputy, you'd spend your life looking over your shoulder. It's a golden rule for any chairman only ever to appoint a deputy who, one, isn't after your job, or two, has unquestionably been over-promoted, or three, is too old to take over from you.'

'Good thinking,' said Emma, 'but there's not a lot I can do to stop him if he can convince a majority of the board to back him. To make matters worse, Seb thinks Mellor may have been in touch with Giles's first wife.'

'Lady Virginia Fenwick?' said Ross, spitting out the words.

'And possibly Alex Fisher as well.'

'Then you'd better start looking over both shoulders.'

—◦—

'Now tell me, revered aunt,' said Seb, 'are you chancellor of the university yet?'

'The Duke of Edinburgh is our chancellor, as you well know,' said Grace.

'Then what about vice chancellor?'

'Not everyone is quite as ambitious as you, Seb. For some of us, doing a worthwhile job, however humble, is reward enough in itself.'

'Then have you thought about principal of your college? After all, no one is more admired by their colleagues.'

'It's kind of you to say so, Sebastian, and I will tell you in confidence that when Dame Elizabeth retired from the post recently, I was approached by one or two people. However, I made it clear that I wasn't born to be an administrator but a teacher, and am happy with my lot.'

'I can't argue with that,' said Seb.

'But tell me, Seb, as you're on your own tonight, should I assume there's still no one special in your life?'

'There hasn't been anyone special, Aunt Grace, since I was stupid enough to lose Samantha.'

'I agree that wasn't your most glorious hour. I realized the first time I met her that she was an exceptional young woman, and on that particular subject I speak with some authority.'

'You were right. I've never met anyone since who even comes close.'

'I'm sorry, Seb, it was tactless of me to raise the subject, but I'm sure, given time, you'll find someone.'

'I wish.'

'Are you still in touch with Samantha? Is there even the slightest chance . . . ?'

'Not a hope. I've written to her several times over the years, but she doesn't reply.'

'Have you thought of going over to America and admitting you were wrong?'

'Every day.'

◄◦►

'How's your campaign to have Anatoly Babakov released progressing?' asked Priscilla.

'I fear progress may not be the right word,' said Harry, who was seated on the opposite side of the table from Giles. 'Mind you, one can never be sure with the Soviets. One day you think they might be about to release him, but the next you're convinced they've thrown away the key.'

'Could anything happen to change that?'

'A change of leadership in the Kremlin might help. Someone who wants the world to know what Stalin was really like. But there's not much chance of that while Brezhnev is in power.'

'But he must know that we know that he knows.'

'He does, but he's just not willing to admit it to the outside world.'

'Does Babakov have a family?'

'His wife escaped from Russia just before he was arrested. She now lives in Pittsburgh. I've been in touch, and I'm hoping to visit her when I'm next in the States.'

'I hope you succeed,' said Priscilla. 'Please don't think even for a moment that we onlookers have forgotten about your campaign. Far from it, we are inspired by your example.'

'Thank you,' said Harry. 'You and Bob have been so supportive over the years.'

'Robert is a great admirer of your wife, as I'm sure you know. It just took me a little longer to appreciate why.'

'What's Bob up to now the company is flourishing again?'

'He's planning to build a new factory. It seems that most of his equipment belongs to the Stone Age.'

'That won't come cheap.'

'No, but I don't think he's got a lot of choice now it looks we're about to join the Common Market.'

'I saw him having dinner in Bristol with Seb and Ross Buchanan.'

'Yes, they're plotting something, but I've only been able to piece together one or two clues. If I was Detective Sergeant Warwick . . .'

'Detective *Inspector* Warwick,' Harry said, smiling.

'Yes, of course, I remember, he was promoted in your last book. No doubt Inspector Warwick would have found out what they were up to some time ago.'

'I may be able to add one or two nuggets of my own,' whispered Harry.

'Then let's swap notes.'

'It's important to remember that Seb has never forgiven Adrian Sloane for appointing himself chairman on the day of Cedric Hardcastle's funeral.'

'In Huddersfield,' said Priscilla.

'Yes, but why's that relevant?'

'Because I know Robert has taken the ferry across the Humber several times in the last couple of months.'

'Could he be visiting another woman, who just happens to own fifty-one per cent of Farthings?'

'Possibly, because Arnold Hardcastle recently stayed with us overnight, and apart from meals, he and Robert never came out of the study.'

'Then Adrian Sloane had better keep both his eyes wide open, because if Bob, Seb and Arnold are working together as a team, heaven help him,' he said, glancing across the table at Priscilla's husband.

–◦–

'Bingham's Fish Paste seems to have fallen out of the headlines lately,' said Gwyneth, turning to the chairman of the company.

'And that's no bad thing,' said Bob. 'Now we can get on with feeding the nation and not titillating the gossip columnists.'

Gwyneth laughed. 'I have a confession to make,' she said. 'We've never had a jar of your fish paste in the house.'

'And I must confess I've never voted Labour, though I might if I lived in Bristol.'

Gwyneth smiled.

'What odds would you put on Giles holding on to his seat?' asked Bob.

'Clinging on by his fingernails seems the likely outcome,' said Gwyneth. 'Bristol Docklands has always been a marginal seat, but the opinion polls suggest that this time it's going to be too close to call. So a lot will depend on who the local Conservatives select as their candidate.'

'But Giles is a popular minister, much admired on both sides of the House. Doesn't that count for anything?'

'About a thousand votes in Griff Haskins's opinion. But his constituency agent never stops reminding me that if the national swing is against you, there's not a lot you can do about it.'

─◈─

'I suppose you have to come up to the Commons fairly regularly,' said Jean Buchanan.

'Not that often actually,' said Griff. 'We agents have a tendency to remain at the coal face, making sure the voters still love the member.' At that moment the dining room door opened, and all conversation stopped as he entered the room.

'No, no, please sit down, I didn't mean to interrupt,' declared a broad Yorkshire accent that hadn't been affected by several years as an Oxford don.

'How kind of you to join us, prime minister,' said Giles, leaping to his feet.

'Only too delighted,' said Harold Wilson. 'It gave me an excuse to escape for a few minutes from a dinner with the executive of the National Union of Mineworkers. Mind you, Giles,' he added, looking around, 'I wouldn't be surprised if we were outnumbered by the Tories in this room. But not to worry, Griff will sort them out.' The prime minister leant across the table and shook hands with Giles's agent. 'And who are these two delightful ladies?'

'My sisters, Emma and Grace,' said Giles.

'I bow before you both,' said the prime minister. 'The first woman chairman of a public company, and the renowned English scholar.' Grace blushed. 'And if I'm not mistaken,' he added, jabbing a finger across the table, 'that's Bob Bingham, the fish-paste king. My mother always had a jar of your paste on the table for what she called high tea.'

'And at Downing Street?' enquired Bob.

'We don't do high tea at Downing Street,' said the prime minister, as he made his way slowly around the table, shaking hands and signing menus.

Giles was touched by how long the prime minister stayed, only leaving when a dutiful PPS reminded him that he was the guest of honour at the miners' dinner where he was due to make a speech. Just before he left, he took Harry to one side and whispered, 'Thank you for your help in Moscow, Mr Clifton. Don't think we've forgotten. And don't give up on Babakov, because we haven't.'

'Thank you, sir,' said Harry, and they all stood again as the prime minister left the room.

After they'd resumed their seats, Jean Buchanan said to Griff, 'It must be such fun being an old friend of the PM.'

'I've only met him once before,' admitted Griff. 'But like an elephant, he never forgets,' he added as Harry stood up, tapped the side of his wine glass with a spoon and waited for silence.

'Fellow guests, I invite you to join me in a toast to my oldest and dearest friend. The man who introduced me to his sister, and is godfather to our son Sebastian. Will you rise and join me in a toast to the Right Honourable Sir Giles Barrington, Her Majesty's first minister of state at the Foreign Office, and a man who still believes he should be the captain of the England cricket team.'

Harry waited for the laughter to die down before he added, 'And we all hope Giles will retain his seat at the next election, and perhaps even fulfil his life's ambition and become foreign secretary.'

Warm applause and cries of 'Hear hear!' echoed around the room as Giles rose to respond.

'Thank you, Harry, and it's wonderful to have not only my family, but my closest and dearest friends around me, who have come together for only one purpose, to remind me just how old I am. I've been blessed with a wonderful family and real friends, and surely any sensible man could wish for nothing more. However, many of you have been kind enough to ask me what I would like for my birthday.' Giles looked slowly around the table before saying, 'To be prime minister, foreign secretary and chancellor of the

Exchequer all at the same time.' Laughter and applause broke out spontaneously before he added, 'But for the moment, I'd be satisfied with holding on to Bristol Docklands at the next election.'

Applause, but no laughter this time.

'No, what I really want is for all of you here tonight, to prosper and flourish –' Giles paused – 'under a Labour government.'

The jeers drowned the cheers, proving the prime minister to be right about Giles being out-numbered by Tories at his own birthday party.

'So let me end by saying, if I don't win, I shall sulk.' The laughter returned. 'A wise man once told me that the secret of a great speech is timing . . .' Giles smiled and sat down, as everyone rose and gave him a standing ovation.

◄○►

'So where are you off to next?' asked Emma as the waiters returned to serve the guests with coffee and After Eight mints.

'East Berlin, a meeting of foreign ministers,' replied her brother.

'Do you think they'll ever tear down that barbaric wall?' asked Grace.

'Not as long as that stooge Ulbricht is in power and simply carries out the bidding of his masters in the Kremlin.'

'And closer to home,' said Emma, 'when do you think the general election will be?'

'Harold wants to go in May, when he's confident we can win.'

'I feel sure you'll hold on to Bristol,' said Emma, 'barring some accident. But I still think the Tories will scrape home with a small majority.'

'And you'll remain loyal to the Labour Party?' Giles asked, turning to his younger sister.

'Of course,' said Grace.

'And you, Emma?'

'Not a chance.'

'Some things never change.'

18

GWYNETH GROANED when the alarm went off, and didn't bother to check what time it was. She had perfected the art of falling back to sleep within minutes of Giles leaving the room. He always took a shower the night before, and laid out the clothes he would need in his dressing room so he wouldn't have to turn on the light and disturb her.

He glanced out of the window overlooking Smith Square. His car was already parked outside the front door. He didn't like to think what hour his driver had to get up to be sure he was never late.

Once Giles had shaved and dressed, he went down to the kitchen, made himself a cup of black coffee and devoured a bowl of cornflakes and fruit. Five minutes later he picked up his suitcase and headed for the front door. Gwyneth only ever asked him one question when he was going away: how many days? Two, he'd told her on this occasion, and she'd packed accordingly. He wouldn't even have to check before he unpacked in Berlin, because he knew everything he needed would be there.

His first wife had been a whore, while his second turned out to be a virgin. Giles tried not to admit, even to himself, that he would have liked a subtle combination of both. Virginia in the bedroom, and Gwyneth everywhere else. He often wondered if other men had the same fantasies. Certainly not Harry, who was even more in love with Emma than he'd been on the day they married. Giles envied that relationship, although that was something else he would never admit, even to his closest friend.

'Good morning, Alf,' said Giles as he climbed into the back of the car.

'Good morning, minister,' replied his driver cheerily.

Alf had been Giles's driver since the day he'd become a minister, and he was often a better source of information about what was happening in the real world than most of his Cabinet colleagues.

'So where are we off to today, sir?'

'East Berlin.'

'Rather you than me.'

'I know how you feel. Now, what have you got for me?'

'The election will be in June, probably the eighteenth.'

'But the press are still predicting May. Where are you getting your information?'

'Clarence, the PM's driver, told me, didn't he?'

'Then I'll need to brief Griff immediately. Anything else?'

'The foreign secretary will announce this morning that he'll be standing down from the Cabinet after the election, whatever the result.'

Giles didn't respond while he considered Alf's casually dropped bombshell. If he could hold on to Bristol Docklands, and if Labour were to win the general election, he must be in with a chance of being offered the

Foreign Office. Only problem: two ifs. He allowed himself a wry smile.

'Not bad, Alf, not bad at all,' he added as he opened his red box and began to look through his papers.

He always enjoyed catching up with his opposite numbers across Europe, exchanging views in corridors, lifts and bars where the *realpolitik* took place, rather than in the endless formal gatherings for which civil servants had already drafted the minutes long before the meeting was called to order.

Alf swept through an unmarked entrance onto runway three at Heathrow and came to a halt at the bottom of the boarding stairs that led up to the aircraft. If Giles didn't retain his seat in the Cabinet after the election, he was going to miss all this. Back to joining baggage queues, check-in counters, passport control, security checks, long walks to the gate, and then an endless wait before you were finally told you could board the plane.

Alf opened the back door and Giles climbed the steps to the waiting aircraft. Don't get used to it, Harold Wilson had once warned him. Only the Queen can afford to do that.

Giles was the last passenger to board and the door was pulled closed as he took his seat in the front row, next to his permanent secretary.

'Good morning, minister,' he said. Not a man who wasted time on small talk. 'Although on the face of it, minister,' he continued, 'this conference doesn't look at all promising, there could be several opportunities for us to take advantage of.'

'Such as?'

'The PM needs to know if Ulbricht is about to be replaced as general secretary. If he is, they'll be sending out smoke signals and we need to find out who's been chosen to replace him.'

'Will it make any difference?' asked Giles. 'Whoever gets the job will still be phoning reverse charges to Moscow before he can take any decisions.'

'While the foreign secretary,' the civil servant continued, ignoring the remark, 'is keen for you to discover if this would be a good time for the UK to make another application to join the EEC.'

'Has De Gaulle died when I wasn't looking?'

'No, but his influence has waned since his retirement last year, and Pompidou might feel the time has come to flex his muscles.'

The two men spent the rest of the flight going over the official agenda, and what HMG hoped to get out of the conference: a nudge here, a wink there, whenever an understanding had been reached.

When the plane taxied to a halt at Berlin's Tegel airport, the British ambassador was waiting for them at the bottom of the steps. With the help of a police escort, the Rolls-Royce whisked them across West Berlin, but came to an abrupt halt when it reached Checkpoint Charlie, as the Western Allies had dubbed the wall's best-known crossing point.

Giles looked up at the ugly, graffiti-covered wall, crowned with barbed wire. The Berlin Wall had been raised in 1961, virtually overnight, to stop the flood of people who were emigrating from East to West. East Berlin was now one giant prison, which wasn't much of an advertisement for Communism. If it had really been the utopia the Communists claimed, thought Giles, it would have been the West Germans who would have had to build a wall to prevent their unhappy citizens from escaping to the East.

'If I had a pick axe . . .' he said.

'I would have to stop you,' said the ambassador. 'Unless of course you wanted to cause a diplomatic incident.'

'It would take more than a diplomatic incident to stop my brother-in-law fighting for what he believes in,' said Giles.

Once their passports had been checked, they were able to leave the Western sector, which allowed the driver to advance another couple of hundred yards before coming to a halt in no-man's-land. Giles looked up at the armed guards in their turrets, staring down grim-faced at their British guests.

They remained parked between the two borders, while the Rolls-Royce was checked from the front bumper to the boot, as if it were a Sherman tank, before they were eventually permitted to enter East Berlin. But without the assistance of a police escort, it took them another hour before they reached their hotel on the other side of the city.

Once they had checked in and been handed their keys, the golden rule was for the minister to swap rooms with his permanent secretary so he wouldn't be troubled by call girls, or have to watch every word he said because his room would certainly be bugged. But the Stasi had caught on to that ruse and now simply bugged both rooms.

'If you want to have a private conversation,' said the ambassador, 'the bathroom, with the taps running, is the only safe place.'

Giles unpacked, showered and came back downstairs

to join some Dutch and Swedish colleagues for a late lunch. Although they were old friends, it didn't stop them pumping each other for information.

'So tell me, Giles, is Labour going to win the election?' asked Stellen Christerson, the Swedish foreign minister.

'Officially, we can't lose. Unofficially, it's too close to call.'

'And if you do win, will Mr Wilson make you foreign secretary?'

'Unofficially, I have to be in with a chance.'

'And officially?' asked Jan Hilbert, the Dutch minister.

'I shall serve Her Majesty's Government in whatever capacity the prime minister thinks fit.'

'And I'm going to win the next Monte Carlo Rally,' said Hilbert.

'And I'm going back to my suite to check over my papers,' said Giles, aware that only debutants sat around drinking just to end up spending the next day yawning. You had to be wide awake if you hoped to catch the one unguarded revelation that often made hours of negotiating worthwhile.

◄○►

The conference opened the following morning with a speech by the East German general secretary, Walter Ulbricht, who welcomed the delegates. It was clear that the contents had been written in Moscow, while the words were delivered by the Soviets' puppet in East Berlin.

Giles leant back, closed his eyes, and pretended to listen to the translation of a speech he'd heard several times before, but his mind soon began to wander. Suddenly he heard an anxious voice ask, 'I hope there's nothing wrong with my translation, Sir Giles?'

Giles glanced round. The Foreign Office had made it clear that, although every minister would have their own interpreter, they came with a health warning. Most of them worked for the Stasi, and any unfortunate remark or lapse in behaviour would undoubtedly be reported back to their masters in the East German Politburo.

What had taken Giles by surprise was not so much the concerned enquiry made by the young woman, as the fact that he could have sworn he detected a slight West Country accent.

'Your translation is just fine,' he said, taking a closer look at her. 'It's just that I've heard this speech, or a slight variation of it, several times before.'

She was wearing a grey shapeless dress that nearly reached her ankles, and that could only have been purchased off the peg from a comrades' cooperative store. But she possessed something you couldn't buy at Harrods, luxuriant auburn hair that had been plaited and wound into a severe bun, to hide any suggestion of femininity. It was as if she didn't want anyone to notice her. But her big brown eyes and captivating smile would have caused most men to take a second look, including Giles. She was like one of those ugly ducklings in a film that you know will turn out in the last scene to be a swan.

It stank of a set-up. Giles immediately assumed she worked for the Stasi, and wondered if he could catch her out.

'You have a slight West Country burr if I'm not mistaken,' he whispered.

She nodded and displayed the same disarming smile. 'My father was born in Truro.'

'Then what are you doing here?'

'I was born in East Berlin. My father met my mother

when he was stationed here with the British Army in 1947.'

'That can't have been met with universal approval,' suggested Giles.

'He had to resign his commission, and he then took a job in Germany so he could be with her.'

'A true romantic.'

'But the story doesn't have a romantic ending, I'm afraid. More John Galsworthy than Charlotte Brontë, because when the wall went up in 1961, my father was in Cornwall visiting his parents and we've never seen him since.'

Giles remained cautious. 'That doesn't make any sense, because if your father is a UK national you and your mother could make an application to visit Britain at any time.'

'We've made thirty-four applications in the past nine years, and those that were answered all came back with the same red stamp, rejected.'

'I'm sorry to hear that,' said Giles. He then turned away, adjusted his headphones and listened to the remainder of the welcoming speech.

When the general secretary finally sat down an hour and twelve minutes later, Giles was one of the few people in the room who was still awake.

He left the conference chamber and joined a subcommittee to discuss the possible lifting of certain sanctions between the two countries. He had a clear brief, as did his opposite number, but during the meeting he had the distinct impression that his interpreter was including the occasional observation that came from the Stasi, and not from the minister. He remained sceptical and cautious about her, although when he looked her up on the briefing notes he saw that her name was Karin Pengelly. So it seemed she was at least telling the truth about her heritage.

Giles soon became used to being followed around by Karin as he moved from meeting to meeting. She continued to pass on everything said by the other side, without the expression on her face ever changing. But Giles's responses were always carefully worded, as he still wasn't sure whose side she was on.

At the end of the first day, Giles felt the conference had yielded some positive results, and not least because of his interpreter. Or was she simply saying what they wanted him to hear?

During the official dinner held at the Palast der Republik, Karin sat directly behind him, translating every word of the interminable, repetitive speeches, until Giles finally weakened.

'If you write a letter to your father, I'll post it to him when I get back to England, and I'll also have a word with a colleague in the immigration office.'

'Thank you, Sir Giles.'

Giles turned his attention to the Italian minister sitting on his right, who was pushing his food around the plate while grumbling about having to serve three prime ministers in one year.

'Why don't you go for the job yourself, Umberto?' suggested Giles.

'Certainly not,' he replied. 'I'm not looking for early retirement.'

◄○►

Giles was delighted when the last course of the endless meal was finally served and the guests were allowed to depart. He said goodnight to some of the other delegates as he left the room. He then joined the ambassador and was driven back to his hotel.

He picked up his key and was back in his suite just after eleven. He'd been asleep for about an hour when there was a tap on the door. Someone obviously willing to ignore the *Do Not Disturb* sign. But that didn't come as a surprise, because the Foreign Office had even issued a briefing note to cover that eventuality. So he knew exactly what to expect and, more important, how to deal with it.

He reluctantly got out of bed, pulled on his dressing gown and went to the door, having already been warned that they would try to produce a lookalike of his wife, but twenty years younger.

When he opened the door he was momentarily stunned. Before him stood the most beautiful blonde, with high cheekbones, deep blue eyes and the shortest leather skirt he'd ever seen.

'Wrong wife,' said Giles once he'd recovered, although he was reminded why he had fallen so hopelessly in love with Virginia all those years ago. 'But thank you, madam,' he said as he took the bottle of champagne. He read the label. 'Veuve Clicquot 1947. Please pass on my compliments to whomever. An excellent vintage,' he added, before closing the door.

He smiled as he climbed back into bed. Harry would have been proud of him.

◄o►

The second day of conference became more and more frenetic as the delegates attempted to close deals so they wouldn't have to return home empty-handed. Giles felt quite pleased when the East Germans agreed to remove their import tariffs on British pharmaceuticals, and delighted, although he tried not to show it, when his French counterpart hinted that if the British Government were to issue an official invitation for the French President to visit Britain in the new year, it would be seriously considered. He wrote down the words 'seriously considered' so there could be no misunderstanding.

As always happens on these occasions, meetings began to run late and to continue into the evening; so Giles ended up scheduling one before dinner, with an East German trade minister, one during, with his Dutch counterpart, and finally one after dinner with Walter Scheel, the West German foreign minister. He asked Karin to join them for dinner, having decided that if she was working for the Stasi, she was a better actress than Peggy Ashcroft. And if she agreed, he just hoped she'd let her hair down.

Karin reminded him that the Dutch minister spoke fluent English, and suggested that they might prefer to dine alone. But Giles thought it would be helpful for her to be there, just in case anything was lost in translation.

He couldn't help wondering if any of his fellow delegates had noticed how often he had turned around during his afternoon session with the trade minister to look more closely at his interpreter, pretending to listen intently to her translation while in fact hoping to be rewarded with that smile. But when she turned up for dinner wearing a stunning off-the-shoulder red silk dress, which certainly hadn't been purchased from a comrades' cooperative store, with her auburn hair hanging loosely below her shoulders, Giles couldn't take his eyes off her, although she continued to feign not to notice.

When he returned to his suite for the final meeting of the evening, Scheel wasted no time in pressing his government's case. 'Your import tax on BMW, Volkswagen and Mercedes is hitting our car industry hard. If you can't lift it, can you at least lower it?'

'I'm afraid that's just not possible, Walter, as we're only a few weeks away from a general election, and the Labour Party is hoping for large donations from Ford, BMC and Vauxhall.'

'You'll have no choice when you become a member of the EEC,' said the German, smiling.

'Amen to that,' said Giles.

'At least I'm grateful for your candid response.' The two men shook hands, and as Scheel turned to leave, Giles put a finger to his lips and followed him out of the room. He looked up and down the corridor before asking, 'Who's going to replace Ulbricht as General Secretary?'

'The Soviets are getting behind Honecker,' said Scheel, 'and frankly I can't see anyone beating him.'

'But he's a weak, sycophantic man, who's never had an original thought in his life,' said Giles, 'and would end up being nothing more than a stooge, just like Ulbricht.'

'Which is precisely why the Politburo is backing him.'

Giles threw his hands up in the air. Scheel could only manage a wry smile. 'See you in London after the election,' he said, before heading off in the direction of the lift.

'Let's hope so,' murmured Giles. When he returned to his room, he was pleased to find that Karin was still there. She opened her bag, took out an envelope and handed it to him.

'Thank you, Sir Giles.'

Giles looked at the name and address on the envelope, placed it in an inside pocket and said, 'I'll post it to your father just as soon as I'm back in England.'

'I know my mother would appreciate that.'

'It's the least I can do,' said Giles as he walked over to the side table, picked up the bottle of champagne and handed it to her. 'A small token of my gratitude for all your hard work. I hope you and your mother will enjoy it.'

'It's very kind of you, Sir Giles,' she whispered, handing the bottle back, 'but I wouldn't get as far as the front door before the Stasi took it away from me,' she added, pointing at the chandelier.

'Then let's at least share a glass together.'

'Are you sure that's wise, Sir Giles, considering—'

'Now that we're on our own, I think you can call me Giles,' he said as he uncorked the bottle and poured two glasses. He raised his. 'Let's hope it won't be too long before you're reunited with your father.'

Karin took a sip and then placed the glass on the table. 'I must go,' she said, and thrust out her hand.

Giles took it and drew her gently towards him. She pushed him away.

'This mustn't happen, Giles, because then you'll only think—'

He started to kiss her before she could say another word. As they kissed, he undid the zip on the back of her dress, and when it fell to the ground he took a pace back, wanting to touch every part of her body at once. He took her back into his arms and when they kissed again, her lips parted as they fell on to the bed. He looked into her brown eyes and whispered, 'If you work for the Stasi, don't tell me until after I've made love to you.'

19

GILES WAS SITTING on the front bench in the House of Commons listening to the foreign secretary deliver a statement to the House on the Test and County Cricket Board's decision to cancel South Africa's England tour, when he was handed a note from the chief whip. *Could I have a word with you following the statement?*

Giles always felt that a summons from the chief whip was rather like being called to the headmaster's study: more likely to be a caning than paeans of praise. Although the chief whip doesn't sit in the Cabinet, his power is disproportionate to his rank. He was the company sergeant major who was there to make sure the troops were kept in line so the officers' lives ran smoothly.

As soon as the foreign secretary had answered the last question from the member for Louth about strengthening government sanctions against South Africa's apartheid regime, Giles slipped out of the chamber into the members' lobby and strolled across to the chief whip's office.

The chief's secretary was clearly expecting him because he was ushered through to the inner sanctum without having to break stride.

As soon as Giles entered the office, he knew from the

look on the chief's face that it had to be a caning, not paeans of praise.

'Not good news, I'm afraid,' said Bob Mellish, taking a large buff-coloured envelope from a drawer in his desk and passing it to Giles.

Giles opened the envelope with trembling fingers and pulled out a set of black and white photographs. He studied them for a few moments before he said, 'It doesn't make any sense.'

'I'm not sure I understand you.'

'I just don't believe Karin was working for the Stasi.'

'Then who else can it have been?' said the chief whip. 'Even if she wasn't on their payroll, God knows what pressure they must have put her under.'

'You have to believe me, Bob, Karin just wasn't like that. I realize I've made a complete fool of myself and let the government and my family down badly. But one thing I'm certain of, Karin is not to blame.'

'I must confess, it's the first time the Stasi have used photographs. They've only ever sent tapes in the past. I'll have to brief the Foreign Office immediately.'

'I can assure you, we never discussed any government business,' said Giles. 'And if anything, she was even more frightened of being caught than I was.'

The chief whip raised an eyebrow. 'Nevertheless, I have to deal with the here and now. I'm assuming these photographs are already in the hands of one of the tabloids, so you'd better prepare yourself for an unpleasant phone call. And I have only one piece of advice, Giles – tell Gwyneth before the news breaks.'

'Should I resign?' said Giles, as he gripped the edge of the desk to try to stop his hands shaking.

'That's not for me to decide. But don't do anything too

hasty. At least wait until you've seen the PM. And let me know the moment the press get in touch with you.'

Giles took one more look at some of the photos of himself and Karin, and still refused to believe it.

◄○►

'How could you, Giles? To fall for such an obvious honey trap,' said Gwyneth. 'Especially after Harry told you what happened to him in Moscow.'

'I know, I know. I couldn't have been more stupid. I'm so sorry for the pain I've caused you.'

'Didn't you give me or your family one moment's thought when this little tart was seducing you?'

'She wasn't a tart,' said Giles quietly.

Gwyneth was silent for some time before she asked, 'Are you saying you knew this woman before all this happened?'

'She was my interpreter.'

'So it was you who seduced her, and not the other way round?'

Giles made no attempt to contradict her. It would have been one lie too many.

'If you'd been set up, or drunk, or just made a fool of yourself, Giles, I might have been able to live with it. But you'd clearly given it some thought before . . .' She stopped mid-sentence and rose from her chair. 'I'm going down to Wales this evening. Please don't try to get in touch with me.'

Giles sat alone as dusk settled over Smith Square and considered the consequences of having told Gwyneth the truth. Not much point if Karin had been nothing more than a Stasi whore. How easy it would have been for him to tell his wife that Karin was just a tart, a one-night stand, that he didn't even know her name. So why hadn't he? Because the truth was, he'd never met anyone quite like her before. Gentle, humorous, passionate, kind and bright. Oh so bright. And if she didn't feel the same way about him, why did she fall asleep in his arms? And why did she make love with him again when they woke in the morning, when she could so easily have stolen away in the night, having done her job? Instead, she chose to take just as big a risk as him and was probably suffering the consequences every bit as much as he was.

◄○►

Every time the phone rang, Giles assumed it would be a journalist on the other end of the line – *We are in possession of some photographs, Sir Giles, and wondered if you'd care to comment . . .*

The phone rang, and he reluctantly picked it up.

'There's a Mr Pengelly on the line,' said his secretary.

Pengelly. It had to be Karin's father. Was he also involved in the set-up? 'Put him through,' said Giles.

'Good afternoon, Sir Giles. My name is John Pengelly. I'm calling to thank you for your kindness in helping my daughter when you were in East Berlin.' The same gentle West Country burr. 'I've just read the letter from Karin that you kindly forwarded. It's the first I've had from her in months. I'd almost given up hope.'

Giles didn't want to tell him why that hope was likely to be short-lived.

'I write to Karin and her mother every week, but I never know how many letters get through. Now you've met her, I feel more confident, and will contact the Home Office again.'

'I've already spoken to the Home Office department that's responsible for immigration. However—'

'That's very kind of you, Sir Giles. My family and I are in your debt, and you're not even my MP.'

'Can I ask you a personal question, Mr Pengelly?'

'Yes, of course, Sir Giles.'

'Do you think it's possible that Karin could be working for the Stasi?'

'No, never. She detests them even more than I do. In fact I keep warning her that her unwillingness to co-operate with the authorities could be the reason they won't grant her a visa.'

'But they gave her a job as an interpreter at an international conference.'

'Only because they were desperate. Karin wrote in her letter there were over seventy delegates from more than twenty countries, and she felt very lucky that she was allocated to you.'

'Not so lucky, because I have to warn you that the press might have got hold of some photographs showing the two of us together, that at best can be described as unfortunate, and at worst—'

'I can't believe it,' Mr Pengelly eventually managed. 'Karin is normally so cautious, she never takes risks. What came over her?'

'She is in no way to blame, Mr Pengelly,' said Giles. 'It was entirely my fault, and I must apologize to you personally, because if the press find out you're Karin's father, they'll make your life hell.'

'They did that when I married her mother,' said Pengelly, 'and I've never regretted it.'

It was Giles's turn to remain silent, as he thought how to respond. 'The truth is quite simple, Mr Pengelly, and

I haven't even been able to share it with my wife.' He paused again. 'I fell in love with your daughter. If I could have avoided it, I most certainly would have and, let me assure you, I am quite willing to go through the same pain you must have endured just to be with her. What makes it worse, I don't even know how she feels about me.'

'I do,' said Pengelly.

◄○►

The call came on a Saturday afternoon, just after four o'clock. It quickly became clear that the *Sunday People* had an exclusive, although Giles accepted that by midnight most editors would be resetting their front pages.

'I assume you've seen the photographs we have in our possession, minister?'

'Yes, I have.'

'Do you wish to make a statement?'

'No, I do not.'

'Will you be resigning from the government?'

'No comment.'

'How has your wife reacted to the news? We understand she's gone to stay with her parents in Wales.'

'No comment.'

'Is it true you're getting divorced?'

Giles slammed down the phone. He couldn't stop shaking as he looked up the chief whip's home number.

'Bob, it's Giles. The story will break in tomorrow's *Sunday People*.'

'I'm so sorry, Giles. For what it's worth, you were a damned good minister and will be sorely missed.'

Giles put down the phone, only one word ringing in his ears – *were*. You were a damned good minister. He took a sheet of House of Commons paper from the letter rack in front of him and began to write.

> *Dear Prime Minister,*
> *It is with great regret . . .*

◄○►

Giles entered the Privy Council office on Whitehall so he could avoid the scrum of Fleet Street hacks waiting for him in Downing Street, or at least those who didn't know about the back door entrance to No.10.

One of the memories he would regale his grandchildren with was that as he entered the Cabinet Room, Harold Wilson was trying unsuccessfully to relight his briar pipe.

'Giles, good of you to drop in, considering what you must be going through. But believe me, and I speak with some experience in these matters, it will blow over.'

'Possibly, prime minister. But it's still the end of my career as a serious politician, which is the only job I've ever really wanted to do.'

'I'm not sure I agree with you,' said Wilson. 'Just think about it for a moment. If you were to hold on to Bristol Docklands at the next election, and I'm still convinced you can, the electorate would have expressed their views in the ballot box, and who am I to disagree with their judgement? And if I'm back in Downing Street, I wouldn't hesitate to ask you to re-join the Cabinet.'

'Two ifs, prime minister.'

'You help me with one, Giles, and I'll see what I can do about the other.'

'But, prime minister, after those headlines . . .'

'I agree, they were not edifying. It was perhaps

unfortunate that you were minister for foreign affairs.'
Giles smiled for the first time in days. 'But several of the
comment pieces,' continued Wilson, 'as well as one or
two leaders, have pointed out that you were an outstanding minister. The *Telegraph*, of all papers, reminded its
readers that you'd won an MC at Tobruk. You somehow
survived that dreadful battle, so what makes you think you
won't survive this one?'

'Because I think Gwyneth is going to divorce me, and
frankly she has good reason to do so.'

'I'm sorry to hear that,' said Wilson, once again trying
to light his pipe. 'But I still think you should go down to
Bristol and test the waters. Be sure to listen to what Griff
Haskins has to say, because when I called him this morning, he left me no doubt that he still wants you to be
the candidate.'

◄○►

'Many congratulations, major,' said Virginia. 'You've been
single-handedly responsible for bringing Giles Barrington
down.'

'But that's the irony,' said Fisher. 'I didn't. It wasn't
our girl who spent the night with him.'

'I'm not following you.'

'I flew to Berlin just as you instructed, and it wasn't
difficult to locate an escort agency with offices on both
sides of the wall. One particular girl came highly recommended. She was paid well, and promised a bonus if she
could supply photographs of the two of them in bed.'

'And there she is,' said Virginia, pointing to a selection
of that morning's papers that normally wouldn't have
found their way into the flat in Cadogan Gardens.

'But that's not her. She rang the following morning

and told me that Barrington had relieved her of a bottle of champagne but then slammed the door in her face.'

'So who's that then?'

'No idea. The agency say they haven't come across her before, and assume she must work for the Stasi. It had sound and surveillance equipment in all the delegates' hotel suites during the conference.'

'But why did he reject your girl, then allow himself to be taken in by this one?'

'That I can't explain,' said Fisher. 'All I am sure about is that your ex-husband isn't necessarily finished.'

'But he resigned this morning. It was the lead story on the morning news.'

'As a minister, yes, but not as a Member of Parliament. And if he were to hold on to his seat at the next election . . .'

'Then we'll just have to make sure he doesn't.'

'How can we do that?'

'I'm so glad you asked that question, major.'

◄○►

'I'm afraid I've been left with no choice but to resign as your Member of Parliament,' said Giles.

'Just because you went to bed with a tart?' said Griff.

'She wasn't a tart,' Giles replied, as he did to everyone who made that assumption.

'If you resign, we may as well hand the seat to the Tories. The PM won't thank you for that.'

'But if the polls are to be believed, the Tories are going to win the seat anyway.'

'We've defied the polls before,' said Griff. 'And the Tories haven't even selected their candidate yet.'

'Nothing is going to persuade me to change my mind,' said Giles.

'But you're the only person who can win the seat,' said Griff as the phone on his desk rang. He picked it up. 'Whoever it is, tell them to bugger off.'

'It's the editor of the *Bristol Evening Post*,' said his secretary.

'And the same applies to him.'

'But he says he has a piece of news you'll want to hear immediately. It's the lead story in tomorrow's paper.'

'Put him on.' Griff listened for some time before he slammed the phone down. 'That's all I need.'

'So what's the news that can't possibly wait?'

'The Tories have announced their candidate.'

'Anyone we know?'

'Major Alex Fisher.'

Giles burst out laughing. 'I can't believe how far you're prepared to go, Griff, just to make sure I stand.'

20

'Good morning, my name is Giles Barrington, and I'm the Labour candidate for Bristol Docklands at the general election on Thursday June eighteenth. Vote Labour. Vote Barrington on June eighteenth. Good morning, my name is . . .'

Giles had fought seven elections in the last twenty-five years, and won all seven of them, gradually increasing his majority to 2,166. The last two had resulted in Labour governments, when the Conservatives hadn't been expected to win Bristol Docklands, and the Liberals knew they couldn't.

The last time Giles had called for a recount was when his opponent was Major Alex Fisher, and on that occasion Giles had won by just four votes, and only after three recounts. It had been a dirty, personal campaign from beginning to end, with Giles's ex-wife Lady Virginia entering the fray when she came down to Bristol to support the major, who she described as 'an honest and decent man'.

Now, fifteen years later, Giles was facing a re-run against the same opponent, and talk of another divorce. Gwyneth, thank heavens, had made it clear that she would not be filing papers until after the election, and although she had no intention of visiting the constituency, she would not be suggesting that anyone should vote for Fisher.

'Thank the Lord for small mercies,' was all Griff Haskins had to say. He didn't raise the subject again.

When the prime minister asked the Queen to dissolve Parliament on 29 May 1970, Giles returned to Bristol the following day to begin the three-week election campaign. As he took to the streets and started canvassing, he was pleasantly surprised by the welcome he received, and by how few people raised the subject of Berlin, or asked where his wife was. The British are not a judgemental lot, Griff observed, although Giles didn't admit to his agent that Karin was rarely out of his thoughts. He wrote to her every night, just before going to bed and, like a schoolboy, eagerly checked the post each morning. But there was never an envelope with an East German stamp on it.

Emma, Harry and Seb, plus the redoubtable Labour Party stalwart Miss Parish, who had taken three weeks off work as she did for every election campaign, regularly accompanied Giles when he was out canvassing. Emma dealt with those women who expressed their doubts about Giles following his resignation from the Cabinet, while Seb concentrated on the eighteen-year-olds, who would be voting for the first time.

But the surprise package was Harry, who proved popular on several levels. There were those constituents who wanted to know how his campaign to have Anatoly Babakov released was coming along, while others wondered what Detective Inspector Warwick would be up to next. Whenever he was asked who he'd be voting for,

Harry always replied, 'Like all sensible Bristolians, I'll be voting for my brother-in-law.'

'No, no,' said Griff firmly. 'Say Giles Barrington, not your brother-in-law. "Brother-in-law" isn't on the ballot paper.'

There was a third group who thought Harry was Bristol's answer to Cary Grant, and told him they would certainly vote for him if he was the candidate.

'I'd rather walk barefoot over hot coals,' Harry would reply, raising his hands in horror.

'Are you jealous, Mum?'

'Certainly not,' said Emma. 'Most of them are middle-aged matrons who simply want to mother him.'

'As long as they vote Labour,' said Griff, 'I don't care what they want to do with him.'

<o>

'Good morning, my name is Giles Barrington, and I'm the Labour candidate for Bristol Docklands at the general election on Thursday June eighteenth. Vote Labour . . .'

Every morning began with a 'prayer meeting' in Griff's office, so the agent could bring the candidate and the core campaign workers up to date, before allocating them their daily tasks.

On the first Monday, Griff opened the meeting by breaking one of his golden rules.

'I think you should challenge Fisher to a debate.'

'But you've always said in the past that a sitting member should never acknowledge the existence of his opponents because it only gives them a platform to air their views and establish themselves as credible candidates.'

'Fisher is a credible candidate,' said Griff. 'He's got a three per cent lead in the polls to prove it, and we desperately need to find some way of eating into his lead.'

'But he'll use the occasion to launch a personal attack on me and capture cheap headlines in the press.'

'Let's hope so,' said Griff, 'because our private polls show that what happened in Berlin is not a high priority for most voters, and our daily postbag confirms it. The public are far more interested in the NHS, unemployment, pensions and immigration. In fact, there are more voters complaining about over-zealous parking wardens in Broadmead than about your nocturnal habits when you're not at home. If you want proof,' he said, extracting some letters from the pile on his desk, 'just listen to any of these. *Dear Sir Giles, if everyone who slept with a tart or had an affair were to vote for you, you'd double your majority. Good luck.*'

'I can see it now,' said Giles. 'Vote for Barrington if you've had an extramarital affair.'

Emma scowled at her brother, clearly disapproving of Griff's casual attitude to Giles's behaviour.

'And here's another one,' said Griff, ignoring Giles's comment. '*Dear Sir Giles, I've never voted Labour before, but I'd prefer to vote for a sinner than for someone like Alex Fisher who poses as a saint. Yours reluctantly,* etc. But this one's my favourite. *Dear Sir Giles, I must say I admire your taste in women. I'm off to Berlin next week and wondered if you could give me her phone number.*'

I only wish I knew her phone number, thought Giles.

◄○►

FISHER TURNS DOWN DEBATE CHALLENGE

'He's made his first mistake,' said Griff, turning the paper round so they could all see the headline on the front page.

'But he's the one with a three per cent lead in the polls,' said Giles. 'That's not a mistake, it's just common sense.'

'Couldn't agree more,' said Griff, 'but it's his reason for turning you down that's the mistake. I quote, "I wouldn't want to be seen in the same room as that man." A foolish error. People don't like personal attacks, so we must take advantage of it. Make it clear that you will turn up, and if he doesn't the electorate can draw their own conclusions.' Griff continued to read the article, and it was not long before he smiled for a second time. 'It's not often that the Liberals come to our aid, but Simon Fletcher has told the *News* that he'll be happy to participate in the debate. But then, he's got nothing to lose. I'll issue a press statement immediately. Meanwhile, you lot get back to work. You're not winning any votes sitting around in my office.'

—◆—

'Good morning, my name is Giles Barrington, and I'm the Labour candidate for Bristol Docklands at the general election on Thursday June eighteenth . . .'

Just as Giles was beginning to feel a little more confident about the outcome, a Gallup Poll in the *Daily Mail* predicted for the first time that Edward Heath and the Tories were on track to win the election with a thirty-seat majority.

'We're thirty-fifth on the list of seats the Tories will need to capture if they hope to get an overall majority,' said Giles.

'Read the small print,' responded Griff. 'The same poll is saying that Bristol Docklands is too close to call. And by the way, have you seen today's *Evening Post*?' He passed the first edition to the candidate.

Giles rather admired the neutral stance the *News* always took during an election campaign, only coming out in favour of a particular candidate on the day before the election, and in the past it hadn't always backed him. But today it broke its rule with a couple of weeks to go. In a leader, the paper made its position clear, below the damning headline:

WHAT'S HE FRIGHTENED OF?

It went on to say that if Major Fisher failed to turn up for next Thursday's debate, they would be recommending that their readers vote Labour, and return Giles Barrington to Westminster.

'Let's pray he doesn't turn up,' said Giles.

'He'll turn up all right,' said Griff, 'because if he doesn't, he'll lose the election. Our next problem is how we handle him when he does.'

'But surely it ought to be Fisher who's worried,' said Emma. 'After all, Giles is a far more accomplished debater, with over twenty years' parliamentary experience.'

'That won't matter a damn on the night,' said Miss Parish, 'if we don't find a way of dealing with the elephant in the room.'

Griff nodded. 'We may have to use our secret weapon.'

'What have you got in mind?' asked Giles.

'Harry. We'll put him in the front row, facing the audience, and get him to read the first chapter of his next book. Then no one will even notice what's happening on stage.'

Everyone laughed except Harry. 'What are you implying?' he asked.

—◦—

'*Good morning, my name is Giles Barrington, and I'm the Labour candidate for Bristol Docklands at the general election on . . .*'

I'LL BE THERE, screamed the headline on the front page of the *Bristol Evening Post* the following day.

Giles read the article that followed, and accepted that the debate might well decide who would be the next Member of Parliament for Bristol Docklands.

Griff agreed and suggested Giles should take time off to prepare as if he was being cross-examined by Robin Day, the BBC's political interrogator. He asked Seb to play the role of Alex Fisher.

'Do you feel that a man with your lack of morals should be standing for Parliament?'

'Whose side are you on, Seb?'

'He's on your side,' said Griff, 'and you'd better have an answer to that question by next Thursday night.'

'May I ask why we haven't seen your wife in the constituency during the election campaign?'

'She's visiting her parents in Wales.'

'That's at least a thousand votes down the drain,' said Griff.

'Tell me, Sir Giles, do you plan to make another trip to Berlin in the near future?'

'That's below the belt, Seb.'

'Which is exactly where Fisher will aim most of his

punches,' said Griff. 'So make sure you keep your guard up.'

'He's right, Seb. Keep on punching.'

◄○►

'Good morning, my name is Giles Barrington, and I'm the Labour candidate for Bristol Docklands . . .'

'They've changed the venue,' said Griff at the morning prayer meeting.

'Why?' asked Giles.

'There's been such a huge demand for tickets that it's been moved from the Guildhall to the Hippodrome Theatre.'

'But the Hippo holds two thousand people,' said Giles.

'I wish it held ten thousand,' said Griff. 'You'll never get a better chance to talk to the voters direct.'

'And at the same time expose Fisher for the fraud he is,' said Seb.

'How many seats have been allocated to us?' asked Griff, turning to Miss Parish.

'Each candidate is entitled to three hundred.'

'Any problem in filling our seats with the faithful?'

'None at all, the phone hasn't stopped for the past week. It could be a Rolling Stones concert. In fact, I've been in touch with my opposite number at the Liberal Party, to see if they've got any spare tickets.'

'They can't be stupid enough to release them to you.'

'It's got nothing to do with stupidity,' said Miss Parish. 'I have a feeling it's something far closer to home.'

'Like what?' said Griff.

'I've no idea, but I'll get to the bottom of it before next Thursday.'

'And what about the remaining tickets?' said Griff. 'Who gets those?'

'First come, first served,' said Miss Parish. 'I'll have a hundred of our people standing in the queue an hour before the curtain goes up.'

'So will the Tories,' said Griff. 'Better make it two hundred, two hours before.'

◄○►

'Good morning, my name is Giles Barrington, and I'm the Labour candidate . . .'

For the next week, Giles didn't let up for one minute, the weekend included. He canvassed, visited pubs, held evening meetings, and attended any gathering where more than half a dozen people were likely to turn up.

On Saturday, he put on his county tie and went to watch Gloucestershire play Middlesex at Nevil Road, but only stayed for about an hour. After walking slowly around the boundary perimeter, making sure all five thousand spectators had seen him, he made his way back to the constituency headquarters on Coronation Road.

On Sunday, he attended matins, communion and evensong in three different churches, but during each sermon his thoughts often strayed back to the debate, testing out arguments, phrases, even pauses . . .

'In the name of the Father . . .'

By Wednesday, Griff's polling was showing that Giles was still a couple of points behind, but Seb reminded him, so was Kennedy before his debate with Nixon.

Every detail of the encounter had been analysed at length. What he should wear, when he should have a haircut, not to shave until an hour before he walked on to the stage and, if he was offered the choice, to speak last.

'Who's chairing the debate?' asked Seb.

'Andy Nash, the editor of the *Evening Post*. We want to win votes, he wants to sell newspapers. Everyone has an angle,' said Griff.

'And be sure you're in bed before midnight,' said Emma. 'You're going to need a good night's sleep.'

Giles did get to bed before midnight, but he didn't sleep as he went over his speech again and again, rehearsing answers to all of Seb's questions. His concentration wasn't helped by Karin regularly barging into his thoughts. He was up by six, and outside Temple Meads station half an hour later, megaphone in hand once again, ready to face the early morning commuters.

'*Good morning, my name is Giles Barrington . . .*'

'Good luck tonight, Sir Giles, I'll be there to support you.'

'I don't live in your constituency, sorry.'

'Where do you stand on flogging?'

'I think I'll give the Liberals a go this time.'

'Don't have a spare fag, do you, guv?'

'*Good morning . . .*'

21

GRIFF PICKED Giles up from Barrington Hall just before six. This was one meeting he couldn't afford to be late for.

Giles was wearing a charcoal-grey single-breasted suit, a cream shirt and a Bristol Grammar School tie. He suspected that Fisher would be wearing his usual blue pinstriped double-breasted suit, a white shirt with a starched collar, and his regimental tie.

Giles was so nervous that he hardly spoke on the journey to the Hippodrome, and Griff remained accommodatingly quiet. He knew the candidate was silently rehearsing his speech.

Thirty minutes later, they pulled up outside the stage door where Giles had once hung around after a matinee of *Pride and Prejudice* to get Celia Johnson's autograph. Griff accompanied his candidate backstage where they were met by Andy Nash, who would be chairing the debate. He looked relieved to see them.

Giles paced up and down in the wings as he waited impatiently for the curtain to go up. Although there was still thirty minutes before the chairman would bang his gavel and call for order, Giles could already hear the buzz of an expectant audience, which made him feel like a finely tuned athlete waiting to be called to the starting line.

A few minutes later, Alex Fisher swept in, surrounded by his entourage, all talking at the tops of their voices. When you're nervous, Giles decided, it reveals itself in many different ways. Fisher marched straight past him, making no attempt to engage him in conversation and ignoring his outstretched hand.

A moment later, Simon Fletcher, the Liberal candidate, strolled in. How much easier it is to be relaxed when you've nothing to lose. He immediately shook hands with Giles and said, 'I wanted to thank you.'

'What for?' asked Giles, genuinely puzzled.

'For not continually reminding everyone that I'm not married, unlike Fisher, who mentions the fact at every opportunity.'

'Right, gentlemen,' said Nash. 'Please gather round, because the time has come to determine the order in which you will speak.' He held out a fist that gripped three straws of differing lengths. Fisher drew the short one, while Fletcher pulled out the longest one.

'You have first choice, Mr Fletcher,' said the chairman.

The Liberal candidate cocked his head to one side and whispered to Giles, 'Where do you want me to go?'

'Second,' Giles replied.

'I'll go second,' said Fletcher. Fisher looked surprised.

'And you, Sir Giles? First or last?'

'Last, thank you, chairman.'

'Right, that's settled. You'll be speaking first, Major Fisher. Let's put our heads above the parapet.'

He led the three candidates out on to the stage, and

it was the only time that evening that the whole audience applauded. Giles looked out into the auditorium where, unlike a theatre production, the lights wouldn't be going down. Two thousand lions had been waiting patiently for the Christians to appear.

He wished he'd stayed at home and was having supper on a tray in front of the TV; anywhere but here. But he always felt like that, even when he addressed the smallest gathering. He glanced across at Fisher to see a bead of sweat appearing on his forehead, which he quickly mopped with a handkerchief from his top pocket. He looked back at the audience and saw Emma and Harry seated in the second row, smiling up at him.

'Good evening, ladies and gentlemen, my name is Andy Nash, and I am editor of the *Bristol Evening Post*. It's my privilege to chair the meeting this evening, which is the only occasion on which all three candidates will appear on the same platform. Now, allow me to explain how the debate will be conducted. Each candidate will make an opening address of six minutes. That will be followed by thirty minutes of questions from the audience. The evening will end with all three candidates summing up for two minutes each. I will now call upon the Conservative candidate, Major Alex Fisher, to address us.'

Fisher made his way purposefully to the centre of the stage and was greeted with warm applause from one section of the audience. He placed his speech on the lectern and immediately began to read it word for word, only occasionally raising his head.

Giles sat nervously in his seat listening carefully as he waited for the sarcastic comment, the barbed innuendo, but none came. Instead, Fisher concentrated on what legislation would be treated as a priority if the Tories formed the next government. He could have been reading out a shopping list that he regularly interspersed with the words 'Time for a change'. At no point did he mention either of his opponents. And then Giles worked out what Fisher was up to. He was not going to indulge in any personal attacks himself; that would be left to his lieutenants, spread evenly throughout the audience. When Fisher returned to his seat, it was not difficult to spot where those supporters were seated from their enthusiastic applause.

The Liberal candidate opened his speech by thanking the packed audience for giving up *Coronation Street* to come and hear him, which was greeted with laughter and warm applause. He then spent the next six minutes discussing local politics, everything from potholes in the roads to rural bus fares. When he returned to his seat, another section of the audience was equally loyal and supportive.

Once Fletcher had sat down, Giles walked to the centre of the stage, although he wasn't as relaxed as he hoped he looked. He placed a postcard on the lectern on which were typed seven headings: Education, Unemployment, Unions, the NHS, Europe, Defence and Bristol.

He barely glanced at the card as he spoke about each subject with confidence and authority, while looking directly at his audience. When he returned to his seat, his supporters rose as one, and a large number of undecided members of the audience joined them. Had the debate ended then, there would have been only one winner, but no sooner had Giles sat down than the chairman called for questions, adding, 'I hope any contributions will be worthy of a debate of this importance, and that no one will resort to personal comments in the hope of getting a cheap headline in tomorrow's paper, because I assure you, as its editor, they won't.'

This statement elicited such a spontaneous round of applause that Giles began to relax for the first time that evening.

'Yes, madam. The lady in the fourth row.'

'With the population growing ever older, can the candidates tell us about their long-term plans for the state pension?'

Giles was back on his feet before the chairman had a chance to decide which candidate should answer the question first.

'The state pension has gone up year on year while the Labour Party has been in power,' he declared, 'because this government considers that a civilized society is one that takes care of its young and old alike.'

Fisher then delivered the party line as outlined in a Central Office brief, after which the Liberal candidate talked about his mother being in an old people's home.

'I'll take you next, sir,' said Nash, pointing to a man in the dress circle who had to wait for some time before a microphone reached him.

'Do all the candidates feel that the United Kingdom should join the Common Market?'

Fisher was well prepared for this question, and reminded the audience of Ted Heath's long-standing commitment to Europe, adding that if the Tories were elected, they would do everything in their power to ensure that Britain became a member of the EEC.

Simon Fletcher reminded the audience it was his party that had pioneered the idea of entry into the Common Market, and how glad he was that the two other parties were now jumping on the Liberal bandwagon.

Giles rose to face the audience. How he would have liked to tell them that when he was in Berlin he had received overtures from the French foreign minister, making it clear that France would welcome a dialogue being opened between the two countries. But any mention of Berlin would have been the red rag one section of the audience was waiting for. So he simply said, 'When it comes to joining the Common Market, I think I can safely say that all three parties are broadly in agreement, so I suspect it will only be a matter of which prime minister finally signs the Treaty of Rome.'

Several more questions on local, national and foreign issues followed without any blows below the belt, and Giles was beginning to think he might be home and dry. 'I'll take two more questions,' said Nash, glancing at his watch. 'Yes, madam, the lady standing near the back.' Giles recognized her immediately.

'Can all three candidates tell us their marital status, and if their wives are with them tonight?' A well-rehearsed question delivered by a seemingly innocent old lady, whom Giles well remembered from her days as a Tory councillor.

This time it was Fisher who was first on his feet, and he delivered an equally well-prepared response. 'Sadly, I've been divorced for some years, but that hasn't stopped me hoping that one day I will find the right partner. But, whatever my marital status, let me assure you that I would never consider becoming involved in a casual sexual relationship.'

A gasp went up in the hall, and one section of the crowd applauded enthusiastically.

The Liberal candidate said, 'I have just as much difficulty finding a girlfriend as I do finding people who will

vote for me, but, like the major, I haven't given up yet.'
This was greeted with laughter and applause.

Giles felt sad that Fletcher wasn't able to be open
about his sexuality, and looked forward to the day when
he could admit that his partner was seated in the front
row, and that they had been living happily together for
many years.

When Giles took his place, he stood to one side of
the lectern, looked directly at the audience and smiled.
'I'm no saint.'

'True!' shouted a Conservative supporter, but he was
greeted only by an embarrassed silence.

'I admit that I've strayed, and, as you all know, that is
why Gwyneth is not here tonight, which I deeply regret.
She has been a loyal and faithful wife, who has played an
active role in the constituency.' He paused for a moment
before adding, 'But when the time comes for you to cast
your vote, I hope you will place on the scales of human
frailty twenty-five years of service to the people of this
great city against one foolish lapse of judgement, because
I would like the honour and privilege of continuing to
serve all of you for many years to come.'

Giles suppressed a smile when the audience began to
applaud, and was just about to return to his seat when
someone shouted, 'Don't you think it's time you told us
more about Berlin?'

A loud undercurrent of chattering broke out in the
hall and the chairman immediately leapt up, but Giles had
already returned to the lectern. He gripped the sides so
no one could see how nervous he was. Two thousand
people looked up expectantly as he faced his inquisitor,
who was still on his feet. Giles waited for complete
silence.

'I'm only too delighted to do so, sir. I found Berlin to be a tragic city divided by a twelve-foot concrete wall crowned in barbed wire. It wasn't built to keep the West Germans out, but to keep the East Germans in, creating the largest prison on earth. Hardly a compelling argument for Communism. But I pray that I will live to see it razed to the ground. I hope that is something we can both agree on, sir.'

The man sank back into his place as Giles returned to his seat with the sound of thunderous applause ringing in his ears.

The final question was about the power of the unions, and both Giles's and Fisher's responses were unconvincing; Giles, because he had lost his concentration, while Fisher hadn't recovered from his demon fast bowler being knocked out of the ground.

Giles had recovered by the time it came to deliver his summing up, and it took him some time to leave the hall, as he had to shake so many outstretched hands. But it was Griff who best summed up the evening.

'We're back in the race.'

22

THE *Bristol Evening Post* made a valiant attempt to present a balanced account of the debate that had taken place at the Hippodrome theatre the previous evening, but you didn't have to read between the lines to be in any doubt who it felt was the winner. Although it had some reservations, the paper recommended that their readers should send Sir Giles Barrington back to the House of Commons.

'We haven't won yet,' said Griff, dropping the paper in the nearest wastepaper basket. 'So let's get back to work. There's still six days, nine hours and fourteen minutes to go before the polls close next Thursday.'

Everyone set about their allotted task, whether it was checking canvass returns, preparing voting sheets for polling day, double-checking who needed a lift to the polling station, answering queries from the public, distributing last-minute leaflets or making sure the candidate was fed and watered.

'Preferably on the move,' said Griff, who returned to his office and continued to work on the eve-of-poll message that would be dropped through the letterbox of every registered Labour supporter the night before the election.

◄◦►

At 5.45 a.m. on polling day Giles was once again standing outside Temple Meads station reminding everyone he shook hands with to 'Vote for Barrington – today!'

Griff had designed a schedule that accounted for every minute of election day until the polls closed at 10.00 p.m. He had allocated Giles ten minutes for a pork pie, a cheese sandwich and half a pint of cider in the most popular pub in the constituency.

At 6.30 p.m., he looked up to the heavens and cursed when it began to rain. Didn't the gods know that between eight and ten in the morning, and five and seven in the evening, were Labour's peak voting times? The Tories always got their vote out between ten and five. From seven o'clock in the evening until ten, when the polls closed, was anybody's guess. The gods must have heard his plea, because the shower only lasted for about twenty minutes.

Giles ended the sixteen-hour day standing outside the gates of the dockyard, making sure that those clocking on for the night shift had already voted. If they hadn't, they were immediately dispatched to the polling station on the other side of the road.

'But I'll be late clocking on.'

'I know the chairman,' said Giles. To those who were coming off duty before going to the pub, Giles kept repeating, 'Make sure you vote before you order your first pint.'

Griff and his team constantly checked their canvass returns so they could 'knock up' those who still hadn't cast their vote and remind them that the polling stations didn't close until ten.

At one minute past ten, Giles shook the last hand and, desperate for a drink, walked down the road to join the dock workers in the Lord Nelson.

'Make mine a pint,' he said, leaning on the bar.

'Sorry, Sir Giles. It's gone ten, and I know you wouldn't want me to lose my licence.'

Two men sitting at the bar grabbed an empty glass and filled it from their own two pints.

'Thank you,' said Giles, raising his glass.

'We're both feeling a little guilty,' one of them admitted. 'We ran in during the shower, so we haven't voted.'

Giles would happily have poured the beer over their heads. Looking around the pub, he wondered how many more votes he'd lost when it was raining.

Harry walked into the Lord Nelson a few minutes later. 'Sorry to drag you away,' he said, 'but Griff has ordered me to take you home.'

'Not a man to be disobeyed,' said Giles, downing his pint.

'So what happens next?' asked Harry as they set off in his car for Barrington Hall.

'Nothing new. The local constabulary will be collecting the ballot boxes from all over the constituency before taking them to the Guildhall. The seals will be broken in the presence of Mr Hardy, the city clerk, and once the ballot papers have been checked, the counting begins. So there's no point in turning up at Council House yet, as we can't expect a result much before three a.m. Griff's picking me up around midnight.'

Giles was dozing in his bath when the front doorbell rang. He climbed slowly out, pulled on a dressing gown and pushed open the bathroom window to see Griff standing on the doorstep below.

'Sorry, Griff, I must have fallen asleep in the bath. Let yourself in and fix yourself a drink. I'll be down as quickly as I can.'

Giles put on the same suit and tie he wore for every count, although he had to admit he could no longer do up the jacket's middle button. He was on his way downstairs fifteen minutes later.

'Don't ask me, because I don't know,' said Griff, as he drove out of the front gates. 'All I can tell you is that if the exit polls are to be believed, the Tories have won by about forty seats.'

'Then it's back to Opposition,' said Giles.

'That's assuming you win, and our polling returns are showing it's too close to call,' said Griff. 'It's 1951 all over again.' Griff didn't say another word until they pulled into the car park outside Council House, when three weeks of pent-up frustration and not a great deal of sleep suddenly came bursting out.

'It's not the thought of losing that I can't stomach,' said Griff. 'It's the thought of Major fucking Fisher winning.'

Giles sometimes forgot how passionately Griff felt about the cause, and how lucky he was to have him as his agent.

'Right,' said Griff, 'now I've got that off my chest, let's report for duty.' He got out of the car, straightened his tie and headed towards Council House. As they walked up the steps together, Griff turned to Giles and said, 'Try and look as if you expect to win.'

'And if I don't?'

'Then you'll have to deliver a speech you've never made before, which will be a new experience for you.' Giles laughed as they entered the packed, noisy room where the count was taking place.

A dozen long trestle tables filled the room, with council officials and selected party representatives seated on both sides, furiously counting or observing. Every time a new black ballot box was emptied on to the tables, a forest of hands stretched out and quickly sorted the names of the candidates into three separate piles, before the counting could begin. Little stacks of ten soon became stacks of a hundred, at which point a red, blue or yellow band was placed around them and they were lined up like infantrymen at the end of the table.

Griff watched the process warily. A simple mistake and a hundred votes could be placed in the wrong pile.

'What do you want us to do?' asked Seb as he and Miss Parish came over to join them.

'Take a table each and report back to me if you spot anything you're not happy about.'

'And what about you?' asked Giles.

'I'll do what I always do,' said Griff, 'scrutinize the votes from the Woodbine Estate and Arcadia Avenue. Once I've checked their returns, I'll be able to tell you who's going to win.'

Griff's team took a table each and, although the process was slow, it was running smoothly. Once Giles had made a complete circuit of the room, deftly avoiding Fisher, he re-joined Griff.

'You're two hundred votes down in Arcadia Avenue, and about two hundred up on the Woodbine Estate, so it's anybody's guess.'

After Giles had done another circuit of the room, only

one thing was certain: Simon Fletcher was going to come third.

A few minutes later, Mr Hardy tapped the microphone in the centre of the stage. The room fell silent and everyone turned to face the town clerk.

'Would the candidates please join me to check the spoilt ballot papers.' A little ceremony Griff always enjoyed.

After the three candidates and their agents had studied the forty-two spoilt papers, they all agreed that twenty-two of them were valid: 10 for Giles, 9 for Fisher and 3 for Fletcher.

'Let's hope that's an omen,' said Griff, 'because as Churchill famously said, one is enough.'

'Any surprises?' asked Seb when they returned to the floor.

'No,' said Griff, 'but I did enjoy one the town clerk rejected, *Will your girlfriend in East Berlin be getting a postal vote?*' Giles managed a smile. 'Back to work. We can't afford one mistake, and never forget 1951 when Seb saved the day.'

Hands began shooting up all around the room to show that the counting had finished on that particular table. An official then double-checked the figures before taking them up to the town clerk, who in turn entered them into an adding machine. Giles could still remember the days when the late Mr Wainwright entered each figure on a ledger, and then three of his deputies checked and double-checked every entry, before he was willing to declare the result.

At 2.49 a.m. the town clerk walked back to the microphone and tapped it once again. The momentary silence was broken only by a pencil falling off a table and rolling across the floor. Mr Hardy waited until it had been picked up.

'I, Leonard Derek Hardy, being the returning officer for the constituency of Bristol Docklands, declare the total number of votes cast for each candidate to be as follows:

Sir Giles Barrington	18,971
Mr Simon Fletcher	3,586
Major Alexander Fisher	18———'

As soon as Giles heard the word eighteen and not nineteen, he felt confident he'd won.

'—994.'

The Tory camp immediately erupted. Griff, trying to make himself heard above the noise, asked Mr Hardy for a recount, which was immediately granted. The whole process began again, with every table checking and rechecking first the tens, then the hundreds and finally the thousands, before once again reporting back to the town clerk.

At 3.27 a.m. he called for silence again. 'I, Leonard Derek Hardy, being the returning officer . . .' Heads were bowed, eyes were closed, while some of those present turned away, unable even to face the stage as they crossed their fingers and waited for the numbers to be read out. '. . . for each candidate to be as follows:

Sir Giles Barrington	18,972
Mr Simon Fletcher	3,586
Major Alexander Fisher	18,993.'

Giles knew that after such a close result he could insist on a second recount, but he did not. Instead, he reluctantly nodded his acceptance of the result to the town clerk.

'I therefore declare Major Alexander Fisher to be the duly elected Member of Parliament for the constituency of Bristol Docklands.'

An eruption of shouting and cheering broke out in one half of the room as the new member was raised on to the shoulders of his party workers and paraded around the hall. Giles walked across and shook Fisher's hand for the first time during the campaign.

After the speeches were over, Fisher triumphant in victory, Giles gracious in defeat, Simon Fletcher pointing out that he'd recorded his highest ever vote, the newly elected member and his supporters went on celebrating throughout the night, while the vanquished drifted away in twos and threes, with Griff and Giles among the last to leave.

'We'd have done it if the national swing hadn't been against us,' said Griff, as he drove the former member home.

'Just twenty-one votes,' said Giles.

'Eleven,' said Griff.

'Eleven?' repeated Giles.

'If eleven voters had changed their minds.'

'And if it hadn't rained for twenty minutes at six thirty.'

'It's been a year of ifs.'

23

GILES FINALLY climbed into bed just before 5 a.m. He switched off the bedside light, put his head on the pillow and closed his eyes, just as the alarm went off. He groaned and switched the light back on. No longer any need to be standing outside Temple Meads station at 6 a.m. to greet the early morning commuters.

My name is Giles Barrington, and I'm your Labour candidate for yesterday's election . . . He switched off the alarm and fell into a deep sleep, not waking again until eleven that morning.

After a late breakfast, or was it brunch, he had a shower, got dressed, packed a small suitcase and drove out of the gates of Barrington Hall just after midday. He was in no hurry, as his plane wouldn't be taking off from Heathrow until 4.15 p.m.

If, another if, Giles had stayed at home for a few more minutes, he could have taken a call from Harold Wilson, who was compiling his resignation honours list. The new leader of the opposition was going to offer Giles the chance to go to the House of Lords and sit on the opposition front bench as spokesman on foreign affairs.

Mr Wilson tried again that evening, but by then Giles had landed in Berlin.

◄○►

Only a few months before, the Rt Hon. Sir Giles Barrington MP had been driven out on to the runway at Heathrow, and the plane took off only after he'd fastened his seat belt in first class.

Now, squeezed between a woman who never stopped chatting to her friend on the other side of the aisle, and a man who clearly enjoyed making it difficult for him to turn the pages of *The Times*, Giles reflected on what he hadn't missed. The two-and-a-half-hour flight seemed interminable, and when they landed he had to dash through the rain to get to the terminal.

Although he was among the first off the plane, he was almost the last to leave baggage reclaim. He had forgotten just how long it could take before your luggage appeared on the carousel. By the time he was reunited with his bag and had been released from customs and finally made it to the front of the taxi queue, he was already exhausted.

'Checkpoint Charlie' was all he said as he climbed into the back of the cab.

The driver gave him a second look, decided he was sane, but dropped him off some hundred yards from the border post. It was still raining.

As Giles ran towards the customs building, carrying his bag in one hand and his copy of *The Times* held over his head in the other, he couldn't help recalling his last visit to Berlin.

When he stepped inside, he joined a short queue, but it still took a long time before he reached the front.

'Good evening, sir,' said a fellow countryman, as Giles handed over his passport and visa.

'Good evening,' said Giles.

'May I ask why you are visiting the Eastern sector, Sir Giles?' the guard enquired politely, while inspecting his documents.

'I'm seeing a friend.'

'And how long do you plan to stay in the Eastern sector?'

'Seven days.'

'The maximum period your temporary visa allows,' the officer reminded him.

Giles nodded, hoping that in seven days' time all his questions would have been answered, and he would at last know if Karin felt the same way as he did. The officer smiled, stamped his passport and said 'Good luck' as if he meant it.

At least the rain had stopped by the time Giles stepped back out of the building. He set out on the long walk across no-man's-land between the two border posts, not in the British Embassy's Rolls-Royce accompanied by the ambassador but as a private citizen representing no one other than himself.

When he saw the guard stationed on the East Berlin border, he didn't need to be reminded that they didn't welcome tourists. He entered another building that hadn't seen a splash of paint since the wall had gone up, and where no one had given a thought for old, tired or infirm visitors who might just want to sit down. Another queue, another wait, longer this time, before he eventually handed over his passport to a young customs officer who did not greet him with good evening, sir, in any language.

The official slowly turned each page of his passport, clearly mystified by how many countries this foreigner had visited in the last four years. After he'd turned the final page, he raised the palm of his right hand in the air, like a traffic policeman, and said, 'Stay', clearly the one word of English he knew. He then retreated to the back of the room, knocked on a door marked KOMMANDANT and disappeared inside.

It was some time before the door opened again, and when it did, a short, bald-headed man appeared. He looked about the same age as Giles, but it was hard to be sure because his shiny, double-breasted suit was so out of date it might have been his father's. His greying shirt was frayed at the collar and cuffs, and his red tie looked as if it had been ironed once too often. But the surprise was his command of English.

'Perhaps you would come with me, Mr Barrington,' were his opening words.

'Perhaps' turned out to be an order, because he immediately turned on his heel and headed towards his office without looking back. The young official lifted the counter lid so Giles could follow him.

The official sat down behind his desk, if a table with a single drawer can be described as a desk. Giles sat opposite him on a hard wooden stool, no doubt a product of the same factory.

'What is the purpose of your visit to East Berlin, Mr Barrington?'

'I'm visiting a friend.'

'And the name of this friend?'

Giles hesitated, as the man continued to stare at him. 'Karin Pengelly.'

'Is she a relative?'

'No, as I said, a friend.'

'And how long are you intending to stay in East Berlin?'

'As you can see, my visa is for one week.'

The official studied the visa for a considerable time, as if hoping to find an irregularity, but Giles had had the document checked by a friend at the Foreign Office who confirmed that every little box had been filled in correctly.

'What is your profession?' asked the official.

'I'm a politician.'

'What does that mean?'

'I used to be a Member of Parliament, and a Foreign Office minister, which is why I've travelled so much in recent years.'

'But you are no longer a minister, or even a Member of Parliament.'

'No, I am not.'

'One moment please.' The official picked up a phone, dialled three numbers and waited. When someone answered, he began a protracted conversation of which Giles couldn't understand a word, but from the man's deferential tone, he was in no doubt that he was addressing someone far more senior than himself. If only Karin had been there to translate for him.

The official began to make notes on the pad in front of him, often followed by the word *Ja*. It wasn't until after several more *Ja*s that he finally put the phone down.

'Before I stamp your visa, Mr Barrington, there are one or two more questions that need to be answered.'

Giles attempted a weak smile as the official looked back down at his pad.

'Are you related to Mr Harry Clifton?'

'Yes, I am. He's my brother-in-law.'

'And are you a supporter of his campaign to have the criminal Anatoly Babakov released from prison?'

Giles knew that if he answered the question honestly, his visa would be revoked. Couldn't the man understand that for the past month he'd been counting the hours until he saw Karin again? He was sure Harry would appreciate the dilemma he was facing.

'I repeat, Mr Barrington, do you support your brother-in-law's campaign to have the criminal Anatoly Babakov released?'

'Yes, I do,' said Giles. 'Harry Clifton is one of the finest men I have ever known, and I fully support his campaign to have the author Anatoly Babakov released.'

The official handed Giles back his passport, opened the drawer of his desk and placed the visa inside.

Giles stood up and, without another word, turned and made his way out of the building, to find it had started raining again. He began the long walk back to the West, wondering if he would ever see Karin again.

SEBASTIAN CLIFTON

1970

24

'DID YOU EVER make a complete fool of yourself when you were my age?' asked Sebastian as they sat drinking on the veranda.

'Not more than once a week, if my memory still serves me,' said Ross Buchanan. 'Mind you, I've improved a little over the years, but not much.'

'But did you ever make such a huge mistake that you've regretted it for the rest of your life?' asked Seb, not touching the brandy by his side.

Ross didn't reply immediately, because he knew only too well what Seb was referring to. 'Nothing I haven't been able to make amends for.' He took a sip of his whisky before adding, 'Are you absolutely convinced you can't win her back?'

'I've written to her several times, but she never replies. I've finally decided I'll have to go to America and find out if she'd even consider giving me a second chance.'

'And there hasn't been anyone else?' said Ross.

'Not in that way,' said Sebastian. 'The occasional fling, too many one-night stands, but frankly Sam was the only woman I loved. She didn't care if I was penniless. I stupidly did. Did you ever have that problem, Ross?'

'Can't pretend I did. When I married Jean, I had twenty-seven pounds, two shillings and four pence in my personal account, but then you weren't allowed an over-draft if you worked as a clerk for the Aberdeen Shipping Company. So Jean certainly didn't marry me for my money.'

'Lucky man. Why didn't I learn from Cedric Hard-castle? A handshake should always be enough to close a deal.'

'Ah, I presume it's Maurice Swann we're now talking about.'

'You know about Mr Swann?'

'Only from what Cedric told me. He was convinced that if you closed the Shifnal Farm deal, you'd keep your side of the bargain. So I must assume you didn't?'

Seb bowed his head. 'That's why Sam left me. I lost her because I wanted to live in Chelsea, and I didn't real-ize she couldn't give a damn where we lived, as long as we were together.'

'It's never too late to admit you're wrong,' said Ross. 'Just pray that Mr Swann is still alive. If he is, you can be sure he'll still be desperate to build his theatre. And Kaufman's, is that enough for you?' asked Ross, changing the subject.

'What do you mean, is it enough?' asked Seb, picking up his brandy.

'It's just that you're the most ambitious young man I've ever come across and I'm not sure you'll be satisfied until you become chairman of the bank.'

'Which bank?'

Ross laughed. 'I've always assumed that it's Farthings you've had your eye on.'

'You're right, and I haven't been idle. On Bob Bingham's advice, I've been picking up shares for the past five years, always investing fifty per cent of the commission I earn on any deal. I already own more than three per cent of Farthings' stock. Once I've got my hands on six per cent, which shouldn't be long now, I intend to take my place on the board and wreak havoc.'

'I wouldn't be too confident about that, because you can be sure Adrian Sloane will have spotted you on his radar and, like a submarine, he'll attack when you least expect it.'

'But what can he do to stop me? The bank's statutes specify that any company or individual who owns six per cent of the stock is automatically entitled to a place on the board.'

'Once you've acquired your six per cent, he'll simply rewrite the statutes.'

'Can he do that?'

'Why not? He appointed himself chairman while we were at Cedric's funeral, so why wouldn't he rewrite the bank's statutes if it meant he could stop you getting on the board? Just because he's a despicable man doesn't mean he isn't a clever one. But frankly, Seb, I think you've got a far bigger problem facing you on the home front.'

'At Kaufman's?'

'No, at Barrington's. I did warn your mother that if she allowed Desmond Mellor to become a director, it would end in tears. He's been on the board for four years, and I'm sure you know he now wants to be deputy chairman.'

'He couldn't make it more obvious,' said Seb. 'But as long as my mother is chairman, he can forget it.'

'I agree, just so long as your mother is chairman. But surely you noticed that he's already begun to park his tanks on your front lawn?'

'What are you talking about?'

'If you read this morning's *Financial Times*, you'll find tucked away under new appointments that Adrian Sloane has invited Mellor to become deputy chairman of Farthings. Now you tell me, what do those two have in common?'

This silenced Seb for the first time.

'An intense dislike of your family. But don't despair,' continued Ross, 'you still have a card up your sleeve that he'll find hard to trump.'

'And what's that?'

'Not what, who. Beryl Hardcastle and her fifty-one per cent of Farthings' stock. Beryl won't consider signing any more documents sent by Sloane that haven't been carefully scrutinized by her son first.'

'So what do you advise?'

'Once you've got six per cent of the bank's stock, you can park *your* tank on Sloane's front lawn and cause havoc.'

'But if I were to get hold of Beryl Hardcastle's fifty-one per cent, I could park a whole army on Sloane's front lawn, and he'd have no choice but to beat a hasty retreat.'

'Nice idea, as long as you know someone with the odd twenty million pounds to spare.'

'How about Bob Bingham?' said Seb.

'Bob's a wealthy man, but I think you'll find that's too much even for him to consider.'

'Saul Kaufman?'

'In his present state of health, I suspect he's a seller not a buyer.'

Seb looked disappointed.

'Try to forget taking over the bank for now, Seb.

Concentrate on becoming a director and making Sloane's life hell.'

Seb nodded. 'I'll go and see him as soon as I'm back from the States.'

'I think there's someone else you should pay a visit to before you go to America.'

◄○►

'What you have to appreciate, Sarah, is that although Macbeth is an ambitious man, Lady Macbeth is the key to him getting his hands on the crown. This was at a time when women's rights didn't exist, and her only hope of having any real influence in Scotland was to convince her weak, vacillating husband he should kill the king while he was a guest under their own roof. So I want to do that scene again, Sarah. Try to remember you're a mean, conniving, evil piece of work, who's trying to get her husband to commit murder. And this time, make sure you convince me, because if you do, you'll convince the audience.'

Sebastian sat at the back of the hall and watched a group of enthusiastic young pupils rehearsing under the watchful eye of Mr Swann. It was a pity that the stage was so small and cramped.

'Much better,' said Swann when they came to the end of the act. 'That will do for today. Tomorrow, I want to start with the Banquo's ghost scene. Rick, you must remember that Macbeth is the only person in the room who can see the ghost. Your guests at the dinner are fearful about what's troubling you, some even think you're losing your mind. And, Sarah, you're trying to convince those same guests that all is well, and despite your husband's strange behaviour there's nothing for them to worry about. And whatever you do, don't ever look at the ghost, because if you should, even once, the spell will be broken. I'll see you all at the same time tomorrow, and be sure you know your lines by then. After Monday, we abandon scripts.'

A groan went up as the actors left the stage and became school children once again, picking up their satchels and books and making their way out of the hall. It amused Seb to see Lady Macbeth clutching Banquo's hand. No wonder Mr Swann had told Sarah not to look at him during the ghost scene. Shrewd man.

Mr Swann didn't turn off the stage lights until he had all the props in place for the banquet scene. He then picked up his well-thumbed script, put it in his old Gladstone bag and headed slowly towards the door. At first he didn't notice that someone was sitting at the back of the room, and he wasn't able to hide his surprise when he saw who it was.

'We're not doing *Othello* this year,' he said. 'But if we were, I wouldn't have to look far to cast Iago.'

'No, Mr Swann, it's Prince Hal you see before you, come on bended knee to beg forgiveness of the King, having made a dreadful mistake from which he may never recover.'

The old man stood still as Sebastian took out his wallet, extracted a cheque and handed it over.

'But this is far more than we agreed on,' the former headmaster said, fumbling for words.

'Not if you still want those new dressing rooms, a proper curtain and not to have to be satisfied with last year's costumes.'

'Not to mention a separate changing room for the girls from Shifnal High,' said Swann. 'But may I ask what you meant, Mr Clifton, when you said you had made a dreadful mistake from which you may never recover?'

'It's a long story,' said Seb, 'and I'll not bore you—'

'I'm an old man with time on my hands,' said Swann, sitting down opposite Seb.

Sebastian told Mr Swann how he'd first seen Samantha at Jessica's graduation ceremony and been struck dumb.

'I can't imagine that happens to you too often,' said Swann with a smile.

'When I next met her, I'd recovered enough to ask her out to dinner. Not long after that I realized I wanted to spend the rest of my life with her.' The old man knew when to remain silent. 'But when she found out that I didn't intend to honour my promise to you, she left me, and returned to America.' He paused. 'I haven't seen her since.'

'Then I would beg you not to make the same mistake I did when I was your age.'

'You made the same mistake?'

'Worse in a way. When I was a young man just down from university, I was offered a job teaching English at a grammar school in Worcestershire. I'd never been happier, until I fell in love with the headmaster's eldest daughter, but didn't have the courage to let her know.'

'Why not?'

'I've always been shy, especially around women, and in any case I was afraid the headmaster wouldn't approve. It must sound silly now, but it was a different world in those days. I moved to another school and later learned that she had never married. I might have been able to live with that if just last year, when I attended her funeral, her younger sister hadn't told me that I was her first and only love, but her father had told her she must do nothing unless I made my feelings known. What a fool I was. A moment wasted, to be followed by a lifetime of regret. Young man, be sure not to make the same mistake. Faint heart ne'er won a lady fair.'

'Robert Burns?' said Seb.

'There's hope for you yet,' said Swann. With the help of his walking stick, the old man rose to his feet and took Seb by the arm. 'Thank you for your generosity. I look forward to the honour of meeting Miss Sullivan.' He turned to face Seb. 'Would you be kind enough to ask her, Mr Clifton, if she would be willing to open the Samantha Sullivan Theatre?'

25

'HI, REVERED PARENT, I'm thinking of going to America on business, and I wondered if—'

'You could sail on the *Buckingham*? Yes, of course, but don't forget Bob Bingham's rule about family members having to pay for their passage. If you can go next week, you could join your father. He's off to New York to see his publisher.'

Sebastian flicked over a page of his diary. 'I'll have to re-arrange a couple of meetings, but yes, that looks fine.'

'And what takes you to the States?'

'A business opportunity that Mr Kaufman wants me to look into.'

The moment Seb put down the phone he felt guilty about not telling his mother the real reason for his trip, as he feared he could well be making a complete fool of himself – once again.

But he had no idea where Sam was living or how he could find out. He was considering the problem when Vic Kaufman walked into his office and took him by surprise.

'Have you noticed my dad repeating himself lately?'

'No, can't say I have,' said Seb. 'Saul's occasionally a little forgetful, but he must be over seventy.'

'When he escaped from Poland he didn't bring a birth certificate with him, but he once let slip that he could remember Queen Victoria's funeral, so he must be nearer eighty. I have to admit I'm a bit worried, because if anything did happen to the old man, frankly, you're not ready to take over yet, and I'm just not good enough.'

It had never crossed Seb's mind that Saul Kaufman wouldn't go on being chairman for ever, and he certainly hadn't considered taking over as chairman of the bank before Vic raised the subject.

Seb now had fourteen staff working for him, most of them older than himself, and his department was the third-largest income provider for the bank, not far behind foreign exchange and commodities.

'Don't worry about it, Vic,' said Seb, trying to reassure him. 'I'm sure your father's got a few more miles left on the clock.'

However, at Seb's weekly meeting with the chairman, Mr Kaufman did ask, on three separate occasions, the name of the client they were representing on one particular land development deal, although Seb knew he'd done business with him on at least two occasions in the past.

Seb had spent so much of his spare time thinking about what was happening at another bank just a few streets away that it hadn't crossed his mind that his future at Kaufman's could not be taken for granted. He tried not to think about the worst-case scenario: the old man having to retire because of ill-health, Farthings making a takeover bid for Kaufman's, and Seb having to write a second resignation letter to the new joint chairman of the two banks.

He even considered cancelling his trip to the States, but he knew that if he didn't leave by the last tide on

Friday evening, he would never have the courage to go through with it.

◄○►

Seb thoroughly enjoyed his father's company on the five-day voyage to New York, not least because, unlike his mother, Harry didn't spend his time asking endless questions Seb didn't want to answer.

They always ate together in the evening, and sometimes at lunch. During the day, his father would lock himself in his cabin, leaving the *Do Not Disturb* sign on his door. He spent hour upon hour going over the final draft of his latest manuscript, which he would hand to Harold Guinzburg within an hour of the ship docking.

So when Seb was taking a brisk walk around the upper deck one morning, he was surprised to find his father reclining in a deckchair, reading his favourite author.

'Does that mean you've finished the book?' he asked as he sat down in the deckchair next to him.

'It does,' said Harry, putting down *Beware of Pity*. 'Now all I have to do is deliver the manuscript to Harold and wait for his opinion.'

'Do you want mine?'

'On my book? No, but on another book, yes.'

'What book are we talking about?'

'*Uncle Joe*,' said Harry. 'Harold has offered Mrs Babakov a hundred-thousand-dollar advance for the world rights, against a fifteen-per-cent royalty, and I'm not sure what to advise her.'

'But is there a chance of anyone ever finding a copy of the book?'

'I used to think there was almost none, but Harold

told me that Mrs Babakov knows where a copy can be found. The only problem is, it's in the Soviet Union.'

'Did she tell him where in the Soviet Union?'

'No. She said she'd only tell me, which is why I'm going on to Pittsburgh once I've seen Harold in New York.'

Harry was surprised by his son's next question.

'Would a hundred thousand dollars be a large sum of money to Mrs Babakov, or is she comfortably off?'

'She escaped from Russia without a penny, so it would change her whole life.'

'Then if you think Mr Guinzburg's offer is fair, my advice is she should accept it. Whenever I want to close a deal, I try to find out how much the other side needs the money, because that will always influence the way I think. If they are desperate for the money, I'm in the driver's seat. If not . . .'

Harry nodded.

'However, there's a caveat in this particular case. Because if you're the only person she's willing to tell where the book is hidden, you can be sure she's also hoping that you'll be the one who'll go and pick it up.'

'But it's in the Soviet Union.'

'Where you're still persona non grata. So whatever you do, don't make any promises.'

'I wouldn't want to let her down.'

'Dad, I know it must be fun to take on the Soviet Empire single-handedly, but it's only James Bond who always triumphs over the KGB. So can we return to the real world, because I also need some advice.'

'Mine?'

'No, Detective Inspector Warwick's.'

'Why, are you planning to murder someone?'

'No, just looking for a missing person.'

'Which is why you're going to the States.'

'Yes. But I don't know where this person lives or how to find out.'

'I think you'll find they have a record of her home address on this ship.'

'How's that possible?'

'Because she travelled with us on the maiden voyage, and would have had to hand in her passport to the purser. So he's almost certain to have her address on his files. It may be a long shot, as it's several years ago, but at least it's somewhere to start. In normal circumstances, I suspect he wouldn't be willing to release personal information about another passenger, but as you're a director of the company, and she was your guest on the trip, I imagine that won't be a problem.'

'How did you know that my missing person was Samantha?'

'Your mother told me.'

'But I didn't tell her.'

'Not in so many words. But I've learnt over the years never to underestimate that woman. Mind you, when it's personal, even she can make mistakes.'

'Like Desmond Mellor?'

'I would never have thought it possible that whoever replaced Alex Fisher could prove even more of a problem.'

'And there's a big difference between Mellor and Fisher,' said Seb. 'Mellor's bright, which makes him far more dangerous.'

'Do you think he has any chance of becoming deputy chairman?'

'I didn't, until Ross Buchanan convinced me otherwise.'

'Maybe that's why Emma's considering the nuclear option, and forcing Mellor to put his cards on the table.'

'Which table?'

'The boardroom table. She's going to let him stand as her deputy, but she'll oppose him and put up her own candidate. If he loses, he'll have no choice but to resign.'

'And if she loses?'

'She'll have to learn to live with it.'

'Who's her candidate?'

'I assumed it must be you.'

'Not a chance. The board would always back Mellor against me, not least because of my age, and that would mean Mother would end up having to resign. Which, come to think of it, might even be part of Mellor's long-term plan. I'm going to have to talk her out of it. And it's not as if that's her only problem at the moment.'

'If you're referring to Lady Virginia and her libel claim, I think that's no longer an issue.'

'How can you be so sure?'

'I can't, but we haven't heard anything on that front for some time. In another twelve months your mother can apply to the courts to have the action struck off the list, but I've advised her against that.'

'Why?'

'When you come across a sleeping snake, don't prod it with a sharp stick in the hope that it will go away, because it's likely to wake up and bite you.'

'And that woman's bite is venomous,' said Seb. 'Mind you, I don't even know why she's suing Mother in the first place.'

'I'll tell you all about it over dinner.'

The ship's purser could not have been more helpful. He was able to supply Sebastian with an address for Miss Samantha Sullivan: 2043 Cable Street, Georgetown, Washington DC, although he couldn't be sure if she was still living there, as she hadn't travelled on the ship since the maiden voyage. Seb hoped 2043 would turn out to be a small apartment where she lived alone or with one of her female colleagues.

He thanked the purser, walked up a couple of flights of stairs to the Grill Room and joined his father for dinner. It wasn't until the steward had cleared away the main course that Seb raised the subject of Virginia's writ.

'Quite dramatic stuff, or at least we all thought so at the time,' said Harry, lighting a Havana cigar, which he couldn't have purchased on an American ship. 'Your mother was addressing the company's AGM, and during questions from the floor Virginia asked if one of the directors of Barrington's had sold all his shares with the intention of bringing down the company.'

'So how did Mother deal with the question?'

'She turned it to her advantage by asking if Virginia was referring to the three occasions on which Alex Fisher, her representative on the board, had sold and then bought back her own shares, while at the same time making a handsome profit.'

'But as that's no more than the truth,' said Seb, 'it's hardly libel.'

'I agree, but your mother couldn't resist prodding the snake with a very sharp stick by adding –' Harry put his cigar down, leant back and closed his eyes – '"If it was your intention to bring the company down, Lady Virginia, you have failed, and failed lamentably, because you were defeated by decent ordinary people who want this company to succeed . . ." no, no,' said Harry, correcting himself, 'her exact words were, "to be a success". The audience cheered, and Virginia stormed out of the room shouting, "You'll be hearing from my solicitor", and indeed we did. But that was some time ago, so let's hope she's been advised to drop the case and has slithered away into the undergrowth.'

'If she has, she'll only be curled up waiting to strike again.'

◄○►

On the last morning of the voyage, Seb joined his father for breakfast, but Harry hardly said a word. He was always the same just before handing in a manuscript to his publishers. The longest three days of his life, he once told Seb, were while he waited to hear Harold Guinzburg's opinion of his latest work.

'But how can you be sure he's being completely honest about how he feels when the last thing he would want is to lose you?'

'I don't listen to a word he says about the book,' admitted Harry. 'I'm only interested in the number of hardback copies he will print for the first impression. He can't bluff that. Because if it's over a hundred thousand this time, it means he thinks he's got a number-one bestseller.'

'And under a hundred thousand?' said Seb.

'Then he's not so sure.'

Father and son walked down the gangway together just over an hour later. One of them was clinging on to a manuscript and heading for a publishing house in Manhattan, while the other took a cab to Penn Station armed with no more than an address in Georgetown.

26

SEBASTIAN STOOD ON the other side of the road clutching a large bunch of red roses. He stared at the front door of a small, single-storey red-brick house. In front, a little square of grass that could have been cut with scissors, was surrounded by begonias. A swept path led up to a recently painted front door with a brass knocker that shone in the late morning sun. So neat, so tidy, and so Samantha.

Why was he fearless whenever he took on Adrian Sloane, or crossed swords with someone over a million-pound deal, when knocking on what might not even prove to be Sam's front door filled him with apprehension? He took a deep breath, crossed the road, walked slowly up the path and knocked tentatively on the door. When it opened, his immediate reaction was to turn and run. It had to be Sam's husband.

'Can I help you?' the man asked, eyeing the roses suspiciously.

'Is Samantha in?' Seb asked, wondering if suspicion would quickly turn to anger.

'She hasn't lived here for over a year.'

'Do you know where she's moved?'

'No idea. Sorry.'

'But she must have left a forwarding address,' said Seb desperately.

'The Smithsonian,' the man replied, 'that's where she works.'

'Thanks,' said Seb, but the door had already closed.

This encounter made him feel a little bolder, and he quickly returned to the street and hailed the first passing cab. During the journey to the Smithsonian, he must have repeated to himself a dozen times, stop being so feeble and just get on with it. The worst she can do is . . .

When he got out of the cab, he found himself standing in front of a very different door: a massive glass panel that never seemed to remain closed for more than a few seconds at a time. He marched into the entrance hall. Three young women in smart blue uniforms were standing behind a reception desk, dealing with visitors' queries.

Seb approached one of them, who smiled when she saw the roses. 'Can I help you?'

'I'm looking for Samantha Sullivan.'

'I'm sorry, I don't know that name, but then I only started last week,' she said, turning to a colleague who had just come off the phone.

'Samantha Sullivan?' she repeated. 'You've just missed her. She left to pick up her daughter from school. She'll be back at ten tomorrow.'

Daughter, daughter, daughter. The word rang in Seb's ears like a discharged bullet. If only he'd known, he wouldn't—

'Would you like to leave a message for her?'

'No, thank you,' he said, as he turned and headed back towards the door.

'You might still catch her at Jefferson Elementary,' said the voice behind him. 'They don't come out until four.'

'Thank you,' repeated Seb, as he pushed his way through the door, but he didn't look back. He walked out of the building and went in search of another cab. One immediately drew up by his side. He climbed in and was about to say Union Station, but the words came out as 'Jefferson Elementary School'.

The driver eased out into the afternoon traffic and tucked in behind a long line of cars.

'I'll double whatever's on the meter if you get me there before four.'

The driver switched lanes, ran the next light and shot through gaps so tight that Seb had to close his eyes. They drew up outside a massive neo-Georgian brick building with four minutes to spare. Seb looked at the meter and handed the driver a ten-dollar bill. He got out of the cab and quickly disappeared behind several little pockets of chatting mothers waiting for their offspring to appear. Shielded by a tree, he checked out the mums one by one, searching for a face he recognized. But he didn't see her.

At four o'clock, a bell rang and the doors opened to disgorge a gaggle of noisy young girls dressed in white shirts, crimson blazers and grey pleated skirts, with school bags swinging by their sides. They ran down the steps and straight to their mothers, as if attracted by magnetism.

Seb looked carefully at the girls. They must have been around five, but how could that be possible when Sam had been in England less than six years ago? And then he saw his little sister charging down the steps. The same mop of wavy black hair, the same dark eyes, the same smile that he could never forget. He wanted to run to her and take her in his arms, but he remained frozen to the spot. She suddenly smiled in recognition, changed direction and ran towards her mother.

Seb stared at the woman who, when he'd first met her, had struck him dumb. Once again he wanted to cry out, but once again he didn't. He just stood and watched as the two of them climbed into a car and, like the other mothers and children, set off on their journey home. A moment later they were gone.

Seb stood there dazed. Why hadn't she told him? He'd never felt sadder or happier in his life. He must win both their hearts, because he would sacrifice anything, everything, to be with them.

The crowd dispersed as the last few children were reunited with their mothers, until finally Seb was left standing on his own, still clutching the bunch of red roses. He crossed another road and entered another door in the hope of finding someone who could tell him where they lived.

He walked down a long corridor, past classrooms on either side that were decorated with pupils' drawings and paintings. Just before he reached a door on which a sign announced *Dr Rosemary Wolfe, Headmistress*, he stopped to admire a child's painting of her mother. It could have been painted by Jessica twenty years ago. The same confident brushwork, the same originality. It was no different this time. Her work was in a different class from anything else on display. He recalled walking down another corridor when he was ten years old, experiencing exactly the same emotion – admiration, and a desire to know the artist.

'Can I help you?' said a stern-sounding voice.

Seb swung round to see a tall, smartly dressed woman bearing down on him. She reminded him of his aunt Grace.

'I was just admiring the paintings,' he said, somewhat

feebly, hoping his exaggerated English accent would throw her off guard. Although she didn't look like the kind of woman who was easily thrown off guard.

'And this one,' Seb added, pointing to *My Mom*, 'is exceptional.'

'I agree,' she said, 'but then Jessica has a rare talent . . . are you feeling all right?' she asked as Seb's cheeks drained of their colour and he staggered forward, quickly steadying himself against the wall.

'I'm fine, just fine,' he said, recovering his composure. 'Jessica, you say?'

'Yes, Jessica Brewer. She's the most accomplished artist we've seen at Jefferson Elementary since I've been headmistress, and she doesn't even realize how talented she is.'

'How like Jessica.'

'Are you a friend of the family?'

'No, I knew her mother when she studied in England.'

'If you tell me your name, I'll let her know you—'

'I'd rather not, headmistress, but I do have an unusual request.' The stern look reappeared. 'I'd like to buy this picture and take it back to England, to remind me of both the mother and her daughter.'

'I'm sorry, but it's not for sale,' said Dr Wolfe, firmly. 'But I'm sure if you were to speak to Mrs Brewer—'

'That's not possible,' said Seb as he bowed his head.

The headmistress's expression softened and she took a closer look at the stranger.

'I'd better be going,' said Seb, 'or I'll miss my train.' He wanted to run, but his legs were so weak he could hardly move. When he looked up to say goodbye, the headmistress was still staring at him.

'You're Jessica's father.'

Seb nodded as the tears welled up uncontrollably. Dr Wolfe walked across, removed the picture from the wall and handed it to the stranger.

'Please don't let them know I was here,' he begged. 'It will be better that way.'

'I won't say a word,' said Dr Wolfe, offering him her hand.

Cedric Hardcastle would have been able to do business with this woman; someone who didn't need to sign a contract to keep her word.

'Thank you,' said Seb, handing her the flowers.

He left quickly, clutching the painting under his arm. Once he was outside, he walked and walked. How stupid he'd been to lose her. Doubly stupid. Like the bad cowboy in a B movie, he knew he had to get out of town, and get out fast. Only the sheriff could know he'd ever been there.

'Union Station,' he said as he climbed in to the back of another cab. He couldn't stop staring at *My Mom*, and would have missed the neon sign if he hadn't happened to look up for a moment.

'Stop!' he shouted. The cab drew in to the kerb.

'I thought you said Union Station. That's another ten blocks.'

'Sorry, I changed my mind.' He paid the driver, stepped out on to the pavement and stared up at the sign. This time he didn't hesitate to walk into the building and straight up to the counter, praying that his hunch was right.

'Which department do you want, sir?' asked the woman standing there.

'I want to buy a photograph of a wedding that I'm sure your paper would have covered.'

'The photographic department is on the second floor,' she said, pointing towards a staircase, 'but you'd better hurry. They'll be closing in a few minutes.'

Seb bounded up the stairs three at a time and charged through some swing doors with PHOTOS stencilled on the bevelled glass. On this occasion, it was a young man looking at his watch who was standing behind a counter. Seb didn't wait for him to speak.

'Did your paper cover the Brewer and Sullivan wedding?'

'Doesn't ring a bell, but I'll check.'

Seb paced back and forth in front of the counter, hoping, willing, praying. At last the young man reappeared carrying a thick folder.

'Seems we did,' he said, dumping the folder on the counter.

Seb opened the buff cover to reveal dozens of photographs and several press cuttings recording the happy occasion: the bride and groom, Jessica, parents, bridesmaids, friends, even a bishop, at a wedding at which he should have been the groom.

'If you'd like to choose a particular photo,' said the young man, 'they're five dollars each, and you can pick them up in a couple of days.'

'What if I wanted to buy every picture in the file. How much would that cost?'

The young man slowly counted them. 'Two hundred and ten dollars,' he said eventually.

Seb took out his wallet, removed three hundred-dollar bills and placed them on the counter. 'I want to take this file away now.'

'I'm afraid that's not possible, sir. But as I said, if you come back in a couple of days . . .'

Seb extracted another hundred-dollar bill, and saw the look of desperation on the young man's face. He knew the deal was all but closed. It was only a matter of how much.

'But I'm not allowed . . .' he whispered.

Before he could finish his sentence Seb placed another hundred-dollar bill on top of the other four. The young man glanced around to see that most of his colleagues were preparing to leave. He quickly gathered up the five bills, stuffed them in a pocket and gave Seb a weak smile.

Seb grabbed the file, left the photo department, walked quickly back down the stairs, through the swing doors and out of the building. He felt like a shoplifter, and continued running until he was sure he had escaped. At last he slowed down, caught his breath and began to follow the signs to Union Station, the painting tucked under one arm, the folder under the other. He bought a ticket on the Amtrak express to New York, and a few minutes later climbed aboard the waiting train.

Sebastian didn't open the folder until the train pulled out of the station. By the time he arrived at Penn Station, he couldn't help wondering if, like Mr Swann, he would regret not telling her for the rest of his life, because Mrs Brewer had only been married for three months.

27

HAROLD GUINZBURG placed the manuscript on the desk in front of him. Harry sat opposite him and waited for his verdict.

Guinzburg frowned when his secretary entered the room and put two steaming hot coffees and a plate of biscuits in front of them, and remained silent while she was in the room. He was clearly enjoying making Harry suffer a few more moments of torture. When the door finally closed behind her, Harry thought he would explode.

The suggestion of a smile appeared on Guinzburg's face. 'No doubt you're wondering how I feel about your latest work,' he said, turning the screw one more notch.

Harry could have happily strangled the damn man.

'Shall we start by giving Detective Inspector Warwick a clue?'

And then buried him.

'A hundred and twenty thousand copies. In my opinion, it's the best thing you've ever done, and I'm proud to be your publisher.'

Harry was so shocked that he burst into tears, and as neither of them had a handkerchief, they both started to laugh. Once they had recovered, Guinzburg spent some time explaining why he'd enjoyed *William Warwick and the Time Bomb* so much. Harry quickly forgot that he'd spent the previous two days endlessly walking the streets of New York agonizing over how his publisher would react. He took a sip of his coffee, but it had gone cold.

'May I now turn your attention to another author,' said Guinzburg, 'namely Anatoly Babakov, and his biography of Josef Stalin.'

Harry placed his cup back on the saucer.

'Mrs Babakov tells me that she's hidden her hus-band's book in a place where no one could possibly find it. Worthy of a Harry Clifton novel,' he added. 'But, as you know, other than to confirm that it's somewhere in the Soviet Union, you're the only person she's willing to tell the exact location.' Harry didn't interrupt. 'My own view,' continued Guinzburg, 'is that you shouldn't become involved, remembering the Communists don't exactly consider you to be a national treasure. So if you do find out where it's hidden, perhaps someone else should go and retrieve it.'

'If I'm not willing to take that risk myself,' said Harry, 'then what was the point of all the years I've spent trying to get Babakov released? But before I decide, let me ask you one question. If I were able to lay my hands on a copy of *Uncle Joe*, what would be your first print run?'

'A million copies,' said Guinzburg.

'And you think it's me who'd be taking a risk!'

'Don't forget that Svetlana Stalin's book, *Twenty Letters to a Friend*, was on the bestseller list for over a year and, unlike Babakov, she never once entered the Kremlin during her father's reign.' Guinzburg opened a drawer of his desk and extracted a cheque for $100,000, made out to Mrs Yelena Babakov. He handed it to Harry. 'If you do find the book, she'll be able to live in luxury for the rest of her life.'

'But if I don't, or if it isn't even there? You'll have spent a hundred thousand dollars and will have nothing to show for it.'

'That's a risk I'm willing to take,' said Guinzburg. 'But then any half-decent publisher is a gambler at heart. Now let's talk about more agreeable things. My beloved Emma, for example, and Sebastian. Not to mention Lady Virginia Fenwick. I can't wait to hear what she's been up to.'

◄◦►

Lunch with his publisher had gone on far too long and Harry only just made it to Penn Station in time to catch the Pennsylvania Flyer. During the first part of the journey to Pittsburgh, he went over every question Guinzburg wanted answered before he could part with his $100,000.

Later, as Harry dozed off, his mind drifted to his last conversation with Sebastian. He hoped his son could win Samantha back, and not just because he'd always liked her. He felt Seb had finally grown up, and that Sam would rediscover the man she'd fallen in love with.

When the train pulled into Union Station, Harry remembered that there was something he'd always wanted to do if he ever went to Pittsburgh. But there would be no time to visit the Carnegie Museum of Art, which Jessica had once told him housed some of the finest Cassatts in America.

He climbed into the back of a yellow cab and asked the driver to take him to Brunswick Mansions on the north side. The address had an air of middle-class gentility about it, but when they came to a halt twenty minutes later Harry discovered the reality was a decaying slum. The cab sped off the moment he had paid the fare.

Harry climbed the well-worn stone steps of a graffiti-covered tenement building. The 'Out of Order' sign hanging from the lift door had a permanent look about it. He walked slowly up the stairs to the eighth floor and went in search of apartment number 86, which was on the far side of the block. Neighbours looked out from their doorways, suspicious of the smartly dressed man who must surely be a government official.

His gentle knock on the door was answered so quickly she must have been waiting for him. Harry smiled down at an old woman with sad, tired eyes and a deeply lined face. He could imagine just how painful her long sep-aration from her husband must have been by the fact that although they were about the same age, she looked twenty years older than him.

'Good afternoon, Mr Clifton,' she said with no trace of an accent. 'Please come in.' She guided her guest down a narrow, uncarpeted corridor into the living room, where a large photograph of her husband, hanging above a shelf of well-thumbed paperbacks, was the sole adornment on otherwise blank walls.

'Please sit down,' she said, gesturing towards one of the two chairs that were the only pieces of furniture in the room. 'It was kind of you to make such a long journey to see me. And I must thank you for your gallant efforts to have my dear Anatoly released. You have proved an indefatigable ally.'

Mrs Babakov talked about her husband as if he was late home from work and would appear at any moment, rather than serving a twenty-year prison sentence more than seven thousand miles away.

'How did you first meet Anatoly?' he asked.

'We both trained at Moscow's Foreign Languages Institute. I ended up teaching English at a local state school, while Anatoly moved into the Kremlin soon after he won the Lenin Medal for coming top of his year. When we were first married, I thought we had everything, that we must have been blessed, we were so lucky, and by most people's standards in Russia, we were. But that changed overnight when Anatoly was chosen to translate the chairman's speeches so they could be used for propaganda purposes in the West.

'Then the chairman's official interpreter fell ill, and Anatoly filled in. A temporary appointment, they told him, and how he wished it had been. But he wanted to impress the country's leader, and he must have done so, because he was quickly promoted to become Stalin's principal interpreter. You'd understand why, if you'd ever met him.'

'Wrong tense,' said Harry. 'You mean I'll understand why when I meet him.'

She smiled. 'When you meet him. That was when his problems began,' she continued. 'He became too close to Stalin, and although he was only an apparatchik, he began to witness things that made him realize what a monster Stalin was. The image presented to the people, of a kind, benevolent favourite uncle, could not have been further from the truth. Anatoly would tell me the most horrendous stories when he came back from work, but never in front of anyone else, even our closest friends. If he had spoken out, his punishment would not have been demotion, he would simply have disappeared like so many thousands of others. Yes, thousands, if they so much as raised an eyebrow in protest.

'His only solace was in his writing, which he knew could never be published until after Stalin's death, and probably not until after his own death. But Anatoly wanted the world to know that Stalin was every bit as evil as Hitler. The only difference being that he'd got away with it. And then Stalin died.

'Anatoly became impatient to let the world know what he knew. He should have waited longer, but when he found a publisher who shared his ideals, he couldn't stop himself. On the day of publication, even before *Uncle Joe* reached the shops, every copy was destroyed. So great were the KGB's fears of anyone discovering the truth that even the presses on which Anatoly's words had been printed were smashed to pieces. The next day he was arrested, and within a week he'd been tried and sentenced to twenty years' hard labour in the gulag for writing a book that no one had ever read. If he'd been an American who'd written a biography of Roosevelt or Churchill, he would have been on every talk show, and his book would have been a bestseller.'

'But you managed to escape.'

'Yes, Anatoly had seen what was coming. A few weeks before publication, he sent me to my mother's in Leningrad and gave me every rouble he had saved, and a proof copy of the book. I managed to get across the border into Poland, but not until I'd bribed a guard with most of Anatoly's life savings. I arrived in America without a penny.'

'And the book, did you bring it with you?'

'No, I couldn't risk that. If I'd been caught and it had

been confiscated, Anatoly's whole life would have served no purpose. I left it somewhere they will never find it.'

—◄◦►—

The three men who had been waiting for her all rose as Lady Virginia entered the room. At last the meeting could begin.

Desmond Mellor sat opposite her, wearing a brown-checked suit that would have been more in place at a greyhound track. On his left was Major Fisher, dressed in his obligatory dark blue pinstriped double-breasted suit, no longer off-the-peg; after all, he was now a Member of Parliament. Opposite him sat the man who was responsible for bringing the four of them together.

'I called this meeting at short notice,' said Adrian Sloane, 'because something has arisen that could well disrupt our long-term plan.' None of them interrupted him. 'Last Friday afternoon, just before Sebastian Clifton travelled to New York on the *Buckingham*, he purchased another twenty-five thousand of the bank's shares, taking his overall position to just over five per cent. As I warned you some time ago, anyone in possession of six per cent of the company's stock is automatically entitled to a place on the board, and if that were to happen, it wouldn't be long before he discovered what we've been planning for the past six months.'

'How much time do you think we've got?' asked Lady Virginia.

'Could be a day, a month, a year, who knows?' said Sloane. 'All we do know for certain is that he only needs another one per cent to claim a place on the board, so we should assume sooner rather than later.'

'How close are we to getting our hands on the old

lady's shares?' enquired the major. 'That would solve all our problems.'

'I have an appointment to see her son Arnold next Tuesday,' said Des Mellor. 'Officially to seek his advice on a legal matter, but I won't tell him my real purpose until he's signed a non-disclosure agreement.'

'Why aren't you making him the offer?' Virginia asked, turning to Sloane. 'After all, you're the chairman of the bank.'

'He'd never agree to do business with me,' said Sloane, 'not after I got Mrs Hardcastle to waive her voting rights on the day of her husband's funeral. But he hasn't come across Desmond before.'

'And once he's signed the non-disclosure agreement,' said Mellor, 'I'll make him an offer of three pounds nine shillings a share for his mother's stock – that's thirty per cent above market value.'

'Surely he'll be suspicious? After all, he knows you're a director of the bank.'

'True,' said Sloane, 'but as the sole trustee of his father's estate, it's his responsibility to get the best possible deal for his mother, and at the moment, she's living off her dividend which I've kept to the minimum for the past two years.'

'After I've reminded him of that,' said Mellor, 'I'll deliver the coup de grâce, and tell him that the first thing I intend to do is remove Adrian as chairman of the bank.'

'That should clinch it,' said the major.

'But what's to stop him getting in touch with Clifton and simply asking for a better price?'

'That's the beauty of the non-disclosure agreement. He can't discuss the offer with anyone other than his mother, unless he wants to be reported to the Bar Council. Not a risk a QC would take lightly.'

'And is our other buyer still in place?' asked the major.

'Mr Bishara is not only in place,' said Sloane, 'but he's confirmed his offer of five pounds a share in writing, and deposited two million pounds with his solicitor to show he's serious.'

'Why is he willing to pay so much over the odds?' asked Lady Virginia.

'Because the Bank of England has recently turned down his application for a licence to trade as a banker in the City of London, and he's so desperate to get his hands on an English bank with an impeccable reputation that he doesn't seem to mind how much he pays for Farthings.'

'But won't the Bank of England object to what is obviously a takeover?' asked Fisher.

'Not if he keeps the same board in place for a couple of years, and I stay on as chairman. Which is why it's so important that Clifton doesn't find out what we're up to.'

'But what happens if Clifton gets his hands on six per cent?'

'I'll also offer him three pounds nine shillings a share,' said Sloane, 'which I have a feeling he won't be able to resist.'

'I'm not so sure,' said Mellor. 'I've noticed a change of attitude recently. He seems to be working to a completely different agenda.'

'Then I'll have to rewrite that agenda.'

―◦―

'The book is where a book should be,' said Mrs Babakov.

'In a bookshop?' Harry guessed.

Mrs Babakov smiled. 'But no ordinary bookshop.'

'If you want to keep that secret, I'll understand, especially if its discovery is likely to bring even greater punishment on your husband.'

'What greater punishment could there be? His last words as he handed me the book were, "I've risked my life for this, and would happily sacrifice it to know it had been published so that the world, and more important the Russian people, can finally be told the truth." So I only have one purpose left in life, Mr Clifton, and that is to see Anatoly's book published, whatever the consequences. Otherwise every sacrifice he's made will have been in vain.' She grasped his hand. 'You'll find it in an antiquarian bookshop that specializes in foreign translations on the corner of Nevsky Prospekt and Bolshaya Morskaya Street in Leningrad,' she said, continuing to grasp Harry's hand like a lonely widow clinging to her only son. 'It's on the top shelf in the farthest corner, between *War and Peace* in Spanish, and *Tess of the d'Urbervilles* in French. But don't look for *Uncle Joe*, because I hid it in the dust jacket of a Portuguese translation of *A Tale of Two Cities*. I don't think too many Portuguese visit that shop.'

Harry smiled. 'And if it's still there, and I'm able to bring it back, are you happy for Mr Guinzburg to publish it?'

'Anatoly would have been proud to be –' she stopped, smiled again and said, 'Anatoly *will* be proud to be published by the same house as Harry Clifton.'

Harry took an envelope from the inside pocket of his jacket and handed it to her. She opened it slowly and extracted the cheque. Harry watched to see her reaction, but she simply put the cheque back in the envelope and returned it to him.

'But surely Anatoly would have wanted you to—'

'Yes, he would,' she said quietly. 'But it's not what I want. Can you imagine the pain he suffers every day? So until he is released, I do not care to live in any degree of comfort. You, of all people, must understand that.'

They sat silently together in the little room, holding hands. As the shadows crept in Harry realized there was no light. She was determined to share her husband's prison. She displayed such dignity that it was Harry who felt embarrassed. Finally, Mrs Babakov stood.

'I've kept you far too long, Mr Clifton. I will understand if you decide not to return to Russia, as you have much to lose. And if you do not, I make only one request: please say nothing, until I have found someone who is willing to carry out the task.'

'Mrs Babakov,' Harry said, 'if the book is still there, I will find it. I will bring it back, and it will be published.'

She embraced him and said, 'I will of course understand if you change your mind.'

Harry felt both sad and exhilarated as he walked back down the eight flights of stairs to the now-deserted sidewalk. He had to walk for several blocks before he was able to hail a cab, and he didn't notice the man following him, dodging in and out of the shadows and occasionally taking a surreptitious photograph.

'Damn,' muttered Harry as the train pulled out of Union Station and began its long journey back to New York. He had been so preoccupied with meeting Mrs Babakov, he'd quite forgotten to visit the Carnegie. Jessica would chastise him. Wrong tense. Jessica would have chastised him.

LADY VIRGINIA FENWICK

1970

28

'I WOULD LIKE TO open this meeting,' said Adrian Sloane, 'by offering my heartiest congratulations to Major Fisher on being elected as a Member of Parliament.'

'Hear, hear,' said Desmond Mellor, patting the new MP on the back.

'Thank you,' said Fisher. 'May I say that I consider it an added bonus that it was Giles Barrington I defeated.'

'And if I have my way,' said Sloane, 'he won't be the only Barrington who's about to suffer a loss. But first, I'm going to ask Desmond to tell us how his meeting with Arnold Hardcastle went.'

'Not well, to begin with, because he clearly wasn't interested in selling his mother's shares, even at the inflated price of three pounds nine shillings. But when I told him that my first action as the majority shareholder would be to sack Adrian and remove him from the board, his whole attitude changed.'

'He took the bait?' said Fisher.

'Of course he did,' said Sloane. 'He hates me as much as you hate Emma Clifton and Giles Barrington, perhaps even more.'

'That's not possible,' said Lady Virginia.

'But the clincher,' said Mellor, 'was when I told him who I intended to appoint as chairman of Farthings in Adrian's place.' Mellor couldn't resist pausing for as long as he felt he could get away with, before saying, 'Ross Buchanan.'

'But one phone call to Buchanan, and he'll know . . .'

'You've forgotten, major, that Hardcastle signed a confidentiality agreement, so he won't be phoning anyone. And I'd love to see his face when he discovers that we're changing the name of the bank from Farthings to Sloane's.'

'Can he still change his mind if someone makes him a better offer for the shares?' asked Lady Virginia.

'It's too late,' said Mellor. 'He's already signed the share transfer certificates, so as long as I pay up within twenty-one days, the stock is mine.'

'And you'll only be out of pocket for a short time,' said Sloane, 'before Hakim Bishara buys the shares, giving you a handsome profit.'

'But if Bishara doesn't pay up, we'll all be left in the lurch,' Virginia reminded them.

'He's been on the phone twice a day wanting updates on everything that's going on. He even postponed a visit to Beirut for a meeting with the Lebanese President. In fact, I'm thinking of upping the price from five pounds to six, but not until the last moment.'

'Isn't that a bit of a risk?' asked Fisher.

'Believe me, he's so desperate to get his hands on Farthings, he'll agree to almost anything. Let's move on to the second part of our plan, which involves you, Lady Virginia, and the timing of your trial, which is crucial.'

'Emma Clifton will be served with pleadings next

week, and my lawyers have told me they anticipate the trial will begin some time in November.'

'That couldn't be better,' said Mellor, checking his diary, 'because the next Barrington's board meeting is in three weeks' time, and I'll insist that Mrs Clifton stands down as chairman, for the good of the company, at least until the trial is over.'

'And there are no prizes for guessing who will take her place during that time,' said Sloane.

'Once I'm in the chair,' said Mellor, 'I will consider it nothing less than my fiduciary duty to let the shareholders know what really happened on the first night of the *Buckingham*'s maiden voyage.'

'But that's always been shrouded in mystery,' said Fisher, looking a little uneasy.

'Not for much longer it won't be. When I first joined the board of Barrington's, Jim Knowles hinted that all had not gone well on that voyage, but however much I pressed him he wouldn't elaborate. Of course, I checked the minutes of the board meeting that was held on the ship later that morning, but all I could find was an apology from the captain for an explosion that took place in the early hours, which he blamed on the Home Fleet, who he claimed were carrying out night exercises in the North Atlantic. One look at the Admiralty records and you'll quickly discover that the Home Fleet was anchored off Gibraltar at the time.'

'So what really happened?' asked Fisher. 'Because I tried to get the truth out of Knowles myself, and even after a few drams he remained tight-lipped.'

'The only thing I could find out,' said Mellor, 'was that he and the other board members had signed a confidentiality agreement. I thought I'd come to a dead end until last month's board meeting when Mrs Clifton made a rash decision without realizing its potential consequences.'

No one asked the obvious question.

'The *Buckingham*'s captain had reported to the board that during its latest voyage the third officer, a Mr Jessel, was found drunk while serving on the bridge, and had been confined to his quarters for the rest of the crossing. Admiral Summers demanded that Jessel be sacked immediately without severance pay or a reference. I supported him because, like all the other board members, he'd forgotten that Jessel was the junior flag officer of the watch on the first night of the maiden voyage, and must have witnessed everything that took place.'

Fisher dabbed his forehead with a handkerchief.

'It wasn't difficult,' continued Mellor, 'to track down Jessel, who is not only out of work, but admitted to being three months behind with his rent. I took him off to the local pub, and it didn't take long to discover that he was still angry and bitter about his dismissal. He went on to claim that he knew things that would bring the company down. A few rums later and he began to elaborate on what those things were, assuming that I'd been sent to make sure he kept his mouth shut, which only made him open it even more. He told me that he saw Harry Clifton and Giles Barrington carrying a large vase of flowers up from one of the first-class cabins to the upper deck. They managed to throw it overboard just moments before it exploded. The following morning three Irishmen were arrested and the captain apologized to the passengers, giving them the Home Fleet story, whereas in truth they were only seconds away from a major disaster that could have killed heaven knows how many people and, quite literally, sunk the company without trace.'

'But why didn't the IRA publicize what really happened?' demanded Fisher nervously.

'Jessel told me that the three Irishmen were arrested later that morning and transported back to Belfast on a Royal Navy ship before being locked up in a Belfast prison on other charges. They've recently been released, and one of their bail conditions is that if they say a word about the *Buckingham* they'll be back in solitary the same day. And let's face it, the IRA don't talk a lot about their failures.'

'But if the IRA are in no position to corroborate the story, and our only witness is a drunk who was dismissed from his post, why would anyone be interested nearly six years later?' asked Fisher. 'And how often,' he added, 'have we read headlines claiming the IRA planned to bomb Buckingham Palace, the Bank of England or the House of Commons?'

'I agree with you, major,' said Mellor, 'but the press may take a very different attitude when, as the new chairman of Barrington's, I decide to put the record straight just weeks before the launch of the *Balmoral* and the announcement of the date of its maiden voyage.'

'But the share price would collapse overnight.'

'And we'll pick them up for almost nothing with the profit we make on the bank deal. With a new board in place and a change of name, we'll soon get the company back to its former status.'

'A change of name?' queried Lady Virginia.

Desmond smiled. 'Mellor Shipping. Adrian gets the bank, and I get a shipping company.'

'And what do I get?' said Virginia.

'Exactly what you always wanted, Virginia, the pleasure of bringing the Barrington family to their knees.

And you still have a vital role to play, because timing will be everything. Another piece of information I picked up at the last board meeting was that Harry and Emma Clifton will be visiting New York next month, which as chairman she does every year. That will be the perfect time for you to let your friends in the press know what they can look forward to at the trial. It's important that you get your side of the story over while she's stuck in the middle of the Atlantic. So by the time Mrs Clifton returns, she'll have to defend herself on two fronts: the shareholders will want to know why, as chairman of a public company, she failed to let them know what really happened that night, and at the same time she'll be having to deal with Virginia's libel case. I predict it won't be long before she joins her father as a footnote in the company's history.'

'One snag,' said Virginia. 'My lawyers only give me a fifty-fifty chance of winning the case.'

'By the time the trial opens,' said Sloane, 'Emma Clifton will have lost whatever credibility she ever had. The jury will be on your side from the moment you enter the witness box.'

'But if I don't win, I'll end up with a hefty legal bill,' persisted Virginia.

'After Mrs Clifton resigns as chairman of Barrington's, I can't see how you lose the case. But in that unlikely eventuality, the bank will happily cover all your costs. Pennies in the grand scheme of things.'

'That doesn't solve the problem of Sebastian Clifton and his six per cent,' chipped in Major Fisher. 'Because if he gets a place on the board, he'll know everything we . . .'

'I've got that covered,' said Sloane. 'I'm going to call Clifton and suggest we meet.'

'Perhaps he'll refuse to see you.'

'He won't be able to resist, and when I offer him five pounds a share for his stock, giving him a hundred per cent profit, he'll roll over. From what I remember of that boy, he forgets any other commitments the moment he sees a chance to make a killing.'

'But if he were to turn down your offer,' said Fisher.

'Then it's plan B,' said Sloane. 'I don't care either way.'

—◦—

'As I explained when we first met, Lady Virginia, in my professional opinion, your chances of winning this case are no better than fifty-fifty, so perhaps it might be wise to drop the action.'

'Thank you for your advice, Sir Edward, but it's a risk I'm willing to take.'

'So be it,' replied her silk. 'But I felt it necessary to place my opinion on the record, so there can be no misunderstanding at a later date.'

'You've made your position abundantly clear, Sir Edward.'

'Then let's begin by looking at the facts of the case as objectively as we can. You either did, or did not, sell, and later buy back, a large number of Barrington's shares with the sole purpose of harming the company.'

'Why would I want to harm the company?'

'Why indeed. I should mention at this juncture that it will be the other side's responsibility to prove that you did, and not ours to prove that you didn't. Nevertheless, on three separate occasions, which coincided with the company having to announce bad news, you sold shares at their peak, and then ten days later when they had fallen in price you returned to the market and repurchased them. Is that a fair assessment?'

'Yes. But I only did so after taking Major Fisher's advice.'

'I think you should avoid mentioning Major Fisher when you're in the witness box.'

'But he's a Member of Parliament.'

'Perhaps this is the time to remind you, Lady Virginia, that lawyers, estate agents and MPs are only just behind tax collectors in the opinion of most jurors.'

'But why shouldn't I mention it, when it's the truth?'

'Because Major Fisher was a director of Barrington's at the time you sold and repurchased the shares, and as he was your representative on the board, the jury won't be in any doubt where you were getting your information from. With that in mind, I shall be advising you not to call Major Fisher, although it might be wise for you to alert him to the possibility of his being called by opposing counsel. If I were them, I would subpoena him.'

Virginia looked anxious for the first time.

'And then, at a later date,' continued Sir Edward, 'you purchased a large holding in Barrington's in order to take your place on the board, at a time when the company was selecting a new chairman.'

'Yes. Major Fisher was my choice to chair the board.'

'That's something else I must advise you against mentioning in the witness box.'

'But why? I thought Major Fisher would make a better chairman.'

'Possibly, but a jury of twelve ordinary citizens selected at random may well feel you were pursuing a vendetta against Mrs Clifton, which would suggest that your original purpose in buying and selling the shares was indeed to harm her and the company.'

'I simply wanted the best qualified person as chairman. In any case, I still don't think a woman is capable of doing the job.'

'Lady Virginia, try to remember that it's likely half the jury will be women, and such an observation will not exactly endear you to them.'

'This is beginning to sound more like a beauty contest than a trial.'

'If you think along those lines, Lady Virginia, you won't go far wrong. Now, we must also assume that the other side will call your former husband Sir Giles Barrington as a witness.'

'Why? He wasn't involved in any way.'

'Except that all these transactions took place after your divorce, and your choice for chairman just happened to be the man who twice stood against him at general elections, which the jury may feel is one coincidence too many.'

'But even if they did call Giles, how can he possibly help their cause? He's an ex-husband, an ex-MP and an ex-minister. He hasn't exactly got a lot going for him.'

'All that may well be true,' said Sir Edward, 'but I have a feeling he would still impress the jury.'

'What makes you say that?'

'He has a great deal of experience as a public speaker, and the dispatch box prepares one well for the witness box. So we can't afford to underestimate him.'

'But the man's a loser,' said Virginia, unable to control her feelings.

'I must stress that any personal attacks on the other side will play into their hands, so please remember to remain calm when you're giving evidence, and play to your strengths. You are the injured party, someone who doesn't understand the ways of the City and who wouldn't have the first idea how to bring a company down.'

'But that will make me appear weak.'

'No,' said Sir Edward firmly, 'that will make you appear vulnerable, which will work in your favour when the jury see you're up against a shrewd, tough business-woman.'

'Whose side are you on?'

'I'm on your side, Lady Virginia, but it is my respon-sibility to be absolutely sure that you know what you're up against. With that in mind, I must ask you once again, are you certain you want to go ahead with this case?'

'Yes, I most certainly am, because there's one piece of evidence that I haven't told you about, Sir Edward, and once it becomes public, I don't think this case will ever get to court.'

29

'MR SLOANE CALLED while you were at lunch,' said Rachel.

'Did he say what he wanted?' asked Seb.

'No, other than that it was a personal matter.'

'I'm sure it is. He's worked out that I've got nearly six per cent of Farthings' stock, so it's suddenly very personal.'

'He suggested you meet at his office at eleven tomorrow. There's space in your diary.'

'Forget it. If he wants to see me, he can damn well come here.'

'I'll ring and find out if that's convenient.'

'I have a feeling it will be, because this time I'm in the driving seat.' Rachel didn't comment, and turned to leave the room. 'You're not convinced, are you, Rachel?' said Seb before she reached the door. She turned back, but before she could offer an opinion he asked, 'What would Cedric have done?'

'He would have given Sloane the impression that he was falling in with his plans, so he would lower his guard.'

'Would he?' said Seb. 'Then tell Sloane to expect me

at eleven tomorrow morning, and add how much I'm looking forward to seeing him.'

'No, that would be overdoing it. But don't be late.'

'Why not?'

'Gives him back the advantage.'

◄○►

Giles wasn't looking forward to returning to the House of Commons for the first time since he'd lost his seat. The policeman at the St Stephen's entrance saluted him.

'Nice to see you, sir. Hope it won't be long before you're back.'

'Thank you,' said Giles as he walked into the building, past Westminster Hall and along the corridor where members of the public wait patiently, hoping to be allocated a seat in the Strangers' Gallery so they can follow the business of the day. Giles marched on past them into Central Lobby, walking briskly so as not to be held up by former colleagues offering their commiserations and adding platitudes they rarely meant.

Passing another policeman, he stepped on to the thick green carpet he'd trodden for so many years. He glanced at the ticker-tape machine that kept members up to date with what was happening around the world, but didn't stop to check the latest headline. On past the members' library, dreading he might bump into one particular member he didn't want to see. He took a left when he reached the office of the Leader of the House, and came to a halt outside a room he hadn't entered for years. He knocked on the door of Her Majesty's Leader of the Opposition, and walked in to find seated at their desks the same two secretaries who had served the former prime minister when he was in Downing Street.

'Nice to see you again, Sir Giles. You can go straight in, Mr Wilson is expecting you.'

Another knock on another door, and he entered the room to see the familiar sight of a man attempting to light his pipe. He gave up when he saw Giles.

'Giles, I've been looking forward to this all day. It's good to see you.'

'And it's good to see you, Harold,' responded Giles, not shaking hands with his colleague in the Palace of Westminster, maintaining a tradition that had been up-held for centuries.

'Such bad luck to lose by only twenty-one votes,' said Wilson. 'I can't pretend I care much for your successor.'

'This place will find him out,' said Giles. 'It always does.'

'And how are you coping with the post-election blues?'

'Not that well. I'm bound to admit, I miss the place.'

'I was sorry to hear about you and Gwyneth. I hope you'll find it possible to remain friends.'

'I hope so too, because I'm to blame. I'm afraid we'd begun to drift apart some time ago.'

'This place doesn't help,' said Harold. 'You need a very understanding wife when you're rarely home before ten o'clock most nights.'

'And what about you, Harold. How are you taking to being Leader of the Opposition again?'

'Like you, not that well. So tell me, what's it like out there in the real world?'

'I'm not enjoying it, and I won't pretend otherwise. When you've been in politics for a quarter of a century, you're not really qualified to do much else.'

'Then why don't we do something about it,' said

Wilson, finally managing to light his pipe. 'I need a front-bench spokesman on foreign affairs in the House of Lords, and I can't think of a better person for the job.'

'I'm flattered, Harold, and I thought that might be the reason you wanted to see me. I've given it a great deal of thought, and I wondered if I might ask you a question before I make a decision.'

'Of course.'

'I don't think Ted Heath is proving to be any better in government than he was in opposition. The voters' view of him as the grocer rather sums it up. And more important, I'm convinced we still have an excellent chance of winning the next election.'

'As my Jewish friends would say, from your lips to God's ears.'

'And if I'm right, it won't be that long before you're back in Number Ten.'

'Amen to that.'

'And both of us know that the real power is in the Commons, not the Lords. Frankly, it's a deluxe old people's retirement home, a reward for party hacks with a record of long service and good conduct.'

'With the possible exception of those who sit on the front bench and revise regulation,' suggested Wilson.

'But I'm only fifty, Harold, and I'm not sure I want to spend the rest of my life waiting to be called to an even higher place.'

'I'd put you to work,' said Wilson, 'and you'd have a place in the shadow cabinet.'

'I'm not sure that's enough, Harold. So I need to ask you, if I contested Bristol Docklands at the next election, and the local association is pressing me to do so, and you formed the next government, would I have a chance of becoming foreign secretary?'

Wilson puffed away on his pipe for a few moments, something he often did if he needed a little time to consider. 'No, not immediately, Giles. That wouldn't be fair on Denis, who as you know is shadowing the post at the moment. But I can guarantee you would be offered a senior Cabinet post, and if you did well, you'd be among the front-runners if the job became available. Whereas if you took up my offer, at least you'd be back in the House. And if you're right, and we win the election, it's no secret that I'd be looking for a Leader of the Lords.'

'I'm a Commons man, Harold, and I don't think I'm quite ready yet to be put out to grass. So it's a risk I'm willing to take.'

'I salute your resolve,' said Wilson. 'And now it's my turn to thank you, because I know you wouldn't be willing to take that risk unless you believed not only that you can win back your seat, but that I have a good chance of returning to Number Ten. However, should you change your mind, just let me know, and then, like your grandfather, you'll be sitting on the red benches as Lord Barrington of . . .'

'Bristol Docklands,' said Giles.

—◦—

Sebastian entered Farthings Bank for the first time since he'd resigned five years before. He walked up to the reception desk and gave the duty clerk his name.

'Ah, yes, Mr Clifton,' the man said checking his list. 'The chairman is expecting you.'

When he said 'the chairman', Seb's immediate thought was of Cedric Hardcastle, and not of the usurper who'd been the reason he resigned. 'Would you be kind enough to sign the visitors' book?'

Seb took a pen from an inside pocket of his jacket and slowly unscrewed the cap, giving himself a little time to study the list of those who'd recently visited the chairman. His eye ran quickly down two columns of names, most of which meant nothing to him. But two of them might as well have had flashing neon lights next to them: Desmond Mellor, who Seb knew Sloane had recently appointed as deputy chairman, so that came as no surprise, but what possible reason could Major Alex Fisher MP have had for visiting the chairman of Farthings? One thing was certain, Sloane wasn't going to tell him. The only other name that caught his eye was that of Hakim Bishara. He was sure he'd read something about Mr Bishara in the *Financial Times* recently, but couldn't remember what.

'The chairman will see you now, sir. His office is on—'

'The top floor,' said Seb. 'Many thanks.'

When Seb stepped out of the lift on the executive floor, he walked slowly down the corridor towards Cedric's old office. He recognized no one, and no one recognized him, but then he knew Sloane hadn't wasted any time in purging Farthings of all Cedric's lieutenants.

He didn't have to knock on Sloane's door because it swung open when he was a couple of paces away.

'Good to see you, Seb,' said Sloane. 'It's been too long,' he added before he ushered him into his office, but didn't risk offering to shake his hand.

The first thing that struck Seb as he entered the chairman's office was that there was no sign of Cedric. No acknowledgement of his thirty years' stewardship of the bank. No portrait, no photograph, no plaque to remind the next generation of his achievements. Sloane had not only replaced him, but had airbrushed him out of existence, like a Soviet politician who'd fallen from favour.

'Have a seat,' said Sloane, as if he was addressing one of the bank's junior clerks.

Seb took a closer look at his adversary. He'd put on a few pounds since they'd last met, but it was cleverly masked by a well-tailored double-breasted suit. One thing that hadn't changed was the insincere smile of a man most people in the City were reluctant to do business with.

Sloane took his seat behind the chairman's desk and didn't waste any more time with banalities.

'Seb, someone as bright as you will already have worked out why I wanted to see you.'

'I assumed you were going to offer me a place on the board of Farthings.'

'That's not exactly what I had in mind.' The false laugh followed, to accompany the insincere smile. 'However, it's been clear for some time that you've been buying the bank's stock on the open market, and you now only need another twenty-two thousand shares to cross the threshold that would allow you to automatically take a place on the board, or to nominate someone else to represent you.'

'Be assured, I'll be representing myself.'

'Which is why I wanted to talk to you. It's no secret that we didn't get on well when you worked under me—'

'Which is why I resigned.'

'It's also why I feel it would be inappropriate for you to be involved in the day-to-day running of the bank.'

'I have absolutely no interest in the day-to-day running of the bank. I assume you have capable staff to carry out that job. That was never my intention.'

'Then what is your intention?' demanded Sloane, barely able to hide his irritation.

'To play a role in ensuring that this bank returns to the high standards it enjoyed under your predecessor, and to be sure that the shareholders are kept informed of what goes on in their name.' Seb decided to roll a small hand grenade across the table and see if it exploded when it reached the other side. 'Because it's clear to me, after reading the minutes of past board meetings, that you are not telling stockholders the whole story.'

'What do you mean by that?' asked Sloane, a little too quickly.

'I think you know all too well what I mean.'

'Perhaps we can make a deal. After all, you always were a brilliant dealer.'

From bully to flatterer with hardly a moment's pause in between. Maurice Swann would have cast Sloane as Richard III, and he could have played it without a script.

'What sort of deal do you have in mind?' asked Seb.

'Over the past five years you must have paid an average of around two pounds ten shillings per share. I'm prepared to double that, and offer you five pounds a share, which I'm sure you'll agree is generous.'

Far too generous, thought Seb. Three pounds should have been his opening bid, and four his closing. Why was Sloane so keen to keep him off the board?

'More than generous,' Seb replied. 'But I still intend to take my place on the board. You see, with me it's personal.'

'Then I shall have to make an official complaint to the Bank of England, pointing out that you have no interest in supporting the bank's long-term aims.'

'Frankly, I'm only interested in finding out what

Farthings' long-term aims are. Which is why I visited the
Bank of England last week and had a long chat with Mr
Craig, the chief compliance officer. He was kind enough
to check the bank's statutes, and has confirmed in writing
that as long as I have a stockholding of six per cent, I'm
entitled to a place on the board. But do by all means give
him a call.'

If Sloane had been a dragon, flames would have been
belching out of his nostrils. 'And if I were to offer you ten
pounds a share?'

Sloane was clearly out of control, so Seb decided to
lob a second grenade. 'Then I'd begin to think the
rumours were true.'

'What rumours?' demanded Sloane.

Did he dare risk taking another pin out? 'Why don't
you ask Desmond Mellor and Alex Fisher what they've
been up to behind your back?'

'How did you know—'

The hand grenade had exploded in Sloane's face, but
Seb couldn't resist one more sortie. 'You have a lot of
enemies in the Square Mile, Sloane, and even one or two
in your own office.'

'It's time for you to leave, Clifton.'

'Yes, I'm sure you're right. But I look forward to
seeing you and your colleagues at next month's board
meeting. I have so many questions for them, particularly
for Mr Mellor, who seems quite happy to open the batting
for both teams.'

Sloane didn't move, but the flush in his cheeks showed
another hand grenade had exploded.

Seb smiled for the first time, rose from his place
and turned to leave, when Sloane lobbed his own hand
grenade.

'I fear I won't be seeing you again for some time, Sebastian.'

'Why not?' demanded Seb, swinging round.

'Because at the last board meeting we passed a resolution stating that any outsider who wished to join the board in future would be required to own ten per cent of the company's stock.'

'You can't do that,' said Seb, defiantly.

'I can and I have,' said Sloane, 'and I feel sure you'll be pleased to hear that Mr Craig, the chief compliance officer at the Bank of England, has given our unanimous resolution his blessing. So I'll see you in about five years' time. But don't hold your breath, Seb, because if you did get hold of ten per cent, we would just have to pass another resolution.'

30

'HOW LONG DO YOU think you'll be in Russia?' Giles asked Harry as he rose from the dining table and led his guests through to the drawing room for coffee.

'Just a few hours, at most overnight.'

'What takes you back there? No one visits that place a second time without a damn good reason.'

'I'm going shopping.'

'Paris, Rome, New York . . .' said Giles, 'but no one goes shopping in Russia, other than the locals.'

'Unless there's something they have in Russia you can't buy in Paris, Rome or New York?' suggested Emma, as she poured her brother a coffee.

'Ah, how slow of me. I should have remembered that Harry's just returned from the States, and Harold Guinzburg wasn't the only person he visited. That's a clue Inspector Warwick wouldn't have missed.'

'I would have put off the trip until after Emma's trial,' said Harry, ignoring Giles's deduction, 'but my visa runs out in a couple of weeks, and the Russian Embassy's warned me there could be a six-month delay before they issue me with a new one.'

'Just be careful,' said Giles. 'The Russians may have

their own Inspector Warwick, who could be sitting waiting for you.' After his own experience in East Berlin, Giles doubted if Harry would get beyond customs but he accepted there was no way he could ever hope to dissuade his brother-in-law once he'd made up his mind.

'I'll be in and out before they realize it,' said Harry, 'so there's nothing for you to be anxious about. In fact, I'm far more worried about the problems Emma's facing.'

'What in particular?' asked Giles as he handed Harry a brandy.

'Desmond Mellor is standing for deputy chairman at next month's board meeting,' said Emma.

'Are you telling me that charlatan's found two directors who are willing to propose and second him?' said Giles.

'Yes, his old friend Jim Knowles, assisted by his even older friend Clive Anscott.'

'But if they fail to get him elected,' said Giles, 'surely all three of them will have to resign? So this could turn out to be a blessing in disguise.'

'Not much of a blessing if they do get him elected,' said Harry.

'Why? What's the worst Mellor can do, even if he does become deputy chairman?' said Giles.

'He could suggest that I stand down until the trial is over,' said Emma, '"for the good of the company".'

'And then the deputy chairman would become acting chairman.'

'But only for a few weeks,' said Harry. 'You'd return once the trial was over.'

'You can't afford to give Mellor that much rope,' said Giles. 'Once you're no longer able to attend board meetings, he'll find a way of making temporary become permanent, believe me.'

'But you could refuse to stand down, Emma, even if he does become your deputy,' suggested Harry.

'I won't be given a lot of choice if I have to spend the best part of a month stuck in the High Court, defending myself.'

'But once you win . . .' said Giles.

'If I win.'

'I can't wait to get in the witness box and tell the jury some home truths about Virginia.'

'We won't be calling you, Giles,' said Emma quietly.

'But I know more about Virginia than—'

'That's exactly what my barrister is worried about. After a few well-chosen words from her ex-husband, the jury might even end up feeling sorry for her, and Mr Trelford, my barrister, says Sir Edward Makepeace, her silk, won't be shy about raising the subject of your second divorce, and what caused it.'

'So who are you going to call?'

'Major Alex Fisher MP.'

'But won't he be a defence witness?'

'Mr Trelford doesn't think so. Fisher could well be as much of a liability for them as you might be for us.'

'Then perhaps the other side will call me?' said Giles, sounding hopeful.

'Let's hope not.'

'I'd pay good money to see Fisher in the witness box,' said Giles, ignoring his sister's barb. 'Remind Mr Trelford that he's got a very short fuse, especially if he's not treated with the respect he feels he deserves, and that was true even before he became an MP.'

'The same can be said of Virginia,' said Harry. 'She

won't be able to resist reminding everyone that she's the daughter of an earl. And there won't be too many of those on the jury.'

'However,' said Giles, 'it would be equally foolish to underestimate Sir Edward. If I may quote Trollope when describing another advocate, he is "as bright as a diamond, and as cutting, and also as unimpressionable".'

'And I may need those same qualities at next month's board meeting when I climb into the ring with Mellor.'

'I have a feeling that Mellor and Virginia must be working together,' said Giles. 'The timing's just a little too convenient.'

'Not to mention Fisher,' added Harry.

'Have you decided yet if you're going to stand against him at the next election?' asked Emma.

'Perhaps it's time to tell you that Harold Wilson has offered me a seat in the Lords.'

'Congratulations!' said Emma, leaping up from her chair and throwing her arms around her brother. 'Some good news at last.'

'And I turned him down.'

'You did what?'

'I turned him down. I told him I wanted one more crack at Bristol Docklands.'

'And one more crack at Fisher, no doubt,' said Harry.

'That would be part of the reason,' admitted Giles. 'But if he beats me again, I'll call it a day.'

'I think you're out of your mind,' said Emma.

'Which is exactly what you said when I first told you twenty-five years ago that I was going to stand for Parliament.'

'As a socialist,' Emma reminded him.

'If it makes you feel any better,' said Giles, 'Sebastian agrees with you.'

'Does that mean you've seen him since he got back from New York?' asked Harry.

'Yes, and before you ask, he clammed up the moment I raised the subject.'

'A pity,' said Harry. 'Such a remarkable girl.'

'But what I can tell you is that when I dropped into his office before taking him out to lunch, I spotted a child's painting on the wall behind his desk that I'd never seen before. It was called *My Mom*, and I could have sworn it was Jessica's hand.'

'A painting of me?' asked Emma.

'No, that's the strange thing,' said Giles. 'It was of Samantha.'

◄o►

'Sloane offered you ten pounds a share?' said Ross Buchanan. 'But that doesn't make any sense. Farthings are trading at two pounds eight shillings this morning.'

'He was simply trying to find out what my limit was,' said Seb. 'Once he realized I wasn't interested, he threw in the towel and lost his temper.'

'That shouldn't have come as a surprise. But why's he so desperate to get his hands on your six per cent?'

'And where do Mellor and Fisher fit in?'

'An unholy alliance that's up to no good, that's for sure.'

'There was another name in the visitors' book that just might provide the answer. Have you ever come across someone called Hakim Bishara?'

'I've never met him,' said Ross. 'But I attended a lecture he gave at the London School of Economics, and

I was mightily impressed. He's Turkish, but was educated in Beirut. He came top in the entrance exam for Oxford, but they didn't offer him a place.'

'Why?'

'It was assumed he must have cheated. After all, how could a boy called Hakim Bishara, the son of a Turkish carpet trader and a Syrian prostitute, possibly beat the cream of the English public school system? So he went to Yale instead, and after he'd graduated he won a scholarship to Harvard Business School, where he's now a visiting professor.'

'So he's an academic?'

'Far from it. Bishara practises what he preaches. When he was twenty-nine he mounted an audacious coup to take over the Beirut Commerce and Trading Bank. It's now one of the most respected financial institutions in the Middle East.'

'So what's he doing in England?'

'For some time now he's been trying to get the Bank of England to grant him a licence to open a branch of BC and T in London, but so far they've always turned him down.'

'Why?'

'The Bank of England doesn't have to give a reason, and don't forget, its committee is made up of the same breed of chinless wonders who prevented Bishara from going to Oxford. But he's not a man who gives up easily. I recently read in the Questor column of the *Telegraph* that he now intends to bypass the committee and take over an English bank. And what bank could be riper for takeover than Farthings?'

'It was staring me in the face, and I didn't spot it,' said Seb.

'When you put two and two together, they usually make four,' said Ross. 'But it still doesn't make a lot of sense to me, because Bishara is happily married, a devout Muslim, who's spent years building a reputation for scrupulous honesty and straight dealing, not unlike Cedric. So why would he be willing to deal with Sloane, who's built a reputation for being unscrupulous and dishonest, and deals from the bottom of the pile?'

'There's only one way I'm going to find out,' said Seb, 'and that's to meet him. Any ideas?'

'Not unless you're a world-class backgammon player, because that's his hobby.'

'I know what to do with a six and a one on the opening throw, but not much more.'

'Well, whenever he's in London he plays regularly at the Clermont Club. He's part of the "Clermont set" – Goldsmith, Aspinall, Lucan. Loners, like him, who don't fit easily into London society. But don't take him on, Seb, unless you want to lose the shirt off your back. Frankly, where Bishara's concerned you don't have a lot going for you.'

'I've got one thing going for me,' said Seb. 'We have something in common.'

◄◦►

'If I were a betting man, Mrs Clifton, the answer to your question would be even money, but the one imponderable in any trial is how people perform once they're in the witness box.'

'Perform? But shouldn't one just be oneself, and tell the truth?'

'Yes, of course,' said Mr Trelford. 'However, I don't

want the jury to feel they are members of a committee that's being chaired by you.'

'But that's what I do,' said Emma.

'Not while you're in the witness box you don't. I want all the men on the jury to fall in love with you, and, if possible, the judge as well.'

'And the women?'

'They must feel you had to struggle to achieve your amazing success.'

'Well, at least that's true. Do you think Sir Edward will be giving Virginia the same advice?'

'Undoubtedly. He'll want to portray her as a damsel in distress, lost in the cruel world of commerce and finance, and trodden on by a bully who's used to having her own way.'

'But that couldn't be further from the truth.'

'I think we'll have to leave the twelve jurors to decide what the truth is, Mrs Clifton. But for now, let's look at the facts in the cold light of day. The first part of your response to Lady Virginia's question at a well-attended public meeting, and as recorded in the company's minutes, we will plead as justification. We will point out that Major Fisher was not only Lady Virginia's chosen vessel on the board, but that it was his inside knowledge as a director of the company that made it possible for her to buy and sell shares to her advantage. Sir Edward will find that hard to refute, and will pass over it as quickly as possible and concentrate on what you added as she was leaving the hall: "If it was your intention to bring the company down, Lady Virginia, then you have failed, and failed lamentably, because you were defeated by decent ordinary people who want the company to be a success." "Decent ordinary people" is our problem, because that's how the jury will see themselves, and Sir Edward will claim that not only is his client a decent, ordinary person, but that the reason she continued to buy Barrington shares was that she had faith in the company, and the last thing she would have wanted was to bring it down.'

'But every time Virginia sold her shares she made a vast profit and put the stability of the company at risk.'

'Indeed, that may well be the case, and I'm hoping that Lady Virginia will attempt to present herself as an innocent when it comes to business matters, and try to persuade the jury that all along she was relying on the expertise of her professional advisor, Major Alexander Fisher.'

'But they were working as a team to bring the company down.'

'Quite possibly, but when she's in the witness box Sir Edward will ask Lady Virginia the one question you avoided answering. "Who were you referring to, Lady Virginia, when you said" –' Mr Trelford pushed his half-moon spectacles up his nose and checked the exact words – '"is it true that one of your directors sold his vast shareholding over the weekend, in an attempt to bring the company down?"'

'But Cedric Hardcastle wasn't trying to bring the company down. The exact opposite. He was attempting to save it, as he would have explained himself had he been able to take his place in the witness box.'

'I'll word this as delicately as I can in the circumstances, Mrs Clifton, but I am relieved that the other side can't call Mr Hardcastle, because we certainly wouldn't have.'

'But why not, when he was a thoroughly decent and honest man?'

'Of that I have no doubt. But Sir Edward will point out that Mr Hardcastle was doing exactly the same thing as you are accusing Lady Virginia of.'

'With the intention of saving the company, not bringing it to its knees.'

'Possibly, but by then you will have lost both the argument and the case.'

'I still wish he were alive today,' said Emma.

'Now, I need you to remember the way you delivered those words, Mrs Clifton, because that's exactly how I want the jury to think of you when they are considering their verdict.'

'I'm not looking forward to this,' admitted Emma.

'Then perhaps it might be wise for you to consider settling the action.'

'Why would I do that?'

'To avoid a high-profile trial with all the attendant publicity, and to get back to your normal life.'

'But that would be admitting she was in the right.'

'Your statement would be worded carefully – "the heat of the moment, possibly a little injudicious at the time, and we offer our sincere apologies".'

'And the financial implications?'

'You would have to pay her costs, my fees, and a small donation to the charity of her choice.'

'Believe me,' said Emma, 'if we were to go down that road, Virginia would see it as a sign of weakness and would be even more determined to go ahead with the action. She doesn't want the case to go away quietly, she wants to be vindicated in court, as well as in the press, preferably with headlines that will humiliate me, day after day.'

'Possibly, but it would be Sir Edward's professional

responsibility also to put the alternative to her: that if she loses the case, she will end up paying your costs as well as his, and, I assure you, there's nothing cheap about Sir Edward Makepeace.'

'She'll ignore his advice. Virginia doesn't believe it's possible she might lose, and I can prove it.' Mr Trelford sat back and listened carefully to what his client had to say. When she had finished, he believed for the first time that they just might have a chance.

31

SEBASTIAN GOT OUT of the car and handed the door-man his keys and a pound note. As he walked up the steps to the entrance of the Clermont, the door was opened for him and he parted with a second.

'Are you a member, sir?' asked the elegantly dressed man standing behind the front desk.

'No,' said Seb, this time slipping the man a five-pound note.

'Just sign here, sir,' the man said, swivelling a form round.

Seb signed where the finger rested and received a temporary membership card. 'The main gaming room is at the top of the stairs on your left, sir.'

Seb walked up the sweeping marble staircase, admiring the dazzling chandelier, the oil paintings and the thick plush carpet. Millionaires must be made to feel at home, he concluded, otherwise they wouldn't be willing to part with their money.

He entered the gaming room but didn't look round, as he wanted the onlookers to believe this was his natural habitat. He strolled across to the bar and climbed on to a leather stool.

'What can I get you, sir?' asked the barman.

'A Campari and soda,' said Seb, as this clearly wasn't a club that served draught ale.

When the drink was placed in front of him, he took out his wallet and placed a pound on the bar.

'There's no charge, sir.'

Establishments that don't charge for drinks have to be making up for the loss in some other ways, thought Seb, leaving the note where it lay. 'Thank you, sir,' said the barman, as Seb swivelled round and slowly took in the 'some other ways'.

Two roulette tables stood next to each other on the far side of the room, and from the large pile of chips in front of each of the players, and their expressionless faces, Seb assumed they were regulars. Hadn't anyone explained to them that they were paying for the marble staircase, the oil paintings, the chandelier and the free drinks? His eyes moved on to the Black Jack tables. At least there the odds were slightly better, because if you could count the court cards, it was even possible to beat the house – but only once, because after that, you'd never be allowed to darken the club's doors again. Casinos like winners, but not consistent ones.

His gaze moved on to two men playing backgammon. One was sipping a black coffee, the other a brandy. Seb turned back to the barman. 'Is that Hakim Bishara playing backgammon?'

The barman looked up. 'Yes, it is, sir.'

Seb took a closer look at the short, pursy, red-cheeked man who looked as if he had to make regular visits to his tailor. He was bald, and his double chin suggested a greater interest in food and drink than weight-training or running. A tall, lithe blonde stood by his side, a hand resting on his shoulder. Seb suspected she was less attracted by the deep lines on his forehead than by the thick wallet in his inside pocket. He wasn't surprised that he kept being rejected by the English establishment. His younger opponent looked like a lamb about to be devoured by a python.

Seb turned back to the barman. 'How do I get a game with Bishara?'

'It's not that difficult if you've got a hundred pounds to throw away.'

'He plays for money?'

'No, for amusement.'

'But the hundred pounds?'

'It's an admission fee that you donate to his favourite charity.'

'Any tips?'

'Yes, sir, you'd be better off giving me fifty quid and going home.'

'But what if I beat him?'

'Then I'll give you fifty quid and I'll go home. Mind you, you'll enjoy his company for the few minutes the game lasts. And if you were to win, he'll donate a thousand pounds to the charity of your choice. He's a real gentleman.'

Despite appearances, thought Seb as he ordered a second drink. He occasionally glanced around at the backgammon table, but it was another twenty minutes before the barman whispered, 'He's free now, sir, waiting for his next victim.'

Seb swung round to see the stout man heave himself out of his chair and begin to walk away with the young woman on his arm.

'But I thought . . .' He looked more closely at the lamb

that had devoured the python. He could hear Cedric saying, 'What did you learn from that, young man?' Bishara looked around forty, perhaps a little older, but his tanned good looks and athletic build suggested that he wouldn't have to continually empty his wallet to attract a beautiful woman. He had thick, wavy black hair and dark penetrating eyes. Had he been penniless, you might have thought he was an out-of-work actor.

Seb slipped off the stool and walked slowly towards him, hoping he looked relaxed and in control, because he wasn't.

'Good evening, Mr Bishara, I wondered if you were free for a game?'

'Not free,' he said, giving Seb a warm smile. 'In fact, rather expensive.'

'Yes, the barman warned me about your terms. But I still want to play you.'

'Good, then have a seat.' Bishara rolled one dice out on to the board.

Seb was painfully aware after the first half a dozen moves that this man was quite simply in another class. It only took a few minutes before Bishara began removing his counters from the board.

'Tell me, Mr . . .'

'Clifton, Sebastian Clifton.'

Bishara reset the board. 'As you are clearly not even a respectable pub player, you must have had a good reason for wanting to give away a hundred pounds.'

'Yes, I did,' said Seb, taking out his cheque book. 'I needed an excuse to meet you.'

'And why, may I ask?'

'Because we have several things in common, one in particular.'

'Clearly not backgammon.'

'True,' said Seb. 'Who should I make the cheque out to?'

'The Polio Society. You haven't answered my question.'

'I thought we might trade information.'

'What makes you think you have any information I might be interested in?'

'Because I saw your name in a visitors' book and thought you just might like to know that I own six per cent of Farthings Bank.'

Seb could tell nothing from the expression on Bishara's face. 'How much did you pay for your shares, Mr Clifton?'

'I've been purchasing Farthings' stock regularly over the past five years, and the price has averaged out at around two pounds.'

'Then it has proved a worthwhile investment, Mr Clifton. Am I to assume you now wish to sell your shares?'

'No. Mr Sloane has already made me an offer of five pounds a share, which I turned down.'

'But you would have made a handsome profit.'

'Only in the short-term.'

'And if I were to offer you more?'

'It would be of no interest to me. I still intend to take my place on the board.'

'Why?'

'Because I began my working life at Farthings as Cedric Hardcastle's personal assistant. After his death, I resigned, and joined Kaufman's.'

'Shrewd old bugger, Saul Kaufman, and a smart operator. Why did you leave Farthings?'

'Let's just say there was a difference of opinion over who should attend funerals.'

'So Sloane wouldn't be happy if you were to join the board?'

'If murder was legal, I'd be dead.'

Bishara took out his cheque book and asked, 'What's your favourite charity?' That was one question Seb hadn't been prepared for.

'The Boy Scouts.'

'Yes, I can believe that,' said Bishara, smiling as he wrote out a cheque, not for a hundred pounds, but for a thousand. 'A pleasure to have met you, Mr Clifton,' he said, as he handed it over. 'I have a feeling we may meet again.'

Seb shook his outstretched hand and was about to leave when Bishara added, 'What was the one thing in particular we have in common?'

'The oldest profession. Except in my case, it was my grandmother, not my mother.'

◄O►

'What's Sir Edward's opinion of your chances of winning the case?' asked the major as Virginia poured him a second gin and tonic.

'He's a hundred per cent certain we can't lose, open-and-shut case were his exact words, and he's convinced the jury will award me substantial damages, possibly as much as fifty thousand.'

'That's good news,' said Fisher. 'Will he be calling me as a witness?'

'No, he says he doesn't need you, although he thinks there's an outside chance the other side may call you. But it's unlikely.'

'That could prove embarrassing.'

'Not if you stick to the simple line that you were my professional advisor when it came to stocks and shares, and that I didn't show a great deal of interest in the details, as I trusted your judgement.'

'But if I were to do that, someone might suggest it was me who was trying to bring the company down.'

'If they were stupid enough to try that line of questioning, Sir Edward would remind the judge that it's not you who's on trial, and because you're a Member of Parliament, Mr Trelford would quickly back off.'

'And you say Sir Edward is certain you can't lose?' asked Fisher, not sounding convinced.

'As long as we all stick to the party line, he says we're home and dry.'

'And he doesn't think it's likely they'll call me?'

'He'd be surprised if they did. But I do feel,' continued Virginia, 'that if, as Sir Edward suggested, I'm likely to be awarded fifty thousand, we should split it down the middle. I've asked my lawyers to draw up an agreement to that effect.'

'That's most generous, Virginia.'

'No more than you deserve, Alex.'

32

SEBASTIAN WAS sitting in the bath when the phone rang. Only one person would have considered calling him at that hour in the morning. Should he jump out of the bath and run into the hall, leaving a small stream in his wake, or should he get on with washing himself, as his mother was sure to call again in a few minutes' time? He stayed put.

He was right, the phone went again while he was in the middle of shaving. This time he walked out into the hall and picked up the receiver. 'Good morning, Mother,' he said, before she'd had a chance to speak.

'Sorry to call you so early, Seb, but I need your advice. How do you think I should vote when Desmond Mellor stands for deputy chairman?'

'I haven't changed my mind since we discussed this subject last night, Mother. If you vote against Mellor and he wins, that will undermine your position. If you abstain and the vote's tied, you'll still have the casting vote. But if you vote for him—'

'I would never do that.'

'Then you have two choices. Personally I'd vote against, so that he if loses he'll have no choice but to

335

resign. By the way, Ross Buchanan doesn't agree with me. He thinks you should abstain and keep your options open. But I don't have to remind you what happened the last time you did that, when Fisher stood for chairman.'

'It's different this time. Mellor's given me his word that he won't vote for himself.'

'In writing?'

'No,' admitted Emma.

'Then it's not a word I'd rely on.'

'Yes, but if I—'

'Mum, if I don't finish shaving, you won't even get my vote.'

'Yes, sorry. I'll think about what you said. See you at the board meeting.'

Seb smiled as he put the phone down. What a complete waste of time that was when he knew she'd already decided to abstain. He checked his watch. Just enough time to grab a bowl of muesli and boil himself an egg.

◄○►

'What did he say?' asked Harry as he passed his wife a cup of tea.

'He said I should vote against, but that Ross thinks I should abstain. So I'm none the wiser.'

'But only last night you told me you were confident of winning.'

'By six votes to four, even if I abstain.'

'Then I think you should abstain.'

'Why?'

'Because I agree with Ross. If you vote against Mellor and lose, it would make your position untenable. However, I'm beginning to think I should postpone my trip to Leningrad until we know the outcome.'

'But if you don't go today,' said Emma, 'you'll have to wait at least six months before you can get another visa. Whereas if you go now, you'll be back well in time for the trial.'

'But if you were to lose the vote today . . .'

'I'm not going to lose, Harry. Six of the directors have given me their word, so there's nothing to worry about. And you gave your word to Mrs Babakov, so you must keep it. In any case, it will be nothing less than a personal triumph when you come home with a copy of *Uncle Joe* under your arm. So start packing.'

◄◊►

Sebastian was putting on his jacket and heading for the door when the phone rang for a third time. He looked at his watch, 7.56, and thought about ignoring it, but turned back, grabbed the phone and said, 'I haven't got time, Mother.'

'It's not your mother,' said Rachel. 'I thought you ought to know that I had a call just after you left the office last night, and I wouldn't have bothered you if she hadn't said it was urgent. I've already called a couple of times this morning, but you were engaged.'

'She?' said Seb.

'A woman called Dr Rosemary Wolfe, phoning from the States. Said you'd know who she was.'

'I most certainly do. Did she leave any message?'

'No, just a number, 202 555 0319. But, Seb, don't forget, they're five hours behind us, so it's only three in the morning in Washington.'

'Thanks, Rachel. Got to dash or I'll be late for the Barrington's board meeting.'

◄◊►

Jim Knowles joined Desmond Mellor for breakfast at the Avon Gorge Hotel.

'It's going to be close,' said Knowles as he sat down opposite Mellor, who stopped speaking while a waitress poured him a coffee. 'My latest calculation is five votes each.'

'Who's changed their mind since yesterday?' asked Mellor.

'Carrick. I convinced him of the importance of having a deputy chairman in place while Mrs Clifton is tied up in a trial that could last for a month, perhaps even longer.'

'Is her vote included in the five?'

'No, because I'm fairly sure she'll abstain.'

'I wouldn't, if I were in her position. And if we win the first vote, what about the second?'

'The second should be easier, as long as you stick to the line that you think it will be for no more than a month. Even the waverers should go along with that.'

'A month will be more than enough to make sure she never returns.'

'But if she loses the trial, it all becomes academic, because then she'll have to resign. Either way, my bet is you'll be chairman a month from today.'

'In which case, Jim, you'll be my deputy.'

'Any news from Virginia on how her case is shaping up?' asked Knowles.

'She rang me yesterday evening. Apparently her barrister has assured her that she can't possibly lose.'

'I've never known a barrister say that before,' said Knowles, 'especially when Alex Fisher might be called as a witness, because I can tell you from past experience, he's not good under fire.'

'Virginia tells me that Sir Edward doesn't intend to call him.'

'Rather proving my point. But once she's won the case, everything should fall neatly into place. That's assuming you've paid Arnold Hardcastle for his mother's shares.'

'Not yet. I don't intend to cough up until the last possible moment. Even I can't afford that sort of outlay for any longer than necessary.'

'Why not ask Sloane to advance you a short-term loan to cover it?'

'I wish I could, but it's against the law for a bank to make a loan for the purpose of buying its own shares. No, I'll get all my money back and make a handsome profit once Bishara completes his part of the deal. If Sloane gets his timing right, it will be a double whammy, because he'll stay on as chairman of the bank and I'll be the new chairman of Barrington's.'

'That's assuming we win today,' said Knowles.

◄○►

Once Sebastian had escaped the rush-hour traffic and turned on to the A40, he checked the clock on his dashboard. He still had a couple of hours to spare, but he didn't need any more holdups. At that moment a red light on the dashboard came on and the petrol indicator began to flicker, which meant he was down to his last gallon. A road sign informed him the next service station was 21 miles away. He knew there was something he'd meant to do last night.

He moved across to the inside lane and maintained a steady fifty miles an hour so he could eke out every last drop of what was left in the tank. He began to pray. Surely the gods weren't on Mellor's side?

◄○►

'Who are you calling?' asked Harry as he zipped up his overnight bag.

'Giles. I'd like to see if he agrees with Ross or Seb. After all, he's still the largest shareholder in the company.'

Harry wondered if he should unpack.

'And don't forget your overcoat,' said Emma.

'Sir Giles Barrington's office.'

'Good morning, Polly. It's Emma Clifton. Could I have a word with my brother?'

'I'm afraid not, Mrs Clifton. He's abroad at the moment.'

'Somewhere exciting, I hope?'

'Not exactly,' said Polly. 'East Berlin.'

—◦—

Seb began to relax when he came off the motorway and drove up the ramp into the petrol station. Once he'd filled up, he realized just how close it must have been. He handed over a ten-pound note for the twelve gallons, and waited for his change.

He was back on the motorway at nine thirty-six. The first sign to Bristol read 61 miles, so he was confident he would still make it with time to spare.

He moved into the outside lane, pleased to see a long stretch of open road ahead of him. His mind drifted from Dr Wolfe, and what could possibly be urgent enough for her to phone him, to his mother, and how she would vote, to Desmond Mellor and what last-minute tricks he would stoop to, and then back to Samantha. Was it possible . . .

When he heard the siren, he assumed it was an ambulance and quickly moved across to the inside lane, but when he looked in his rear-view mirror he saw a police car with lights flashing bearing down on him. He slowed down, willing it to shoot past, but it drew up alongside him and the driver indicated that he should pull over on to the hard shoulder. Reluctantly, he obeyed.

The police car pulled up in front of him and two policemen climbed out and walked slowly towards him. The first was carrying a thick leather notebook, the second what looked like a briefcase. Seb wound down the window and smiled.

'Good morning, officers.'

'Good morning, sir. Were you aware that you were travelling at almost ninety miles an hour?'

'No, I wasn't,' admitted Seb. 'I'm very sorry.'

'Could I see your driving licence, sir?'

Seb opened the glove compartment, took out his licence and handed it to the policeman, who studied it for some time before saying, 'Would you be kind enough to step out of the car, sir.'

Seb got out as the other policeman opened his briefcase and extracted a large yellow balloon-like bag attached to a tube. 'This is a breathalyser, sir, and I have to ask if you are willing to be tested to see if you are above the legal limit.'

'At ten o'clock in the morning?'

'It's standard procedure for a speeding offence. If you choose not to do so, I shall have to ask you to accompany me to the nearest police station.'

'That won't be necessary, officer, I'm quite happy to take the test.'

He carried out the instructions to the letter, well aware that he'd only had two Campari and sodas the previous night. Once he'd blown into the tube twice – evidently he didn't blow hard enough the first time – the two officers studied the orange indicator for some time, before one of them pronounced, 'No problem there, sir, you're well below the limit.'

'Thank God for that,' said Seb, climbing back into his car.

'Just a moment, sir, we're not quite finished. We still have a couple of forms to fill in. Your name, please, sir?'

'But I'm in a hurry,' said Seb, regretting his words the moment he'd said them.

'We'd gathered that, sir.'

'Sebastian Clifton.'

'Home address?'

When the officer had finally filled in the answer to the last question, he handed Seb a speeding ticket, saluted and said, 'Have a good day, sir, and please drive more carefully in the future.'

Sebastian glanced desperately at the little clock on the dashboard, but it faithfully recorded the correct time. In forty minutes, his mother would be calling the board meeting to order, and he couldn't help remembering that the election of a new deputy chairman was the first item on the agenda.

◄○►

Lady Virginia took her time telling Sir Edward what really happened on the first morning of the *Buckingham*'s maiden voyage.

'Fascinating,' he said. 'But it's not something we can use in evidence.'

'Why not? Mrs Clifton wouldn't be able to deny it, and then she'd have to resign as chairman of Barrington's and we couldn't lose the case.'

'Possibly not, but the judge would rule the evidence

as inadmissible. And that's not the only reason we couldn't use it.'

'What more do you need?' asked Virginia.

'A witness who wasn't dismissed for being drunk on duty, and who clearly bears a grudge against the company, and a director who would be willing to stand in the witness box and give evidence under oath.'

'But it's no more than the truth.'

'It may well be, but tell me, Lady Virginia, have you read Harry Clifton's latest novel?'

'Certainly not.'

'Then be thankful that I have, because in *Inspector Warwick and the Time Bomb* you will find almost word for word the story you've just told me. And you can be sure that at least one or two members of the jury will also have read it.'

'But surely that would only strengthen our case?'

'More likely we'd be laughed out of court.'

◄○►

Emma looked slowly around the table. Every director was in place except Sebastian. But never in her eleven years as chairman of Barrington's had she failed to begin a meeting on time.

Philip Webster, the company secretary, opened proceedings by reading the minutes of the previous meeting. Far too quickly in Emma's opinion. 'Are there any matters arising from the minutes?' she asked hopefully. There were none.

'So let us move on, to item number one, the election of a deputy chairman. Desmond Mellor has been proposed by Jim Knowles and seconded by Clive Anscott. Before I call for a vote, does anyone have any questions?'

Mellor shook his head and Knowles said nothing, both well aware that Sebastian Clifton might appear at any moment. Emma stared hopefully at the admiral, but he looked as if he'd fallen asleep.

'I think we've all had more than enough time to consider our position,' said Anscott.

'I agree,' said Knowles. 'Let's get on with the vote.'

'Before we do so,' said Emma, 'perhaps Mr Mellor would care to address the board on why he feels he's the right man to be deputy chairman of Barrington's.'

'I don't think that will be necessary,' said Mellor, who had spent some considerable time preparing a speech, which he now had no intention of delivering. 'I leave my record to speak for itself.'

As Emma had now run out of delaying tactics, she was left with no choice but to call on the company secretary to carry out the roll call.

Webster rose from his place and read out the names of each director, starting with the chairman, Mrs Clifton.

'I shall abstain,' said Emma.

'Mr Maynard?'

'For.'

'Mr Dixon?'

'Against.'

'Mr Anscott?'

'For.'

'Mr Knowles?'

'For.'

'Mr Dobbs?'

'Against.'

He too had kept his word. Emma kept looking towards the door.

'Mr Carrick?'

'For.'

Emma looked surprised. The last time they'd spoken, Carrick had given her his assurance that he wouldn't be supporting Mellor. Who had been the last person to sit on that particular cushion, she wondered.

'Admiral Summers?'

'Against.'

Not a man to desert his friends.

'Mr Clifton?'

Webster looked around the table and, satisfied that Sebastian wasn't present, wrote *Absent* by his name.

'Mr Bingham?'

'Against.'

No surprise. He disliked Mellor almost as much as she did.

Emma smiled. Four all. As chairman, she wouldn't hesitate to exercise her casting vote to stop Mellor becoming deputy chairman.

'And finally, Mr Mellor?' said the company secretary.

'For,' he said firmly.

Emma was momentarily stunned. But turning to Mellor, she eventually managed, 'You told me only yesterday that you would be abstaining, which is why I did so myself. Had I known of this change of heart—'

'Since I spoke to you yesterday evening,' said Mellor, 'one or two of my colleagues have pointed out that the company's statutes allow a board member to vote for himself when standing for office. Reluctantly, I allowed them to convince me that I should do so.'

'But you gave me your word.'

'I did call you at home, several times this morning, chairman, but the line was always busy.'

Not something Emma was able to contradict. She sank back into her chair.

Mr Webster carefully double-checked the list, but Emma already knew the result and its consequences.

'By a vote of five to four, Mr Mellor is elected deputy chairman.'

Some people around the table smiled and said, 'Hear, hear.' Others remained silent.

Seb had been right. She should have voted against Mellor in the first place, and then she could have defeated him with her casting vote. But where was Seb, whose vote would have made that unnecessary? How could he have let her down when she most needed him? And then she froze, and stopped being the chairman of a public company and reverted to being a mother. Was it possible her son had been involved in another dreadful accident? Emma couldn't bear the thought of going through all that again. She'd far rather lose the vote than . . .

'Item number two,' said the company secretary. 'To select a launch date for the MV *Balmoral*, and for the opening of the first booking period for her maiden voyage to New York.'

'Before we move on to item two,' said Mellor, rising from his place to deliver a speech that had also been well prepared, 'I consider it nothing less than my duty to remind the board that Mrs Clifton is about to face a most unpleasant trial that has already attracted considerable media attention. Of course, we all hope, and expect, that our chairman will be able to dismiss the serious charges levelled against her. However, should Lady Virginia Fenwick succeed in proving her case, obviously Mrs Clifton would have to consider her position. With that in mind, it might be prudent for her to temporarily, and I stress the word temporarily, step down as chairman until the trial is over.' He paused for a moment and looked at each of his fellow directors in turn before adding, 'I hope it won't be necessary to call a vote on this occasion.'

Emma could sense that if it was put to a vote, the board were, with one or two exceptions, broadly in agreement with the new deputy chairman's proposal. She gathered up her things and quietly left the room.

Mellor was about to move into her chair when Admiral Summers rose from his place, and fixed him with a stare as if he were a German U boat commander, before saying, 'This is not the board I joined twenty years ago, and I no longer care to be a member of it.'

As he left the room, Bob Bingham and David Dixon joined him.

When the door closed behind them, Mellor turned to Knowles and said, 'That's a bonus I hadn't anticipated.'

SEBASTIAN CLIFTON

1970

33

'WHAT DO I TELL your father when he phones to ask me how the board meeting went?'

'The truth. He'll expect nothing less.'

'But if I do, he'll turn around and come straight back home.'

'Why, where is he?'

'At Heathrow, waiting to board a flight to Leningrad.'

'How unlike him to leave when—'

'It's my fault. I told him we couldn't possibly lose the vote, and he took my word for it.'

'And we wouldn't have done if I'd arrived on time.'

'True enough. Perhaps it would have been more sensible if you'd come down the night before,' said Emma.

'And if you'd taken my advice, none of this would have happened,' snapped Seb.

Both of them remained silent for some time.

'How important is Dad's trip to Leningrad?'

'Every bit as important as this morning's vote was for me. He's been preparing for it for weeks, and if he doesn't go now, he won't get another chance for a very long time, if ever. Anyway, he's only going to be away for a couple of days.' She looked at her son. 'Perhaps you could take the call when he phones.'

'And say what?' asked Seb. 'If he asks me how the meeting went, I'll have to tell him the truth otherwise he'll never trust me again.' He brought the car to a halt outside the Manor House. 'What time did you say he was likely to call?'

'His flight's at four, so I suppose it will be some time around three.'

Seb looked at his watch. 'Don't worry, I'll come up with something by then.'

◄o►

Harry didn't need to check in his luggage because he'd only brought an overnight bag. He knew exactly what he needed to do from the moment he landed and he would have more than enough time to fine-tune his plan on the long flight across the continent. If the impossible had happened and Emma had lost the vote, then it wouldn't matter anyway, because he'd be taking the next train back to Bristol.

'This is the first call for all passengers on BOAC flight 726 to Leningrad. Would you please make your way to gate number three where the flight is now boarding.'

Harry strode across to the nearest phone booth, clutching a handful of coins. He dialled his home number and fed in enough money to allow him three minutes.

'Bristol 4313,' said a voice he recognized immediately.

'Seb, hi. What are you doing at home?'

'Helping Mum celebrate. I'll go and get her so she can tell you the good news herself.'

'This is the second call for passengers travelling to Leningrad on BOAC flight number . . .'

'Hello, darling,' said Emma. 'I'm so glad you called, because—' The line went dead.

'Emma, are you there?' There was no reply. 'Emma?' he tried again, but there was still no response and he didn't have enough coins left over to call a second time.

'This is the third and final call for passengers on BOAC flight 726 to Leningrad.'

Harry replaced the receiver, trying to recall Seb's exact words – 'Helping Mum celebrate. I'll go and get her so she can tell you the good news herself.' When Emma had come on the line, she had sounded unusually cheerful. She must have won the vote, Harry concluded. Despite this, he hesitated for a moment.

'Would Mr Harry Clifton please make his way to gate number three, as the gate is about to close.'

—◦—

'What are we celebrating?' asked Emma.

'I don't know,' said Seb, 'but I'll think of something by the time Dad gets back from Russia. But for now we have to concentrate on more immediate problems.'

'There's not much we can do until the trial is over.'

'Mother, you must stop acting like a Girl Guide, and begin to think like Mellor and Knowles.'

'And what are they thinking at this moment?'

'That it couldn't have gone better for them if they'd planned it. Not only did they get rid of you, but three of your most trusted lieutenants at the same time.'

'Three honourable men,' said Emma.

'Just like Brutus, and look where that got him.'

'I wish I'd still been in the boardroom when Admiral Summers—'

'You're back in your Girl Guide uniform, Mother.

Now snap out of it, and listen carefully. The first thing you must do is ring Admiral Summers, Bob Bingham and Mr Dixon, and tell them that under no circumstances are they to resign from the board.'

'But they walked out, Seb. Knowles and Mellor won't give a damn why they did.'

'But I do give a damn, because I only care about the three votes we would sacrifice for the sake of a pointless gesture. If they were to remain on the board, with my vote, yours and Dobbs's, we'd have six votes to their five.'

'But I won't be in the chair again until after the trial. Have you forgotten that I stood down?'

'No, you didn't. You just walked out of the meeting. So you can walk back in again, because if you don't, you won't be chairman after the trial, win or lose.'

'You're a devious individual, Sebastian Clifton.'

'And as long as Mellor and Knowles don't work that out, we're still in with a chance. But first, you've got three calls to make. Because, believe me, Mellor and Knowles will only ever accept defeat if we win every vote.'

'Perhaps you should be chairman,' said Emma.

'All in good time, Mother. But what I need you to do now is get straight on the phone to Admiral Summers, because he's probably already written his resignation letter. Let's just hope he hasn't posted it.'

Emma picked up the phone book and began flicking through the S's.

'And if you need me for anything, I'll be in the library making a long-distance call,' said Seb.

—◇—

Adrian Sloane was standing in the entrance hall of Farthings Bank at five minutes to eleven. No one could remember the chairman ever coming down to meet a guest before.

Mr Bishara's Bentley drew up outside the bank four minutes later and a doorman rushed across to open the car's back door. As Bishara and his two colleagues entered the building, Sloane stepped forward to greet him.

'Good morning, Mr Bishara,' he said as they shook hands. 'Welcome to your bank.'

'Thank you, Mr Sloane. I'm sure you'll remember Mr Moreland, my lawyer, and Mr Pirie, my chief accountant.'

'Of course,' said Sloane, shaking hands with both men. He then guided his guests towards a waiting lift as the staff burst into well-rehearsed applause to welcome their new president.

Bishara gave a slight bow and smiled at the three young porters who stood behind the reception desk. 'That's where I began my banking career,' he said to Sloane as he stepped into the lift.

'And now you're about to become the owner of one of the City's most respected financial institutions.'

'A day I have looked forward to for many years,' admitted Bishara. A statement that made Sloane feel even more confident that he could forge ahead with his change of plan.

'When we reach the executive floor we'll go straight through to the boardroom, where the offer documents have been prepared and await your signature.'

'Thank you,' said Bishara, as he stepped out into the corridor. When he entered the boardroom, the bank's eight directors rose as one and waited for him to take his place at the head of the table before they sat back down. A butler served Bishara with a cup of his favourite Turkish coffee, black and steaming hot, and two McVitie's shortbread biscuits, also his favourite. Nothing had been left to chance.

Sloane took a seat at the other end of the table.

'On behalf of the board, Mr Bishara, allow me to welcome you to Farthings Bank. With your permission, I will take you through the procedure for the exchange of ownership.'

Bishara took out his fountain pen and placed it on the table.

'In front of you are three copies of the offer document, as approved by your lawyers. Both sides have made small emendations, but nothing of any real consequence.' Mr Moreland nodded his agreement.

'I thought it might be helpful,' continued Sloane, 'if I were to highlight the most important issues we have agreed on. You will become the president of Farthings Bank, and can nominate three directors to represent you on the board, one of whom will be appointed deputy chairman.'

Bishara smiled. They weren't going to like who he had in mind for deputy chairman.

'I will remain as chairman for a period of five years, and the eight board members present here today will also have their contracts renewed for a further five years. And, finally, the sum agreed upon for the takeover is twenty-nine million eight hundred thousand pounds, which values each share at five pounds.'

Bishara turned to his lawyer, who handed him a banker's draft for the full amount. He placed it on the table in front of him. The sight of it almost caused Sloane to change his mind.

'However,' said Sloane, 'something has arisen in the

past twenty-four hours that has made it necessary to make a small adjustment to the contract.'

Bishara could have been playing backgammon at the Clermont for all Sloane could tell from the expression on his face.

'Yesterday morning,' continued Sloane, 'we had a call from a well-established City institution which offered us six pounds a share. In order to prove their credibility, they placed the full amount in escrow with their solicitors. This offer placed me and the board in a most invidious position, as we are no more than the servants of our shareholders. However, we held a board meeting earlier this morning and it was unanimously agreed that if you were able to match the offer of six pounds a share, we would dismiss the rival bid and honour our original agreement. We have therefore adjusted the offer document to show this change, and have entered the new figure of thirty-five million, seven hundred and sixty thousand pounds.' Sloane gave Bishara an ingratiating smile, and added, 'Given the circumstances, I hope you will consider this an acceptable solution.'

Bishara smiled. 'Firstly, Mr Sloane, allow me to thank you for your courtesy in giving me this opportunity to equal the counter-bid made by a third party.' Sloane smiled. 'However, I must point out that we agreed on the sum of five pounds a share almost a month ago, and as I put down a deposit with my solicitors in good faith, this comes as something of a surprise.'

'Yes, I must apologize for that,' said Sloane. 'But you will understand the dilemma I faced, remembering that we have a fiduciary duty to our stockholders.'

'I don't know what your father did for a living, Mr Sloane,' said Bishara, 'but mine was a carpet trader in

Istanbul, and one of the many things he taught me in my youth was that once a price had been agreed upon, coffee was served, and you then sat around for some time pretending to like each other; the equivalent of an Englishman's handshake followed by lunch at his club. So my offer of five pounds a share is still on the table, and if you decide to take it up I will happily sign the agreement.'

All eight board members turned and looked at the chairman, willing him to accept Bishara's offer. But Sloane simply smiled, convinced that the carpet-trader's son was bluffing.

'If that is your final offer, Mr Bishara, I fear I will have to accept the counter-bid. I only hope that we can part as friends.'

The eight directors turned their attention to the other end of the table. One of them was sweating.

'Clearly the morals of City bankers are not those I was taught sitting at my father's feet in the bazaars of Istanbul. Therefore, Mr Sloane, you have left me with no choice but to withdraw my offer.'

Sloane's lips began to quiver as Bishara handed the banker's draft back to his lawyer, rose slowly from his place, and said, 'Good day, gentlemen. I wish you a long and successful relationship with your new owner, whoever that might be.'

Bishara left the boardroom flanked by his two advisors. He did not speak again until they were seated in the back of his Bentley, when he leant forward and said to his driver, 'Change of plan, Fred, I need to call Kaufman's Bank.'

◄o►

'Could you put me through to Dr Wolfe,' said Seb.
    'Who is calling?'

'Sebastian Clifton.'

'Mr Clifton, how kind of you to call back. I only wish it were in happier circumstances.'

Seb's legs gave way, and he collapsed into the chair behind his father's desk, desperate to find out if anything had happened to Samantha or Jessica.

'Sadly,' continued Dr Wolfe, 'Samantha's husband, Michael, recently suffered a stroke while on a flight from Chicago back to Washington.'

'I'm very sorry to hear that.'

'By the time they got the poor man to a hospital, he had lapsed into a coma. How differently things might have turned out if it had happened an hour earlier or an hour later. This all took place some weeks ago, and his doctors are not optimistic about his recovery. In fact, they have no way of knowing how long he will remain in his present state. But that was not the purpose of my call.'

'I'm guessing that it's Jessica you called about, and not her step-father.'

'You're right. The truth is that medical bills in this country are quite horrendous, and although Mr Brewer held a high-ranking post in the State Department and was well covered by his health insurance, the expense of the round-the-clock nursing his condition requires has resulted in Samantha deciding to withdraw Jessica from Jefferson Elementary at the end of this term, as she can no longer afford our fees.'

'I'll cover them.'

'That is most generous of you, Mr Clifton. However, I should tell you that our fees are fifteen hundred dollars a semester, and Jessica's extra-curricular activities last semester came to a further three hundred and two dollars.'

'I'll wire you two thousand dollars immediately, and then perhaps you'll be kind enough to bill me at the end of every semester. However, that is on condition that neither Samantha nor Jessica ever finds out that I'm involved in any way.'

'I had a feeling you might say that, Mr Clifton, and I think I've come up with a strategy that would protect your anonymity. If you were to endow an art scholarship with an annual donation of, say, five thousand dollars, it would then be up to me to select which pupil should be the beneficiary.'

'A nice solution,' said Seb.

'I feel sure your English master would have approved of your correct use of the word nice.'

'My father, actually,' said Seb. 'Which reminds me, when my sister needed canvases, paints, drawing paper, brushes or even pencils, my father always made sure they were of the highest quality. He used to say it mustn't be our fault if she didn't succeed. I want the same for my daughter. So if five thousand isn't enough, Dr Wolfe, don't hesitate to give her anything she needs and I'll cover the extra costs. But I repeat, neither mother nor daughter must ever find out who made this possible.'

'It won't be the first secret of yours I've kept, Mr Clifton.'

'I apologize,' said Seb, 'and also for my next question. When do you retire, Dr Wolfe?'

'Not long after your daughter will have won the Hunter Prize Scholarship to the American College of Art, which will be a first for Jefferson Elementary.'

34

HARRY WAS CHECKING his traveller's cheques when the stewardess began her final round, making sure the first-class passengers had fastened their seat belts as the plane began its descent into Leningrad.

'Excuse me,' said Harry. 'Do you know when your next flight back to London is?'

'This aircraft has a four-hour turnaround, and is scheduled to return to London at nine ten this evening.'

'That's a bit rough on you, isn't it?'

'No,' she said, suppressing a smile. 'We always have a stopover in Leningrad. So if you were to return on this evening's flight, you'd be served by a completely different crew.'

'Thank you,' said Harry. 'That's most helpful.' He looked out of the cabin window to watch Tolstoy's favourite city looming larger by the second, although he suspected the great author would have been appalled by its change of name. As he heard the hydraulics lowering the wheels into place he wondered if there would be enough time for him to carry out his shopping spree and be back on board before the cabin door was locked.

When the wheels touched the ground, Harry felt a

surge of adrenalin he'd only previously experienced when he'd been behind enemy lines during the war. He sometimes forgot that was nearly thirty years ago, when he was a stone lighter and a whole lot nimbler. Well, at least this time he wouldn't be expected to face a regiment of Germans advancing towards him.

After leaving Mrs Babakov, he had committed everything she had said to memory. He hadn't written anything down for fear of someone discovering what he had planned. He had told no one other than Emma the real reason he was visiting Leningrad, although Giles had worked out that he must be going there to collect the book – although 'collect' was the wrong verb.

As the plane bumped along the pot-holed runway he estimated that it would be at least an hour before he cleared customs and was able to convert some sterling into the local currency. In fact, it took an hour and fourteen minutes, despite his only having an overnight bag and exchanging ten pounds for twenty-five roubles. He then had to join the end of a long taxi queue, because the Russians hadn't quite got the hang of free enterprise.

'The corner of Nevsky Prospekt and Bolshaya Morskaya Street,' he instructed the driver in his native tongue, hoping he would know where it was. All those hours learning Russian, when in truth he would only need a few well-honed phrases, as he intended to be on his way back to England in a few hours, mission completed, as his old commanding officer would say.

During the drive into the city they passed the Yusupov Palace, when Harry's thoughts turned to Rasputin. The arch manipulator might have enjoyed his little subterfuge. Harry only hoped he wouldn't end up being poisoned, wrapped in a carpet and then dropped through an ice-hole in the Malaya Nevka river. He realized that if he was going to be back at the airport in time to board the 21.10 to Heathrow, he would only have twenty or thirty minutes to spare. But that should be more than enough.

The taxi driver stopped outside an antiquarian bookshop and pointed to the meter. Harry took out a five-rouble note and handed it to him.

'I don't expect to be long, so would you be kind enough to wait?'

The driver pocketed the note and gave him a curt nod.

The moment Harry stepped inside the shop, he could see why Mrs Babakov had chosen this particular establishment in which to secrete her treasure. It was almost as if they didn't want to sell anything. An elderly woman was seated behind the counter, her head in a book. Harry smiled at her, but she didn't even look up when the bell rang above the door.

He took a couple of books down from a nearby shelf and pretended to peruse them as he edged his way slowly to the back of the shop, his heart beating a little faster with each step he took. Would it still be there? Had someone already bought it, only to discover when they got home that they'd got the wrong book? Had another customer captured the prize and destroyed *Uncle Joe* for fear they might be caught with it? He could think of a dozen reasons why the three-thousand-mile round trip could turn out to be a wasted journey. But for the moment, hope still triumphed over expectation.

When he finally reached the bookcase on which Mrs Babakov had said she'd hidden her husband's work, he closed his eyes and prayed. He opened his eyes to find that *Tess of the d'Urbervilles* was no longer in its place; just a gap covered with a thin layer of dust between *A Tale of Two Cities* and *Daniel Deronda*. Mrs Babakov had made no mention of *Daniel Deronda*.

He glanced back towards the counter, to see the old woman turning a page. Standing on tiptoe, he stretched up and eased *A Tale of Two Cities* off the top shelf, accompanied by a shower of dust that sprinkled down on him. When he opened it, he thought he might have a heart attack, because it was not a copy of Dickens's work but a slim volume by Anatoly Babakov.

Not wishing to draw attention to his prize, he took two other novels from the same shelf, *Greenmantle* by John Buchan and *Jamaica Inn* by Daphne du Maurier, and pretended to browse as he made his way slowly towards the counter. He almost felt guilty interrupting the old woman as he placed the three books on the counter in front of her.

She opened each of them in turn and checked the prices. Mrs Babakov had even pencilled in the price. If she'd turned one more page, he would have been caught. She didn't. Using her fingers as an adding machine, she said, 'Eight roubles.'

Harry handed her two five-rouble notes, having been warned when he was in Moscow for the conference that shopkeepers had to report anyone who attempted to purchase goods with foreign currency and, more important, that they were to refuse the sale and confiscate the money. He thanked her as she handed him his change. By the time he left the shop, she'd turned another page.

'Back to the airport,' said Harry as he climbed into the waiting taxi. The driver looked surprised, but swung obediently round and set out on the return journey.

Harry opened the book once again to check that it hadn't been an illusion. The thrill of the chase was replaced by a feeling of triumph. He turned to the first page and began reading. All those hours spent studying Russian were finally proving worthwhile. He turned the page.

An early evening traffic jam meant the journey back to the airport took far longer than he'd originally anticipated. He began to check his watch every few minutes, fearful that he might miss the plane. By the time the taxi dropped him at the airport, he had reached chapter seven and the death of Stalin's second wife. He handed another five roubles to the driver and didn't wait for the change, but ran into the airport and followed the signs for the BOAC counter.

'Can you get me on the nine ten back to London?'

'First or economy?' asked the booking clerk.

'First.'

'Window or aisle?'

'Window, please.'

'Six A,' she said, handing him a ticket.

It amused Harry that he would be flying back in the same seat he'd occupied for the incoming flight.

'Do you have any luggage to check in, sir?'

'No, just this,' he said, holding up his bag.

'The flight is due to take off shortly, sir, so it might be wise to make your way through to customs.'

Harry wondered how many times a day she delivered that particular line. He was happy to obey her suggestion and, as he passed a bank of telephones, his thoughts turned to Emma and Mrs Babakov, but he would have to wait until he was back in London before he could tell them the news.

He was only a couple of strides away from passport control when he felt a firm hand on his shoulder. He turned to find two heavily built young policemen standing on either side of him.

'Would you come with me,' said one of the officers, confident that Harry spoke Russian.

'Why?' asked Harry. 'I'm on my way back to London and I don't want to miss my flight.'

'We just need to check your bag. If there are no irregularities, you'll have more than enough time to catch your flight.'

Harry prayed they were looking for drugs, cash or contraband, as they gripped him firmly by the arm and led him away. He considered making a dash for it. Perhaps twenty years ago . . .

The policemen stopped outside an unmarked door, unlocked it and shoved Harry inside. The door slammed behind him and he heard a key turning in the lock. He looked around the room. A small table, two chairs and no windows. Nothing on the walls other than a large black and white photograph of Comrade Brezhnev, chairman of the party.

Moments later, he heard the key turning in the lock again. Harry already had half a story prepared about having come to St Petersburg to visit the Hermitage. The door opened and a man entered. The sight of this tall, elegantly dressed officer caused Harry to feel apprehensive for the first time. He was wearing a dark green uniform with three gold stars on his epaulettes and too many medals on his chest to suggest that he might be easily intimidated. Two very different men followed him in, whose appearance seemed to disprove Darwin's theory of evolution.

'Mr Clifton, my name is Colonel Marinkin and I am the officer in charge of this investigation. Please open your bag.' Harry unzipped the bag and stood back. 'Place all the contents on the table.'

Harry took out his wash bag, a pair of pants, a pair of socks, a cream shirt, just in case he had to stay overnight, and three books. The colonel only seemed interested in the books, which he studied for a few moments before placing two of them back on the table.

'You may pack your bag, Mr Clifton.'

Harry let out a long sigh as he returned his belongings to the bag. At least the whole exercise hadn't been a complete waste of time. He knew the book existed, and he'd even read seven chapters, which he would write out on the plane.

'Are you aware of what this book is?' asked the colonel, holding it up.

'*A Tale of Two Cities*,' said Harry, 'among my favourites but not considered to be Dickens's masterpiece.'

'Don't play games with me,' said Marinkin. 'We are not the complete fools you arrogant English take us for. This book, as you well know, is *Uncle Joe* by Anatoly Babakov, which you have been trying to get hold of for some years. Today you almost succeeded. You planned everything down to the finest detail. First you visit Mrs Babakov in Pittsburgh to learn where she had hidden the book. On returning to Bristol, you brush up your Russian, even impressing your tutor with your grasp of our language. You then fly to Leningrad just a few days before your visa is due to expire. You enter the country carrying only an overnight bag, the contents of which suggest you didn't plan even to stay overnight, and you change just ten pounds into roubles. You ask a taxi driver to take you to an obscure antiquarian bookshop in the centre of the city. You purchase three books, two of which you could have picked up in any bookshop in England. You ask the driver to take you back to the airport and you check yourself in on the next flight home, even the same seat. Who do you imagine you're fooling? No, Mr Clifton, your luck has run out, and I am placing you under arrest.'

'On what charge?' asked Harry. 'Buying a book?'

'Save it for the trial, Mr Clifton.'

'Would those passengers travelling to London on BOAC flight number . . .'

◄○►

'There's a Mr Bishara on line three,' said Rachel. 'Shall I put him through?'

'Yes,' said Seb, then placed a hand over the mouthpiece and asked his two colleagues if they could leave him for a few minutes.

'Mr Clifton, I think it's time we had another game of backgammon.'

'I'm not sure I can afford it.'

'In exchange for a lesson, I ask for nothing more than information.'

'What do you need to know?'

'Have you ever come across a man by the name of Desmond Mellor?'

'Yes, I have.'

'And your opinion of him?'

'On a scale of one to ten? One.'

'I see. And what about a Major Alex Fisher MP?'

'Minus one.'

'Do you still own six per cent of Farthings Bank?'

'Seven per cent, and those shares are still not for sale.'

'That's not why I asked. Shall we say ten o'clock to-night at the Clermont?'

'Could we make it a little later? I'm taking my aunt Grace to see *Death of a Salesman* at the Aldwych, but she always likes to catch the last train back to Cambridge, so I could be with you around eleven.'

'I'm delighted to be stood up in favour of your aunt, Mr Clifton. I look forward to seeing you at eleven at the Clermont – where we can discuss *Death of a Salesman*.'

35

'ARROGANCE AND GREED is the answer to your question,' spat out Desmond Mellor. 'You had a banker's draft, cash in hand, but you still weren't satisfied. You wanted more, and because of your stupidity, I'm facing bankruptcy.'

'I'm sure it's not that bad, Desmond. After all, you still own fifty-one per cent of Farthings, not to mention your other considerable assets.'

'Let me spell it out for you, Sloane, so you're not under any illusions as to what I'm up against and, more important, what I expect you to do about it. I purchased, on your advice, fifty-one per cent of the bank's stock from Arnold Hardcastle, at a price of three pounds nine shillings a share, which cost me just over twenty million pounds. In order to raise that sum, I had to borrow eleven million from my bank, using the shares, all my assets including two homes, as well as having to sign a personal guarantee. Farthings' shares are on the market this morning at two pounds eleven shillings, which means I'm showing a shortfall of over five million pounds, for a deal you said we couldn't lose on. It's just possible I may avoid going bankrupt, but I'll certainly be wiped out if I have to put my shares on the market now. Which, I repeat, is because of your arrogance and greed.'

'That isn't entirely fair,' said Sloane. 'At the board meeting last Monday, we all agreed, you included, to put the asking price up to six pounds.'

'True, but the carpet-trader's son called your bluff. He was still willing to go ahead at five pounds a share, which would have got me off the hook and provided us all with a handsome profit. So the least you can do is buy my shares for three pounds and nine shillings, and get me out of a situation you're responsible for.'

'But as I've already explained, Desmond, much as I'd like to help, what you're suggesting would be breaking the law.'

'That didn't seem to worry you when you told Bishara that you had a bid of six pounds on the table from a "well-established City institution", when no such third party existed. I think you'll find that's also against the law.'

'I repeat, we all agreed—'

The phone on Sloane's desk began to ring. He pressed the intercom and barked, 'I told you, no interruptions.'

'It's Lady Virginia Fenwick, and she says it is urgent.'

'I can't wait to hear what she's got to say,' said Mellor.

'Good morning, Lady Virginia,' said Sloane, trying to keep the impatience out of his voice. 'How nice to hear from you.'

'You may not feel that way when you know why I'm calling,' said Virginia. 'I've just received a pre-trial invoice from my solicitors for twenty thousand pounds that has to be settled before the first day of proceedings. You will recall, Adrian, giving me your word that you would cover the costs of my trial. Pennies, in the grand scheme of things, if I remember your words correctly.'

'I did indeed say that, Lady Virginia. But you will also remember that the offer depended on the successful outcome of our negotiations with Mr Bishara, so I'm afraid—'

'But Major Fisher tells me you only have yourself to blame for that remarkable lack of judgement. You may take this as you wish, Mr Sloane, but if you do not keep your word and cover my legal costs, let me warn you that I am not without influence in the City . . .'

'Are you threatening me, Lady Virginia?'

'As I said, Mr Sloane, you may take it as you wish.'

◄o►

Virginia slammed down the phone and turned to Fisher. 'I'll give him a couple of days to come up with the twenty thousand, otherwise—'

'That man won't part with a penny unless you have a written agreement, and perhaps not even then. It's the way he treats everyone. He promised me a place on the board of Farthings but since the Bishara deal fell through, I haven't heard a word from him.'

'Well, I can promise you that he won't be working in the City for much longer if I have anything to do with it. But I'm sorry, Alex, I'm sure that wasn't the reason you wanted to see me.'

'No, it wasn't. I thought you ought to know that I was issued with a subpoena this morning from Mrs Clifton's solicitors, putting me on notice that they intend to call me as a witness at your trial.'

◄o►

'I'm sorry I'm late,' said Seb as he climbed on to the bar-stool. 'When we came out of the theatre, it was raining and I couldn't find a taxi, so I had to drive my aunt to King's Cross to make sure she didn't miss the last train.'

'Worthy of a boy scout,' said Bishara.

'Good evening, sir,' said the barman. 'Campari and soda?'

Seb was impressed, as he'd only visited the club once before. 'Yes,' he replied, 'thank you.'

'And what does your aunt do in Cambridge?' asked Bishara.

'She's an English don at Newnham, the family's blue stocking. We're very proud of her.'

'You're so unlike your fellow Englishmen.'

'What makes you say that?' asked Seb as a Campari and soda was placed in front of him.

'You treat everyone as an equal, from the barman to your aunt, and you don't patronize foreigners, like myself. So many Englishmen would have said, my aunt teaches English at Cambridge University, but you took it for granted that I knew what a don is, that Newnham is one of the five women's colleges at Cambridge, and that a blue stocking is a girl who aspires to learning. Unlike that patronizing idiot Adrian Sloane, who, because he went to Harrow, thinks he's well educated.'

'I get the impression you dislike Sloane almost as much as I do.'

'Possibly more, after his latest con trick when he tried to sell me his bank.'

'But it's not his bank to sell. At least not as long as Cedric Hardcastle's widow still owns fifty-one per cent of the stock.'

'But she doesn't any longer,' said Bishara. 'Desmond Mellor has recently purchased all her shares.'

'That's not possible,' said Seb. 'Mellor's a wealthy man,

but he's not in that league. He'd need twenty million before he could get his hands on fifty-one per cent of Farthings' stock, and he doesn't have that sort of money.'

'Could that be the reason the man who was sweating when I was in the Farthings boardroom wants to see me?' said Bishara, almost as if he was speaking to himself. 'Has Mellor overstretched himself, and now that my offer is no longer on the table, does he need to offload his shares?'

'What offer?' said Seb, not touching his drink.

'I agreed to pay five pounds a share for what must have been Arnold Hardcastle's stock, or to be more accurate, his mother's. I was just about to sign the contract when Sloane decided to raise the price to six pounds. So I withdrew my offer, packed up my tent, gathered up my camels and headed back into the desert.'

Seb laughed. 'But at five pounds he and Mellor would both have made a small fortune.'

'That's my point, Mr Clifton. You would have honoured the deal, not tried to change the price at the last moment. But Sloane only thinks of me as a carpet trader he can take advantage of. But if I can get two questions answered before I see Mellor tomorrow, I could still take over Farthings and, unlike Sloane, I would welcome you on to the board.'

'What do you need to know?'

'*Was* it Mellor who purchased Mrs Hardcastle's shares and, if so, how much did he pay for them?'

'I'll give Arnold Hardcastle a call first thing in the morning. But I must warn you, he's a lawyer by profession, and although he hates Sloane almost as much as I do, he would never compromise a client's confidentiality. But that won't stop me trying. What time's your meeting with Mellor?'

'Twelve o'clock, at my office.'

'I'll ring you as soon as I've spoken to Arnold Hardcastle.'

'Thank you,' said Bishara. 'Now on to more important matters. Your first lesson in the dubious art of backgammon. One of the few games you English didn't invent. The most important thing to remember about backgammon is that it's all about percentages. As long as you can calculate the odds after each throw of the dice, you can never be beaten by an inferior opponent. Luck only comes into the equation when two players are equal.'

'Not unlike banking,' said Seb as the two men took their seats on opposite sides of the board.

◄○►

When Harry opened his eyes, he had such a splitting headache that it was some time before he could focus. He tried to raise his head but he didn't have the strength. He lay still, feeling as if he was coming round after an anaesthetic. He opened his eyes again and looked up at the ceiling. A concrete block with several cracks in it, one producing a slow drip of water, like a tap that hadn't been properly turned off.

He turned his head slowly to his left. The condensation on the wall was so close that he could have touched it if he hadn't been handcuffed to the bed. He turned the other way, to see a door with a square window in it, through which he could, like Alice, have escaped if there hadn't been three iron bars across it, and two guards standing on the other side.

He tried to move his feet, but they were also clamped to the bed. Why such precautions for an Englishman who had been caught with a banned book? Although the first seven chapters had been fascinating, he sensed that he hadn't yet discovered the real reason every copy had been destroyed, which only made him even more determined to read the remaining fourteen chapters. They might also explain why he was being treated as if he were a double agent or a mass murderer.

Harry had no way of knowing how long he'd been in the cell. His watch had been removed, and he couldn't even be sure if it was night or day. He started singing 'God Save the Queen', not as an act of defiant patriotism but more because he wanted to hear the sound of his own voice. Actually, if you'd asked him, Harry would have admitted he preferred the Russian national anthem.

Two eyes peered through the bars but he ignored them and continued singing. Then he heard someone shouting a command, and moments later the door swung open and Colonel Marinkin reappeared, accompanied by his two Rottweilers.

'Mr Clifton, I must apologize for the state of your accommodation. It's just that we didn't want anyone to know where you were before we released you.'

The words 'released you' sounded to Harry like Gabriel's horn.

'Let me assure you, we have no desire to keep you any longer than necessary. Just some paperwork to complete, and a statement for you to sign, and then you can be on your way.'

'A statement? What kind of statement?'

'More of a confession,' admitted the colonel. 'But once you've signed it, you'll be driven back to the airport and be on your way home.'

'And if I refuse to sign it?'

'That would be remarkably foolish, Mr Clifton,

because you would then face a trial at which the charge, the verdict and the sentence have already been decided. You once described a show trial in one of your books. You will be able to give a much more accurate portrayal when you write your next novel –' he paused – 'in twelve years' time.'

'What about the jury?'

'Twelve carefully selected party workers, whose vocabulary only needs to stretch to the word guilty. And just to let you know, your current accommodation is five star compared to where you would be going. No dripping ceilings, because the water is frozen night and day.'

'You'll never get away with it.'

'You're so naïve, Mr Clifton. You have no friends in high places here to take care of you. You are a common criminal. There will be no solicitor to advise you, and no QC to argue your case in front of an unbiased jury. And unlike America, there is no jury selection, and we don't even have to pay the judges to get the verdict we want. I will leave you to consider your options, but in my opinion, it is a simple choice. You can fly back to London, first class on BOAC, or take a cattle train to Novaya Uda that only has straw class, and which I'm afraid you'd have to share with several other animals. And I feel I should warn you, it's a prison from which no one has ever escaped.'

Wrong, thought Harry, as he recalled from chapter three of *Uncle Joe* that it was the jail Stalin was sent to in 1902, and from which he had escaped.

36

'HOW ARE YOU, my boy?'

'Well, thank you, Arnold. And you?'

'Never better. And your dear mother?'

'Preparing herself for next week's trial.'

'Not a pleasant experience to have to go through, especially when there's so much at stake. Talk in chambers is that it's too close to call, but the odds are shortening on your mother, as nobody thinks Lady Virginia will endear herself to the jury. She'll either patronize them, or insult them.'

'I was rather hoping both.'

'Now, why are you calling, Sebastian, because I usually charge by the hour, not that I've started the clock yet.'

Seb would have laughed, but he suspected Arnold wasn't joking. 'Word in the City is that you've sold your shares in Farthings Bank.'

'Mother's shares, to be accurate, and only after I was made an offer that it would have been extremely foolish to turn down. Even then I only agreed when I was assured that Adrian Sloane would be removed as chairman, and Ross Buchanan would take his place.'

'But that's not going to happen,' said Seb. 'Sloane's

representative lied to you, and I can prove it if you felt able to answer a couple of questions.'

'Only if they don't involve a client I represent.'

'Understood,' said Seb, 'but I hoped you'd be able to tell me who bought your mother's shares and how much he paid for them.'

'I can't answer that, as it would break client confidentiality.' Seb was about to curse when Arnold added, 'However, were you to suggest the name of Sloane's representative, and were I to remain silent, you could draw your own conclusions. But, Sebastian, let me make it clear, one name and one name only. This is not a raffle.'

'Desmond Mellor.' Seb held his breath for several seconds, but there was no response. 'And is there any chance you'll let me know how much he paid for the shares?'

'Under no circumstances,' said Arnold firmly. 'And now I must dash, Seb. I'm off to see my mother in Yorkshire, and if I don't leave immediately I'll miss the 3.09 to Huddersfield. Do give your mother my kindest regards and wish her luck for the trial.'

'And please pass on my best wishes to Mrs Hardcastle,' said Seb, but the line had already gone dead.

He checked his watch. It was just after ten, which didn't make any sense. Seb picked up the phone again and dialled Hakim Bishara's private line.

'Good morning, Sebastian. Did you have any luck getting your distinguished QC to answer my two questions?'

'Yes, and I think so.'

'Curiouser and curiouser.'

'He confirmed that it was Desmond Mellor who

bought the stock, and I think the price he paid was three pounds and nine shillings per share.'

'Why can't you be sure? He either told you the price, or he didn't.'

'He neither did, nor didn't. But what he did say was that he had to leave immediately or he'd miss the 3.09 to Huddersfield, and as it's just after ten a.m., and Euston is only twenty minutes away by taxi . . .'

'Clever man, your Mr Hardcastle, because I'm sure we won't have to check whether or not there actually is a 3.09 to Huddersfield. Congratulations. I suspect no one other than you would have been able to get that information out of him. So as they say in my country, I will be forever in your debt, until you have been repaid in full.'

'Well, now you mention it, Hakim, there is something you may be able help me with.'

Bishara listened carefully to Seb's request. 'I'm not sure that your scout master would have approved of what you're suggesting. I'll see what I can do, but I make no promises.'

◄◦►

'Good morning, Mr Mellor. I think you've already met my lawyer, Jason Moreland, and my chief accountant, Nick Pirie.'

Mellor shook hands with both men before joining them around an oval table.

'As you're on the board of Farthings,' said Bishara, 'I can only assume you come here as an emissary of Mr Sloane.'

'Then you assume wrongly,' said Mellor. 'He's the last man I would be willing to represent in any negotiation.

Sloane made a complete ass of himself when he turned down your offer.'

'But he told me he had an offer of six pounds on the table, from a well-established City institution.'

'And you knew that wasn't true, which is why you walked away.'

'And you are willing to walk back, because they were never his shares to sell in the first place.'

'The truth is,' said Mellor, 'he was playing Russian roulette with my bullet, and it turned out to be a blank. However, I am willing to sell you fifty-one per cent of the bank's stock for the five pounds a share you originally offered.'

'Originally offered is correct, Mr Mellor. But that offer is no longer on the table. After all, I can buy Farthings on the open market for two pounds and eleven shillings a share, and have been doing so for several weeks.'

'Not the fifty-one per cent you want, which would give you overall control of the bank. In any case, I can't afford to sell them at that price.'

'No,' said Bishara, 'I'm sure you can't. But you can afford to sell them for three pounds and nine shillings a share.'

Mellor's mouth opened, and didn't close for some time. 'Could you make it four pounds?'

'No, I could not, Mr Mellor. Three pounds and nine shillings is my final offer.' Bishara turned to his chief accountant who handed him a banker's draft for £20,562,000. He placed it on the table.

'I may be wrong, Mr Mellor, but I have a feeling you can't afford to make the same mistake twice.'

'Where do I sign?'

Mr Moreland opened a file and placed three identical contracts in front of Mellor. Once he'd signed them, he thrust out a hand and waited for the banker's draft to be passed across to him.

'And like Mr Sloane,' said Bishara as he took the top off his fountain pen, 'before I can add my signature to the contract, I require one small amendment that I have promised for a friend.'

Mellor stared defiantly at him. 'And what might that be?'

The lawyer opened a second file, took out a letter and placed it in front of Mellor. He read it slowly.

'I can't sign this. Never.'

'I'm sorry to hear that,' said Bishara, picking up the banker's draft and handing it back to his chief accountant.

Mellor didn't move, but when he began to sweat, Bishara realized it was only a matter of time.

'All right, all right,' said Mellor. 'I'll sign the damn letter.'

The lawyer double-checked the signature before placing the letter back in his file. Bishara then signed all three contracts, and the accountant handed Mellor one copy and the banker's draft for £20,562,000. Mellor left without another word. He didn't even thank Bishara, nor did he shake hands.

'If he'd called my bluff,' said Bishara to his lawyer once the door had closed, 'I would have settled without him having to sign the letter.'

Harry studied the statement they expected him to read out in court. He would have to confess to being a British agent who worked for MI5. If he did so, he would be released immediately and deported back to his homeland, never to be allowed to return to the Soviet Union.

Of course, his family and friends would dismiss the statement for what it was worth. Others might feel he'd been left with little choice. But then there would be the majority who didn't know him. They would assume that it was true, and that his fight for Babakov had been nothing more than a smokescreen to cover his espionage. One signature, and he would be free but his reputation would be shattered and, more important, Babakov's cause would be lost for ever. No, he wasn't willing to sacrifice his reputation, or Anatoly Babakov, quite that easily.

He tore up the confession and threw the little pieces of paper high in the air, like confetti waiting for a bride.

When the colonel returned an hour later armed only with a pen, he stared in disbelief at the scraps of paper strewn across the floor.

'Only an Englishman could be that stupid,' he remarked, before turning and marching back out of the cell, slamming the door behind him.

He's got a point, thought Harry, then closed his eyes. He knew exactly how he intended to pass any unfulfilled hours. He would try to recall as much as possible of the first seven chapters of Uncle Joe. He began to concentrate. Chapter One . . .

Josef Stalin was born Iosif Vissarionovich Dzhugashvili in Gori, Georgia, on 18 December 1878. As a child, he was known as Soso, but when he became a young revolutionary he adopted the pseudonym Koba, after a fictional Robin Hood figure he wanted to be compared with, although in fact he was more like the Sheriff of Nottingham.

*As he rose through the ranks of the party, and his
influence grew, he changed his name to Stalin
('Man of Steel'). But . . .*

◄○►

'Some good news at last,' said Emma, 'and I wanted you
to be the first to know.'

'Lady Virginia has fallen into a concrete mixer, and is
now part of a high rise in Lambeth?' suggested Seb.

'Not quite that good, but almost.'

'Dad's home and he's got a copy of *Uncle Joe*?'

'No, he's still not back, although he promised he
wouldn't be more than a couple of days.'

'He told me he might visit the Hermitage and see
some of the other sights while he was over there, so no
need to worry. But come on, Mum, what's your news?'

'Desmond Mellor has resigned from the board of
Barrington's.'

'Did he give a reason?'

'He was pretty vague – just said it was for personal
reasons, and that he wished the company every success in
the future. He even sent his best wishes for the trial.'

'How considerate of him.'

'Why do I get the distinct impression my news doesn't
come as a surprise to you?' said Emma.

◄○►

'Chairman, Mr Clifton has arrived. Shall I send him in?'

'Yes, do.' Sloane leaned back in his chair, delighted
that Clifton had finally come to his senses. But he still
intended to give him a hard time.

A few seconds later his secretary opened the door

and stood aside to allow Sebastian to enter the chairman's office.

'Let me say at the outset, Clifton, that my offer of five pounds a share for your six per cent is no longer on the table. But as a sign of goodwill, I'm prepared to offer you three pounds a share, which is still considerably above this morning's market price.'

'It is indeed, but my shares are still not for sale.'

'Then why are you wasting my time?'

'I hope I'm not wasting your time, because as the new deputy chairman of Farthings Bank, I'm here to carry out my first executive action.'

'What the hell are you talking about?' said Sloane, leaping up from behind his desk.

'At twelve thirty this afternoon, Mr Desmond Mellor sold his fifty-one per cent shareholding in Farthings to Mr Hakim Bishara.'

'But, Sebastian—'

'Which also made it possible for Mr Mellor to finally keep his word.'

'What are you getting at?'

'Mellor promised Arnold Hardcastle that you would be removed from the board, and Ross Buchanan would be the next chairman of Farthings.'

HARRY AND EMMA

1970

37

'WHERE'S HARRY?' one of the journalists shouted as the taxi pulled up outside the Royal Courts of Justice and Emma, Giles and Sebastian stepped out.

The one thing Emma hadn't prepared herself for was twenty or thirty photographers lined up behind two makeshift barriers on either side of the court entrance, bulbs flashing. Journalists hollered questions, even though they didn't expect them to be answered. The most persistent was, 'Where's Harry?'

'Don't respond,' said Giles firmly.

If only I knew, Emma wanted to tell them as she walked through the press gauntlet, because she'd thought of little else for the past forty-eight hours.

Seb ran ahead of his mother and held open the door to the law courts so her progress would not be impeded. Mr Trelford, in his long black gown and carrying a faded wig, was waiting for her on the other side of the double door. Emma introduced her brother and son to the distinguished advocate. If Trelford was surprised that Mr Clifton was not in attendance, he didn't show it.

The silk led them up the wide marble staircase, taking

Emma through what would happen on the first morning of the trial.

'Once the jury has been sworn in, the judge, the Honourable Mrs Justice Lane, will address them on their responsibilities, and when she has finished she will invite me to make an opening statement on your behalf. When I've done so, I will call my witnesses. I shall start with you. First impressions are very important. Juries often make up their minds in the first two days of a trial, so like an opening batsman, if you score a century, it will be the only thing they'll remember.'

When Trelford held open the door of court fourteen, the first person Emma saw as she entered the courtroom was Lady Virginia with her leading counsel, Sir Edward Makepeace, huddled in a corner, deep in conversation.

Trelford guided Emma to the other side of the court, where they took their places on the front bench, with Giles and Seb in the second row, directly behind them.

'Why isn't her husband with her?' asked Virginia.

'I have no idea,' said Sir Edward, 'but I can assure you, it will have no bearing on the case.'

'I wouldn't be so sure of that,' said Virginia as the clock behind them quietly struck ten.

A door to the left of the royal crest opened and a tall, elegant woman appeared wearing a long red robe and full-bottomed wig, ready to rule over her domain. Everyone in the well of the court immediately rose and bowed. The judge returned their bow before taking her place in the high-backed chair in front of a desk covered in copious legal documents and leather-bound volumes on the laws of defamation. Once everyone had settled, Dame Elizabeth Lane turned her attention to the jury.

'Allow me to begin,' she said, giving them a warm

smile, 'by making it clear from the outset that you are the most important people in this courtroom. You are the proof of our democracy and the sole arbiters of justice, because it is you, and you alone, who will decide the outcome of this case. But let me offer you a word of advice. You cannot have failed to notice that there is considerable press interest in this case, so please avoid the media's accounts of it. Only your opinion matters. They may have millions of readers, viewers and listeners, but they don't have a single vote in this courtroom. The same applies to your family and friends, who may not only have opinions on the case but be all too happy to express them. But unlike you,' the judge continued, her eyes never leaving the jury, 'they will not have heard the evidence and therefore cannot offer an informed and unbiased opinion.

'Now, before I explain what is about to happen, I will remind you of the Oxford English Dictionary definition of the word libel: *A false, undeserved, discredit on a person or country.* In this case, you will have to decide whether or not Lady Virginia Fenwick has suffered such a defamation. Mr Trelford will begin proceedings by making an opening statement on behalf of his client, Mrs Clifton, and as the trial progresses I will keep you fully briefed. Should a matter of the law arise, I will stop proceedings and explain its relevance to you.'

Dame Elizabeth turned her attention to counsel's bench. 'Mr Trelford, you may proceed with your opening statement.'

'I am obliged, my lady.' Trelford rose from his place, once again giving her a slight bow. Like the judge, he turned to face the jury before he began his submission. He opened a large black file in front of him, leant back, held the lapels of his gown and gave the seven men and five women of the jury if anything an even warmer smile than the judge had managed a few minutes before.

'Members of the jury,' he began. 'My name is Donald Trelford, and I represent the defendant, Mrs Emma Clifton, while my learned friend Sir Edward Makepeace represents the plaintiff, Lady Virginia Fenwick.' He gave a cursory nod in their direction. 'This,' he continued, 'is a case of both slander and libel. The slander arises because the words in contention were delivered during a heated exchange, when the defendant was taking questions at the annual general meeting of the Barrington Shipping Company, of which she is chairman, and the libel arises because those words were later recorded in the minutes of that meeting.

· 'Lady Virginia, a shareholder of the company, was sitting in the audience that morning and when questions arose she asked Mrs Clifton: "Is it true that one of your directors sold his vast shareholding over the weekend, in an attempt to bring the company down?" Shortly afterwards, she followed this with another question: "If one of your directors was involved in such an action, shouldn't he resign from the board?" Mrs Clifton replied, "If you're referring to Major Fisher, I asked him to resign last Friday when he came to visit me in my office, as I'm sure you already know, Lady Virginia." Lady Virginia then asked, "What are you insinuating?" And Mrs Clifton responded, "That on two separate occasions when Major Fisher represented *you* on the board, you allowed him to sell all your shares over a weekend, and then, after you'd made a handsome profit, you bought them back during the three-week trading period. When the share price recovered and reached a new high, you carried out the same exercise a second time, making an even larger profit.

If it was your intention to bring the company down, Lady Virginia, then . . . you have failed, and failed lamentably, because you were defeated by decent ordinary people who want this company to be a success."

'Now, members of the jury, it is Mrs Clifton's response that is the subject of this action, and it is up to you to decide if Lady Virginia was libelled or if my client's words were, as I contend, no more than fair comment. For example,' continued Trelford, still looking directly at the jury, 'if one of you were to say to Jack the Ripper, "You're a murderer," that unquestionably would be fair comment, but if Jack the Ripper were to say to any one of you sitting on the jury, "You're a murderer," and if the allegation was then printed in a newspaper, that would undoubtedly be both libel and slander. This case, however, requires a finer judgement.

'So let us look at the relevant words again. "If it was your intention to bring the company down, Lady Virginia, then . . . you have failed, and failed lamentably, because you were defeated by decent ordinary people who want this company to be a success." Now, what did Mrs Clifton mean when she said those words? And is it possible that Lady Virginia over-reacted to them? I suspect that, having only heard those words delivered by me, you will not feel able to reach a conclusion until you have heard all the evidence in this case, and seen both the plaintiff and the defendant in the witness box. With that in mind, my lady, I will call my first witness, Mrs Emma Clifton.'

◄o►

Harry had become used to the continual presence of the two guards in their bottle-green uniforms stationed out-side the door of his cell. He did not know how much time

393

had passed since that door had last been opened, but he had reached about halfway through chapter three, and a story that still made him laugh.

> *Yakov Bulgukov, the Mayor of Romanovskaya, faced a potentially dangerous problem when he decided to build a massive statue in honour of Stalin . . .*

It was so cold Harry couldn't stop himself from shivering. He tried to snatch a few moments of glorious sleep, but just as he was slipping into unconsciousness the cell door was suddenly flung open. For a moment he wasn't sure if it was real or just part of his dream. But then the two guards removed the shackles from his arms and legs, pulled him off the mattress and dragged him out of the cell.

When they reached the bottom of a long flight of stone steps, Harry made a determined effort to climb them, but his legs were so weak they gave way long before the three of them reached the top step. Still the guards kept propelling him forward along a dark corridor until he wanted to scream out in pain, but he refused to give them that satisfaction.

Every few steps he passed armed soldiers. Hadn't they got anything better to do with their time, thought Harry, than guard a fifty-year-old man who was literally on his last legs? On and on until at last they reached an open door. He was pushed inside, landing unceremoniously on his knees.

Once he'd caught his breath, Harry tried to haul himself to his feet. Like a cornered animal, he looked around a room that must, in better times, have been a classroom: wooden benches, small chairs and a raised platform at one end with a large table and three high-backed chairs behind it. The blackboard on the back wall confirmed the room's original purpose.

He summoned up all his strength and managed to pull himself up on to one of the benches. He didn't want them to think he was broken. He began to study the layout of the room more carefully. On the right of the stage were twelve chairs, in two straight lines of six. A man who wasn't in uniform but wore a grey, ill-fitting suit that any self-respecting tramp would have rejected was placing a single sheet of paper on each of the chairs. Once he'd performed this task, he sat down on a wooden chair opposite what Harry assumed was the jury box. Harry took a closer look at the man and wondered if he was the clerk of the court, but he just sat there, clearly waiting for someone to appear.

Harry turned round to see more green uniforms wearing heavy greatcoats standing at the back of the room, as if waiting for the prisoner to try to escape. If only one of them had heard of Saint Martin, he might have taken pity and cut his coat in half to share it with the freezing man from another country.

As he sat there waiting, waiting for he knew not what, Harry's thoughts turned to Emma, as they had done so often between stolen moments of sleep. Would she understand why he couldn't sign the confession and allow them to hammer another nail into Babakov's coffin? He wondered how her own trial was progressing, and felt guilty for not being by her side.

His thoughts were interrupted when a door on the far side of the room swung open and seven women and five men entered and sat in their allocated places, giving the distinct impression this wasn't the first time they had performed the task.

Not one of them as much as glanced in his direction, which didn't stop Harry staring at them. Their blank faces suggested they had only one thing in common: their minds had been confiscated by the State, and they were no longer expected to have opinions of their own. Even in that moment of darkness, Harry reflected on what a privileged life he'd led. Was it possible that among these blank-faced clones there was a singer, an artist, an actor, a musician, even an author, who had never been given the opportunity to express their talent? Such is the lottery of birth.

Moments later, two other men entered the room, made their way to the front bench and sat down, facing the stage, with their backs to him. One of them was in his fifties, far better dressed than anyone else in the room. His suit fitted, and he had an air of confidence that suggested he was the sort of professional even a dictatorship requires if a regime is to run smoothly.

The other man was much younger, and kept looking around the courtroom as if he was trying to find his bearings. If these two were the counsel for the state and for the defence, it wasn't difficult for Harry to work out which of them would be representing him.

Finally, the door behind the platform opened so the principal actors could make their entrance: three of them, one woman and two men, who took their seats behind the long table on the centre of the stage.

The woman, who must have been about sixty and had fine grey hair tightly pinned up in a bun, could have been a retired headmistress. Harry even wondered if this had once been her classroom. She was clearly the most senior person present because everyone else in the room was looking in her direction. She opened the file in front of her and began to read out loud. Harry silently thanked his Russian tutor for the hours she'd spent making him read the Russian classics before getting him to translate whole chapters into English.

'The prisoner' – Harry had to assume she was referring to him, although she had not once acknowledged his presence – 'recently entered the Soviet Union illegally' – Harry would have liked to take notes, but he hadn't been supplied with a pen or paper so he would have to rely on his memory, assuming he would even be given the chance to defend himself – 'with the sole purpose of breaking the law.' She turned to the jury and did not smile. 'You, comrades, have been selected to be the arbiters of whether the prisoner is guilty or not. Witnesses will come forward to assist you in making that judgement.'

'Mr Kosanov,' she said, turning to face counsel, 'you may now present the State's case.'

The older of the two men seated on the front bench rose slowly to his feet.

'Comrade commissioner, this is a straightforward case that should not trouble the jury for any length of time. The prisoner is a well-known enemy of the State, and this is not his first offence.'

Harry couldn't wait to hear what his first offence had been. He soon found out.

'The prisoner visited Moscow some five years ago as a guest of our country and took cynical advantage of his privileged status. He used the opening speech at an international conference to mount a campaign for the release of a self-confessed criminal who had previously pleaded guilty to seven offences against the State. Anatoly Babakov will be well known to you, comrade commissioner, as the author of a book about our revered leader, Comrade

Chairman Stalin, for which he was charged with seditious libel and sentenced to twenty years' hard labour.

'The prisoner repeated these libels despite the fact that it was pointed out to him on more than one occasion that he was breaking the law' – Harry couldn't recall that, unless the scantily dressed young woman who'd visited him in his hotel room in the middle of the night was meant to have delivered the message, along with the bottle of champagne – 'but for the sake of international relations, and to demonstrate our magnanimity, we allowed him to return to the West, where this kind of libel and slander is part of everyday life. We sometimes wonder if the British remember we were their allies during the last war and that our leader at the time was none other than Comrade Stalin.

'Earlier this year, the prisoner travelled to the United States for the sole purpose of making contact with Babakov's wife, who defected to the West days before her husband was arrested. It was the traitor, Yelena Babakov, who told the prisoner where she had hidden a copy of her husband's seditious book. Armed with this information, the prisoner returned to the Soviet Union to complete his mission: locate the book, smuggle it back to the West and have it published.

'You may ask, comrade commissioner, why the prisoner was willing to involve himself in such a risky venture. The answer is quite simple. Greed. He hoped to make a vast fortune for himself and Mrs Babakov by peddling these libels to whoever would publish them, even though he knew the book was pure invention from beginning to end, and written by a man who'd only met our revered former leader on one occasion when he was a student.

'But thanks to some brilliant detective work carried

out by Colonel Marinkin, the prisoner was arrested while trying to escape from Leningrad with a copy of Babakov's book in his overnight bag. In order that the court can fully understand the lengths to which this criminal was willing to go to undermine the State, I will call my first witness, Comrade Colonel Vitaly Marinkin.'

38

EMMA THOUGHT her legs would give way as she walked
the short distance to the witness box. When the clerk
of the court handed her a Bible, everyone could see her
hands were shaking, and then she heard her voice.

'I swear by Almighty God that the evidence I give
shall be the truth, the whole truth, and nothing but the
truth, so help me God.'

'Would you please state your name for the record,'
said Mr Trelford.

'Emma Grace Clifton.'

'And your occupation?'

'I am chairman of the Barrington Shipping Company.'

'And how long have you been chairman of that distinguished company?'

'For the past eleven years.'

Emma could see Mr Trelford's head jerking from
right to left, and then she recalled his words, 'Listen to
my questions carefully, but always address your answers
to the jury.'

'Are you married, Mrs Clifton?'

'Yes,' said Emma, turning to the jury, 'for nearly twenty-
five years.'

Mr Trelford would have liked her to add, 'My husband Harry, our son Sebastian and my brother Giles are all present in the court.' She could then turn to face them and the jury would realize they were a happy and united family. But Harry wasn't there, in fact Emma didn't even know where he was, so she continued to look at the jury. Mr Trelford moved quickly on. 'Can you please tell the court when you first met Lady Virginia Fenwick?'

'Yes,' said Emma, returning to her script, 'my brother Giles . . .' This time she did look across at him, and like an old pro, he smiled first at his sister and then at the jury. 'My brother Giles,' she repeated, 'invited my husband Harry and myself to dinner to meet the woman he'd just become engaged to.'

'And what was your first impression of Lady Virginia?'

'Stunning. The kind of beauty you normally associate only with film stars or glamorous models. It quickly became clear to me that Giles was totally infatuated with her.'

'And did you, in time, become friends?'

'No, but to be fair we were never likely to become bosom pals.'

'Why do you say that, Mrs Clifton?'

'We didn't share the same interests. I've never been part of the hunting, shooting and fishing set. Frankly, we come from different backgrounds, and Lady Virginia mixed in a circle I would never normally have come across.'

'Were you jealous of her?'

'Only of her good looks,' said Emma with a broad grin. This was rewarded with several smiles from the jury box.

'But sadly, your brother and Lady Virginia's marriage ended in divorce.'

'Which didn't come as a surprise, at least not to anyone on our side of the family,' said Emma.

'And why was that, Mrs Clifton?'

'I never felt she was the right person for Giles.'

'So you and Lady Virginia didn't part as friends?'

'We'd never been friends in the first place, Mr Trelford.'

'Nevertheless, she came back into your life a few years later?'

'Yes, but that wasn't by my choice. Virginia started buying a large number of Barrington's shares, which came as a surprise to me, as she'd never previously shown any interest in the company. I didn't give it a great deal of thought until the company secretary informed me that she owned seven and a half per cent of the stock.'

'Why was seven and a half per cent so important?'

'Because it entitled her to a place on the board.'

'And did she take up that responsibility?'

'No, she appointed Major Alex Fisher to represent her.'

'Did you welcome this appointment?'

'No, I did not. From the first day, Major Fisher made it abundantly clear that he was only there to carry out Lady Virginia's wishes.'

'Can you be more specific?'

'Certainly. Major Fisher would vote against almost any proposal I recommended to the board, and often came up with his own ideas, which he must have known could only damage the company.'

'But in the end, Major Fisher resigned.'

'If he hadn't, I would have sacked him.'

Mr Trelford frowned, not pleased that his client had come off-piste. Sir Edward smiled and made a note on the pad in front of him.

'I would now like to move on to the AGM held at the Colston Hall in Bristol, on the morning of August twenty-fourth, 1964. You were in the chair at the time, and—'

'Perhaps Mrs Clifton can tell us in her own words, Mr Trelford,' suggested the judge. 'And not be continually prompted by you.'

'As you wish, my lady.'

'I had just presented the annual report,' said Emma, 'which I felt had gone rather well, not least because I had been able to announce the date for the launch of our first luxury liner, the MV *Buckingham*.'

'And if I recall,' said Trelford, 'the naming ceremony was to be performed by Her Majesty the Queen Mother—'

'Clever, Mr Trelford, but don't try my patience.'

'I apologize, my lady, I just thought—'

'I know exactly what you were thinking, Mr Trelford. Now please let Mrs Clifton be her own spokesman.'

'At the end of your speech,' said Trelford, turning back to his client, 'you took questions from the floor?'

'Yes, I did.'

'And among those who asked a question was Lady Virginia Fenwick. As the outcome of this trial rests on that exchange, I will, with your permission, my lady, read out to the court the words spoken by Mrs Clifton that are the cause of this trial. In reply to a question from Lady Virginia she said, "If it was your intention to bring the company down, Lady Virginia, . . . then you have failed, and failed lamentably, because you were defeated by decent ordinary people who want this company to be a success." Now that you hear those words again in the cold light of day, Mrs Clifton, do you regret them?'

'Certainly not. They were nothing more than a statement of fact.'

'Then it was never your intention to defame Lady Virginia?'

'Far from it. I simply wanted the shareholders to know that Major Fisher, her representative on the board, had been buying and selling the company's shares without informing me or any other of his colleagues.'

'Quite so. Thank you, Mrs Clifton. No more questions, my lady.'

'Do you wish to cross-examine this witness, Sir Edward?' asked Mrs Justice Lane, well aware of what his answer would be.

'I most certainly do, my lady,' said Sir Edward, rising slowly from his place and adjusting his ancient wig. He checked his first question before leaning back and giving the jury his most avuncular smile, in the hope that they would look upon him as a respected family friend from whom everyone seeks advice.

'Mrs Clifton,' he said, turning to face the witness box, 'let's not mince words. The truth is that you were against Lady Virginia marrying your brother from the moment you met. In fact, isn't it the case that you'd made up your mind to dislike her even before you'd met?'

Trelford was surprised. He hadn't thought Eddie would plunge the dagger in quite so quickly, although he had warned Emma that her cross-examination was not going to be a pleasant experience.

'As I said, Sir Edward, we were not natural friends.'

'But isn't it the case that you set out from the start to make her an enemy?'

'I wouldn't go that far.'

'Did you attend the wedding of your brother and Lady Virginia?'

'I was not invited.'

'Were you surprised at that, after the way you'd treated her?'

'Disappointed, rather than surprised.'

'And your husband,' said Sir Edward, taking his time to look around the courtroom as if he was trying to find him, 'was he invited?'

'Not one member of the family received an invitation.'

'And why do you think that was?'

'You'll have to ask your client, Sir Edward.'

'And I intend to do so, Mrs Clifton. May I now turn to the death of your mother. I understand there was a dispute over her will.'

'Which was settled in the High Court, Sir Edward.'

'Yes, indeed it was. But correct me if I'm wrong, as I am sure you will, Mrs Clifton, you and your sister Grace inherited almost the entire estate, while your brother, Lady Virginia's husband, ended up with nothing.'

'That was not my choice, Sir Edward. In fact, I tried to talk my mother out of it.'

'We only have your word for that, Mrs Clifton.'

Mr Trelford was quickly on his feet. 'My lady, I must protest.'

'Yes, yes, Mr Trelford, I agree. Sir Edward, that was uncalled for.'

'I apologize, my lady. May I ask you, Mrs Clifton, if Sir Giles was shocked by your mother's decision?'

'Sir Edward,' said the judge, even before Mr Trelford could get to his feet.

'I do apologize, my lady. I'm just an old seeker after the truth.'

'It was a terrible shock for all of us,' said Emma. 'My mother adored Giles.'

'But, like you, she clearly didn't adore Lady Virginia, otherwise she would presumably have made provision for him in her will.' Sir Edward quickly added, 'But let us move on. Your brother and Lady Virginia's marriage was sadly to end in divorce, on the grounds of his adultery.'

'As you well know, Sir Edward,' said Emma, trying to restrain herself, 'those were the days when a man had to spend a night in a Brighton hotel with a hired woman before the courts would grant him a divorce. Giles did so at Virginia's request.'

'I am so sorry, Mrs Clifton, but on the divorce petition, it merely says adultery. But at least we now all know how you react when you feel strongly about something.'

One look at the jury and it was clear that Sir Edward had made his point.

'One final question concerning the divorce, Mrs Clifton. Was it a cause of celebration for you and your family?'

'My lady,' said Trelford, leaping to his feet.

'Sir Edward, you are once again overstepping your brief.'

'I'll try hard not to transgress in future, my lady.'

But when Trelford looked at the jury, he knew that Sir Edward would have felt the reprimand had served its purpose.

'Mrs Clifton, let us move on to more important matters, namely what you said and what you meant when my client put a perfectly legitimate question to you at the annual general meeting of the Barrington Shipping Company. In the interests of accuracy, I will repeat Lady Virginia's question: "Is it true that one of your directors sold his vast shareholding over the weekend, in an attempt to bring the company down?' If I may say so, Mrs Clifton, you deftly and quite brilliantly avoided answering that question. Perhaps you'd care to do so now?'

Emma glanced over at Trelford. He had advised her not to answer the question so she remained silent.

'Perhaps I can suggest that the reason you didn't want to answer that particular question was because Lady Virginia went on to ask, "If one of your directors was involved in such an exercise, shouldn't he resign from the board?" Your reply was, "If you are referring to Major Fisher . . ." although she wasn't, as you knew only too well. She was talking about your close friend and colleague, Mr Cedric Hardcastle, was she not?'

'One of the finest gentlemen I've ever known,' said Emma.

'Was he indeed?' said Sir Edward. 'Well then, let us examine that statement more closely, shall we, because it seems to me that what you were suggesting is that when your close friend – one of the "finest men" you've ever known – sold his shares overnight, he did so in order to *help* the company, but when Lady Virginia sold her shares she was doing it to *harm* the company. Perhaps the jury might feel that you can't have it both ways, Mrs Clifton, unless of course you can find a weakness in my argument, and explain to the court the subtle distinction between what Mr Hardcastle did on behalf of the company and what Major Fisher did on behalf of my client?'

Emma knew she couldn't justify what Cedric had done in good faith, and that the reason he'd sold his shares would be extremely difficult to explain to the jury. Trelford had advised her, when in doubt, simply don't reply, especially if the answer would damn her.

Sir Edward waited for some time before he said, 'Well, as you seem unwilling to answer that question, perhaps we should move on to what you said next? "If it was your intention to bring the company down, Lady Virginia, then . . . you have failed, and failed lamentably, because you were defeated by decent ordinary people who want this company to be a success." Can you deny, Mrs Clifton, that what you were suggesting to a packed audience in the Colston Hall in Bristol that morning was that Lady Virginia is not a decent ordinary person?' He emphasized the last three words.

'She's certainly not ordinary.'

'I agree with you, Mrs Clifton, she's extraordinary. But I put it to the jury that the suggestion that my client is not decent, and that her purpose was to bring your company down, is libellous, Mrs Clifton. Or is that, in your view, also nothing more than the truth?'

'I meant what I said,' Emma replied.

'And so convinced were you of your righteousness that you insisted your words be recorded in the minutes of the AGM.'

'Yes, I did.'

'Did the company secretary advise against this course of action at the time?'

Emma hesitated.

'I can always call Mr Webster to give evidence,' said Sir Edward.

'I believe he may have done so.'

'Now why would he have done that, I wonder?' said Sir Edward, his voice heavy with sarcasm. Emma continued to stare at him, well aware that he wasn't expecting her to reply. 'Could it have been that he didn't want you to add libel to the slander you had already committed?'

'I wanted my words to be on the record,' said Emma.

Trelford bowed his head, as Sir Edward said, 'Did you indeed? So we have established, have we not, Mrs Clifton, that you took against my client on the day you met her, that this intense dislike was compounded when you were not invited to your brother's wedding, and that years later at your company's AGM, in front of a packed audience of the shareholders, you sought to humiliate Lady Virginia by suggesting she was not a decent ordinary person, but someone who wanted to bring the company down. You then went on to overrule your company secretary in order to ensure that your slanderous words were repeated in the minutes of the AGM. Isn't the truth, Mrs Clifton, that you were simply seeking revenge on an ordinary decent human being, who is now asking for nothing more than retribution for your ill-considered words? I think the Bard best summed it up when he said, *He that filches from me my good name, robs me of that which not enriches him, and makes me poor indeed.*'

Sir Edward continued to glare at Emma, while holding on to the lapels of his ancient, well-worn gown. When he felt he had created the desired effect, he turned to the judge and said, 'I have no more questions, my lady.'

When Trelford looked at the jury, he thought they might burst into applause. He decided that he would have to take a risk, one that he wasn't sure the judge would let him get away with.

'Do you have any further questions for your client, Mr Trelford?' asked Mrs Justice Lane.

'Just one, my lady,' said Trelford. 'Mrs Clifton, Sir Edward raised the question of your mother's will. Did she ever confide her feelings about Lady Virginia to you?'

'Mr Trelford,' interrupted the judge before Emma could reply, 'as you well know, that would be hearsay, and inadmissible.'

'But my mother recorded her opinion of Lady Virginia in her will,' said Emma, looking up at the bench.

'I'm not sure I fully understand you, Mrs Clifton,' said the judge.

'In her will, she spelt out her reasons for not leaving anything to my brother.'

Trelford picked up the will and said, 'I could read out the relevant passage, my lady. If you felt it might help,' he added, trying to sound like an innocent schoolboy.

Sir Edward was quickly on his feet. 'This is undoubtedly nothing more than another libel, my lady,' he said, knowing only too well what Trelford was referring to.

'But this is a public, notarized document,' said Trelford, waving the will under the noses of the journalists sitting in the press box.

'Perhaps I should read the words concerned before I make a judgement,' said Mrs Justice Lane.

'Of course, my lady,' said Trelford. He handed the will to the clerk of the court, who in turn passed it up to the judge.

As Trelford had only highlighted a couple of lines, Mrs Justice Lane must have read them several times before she finally said, 'I think on balance this piece of evidence is inadmissible as it could well be taken out of context. However, Mr Trelford,' she added, 'if you wish me to adjourn proceedings so that you can argue a point of law, I will be happy to clear the court in order that you may do so.'

'No, thank you, my lady. I am happy to accept your judgement,' said Trelford, well aware that the press, several of whom were already leaving the court, would have the relevant passage on their front pages in the morning.

'Then let us move on,' said the judge. 'Perhaps you would like to call your next witness, Mr Trelford.'

'I am unable to do so, my lady, as he is currently attending a debate in the House of Commons. However, Major Fisher will be available to appear at ten o'clock tomorrow morning.'

39

HARRY WATCHED from his wooden bench in the third row as Colonel Marinkin entered the makeshift court-room. He stood to attention in front of the state prosecutor, saluted and remained standing.

Marinkin was dressed in a smarter uniform than the one Harry remembered from the time he was arrested; the one for special occasions, no doubt. The six buttons on his tunic shone, the crease in his trousers was sharp, and his boots were so finely polished that had he looked down, he would have seen his reflection in them. His five rows of medals would have left no one in any doubt that he had stared the enemy in the eye.

'Colonel, could you tell the court when you first became aware of the defendant?'

'Yes, comrade prosecutor. He came to Moscow some five years ago as the British representative at an inter-national book conference and gave the keynote speech on the opening day.'

'Did you hear that speech?'

'Yes I did, and it became clear to me that he believed the traitor Babakov had worked for many years inside the Kremlin and was a close associate of the late Comrade

Stalin. In fact, so persuasive was his argument that by the time he sat down almost everyone else in that hall also believed it.'

'Did you attempt to make contact with the defendant while he was in Moscow?'

'No, because he was travelling back to England the following day, and I confess I assumed that, like so many campaigns the West gets worked up about, it would only be a matter of time before another one came along to occupy their impatient minds.'

'But this particular cause didn't go away.'

'No, the defendant had clearly convinced himself that Babakov was telling the truth, and that if his book could be published the whole world would also believe him. Earlier this year, the defendant travelled to the United States on a luxury liner, owned by his wife's family. On arrival in New York, he visited a well-known publisher, no doubt to discuss the publication of Babakov's book, because the following day he boarded a train to Pittsburgh with the sole purpose of meeting the defector Yelena Babakov, the wife of the traitor. I have in this folder several photographs taken during this visit to Pittsburgh by one of our agents.'

Marinkin handed the folder to the judge's clerk, who passed it to the tribunal chairman. The three judges studied the photographs for some time before the chairman asked, 'How much time did the prisoner spend with Mrs Babakov?'

'Just over four hours. He then returned to New York. The following morning he visited his publisher once again, and later that day boarded the ship owned by his wife's family and travelled back to England.'

'Once he had returned, did you continue to maintain a high level of surveillance?'

'Yes. One of our senior operatives monitored his daily activities and reported that the defendant had enrolled for a Russian language course at Bristol University, not far from where he lives. One of my agents signed up for the same course and reported that the accused was a conscientious student, who studied far harder than any of his classmates. Shortly after he'd completed the course, he flew to Leningrad, just weeks before his visa expired.'

'Why didn't you arrest him immediately he arrived in Leningrad and put him on the next plane back to London?'

'Because I wanted to discover if he had any associates in Russia.'

'And did he?'

'No, the man's a loner, a romantic, someone who would have been more at home in ancient times when, like Jason, he would have gone in search of the Golden Fleece, which, for him in the twentieth century, was Babakov's equally fictitious story.'

'And was he successful?'

'Yes, he was. Babakov's wife had evidently told him exactly where he could find a copy of her husband's book, because no sooner had he arrived in Leningrad than he took a taxi to the Pushkin antiquarian bookshop on the outskirts of the City. It took him only a few minutes to locate the book he was looking for, which was concealed inside the dust jacket of another title, and must have been exactly where Mrs Babakov had told him it would be. He paid for the book and two others, then instructed the waiting taxi to take him back to the airport.'

'Where you arrested him?'

'Yes, but not immediately, because I wanted to see if he had an accomplice at the airport he would try to pass the book on to. But he simply bought a ticket for the same plane he had flown in on. We arrested him just before he attempted to board it.'

'Where is the book now?' asked the president of the tribunal.

'It has been destroyed, comrade chairman, but I have retained the title page for the records. It may interest the court to know that it appears to have been a printer's proof, so it was possibly the last copy in existence.'

'When you arrested the defendant, how did he react?' asked the prosecutor.

'He clearly didn't realize the severity of his crime because he kept asking on what charge he was being held.'

'Did you interview the taxi driver?' asked the prosecutor, 'and the elderly woman who worked in the bookshop, to see if they were in league with the defendant?'

'Yes, I did. Both turned out to be card-carrying members of the party, and it quickly became clear they had no earlier association with the defendant. I released them after a short interview, as I felt the less they knew about my enquiries the better.'

'Thank you, colonel. I have no more questions,' said the prosecutor, 'but my colleague may have,' he added before he sat down.

The chairman glanced in the direction of the young man who was seated at the other end of the bench. He rose and looked at the senior judge, but said nothing.

'Do you wish to cross-examine this witness?' she asked.

'That won't be necessary, comrade chairman. I am

quite content with the evidence presented by the chief of police.' He sat back down.

The chairman turned her attention back to the colonel.

'I congratulate you, comrade colonel, on a thoroughly comprehensive piece of detective work,' she said. 'But is there anything you would like to add that might assist us to make our judgement?'

'Yes, comrade. I am convinced that the prisoner is merely a naïve and gullible idealist, who believes that Babakov actually worked in the Kremlin. In my opinion he should be given one more chance to sign a confession. If he does so, I will personally supervise his deportation.'

'Thank you, colonel, I will bear that in mind. Now you may return to your important duties.'

The colonel saluted. As he turned to leave the room, he glanced briefly at Harry. A moment later he was gone.

That was the moment Harry realized that this was a show trial with a difference. Its sole purpose was to convince him that Anatoly Babakov was a fraud, so that he would return to England and tell everyone the truth, as it was being played out in that courtroom. But the carefully orchestrated charade still required him to sign a confession, and he wondered just how far they would go to achieve their aim.

'Comrade prosecutor,' said the tribunal chairman, 'you may now call your next witness.'

'Thank you, comrade chair,' he said, before rising once again. 'I call Anatoly Babakov.'

40

GILES SAT DOWN to breakfast and began to go through the morning papers. He was on his second cup of coffee by the time Sebastian joined him.

'How do they read?'

'I think a theatre critic would describe the opening day as having mixed reviews.'

'Then perhaps it's a good thing,' said Seb, 'that the judge instructed the jury not to read them.'

'They'll read them, believe me,' said Giles. 'Especially after the judge refused to let Trelford tell them what my mother had to say about Virginia in her will. Pour yourself a coffee and I'll read it to you.' Giles picked up the *Daily Mail* and waited for Seb to return to the breakfast table before he put his glasses back on and began to read. '"The remainder of my estate is to be left to my beloved daughters Emma and Grace to dispose of as they see fit, with the exception of my Siamese cat, Cleopatra, who I leave to Lady Virginia Fenwick, because they have so much in common. They are both beautiful, well-groomed, vain, cunning, manipulative predators, who assume that everyone else was put on earth to serve them, including my besotted son, who I can only pray will break from the spell she has cast on him before it is too late."'

'Bravo,' said Seb when his uncle had put the paper down. 'What a formidable lady. We could have done with her in the witness box. But what about the broadsheets, how are they reporting it?'

'The *Telegraph* is hedging its bets, although it does praise Makepeace for his forensic and analytical cross-examination of Emma. *The Times* speculates about why the defence rather than the prosecution is calling Fisher. You'll see it under the headline "Hostile Witness",' said Giles, sliding *The Times* across the table.

'I have a feeling Fisher won't get mixed reviews.'

'Just be sure to keep staring at him while he's in the witness box. He won't like that.'

'Funnily enough,' said Seb, 'one female member of the jury keeps staring at me.'

'That's good,' said Giles. 'Be sure to smile at her occasionally, but not too often in case the judge notices,' he added as Emma walked into the room.

'How are they?' she asked, looking down at the papers.

'About as good as we could have expected,' said Giles. 'The *Mail* has turned Mother's will into folklore, and the serious journalists want to know why Fisher is being called by us and not them.'

'They'll find out soon enough,' said Emma, taking a seat at the table. 'So which one should I start with?'

'Perhaps *The Times*,' said Giles, 'but don't bother with the *Telegraph*.'

'Not for the first time,' said Emma, picking up the *Telegraph*, 'I wish I could read tomorrow's papers today.'

—◦—

'Good morning,' said Mrs Justice Lane once the jury had settled. 'Proceedings will begin today with a rather unusual occurrence. Mr Trelford's next witness, Major Alexander Fisher MP, is not giving evidence by choice, but has been subpoenaed by the defence. When Mr Trelford applied for a subpoena, I had to decide if his evidence was admissible. On balance, I concluded that Mr Trelford did have the right to call Major Fisher, as his name is mentioned during the exchange between Mrs Clifton and Lady Virginia that is at the core of this case, and he may therefore be able to throw some light on the situation. You must not, however,' she emphasized, 'read anything into the fact that Major Fisher wasn't included on Sir Edward Makepeace's list of witnesses.'

'But they will,' whispered Giles to Emma.

The judge looked down at the clerk of the court. 'Has Major Fisher arrived?'

'He has, my lady.'

'Then please call him.'

'Call Major Alexander Fisher MP,' bellowed the clerk.

The double doors at the back of the courtroom swung open and in marched Fisher, with a swagger that took even Giles by surprise. Clearly becoming a Member of Parliament had only added to his considerable self-esteem.

He took the Bible in his right hand and delivered the oath, without once looking at the card the clerk held up for him. When Mr Trelford rose from his place, Fisher stared at him as if he had the enemy in his sights.

'Good morning, Major Fisher,' said Trelford, but received no response. 'Would you be kind enough to state your name and occupation for the court records?'

'My name is Major Alexander Fisher, and I am the

Member of Parliament for Bristol Docklands,' he said, looking directly at Giles.

'At the time of Barrington Shipping's annual general meeting that is the subject of this libel, were you a director of the company?'

'I was.'

'And was it Mrs Clifton who invited you to sit on the board?'

'No, it was not.'

'So who was it who asked you to represent them as a director?'

'Lady Virginia Fenwick.'

'And why, may I ask? Were you friends, or was it simply a professional relationship?'

'I would like to think both,' said Fisher, glancing down at Lady Virginia, who nodded and smiled.

'And what particular expertise did you have to offer Lady Virginia?'

'I was a stockbroker by profession before I became an MP.'

'I see,' said Trelford. 'So you were able to offer advice to Lady Virginia on her share portfolio, and because of your wise counsel, she invited you to represent her on the board of Barrington's.'

'I couldn't have put it better myself, Mr Trelford,' said Fisher, a smug smile appearing on his face.

'But are you sure that was the only reason Lady Virginia selected you, major?'

'Yes, I am sure,' barked Fisher, the smile disappearing.

'I'm just a little puzzled, major, how a stockbroker based in Bristol becomes a professional advisor to a lady living in London, who must have access to any number of leading stockbrokers in the City. So perhaps I should ask how you first met.'

'Lady Virginia supported me when I first stood for Parliament as the Conservative candidate for Bristol Docklands.'

'And who was the Labour candidate at that election?'

'Sir Giles Barrington.'

'Lady Virginia's ex-husband and Mrs Clifton's brother?'

'Yes.'

'So now we know why Lady Virginia chose you as her representative on the board.'

'What are you suggesting?' snapped Fisher.

'Quite simply, that if you had stood for Parliament in any other constituency, you would never have come across Lady Virginia.' Mr Trelford looked at the jury while he waited for Fisher's reply, because he was confident none would be forthcoming. 'Now that we have established your relationship with the plaintiff, let us consider the value and importance of your professional advice. You will recall, major, that I earlier asked you if you advised Lady Virginia on her share portfolio, and you confirmed that you did.'

'That is correct.'

'Then perhaps you can tell the jury which shares, other than Barrington Shipping, you advised her ladyship on?' Again, Mr Trelford waited patiently, before he spoke again. 'I suspect the answer is none, and that her only interest in you was as an insider, to let her know what was going on at Barrington's, so both of you could take advantage of any information to which you were privy as a board member.'

'That is an outrageous suggestion,' said Fisher, looking up at the judge. But she remained impassive.

'If that is the case, major, could you deny that on three separate occasions you advised Lady Virginia to sell her shares in Barrington's – I have the dates, the times and the amounts in front of me – and on each occasion, just a couple of days later the company announced some bad news.'

'That is what advisors are for, Mr Trelford.'

'And then some three weeks after that you bought the shares back, which I would suggest was for two reasons. First, to make a quick profit, and second, to be sure that she retained her seven and a half per cent of the company's stock so you didn't lose your place on the board. Otherwise you wouldn't have been privy to any more inside information, would you?'

'That is a disgraceful slur on my professional reputation,' barked Fisher.

'Is it?' said Trelford, holding up a sheet of paper for everyone to see, before reading out the figures in front of him. 'On the three transactions in question, Lady Virginia made profits of £17,400, £29,320, and £70,100 respectively.'

'It's not a crime to make a profit for one's client, Mr Trelford.'

'No, it most certainly is not, major, but why did you need to use a broker in Hong Kong to carry out these transactions, a Mr Benny Driscoll?'

'Benny is an old friend who used to work in the city, and I am loyal to my friends, Mr Trelford.'

'I'm sure you are, major, but were you aware that at the time of your dealings, the Irish Garda had a warrant out for Mr Driscoll's arrest for fraud and share manipulation?'

Sir Edward was quickly on his feet.

'Yes, yes, Sir Edward,' said Mrs Justice Lane. 'I do hope, Mr Trelford, you are not suggesting that Major Fisher was aware of this warrant but was still willing to do business with Mr Driscoll?'

'That would have been my next question, my lady,' said Trelford, the innocent schoolboy look returning.

'No, I did not know,' protested Fisher, 'and had I done so, I certainly wouldn't have continued to deal with him.'

'That's reassuring,' said Trelford. He opened a large black file in front of him and took out a single sheet of paper, covered in figures. 'When you purchased shares on behalf of Lady Virginia, how were you paid?'

'On commission. One per cent of the buying or selling price, which is standard practice.'

'Very right and proper,' said Trelford, making a show of putting the sheet of paper back in his file. He then extracted a second sheet, which he studied with equal interest. 'Tell me, major, were you aware that on each occasion after you had asked your loyal friend, Mr Driscoll, to carry out these transactions for Lady Virginia, he also bought and sold shares in Barrington's on his own behalf, which he must have known was illegal.'

'I had no idea he was doing that, and I would have reported him to the Stock Exchange had I been aware of it.'

'Would you indeed? So you had no idea that he made several thousand pounds piggy-backing your transactions?'

'No, I did not.'

'And that he has recently been suspended by the Hong Kong Exchange for unprofessional conduct?'

'I was not aware of that, but then I haven't dealt with him for several years.'

'Haven't you?' said Trelford, returning the second sheet to his file and taking out a third. He adjusted his glasses and studied a row of figures on the page in front of him before saying, 'Did you also, on three separate occasions, buy and sell shares for yourself, making a handsome profit each time?'

Trelford continued to stare at the sheet of paper he held in his hand, painfully aware that all Fisher had to say was 'I did not', and his bluff would have been called. However, the major hesitated, just for a moment, which allowed Trelford to add during the brief silence, 'I don't have to remind you, Major Fisher, as a Member of Parliament, that you are under oath, and of the consequences of committing perjury.' Trelford continued to study the row of figures in front of him.

'But I didn't make a profit on the third transaction,' Fisher blurted out. 'In fact, I made a loss.'

A gasp went up around the court, followed by an outbreak of chattering. Trelford waited for complete silence before he continued. 'So you made a profit on the first two transactions, major, but suffered a loss on the third?'

Fisher shuffled uneasily in the box, but made no attempt to reply.

'Major Fisher, you stated earlier to the court that it's not a crime to make a profit for one's client,' said Trelford, looking down at a scribbled note to check the major's exact words.

'Yes, I did,' said Fisher, trying to recover.

'But as a qualified stockbroker you will have known

that it was a crime,' continued Trelford, picking up a thick red leather-bound volume from the bench in front of him and opening it at a page marked with a slip of paper, 'to trade shares in a company of which you sit on the board.' Trelford read out the exact words: *unless you have informed the chairman of that company and sought legal guidance*'. He let his words sink in, before slamming the book shut and asking quietly, 'Did you inform Mrs Clifton, or seek legal guidance?'

Fisher gripped the sides of the witness box to stop his hands from shaking.

'Can you tell the court how much profit you made when you bought and sold your Barrington's shares?' asked Trelford as he continued to look down at a hotel bill from his recent trip to Hong Kong. He waited for some time before he placed the receipt back in his file, looked up at the judge and said, 'My lady, as Major Fisher seems unwilling to answer any more of my questions, I see no purpose in continuing.' He sat down and smiled at Emma.

'Sir Edward,' said Mrs Justice Lane, 'do you wish to cross-examine this witness?'

'Just a couple of questions, if I may,' said Sir Edward, sounding unusually subdued.

'Major Fisher, is there any suggestion that Lady Virginia Fenwick was aware that you were trading in Barrington's shares on your own behalf?'

'No, sir.'

'Correct me if I'm wrong, but you were simply her advisor, and all the transactions carried out in her name were conducted within the full rigours of the law?'

'They were indeed, Sir Edward.'

'I am obliged to you for that clarification. No more questions, my lady.'

The judge was writing furiously while Fisher remained motionless in the witness box, looking like a rabbit caught in the headlights. Finally she put her pen down and said, 'Before you leave the court, Major Fisher, I must tell you that I intend to send a transcript of your evidence to the Department of Public Prosecutions, so they can decide if any further legal action should be taken.'

As the major stepped out of the witness box and made his way out of the courtroom, the press corps deserted their benches and followed him out into the corridor like a pack of baying hounds pursuing a wounded fox.

Giles leaned forward, patted Trelford on the back and said, 'Well done, sir. You crucified him.'

'Him, yes, but not her. Thanks to those two carefully worded questions from Sir Edward, Lady Virginia lives to fight another day.'

41

SOMETHING WAS WRONG. Surely this couldn't possibly be Anatoly Babakov. Harry stared at the frail skeleton of a man who shuffled into the courtroom and collapsed on to the stool opposite the state prosecutor.

Babakov was dressed in a suit and shirt that hung on him as if he were a coat hanger. They were both several sizes too large for him, and Harry's first thought was that he must have borrowed them from a stranger that morning. And then he realized that they were Babakov's own suit and shirt; he just hadn't worn them since the day he'd been sent to prison, all those years ago. His hair was thinning, and the few strands left were steel grey. His eyes, also grey, had sunk back into their sockets, and his skin was lined and parched, not from the heat of the sun, but from endless hours of exposure to the frozen winds born on the Siberian plains. Babakov looked about seventy, even eighty, although Harry knew they were contemporaries so he couldn't be much more than fifty.

The state prosecutor rose from his place; the sycophant replaced by the bully. He looked right through Babakov and addressed him with a cold arrogance, so different from the manner afforded to the comrade colonel when he'd been in the witness box.

'Tell the court your name and number,' he demanded.

'Babakov, seven-four-one-six-two, comrade prosecutor.'

'Do not address me in that familiar manner.'

The prisoner bowed his head. 'I apologize, sir.'

'Before you were convicted, Babakov, what was your occupation?'

'I was a school teacher in the seventh district of Moscow.'

'How many years did you teach at that school?'

'Thirteen years, sir.'

'And the subject you taught?'

'English.'

'What were your qualifications?'

'I graduated from the Foreign Languages Institute in Moscow in 1941.'

'So after graduating, your first job was as a school teacher, and you've never worked anywhere else?'

'No, sir, I have not.'

'During those thirteen years as a school teacher, did you ever visit the Kremlin?'

'No, I did not, sir. Never.'

The vehemence with which Babakov said 'Never' was a clear indication to Harry that he regarded this mock trial as worthy only of ridicule. Every Soviet schoolchild had visited the Kremlin at some time to pay homage at Lenin's tomb. If Babakov had been a schoolmaster he would even have supervised such visits. Harry had no way of letting him know that he'd got the message without breaking the thin shell of deception.

'At any time did you ever meet our revered leader

the chairman of the Presidium Council, Comrade Stalin?'
continued the state prosecutor.

'Yes, on one occasion when I was a student he visited
the Foreign Languages Institute to present the annual
state awards.'

'Did he speak to you?'

'Yes, he congratulated me on being awarded my
degree.'

Harry knew Babakov had won the Lenin medal
and come top of his class. Why didn't he mention that?
Because it wasn't part of the well-prepared script he had
been given, and which he was sticking to. The answers
had probably been written by the same person who was
asking the questions.

'Other than that brief encounter, did you ever come
across Comrade Stalin again?'

'No, sir, never.' Once again, he exaggerated the word
'never'.

Harry was beginning to form a plan in his mind. If it
was to work, he would have to convince those three stony-
faced comrades sitting in judgement that he believed
every word Babakov was uttering, and was appalled ever
to have been taken in by the man.

'I should now like to move on to 1954, when you
attempted to have a book published, in which you claimed
that you had worked on the president's private staff for
thirteen years as his personal interpreter, when in fact
you had never once entered the Kremlin. What made you
think you could possibly get away with such a deception?'

'Because, like me, no one who worked at the Sarkoski
Press had ever been inside the Kremlin. They had only
seen Comrade Stalin from a distance when he reviewed
our troops at the May Day parade. So it wasn't difficult

to convince them that I had been a member of his inner circle.'

Harry shook his head in disgust and frowned at Babakov, hoping he wasn't overdoing it. He saw the chairman make a note on the pad in front of her. Was there even the suggestion of a smile?

'And is it also true that you planned to defect, in the hope of having your book published in the West, with the sole purpose of making a large sum of money?'

'Yes, I thought that if I could fool the people at the Sarkoski Press, how much easier it would be to convince the Americans and the British that I had been a party official working alongside the chairman. After all, how many people from the West have ever visited the Soviet Union, let alone spoken to the comrade chairman, who everyone knows didn't speak a word of English?'

Harry put his head in his hands and, when he looked up, he stared at Babakov with contempt. The chairman made another note on her pad.

'Once you'd completed the book, why didn't you defect at the first opportunity?'

'I didn't have enough money. I had been promised an advance on the day of publication, but I was arrested before I could collect it.'

'But your wife did defect.'

'Yes, I sent her ahead of me with our life savings, hoping I would be able to join her later.'

Harry was appalled by how the prosecutor was mixing half-truths with lies, and wondered how they could possibly think, even for a moment, that he might be deceived by this pantomime. But that was their weakness. Clearly all of them were taken in by their own propaganda, so he decided to play them at their own game.

He nodded whenever the prosecutor seemed to have scored a point. But then he recalled his drama teacher at school chastising him, on more than one occasion, for overacting, so he reined it in.

'Did your wife take a copy of the book with her?' demanded the prosecutor.

'No. It hadn't been published by the time she left, and in any case she would have been searched when she tried to cross the border, and if she'd had the book with her she would have been arrested and sent straight back to Moscow.'

'But thanks to some brilliant detective work, you were arrested, charged and sentenced before even one copy of your book reached the shops.'

'Yes,' said Babakov, bowing his head again.

'And when you were charged with offences against the State, how did you plead?'

'Guilty to all charges.'

'And the people's court sentenced you to twenty years' hard labour.'

'Yes, sir. I was lucky to receive such a light sentence for the despicable crime I had committed against the nation.'

Once again Harry realized that Babakov was letting him know he considered the whole trial to be a sham. But it was still important for Harry to look as if he was being taken in by the play within a play.

'That concludes my examination of this witness, comrade chairman,' said the prosecutor, who then bowed low and sat down.

The chairman glanced at the young man who was seated at the other end of the bench.

'Do you have any questions for this witness?'

The young man rose unsteadily to his feet. 'No, I do not, comrade chairman. The prisoner Babakov is clearly an enemy of the state.'

Harry felt sorry for the young man, who probably believed every word he'd heard in the courtroom that morning. Harry gave a slight nod to show he also agreed, although the young man's inexperience had once again given the game away. If he had read more Chekhov he would have realized that silence can often be more powerful than the spoken word.

'Take him away,' said the tribunal chairman.

As Babakov was led out of the courtroom, Harry bowed his head as if he no longer wanted anything to do with the man.

'Comrades, it has been a long day,' said the chairman, turning to the jury. 'As Monday is a national holiday, on which we will all remember those brave men and women who sacrificed their lives in the Siege of Leningrad, this court will not reconvene until Tuesday morning, when I will sum up the State's position, so you can decide if the prisoner is guilty.'

Harry wanted to laugh. He wasn't even going to be allowed to give evidence, but he was now well aware that this was a tragedy, not a comedy, and he still had his part to play.

The tribunal president rose from her chair and led her colleagues out of the courtroom. No sooner had the door closed behind them than two prison guards grabbed Harry by the arms, and dragged him out of the room.

As he had nearly four days of solitude ahead of him, he was already looking forward to the challenge of seeing how much more he could remember of *Uncle Joe*. Chapter three. He began mouthing the words as they bundled him out of court.

> *Stalin not only made history, but was also happy to rewrite it, and there is no better example than the way he treated his family. His second wife, Nadya, took her own life because 'she would rather die than remain married to such an evil tyrant'. On hearing of her death, Stalin immediately ordered that her suicide was to remain a state secret, as he feared the truth would bring him disgrace in the eyes of his comrades and enemies alike . . .*

One of the guards unlocked the heavy cell door and his colleague pushed the prisoner inside.

Even as he fell on the floor, Harry sensed that he was not alone in the cell. He looked up and saw him hunched in the corner, a forefinger pressed firmly to his lips.

'Speak only in English,' were Babakov's first words.

Harry nodded, and looked back to see one of the guards staring through the bars. The charade was still being played out. He crouched down a few feet away from Babakov.

'They need to believe you were convinced by everything you've just witnessed,' Babakov whispered. 'If they do, they'll allow you to go home.'

'But how will that help you?' asked Harry. 'Especially if I have to sign a confession saying that I accept you made it all up.'

'Because I can tell you how to get your hands on a copy of *Uncle Joe* without being caught.'

'Is that still possible?'

'Yes,' said Babakov.

After listening carefully to his new cellmate's whispered explanation, Harry smiled. 'Why didn't I think of that?'

◄○►

'I appreciate you finding the time to see me,' said Griff, 'especially while you're in the middle of your sister's trial.'

'Urgent isn't a word you use often,' said Giles, 'and as you caught the first train to London, I assumed it had to be serious.'

'It won't become public for a few days,' said Griff, 'but my mole in the local Tory party office tells me there's going to be a meeting of their executive committee this evening, and there's only one item on the agenda. To call for the member's resignation.'

'And that would mean a by-election,' said Giles thoughtfully.

'Which is why I caught the first train to London.'

'But Conservative Central Office would never allow Fisher to resign while the government are so far behind in the opinion polls.'

'They won't have a lot of choice if the press goes on calling Fisher "the galloping major", and you know only too well what that lot are like, once they smell blood. Frankly, I can't see Fisher lasting more than a few days. So the sooner you get back down to the constituency, the better.'

'I will, the moment the trial's over.'

'When is that likely to be?'

'A few more days. A week at the most.'

'If you could come down at the weekend, be seen shopping in Broadmead on Saturday morning, go and watch City play in the afternoon, and then attend Matins at St Mary Redcliffe on Sunday, it would remind people you're still alive and kicking.'

'If there is a by-election, how would you rate my chances?'

'Of being re-selected as the candidate, or of winning the seat back?'

'Both.'

'You're still just about favourite to be the candidate, although several women on the executive keep raising the fact that you've had two marriages break down. But I'm working on them, and it helps that you turned down a place in the Lords because you wanted to fight the seat again.'

'I told you that in the strictest confidence,' said Giles.

'And I told all sixteen members of the executive committee in the strictest confidence,' replied Griff.

Giles smiled. 'And my chances of winning back the seat?'

'A poodle wearing a red rosette would win the by-election if all Ted Heath can come up with is to call a state of emergency every time there's a strike.'

'Then perhaps it's time to tell you my other news.'

Griff raised an eyebrow.

'I'm going to ask Karin to marry me.'

'Could it possibly be after the by-election,' begged Griff.

42

FOR EVERYONE involved in the libel trial, it turned out to be a long weekend.

Following a short consultation with Mr Trelford immediately after the court had been adjourned for the day, Giles drove Emma down to Gloucestershire.

'Would you prefer to stay at the hall over the weekend? Marsden will take care of you.'

'It's kind of you to offer,' said Emma, 'but I ought to be at home just in case Harry calls.'

'I think that's unlikely,' said Giles quietly.

'Why?' demanded Emma.

'I visited Sir Alan at Number Ten before the court resumed yesterday morning, and he told me Harry had booked himself on to a BOAC flight last Friday evening, but never boarded the plane.'

'Then they must have arrested him.'

'I fear so.'

'Why didn't you tell me immediately?'

'Moments before you went into the witness box? I don't think that would have been helpful.'

'Did Sir Alan have any other news?'

'He told me that if we haven't heard from Harry by

Monday morning, the foreign secretary will call in the Russian ambassador and demand an explanation.'

'What good will that do?'

'He'll realize that Harry will be on the front page of every paper around the world the next day if they don't release him, which is the last thing the Russians will want.'

'Then why arrest him in the first place?' demanded Emma.

'They're up to something, but even Sir Alan can't work out what it is.'

Giles didn't tell Emma about his recent experience when he'd tried to enter East Berlin, not least because he'd assumed that Harry was unlikely to get beyond passport control and would have been frogmarched back on to the next plane to Heathrow. It made no sense that they would detain the president of English PEN without good reason. Even the Soviets don't like bad publicity if they can possibly avoid it. Like Sir Alan, he couldn't work out what they were up to.

◄◦►

During a sleepless weekend, Emma occupied herself answering letters, reading, even polishing some of the family silver, but she was never more than a few paces away from the phone.

Sebastian rang on Saturday morning and when she heard his voice she thought for a moment, just a moment, that it was Harry.

◄◦►

'It's ours to lose,' was the expression Sir Edward used during the consultation with Lady Virginia in his chambers on the Friday evening. He advised her to spend a quiet weekend, no late nights, and not to drink too much. She had to be rested, calm and ready to do battle with Trelford when she stepped into the witness box on Monday morning.

'Just confirm that you always allowed Major Fisher, your professional advisor, to handle anything to do with Barrington's.' 'At arm's length,' was the phrase he kept repeating. 'You've never heard of Mr Benny Driscoll, and it came as a great shock when you discovered that Cedric Hardcastle had been dumping all his shares on the market the weekend before the AGM. You simply felt, as a stock-holder, that Mrs Clifton should tell you the truth and not fob you off with a self-serving platitude. And whatever you do, don't rise to Trelford's bait, because he'll try to tickle you under the chin like a trout. Swim in the deep water and don't be tempted to come up to the surface because, if you do, he'll hook you and slowly reel you in. And finally, just because things have gone well for us so far, that doesn't mean you should become over-confident. I've seen far too many cases lost on the last day of the trial by a client who thought they'd already won. Remember,' he repeated, 'it's ours to lose.'

◄○►

Sebastian spent most of his weekend at the bank, trying to catch up with a backlog of unanswered correspondence and dozens of 'urgent' queries that Rachel had left in his in-tray. It took all of Saturday morning just to tackle the first pile.

Mr Bishara's inspired choice as the new chairman of Farthings had been greeted in the City with acclamation, which made Seb's life much easier. A few customers closed their accounts when Sloane departed, but many more returned when they discovered his successor would be Ross Buchanan: an experienced, shrewd operator, with bottom, was how the *Sunday Times* described him.

Sebastian called his mother just before lunch on Saturday and tried to reassure her that there was nothing for her to worry about.

'He probably can't get through. Can you imagine what the Russian telephone service must be like?'

But he wasn't convinced by his own words. His father had expressly told him he would be back in time for the trial, and he couldn't help remembering one of his papa's favourite maxims, 'There's only one excuse to be late for a lady: death.'

Seb grabbed a quick lunch with Vic Kaufman, who was worried about his own father, but for a different reason. It was the first time he'd mentioned Alzheimer's.

'I'm becoming painfully aware that Dad is a one-man band. He beats the big drum while the rest of us are occasionally allowed to bang the cymbals. Perhaps the time has come for Farthings and Kaufman's to consider a merger.'

Seb couldn't pretend that the idea hadn't crossed his mind since he'd become deputy chairman, but Vic's suggestion couldn't have come at a worse time, while he had so many other things on his mind.

'Let's talk about it as soon as the trial is over. And by the way,' Seb added, 'be sure to keep a close eye on Sloane because rumour in the city is that he's also showing a keen interest in your father's health.'

Seb was back behind his desk just after two o'clock and went on attacking the pile of unopened mail for the rest of the day. He didn't get home until after midnight.

A security man let him into the bank on Sunday

morning, but it wasn't until late on Sunday afternoon that he came across a cream envelope marked *PRIVATE & CONFIDENTIAL*, with six George Washington stamps in the top right-hand corner. He ripped it open and read a letter from Rosemary Wolfe. How could he possibly take time off to go to America now? How could he possibly not?

◄◦►

Giles did as he was told. He spent Saturday morning walking up and down Broadmead carrying a large, empty Marks and Spencer shopping bag. He shook hands with anyone who stopped to talk to him about the dreadful Conservative government, and that awful Ted Heath. If anyone raised the subject of Major Fisher, he remained diplomatic.

'I wish you were still our MP.'

'If only I'd known, I would never have voted for him.'

'It's a scandal. The damn man ought to resign,' to which Giles responded with a well-prepared reply: 'That's a decision for Major Fisher and his constituency party to make, so we'll just have to wait and see.'

Later, he sat at the bar of a packed, noisy pub and had a ploughman's lunch with Griff, washed down with a pint of Somerset cider.

'If Fisher resigns and a by-election is called,' said Griff, 'I've already told the *Bristol Evening Post* that the local Labour party won't be interviewing anyone other than the former member.'

'Cheers,' said Giles, raising his glass. 'How did you manage that?'

'Twisted a few arms, made the odd threat, offered the occasional bribe, and promised the chairman an MBE.'

'Nothing new then?'

'Except that I did remind the committee that if the Tories are going to have a new name on the ballot paper, perhaps we should stick with one the voters are familiar with.'

'What are you doing about the increased aircraft noise what's comin' out of Filton? It's a bloody disgrace!'

'I'm no longer your MP,' Giles reminded the man politely as he headed towards the door.

'I didn't know that. When did that happen?'

Even Griff had the grace to laugh. After they had left the pub they both donned their red and white scarves and along with six thousand other supporters watched Bristol City beat Birmingham City 2–1.

In the evening, Emma came to Barrington Hall for dinner, but she wasn't very good company. She left long before Marsden served coffee.

Giles settled down in his grandfather's favourite chair in the drawing room, a brandy in one hand, a cigar in the other. He was thinking about Karin when the phone rang. He grabbed it, hoping to hear Harry's voice on the other end of the line, but it was Griff. Who else would call him at that time of night? When Griff told him the news about Fisher, Giles felt sorry for the man for the first time in his life.

◄○►

Mr Trelford spent his weekend preparing for Lady Virginia's cross-examination. But it wasn't proving easy. She would have learnt from Fisher's mistake, and he could hear Eddie Makepeace advising her to remain calm at all times and not to let him goad her. However hard he tried, he couldn't come up with a ploy to break through her defence.

The wastepaper basket was full, and the A4 pad in front of him was blank. How could he demonstrate to the jury that Emma's mother had been right when she compared Virginia to her Siamese cat, Cleopatra? *They are both beautiful, well-groomed, vain, cunning, manipulative predators, who assume that everyone else was put on earth to serve them.*

It was two o'clock in the morning and he was going over some old Barrington's boardroom minutes when he came up with a new line of questioning.

‐‐◦‐‐

Major Fisher had driven out of the Commons car park soon after the House had risen on Friday afternoon. One or two colleagues had wished him luck, but they didn't sound convincing. As he drove down to the West Country, he thought about the letter he would have to write if his local executive committee didn't support him.

He remained in his flat all the next day, not turning the front page of the morning papers, not bothering with breakfast or lunch as the lonely hours ticked by. Long before the sun was over the yardarm he began opening bottles and draining them. During the evening, he sat by the phone and waited impatiently to hear how the committee had voted on the No Confidence motion. He returned to the kitchen, opened a tin of pilchards, but left them on the table, untouched. He sat down in the drawing room to watch an episode of *Dad's Army*, but didn't laugh. Finally, he picked up a copy of Friday's *Bristol Evening Post*, and looked again at the front-page headline:

LOCAL CONSERVATIVES TO DECIDE FATE
OF MP. SEE LEADER, PAGE ELEVEN.

He turned to page eleven. He and the editor had always been on good terms, so he had rather hoped . . . but he didn't get beyond the headline,

DO THE HONOURABLE THING, MAJOR

He tossed the paper aside and didn't turn on the light as the sun disappeared behind the highest building.

The phone rang at twelve minutes past ten. He grabbed the receiver, and immediately recognized the voice of the local party chairman. 'Good evening, Peter.'

'Good evening, major. I won't beat about the bush. I'm sorry to say that the committee didn't support you.'

'Was it close?'

'I'm afraid not,' said Maynard. 'It was unanimous. So it might be wise for you to write a letter offering your resignation rather than waiting for the executive committee to formally de-select you. So much more civilized that way, don't you think? I am sorry, Alex.'

No sooner had he put the phone down than it rang again. It was a reporter from the *Post* asking him if he wanted to comment on the unanimous decision to call for his resignation. He didn't even bother to say 'No comment' before slamming the phone back down.

In an alcoholic blur, he walked unsteadily through to his study, sat down and placed his head in his hands while he thought about the wording of the letter. He took a sheet of House of Commons paper from the letter rack and began to write. When he'd finished, he waited for the ink to dry before he folded it, sealed it in an envelope and placed it on his desk.

He leant down and opened the bottom drawer of his desk, took out his service revolver, put the muzzle in his mouth and pulled the trigger.

43

THE COURTROOM was packed, the two combatants ready. All that was needed was for the bell to ring so the first punch could be landed.

On one side of the ring sat Mr Trelford, who was going over the order of his questions for the last time. Giles, Emma and Seb sat behind him, talking quietly, making sure they didn't disturb him.

Giles looked up as a police constable entered the courtroom, walked across to counsel's bench and handed Mr Trelford an envelope. The word *URGENT* was written below his name. Trelford opened it, extracted a letter and read it slowly. Giles learnt nothing from the expression on the barrister's face, but he recognized the familiar green portcullis crest at the head of the paper.

Sir Edward sat alone with his client on the other side of the ring, delivering his final instructions. 'Be calm, take your time before answering each question,' he whispered. 'You're not in a hurry. Face the jury, and never forget that they are the only people in the room who matter.'

The crowd fell silent, and everyone rose when the bell rang for the first round and the referee entered the ring. If Mrs Justice Lane was surprised to find the press and public galleries of her courtroom packed on a Monday morning, she didn't show it. She bowed, and everyone in the well of the court returned the compliment. Once they'd all settled back into their seats, with only Sir Edward still standing, she invited the eminent silk to call his first witness.

Virginia walked slowly up to the witness box, and when she took the oath, she could barely be heard. She wore a black tailored suit that emphasized her slim figure, a black pillbox hat, no jewellery and little make-up, clearly wanting to remind all those present of Major Fisher's untimely death. Had the jury retired there and then to deliver their verdict, the result would have been unanimous, and Sir Edward would happily have settled for that.

'For the record, would you tell the court your name and where you live,' asked Sir Edward, as he adjusted his wig.

'Virginia Fenwick. I live alone in a modest flat in Cadogan Gardens, SW3.'

Giles smiled. My name is Lady Virginia Alice Sarah Lucinda Fenwick, only daughter of the ninth Earl of Fenwick, and I have homes in Scotland and Tuscany, and a large apartment on three floors in Knightsbridge, with a butler, maid and chauffeur, would have been more accurate.

'Can I confirm that you were formerly married to Sir Giles Barrington, from whom you are now divorced?'

'Sadly yes,' said Virginia, turning towards the jury. 'Giles was the love of my life, but his family never considered me good enough for him.'

Giles would have happily throttled the woman, while Emma wanted to jump up and protest. Mr Trelford crossed out four of his well-prepared questions.

'But despite that, and all you've been put through, you still don't bear a grudge against Mrs Clifton?'

'No, I do not. In truth, it was with a heavy heart that I finally issued this writ, because Mrs Clifton has many admirable qualities, and has unquestionably been an outstanding chairman of a public company, making her a role model for aspiring professional women.'

Mr Trelford began to write out some new questions.

'Then why did you issue the writ?'

'Because she accused me of wilfully attempting to destroy her family company. Nothing could be further from the truth. I simply wanted to know on behalf of ordinary shareholders, like myself, if one of her directors had disposed of all his stock the weekend before the AGM, because in my opinion that would have greatly harmed the company. But rather than answer my question, she chose to belittle me, giving everyone in that crowded hall the impression that I didn't know what I was talking about.'

'Word perfect,' said Giles under his breath, which caused Mr Trelford to smile. He turned and whispered, 'I agree, but then while Sir Edward is on his feet, she knows what questions to expect. She'll have no crib sheet to rely on when I cross-examine her.'

'In particular,' continued Sir Edward, 'you are referring to Mrs Clifton's reply to the quite valid question you raised at the AGM.'

'Yes. Rather than answer that question, she decided to humiliate me and ruin my reputation, in front of a packed audience, many of them my friends. I was left with no alternative but to seek the recourse of the law.'

'And you were referring on that occasion, not to Major Fisher, as Mrs Clifton erroneously suggested, but to Mr Cedric Hardcastle, who, as you pointed out, sold his entire stock over the weekend before the AGM, thus placing the company in jeopardy.'

'That is correct, Sir Edward.'

'Did she really just flutter her eyelids?' whispered Giles.

'And the late Major Fisher was one of your financial advisors?'

'Yes, and whenever he recommended I should buy or sell shares, I followed his advice. I always found him honest, trustworthy and utterly professional.'

Emma couldn't bring herself to look at the jury. Giles did, to find they were hanging on Virginia's every word.

Sir Edward lowered his voice, like a great thespian demanding silence before he delivered his closing line. 'Let me finally ask you, Lady Virginia, if you have any regrets about issuing this libel writ against Mrs Clifton?'

'Yes, I do, Sir Edward. The tragic and unnecessary death of my dear friend, Major Alex Fisher, makes the outcome of this trial unimportant. If by withdrawing this action I could have saved his life, I would have done so without hesitation.' She turned to the jury, took a handkerchief from her sleeve and dabbed away an imaginary tear.

'I am sorry you have been put through this ordeal, Lady Virginia, so soon after the death of your friend and advisor Major Fisher. No more questions, my lady.'

If they had been alone together in chambers, Trelford would have congratulated his learned friend on a quite masterful cross-examination. He opened his file to see the words Giles had advised, written at the top of the first page. *MAKE HER LOSE HER TEMPER.* He then looked down at his first question, newly minted.

'Lady Virginia,' he said, emphasizing the word 'lady', 'you told the court of your admiration for Mrs Clifton, and your devotion to her brother Sir Giles Barrington, but despite that, you didn't invite a single member of the Barrington or Clifton families to attend your wedding to Sir Giles.'

'That was a shared decision, Mr Trelford. Giles felt every bit as strongly about it as I did.'

'If that is the case, Lady Virginia, perhaps you could explain your father's words at the time of the wedding, recorded in the *Daily Express* by William Hickey: *My daughter was ready to call off the whole thing if Giles hadn't agreed to her demands.*'

'Gossip column tittle-tattle, written to sell newspapers, Mr Trelford. Frankly, I'm surprised you feel the need to resort to such tactics.'

Sir Edward couldn't resist a smile. His client had clearly seen that one coming.

'And later, in your evidence,' said Trelford, moving swiftly on, 'you went on to blame Mrs Clifton for your divorce.'

'She can be a very determined woman,' said Virginia, 'as I'm sure you yourself have discovered.'

'But surely your divorce had nothing to do with Mrs Clifton, but was rather caused by the quarrels you had with your husband about him being cut out of his mother's will?'

'That is not true, Mr Trelford. Giles's inheritance never interested me. I married him for richer, for poorer, and frankly, since you mention it, I was richer than he was.'

This caused enough laughter in court for the judge to scowl menacingly down from her bench.

'So it wasn't you who insisted that Sir Giles should issue a writ against his own sister, disputing the validity of his mother's will? That was another shared decision?'

'No, that was Giles's decision. I think I advised against it at the time.'

'Perhaps you'd like to reconsider that answer, Lady Virginia, as I can always call Sir Giles as a witness, and ask him to set the record straight.'

'Well, I admit that I felt Giles had been treated rather shabbily by his family, and that he had the right at least to question the validity of his mother's will, as it had been rewritten while the poor lady was in hospital, only days before she died.'

'And what was the court's decision on that occasion?'

'The judge came down in favour of Mrs Clifton.'

'No, Lady Virginia, he did not. I have Mr Justice Cameron's judgement to hand. He ruled that the will was valid, and that Mrs Clifton's mother was of sound mind when she executed it. Which is particularly relevant, considering what she had to say about you at the time.'

Sir Edward was quickly on his feet.

'Mr Trelford,' said the judge sharply, before Sir Edward could offer an opinion, 'we have already travelled down that road and it came to a dead end. Do I make myself clear?'

'I apologize, my lady. Would you have any objection to my asking Lady Virginia if I could read out—'

'Yes, I would, Mr Trelford. Move on,' she said sharply.

Trelford glanced across at the jury. As it was clear from the looks on their faces they had ignored the judge's instruction not to read any newspaper reports of the case and must have been well aware of what Mrs Clifton's mother thought of Lady Virginia, he was happy to obey the judge's wishes and to move on.

'Lady Virginia, are you aware that despite the learned judge's ruling in favour of Mrs Clifton and her sister, Dr Grace Barrington, they both agreed that their brother could go on living at their family home in Gloucestershire, as well as at the London house in Smith Square, while Mrs Clifton and her husband continued to reside at their more modest Manor House?'

'I have no idea what Giles's domestic arrangements were after I divorced him for adultery, let alone what Mrs Clifton was up to.'

'You had no idea what Mrs Clifton was up to,' repeated Mr Trelford. 'In which case, Lady Virginia, you must have either a very short or a very selective memory, because only a few moments ago you told the jury how much you admired Mrs Clifton. Allow me to remind you of your exact words.' He slowly turned back a page of his file. '"Emma has many admirable qualities, and has unquestionably been an outstanding chairman of a public company, making her a role model for aspiring professional women." That wasn't always your opinion, was it, Lady Virginia?'

'My opinion of Mrs Clifton has not changed, and I stand by what I said.'

'Did you purchase seven and a half per cent of Barrington's stock?'

'Major Fisher did on my behalf.'

'For what purpose?'

'As a long-term investment.'

'And not because you wanted to take a seat on the board of the company?'

'No. Major Fisher, as you well know, represented my interests on the board.'

'Not in 1958 he didn't, because in that year you turned up at an Extraordinary General Meeting of Barrington's in Bristol, claiming your right to sit on the board and to vote on who should be the company's next chairman. For the record, Lady Virginia, who did you vote for?'

'I voted for Major Fisher.'

'Or do you mean you voted against Mrs Clifton?'

'Certainly not. I listened to both their presentations most carefully and decided on balance in favour of Major Fisher, rather than Mrs Clifton.'

'Well then, clearly you have forgotten what you said on that occasion, but as it was recorded in the minutes of the meeting, allow me to remind you. *I don't believe that women were put on earth to chair boards, take on trade union leaders, build luxury liners or have to raise vast sums of money from bankers in the City of London.* Hardly a ringing endorsement for aspiring professional women.'

'Perhaps you should read on, Mr Trelford, and not be quite so selective in your quotations.'

Trelford looked beyond the paragraph he'd underlined, and hesitated.

Mrs Justice Lane gave him a nudge. 'I would like to hear what else Lady Virginia had to say on that occasion.'

'And so would I,' said Sir Edward, loud enough for everyone in court to hear.

Trelford reluctantly read out the next couple of lines. *'I shall be supporting Major Fisher, and I only hope that Mrs Clifton will accept the major's generous offer to serve as his deputy.'* Mr Trelford looked up.

'Please keep going, Mr Trelford,' prompted Lady Virginia.

'I came here with an open mind, willing to give her the benefit of the doubt, but sadly she has not lived up to my expectations.'

'I think you'll find, Mr Trelford,' said Virginia, 'that it's you who has either a very short or a very selective memory, not me.'

Sir Edward applauded, although his hands didn't actually touch.

Mr Trelford quickly changed the subject. 'Shall we move on to Mrs Clifton's words which you claim were libellous and belittled you?'

'I'm quite happy to do so.'

'If it was your intention to bring the company down, Lady Virginia,' continued Trelford, as if he hadn't been interrupted, *'then . . . you have failed, and failed lamentably, because you were defeated by decent ordinary people who want this company to be a success.* Now, Major Fisher admitted that he carried out his dealings in Barrington's shares simply to make money, which in his case was illegal—'

'In his case, but not in mine,' said Lady Virginia. 'In my case he was simply acting on my behalf. For all I know, he was giving exactly the same advice to several other clients.'

'So Major Fisher was not a close friend, who kept you in touch with what was happening on the board of Barrington's, but simply a professional advisor?'

'Even if we were friends, Mr Trelford, when it came to business matters, everything he did on my behalf was conducted at arm's length.'

'I would suggest, Lady Virginia, that when it came to business matters, far from being conducted at arm's length, it was very much hands-on, and, just as Mrs

Clifton suggested, the two of you planned on three separate occasions to try to bring the company down.'

'Mr Trelford, I think you are confusing me with Mr Cedric Hardcastle, a director of the company, who sold all his stock over the weekend before the AGM. When I asked Mrs Clifton a perfectly legitimate question about who that director was, she seemed to have conveniently forgotten his name. Someone else with either a very short or a very selective memory.'

Sir Edward's smile was growing broader by the minute, while Trelford was sounding less and less assured. He quickly turned another page.

'We all regret the tragic death of Major Fisher . . .'

'I certainly do,' said Virginia. 'And as I said earlier, which I'm confident you will have recorded word for word, Mr Trelford, I would never have considered issuing a writ in the first place if I had thought even for a moment that it could have resulted in the tragic and unnecessary death of my dear friend.'

'I do indeed remember your words, Lady Virginia, but I wonder if you noticed that just before proceedings opened this morning, a policeman entered this court and handed me a letter?'

Sir Edward edged forward in his seat, ready to pounce.

'Would it surprise you to know it was addressed to me, and that it was from your dear friend, Major Fisher?'

If Mr Trelford had wanted to go on speaking, his words would have been drowned out by a cacophony of noise that came from all corners of the courtroom. Only the judge and the jury remained impassive. He waited for complete silence before he continued.

'Lady Virginia, would you like me to read out to the

court the last words your dear friend Major Fisher wrote, moments before he died?'

Sir Edward leapt up. 'My lady, I have not seen this letter in the bundle of evidence, and therefore have no idea if it's admissible or even authentic.'

'The blood stain on the envelope would suggest its authenticity, my lady,' said Trelford, waving the envelope in front of the jury.

'I haven't seen the letter either, Sir Edward,' said the judge, 'so it certainly isn't admissible as evidence until I say so.'

Trelford was quite happy for them to go on discussing the legal niceties as to whether the letter was admissible or not, well aware that he had made his point without having to produce any evidence.

Giles studied the sphinx-like expression on Trelford's face and couldn't be sure if Emma's counsel even wanted the letter to be read out in court, but following what had started out as a triumphant morning for Lady Virginia, he had once again sown a seed of doubt in the jury's minds. Everyone in the court's eyes were on him.

Mr Trelford tucked the envelope back into an inside pocket of his jacket. He smiled up at the judge, and said, 'No more questions, my lady.'

44

WHEN THE CELL DOOR swung open on Tuesday morning, two guards marched in to find Harry and Babakov sitting on the floor in opposite corners of the cell, not speaking.

They grabbed Babakov and, as they dragged him out of the cell, Harry bowed his head as if he wanted nothing to do with the man. A moment later two more guards appeared, walking at a more leisurely pace. Although they took Harry firmly by the arms, they didn't jostle, push or drag him out of the cell, which made him wonder if it was just possible that Babakov's plan had worked. However, the guards didn't let go of Harry as they led him up the stairs, along the corridor and into the courtroom, as if they feared he might try to make a run for it. But where would he run, and just how far did they imagine he would get?

Harry had insisted that Babakov sleep on the one thin mattress in their cramped cell, but the Russian had refused, explaining that he couldn't afford to get used to such luxury when he would be returning to a stone floor in Siberia on Tuesday night. Sleeping on the straw that was liberally scattered over the floor was quite enough luxury for one weekend. The truth was, neither of them had slept for any length of time, which brought back memories for Harry of his days behind enemy lines. By the time the guards came to collect them on the Tuesday morning, they were both mentally and physically exhausted, having used every available hour for the challenge they had set themselves.

When the two guards accompanied Harry into the court, he was surprised to find the chief prosecutor and the jury already in their places. He hardly had time to catch his breath before the door at the back of the room opened and the three judges entered and returned to their seats on the raised dais.

Once again, the tribunal chairman didn't even glance in Harry's direction, but immediately turned to the jury. She opened a file in front of her and began what Harry assumed was her summing up. She only spoke for a few minutes, rarely raising her head from the text. Harry could only wonder who had written it, and when.

'Comrades, you have heard all the evidence, and have had more than enough time to consider your verdict. Can there be any doubt that the prisoner is guilty of the crimes he has been charged with, and that he deserves to be sentenced to a long term of imprisonment? The jury will be interested to learn that this will not be the prisoner's first experience of jail. He has already served a sentence for murder in the United States, but do not let that influence you, because it is you, and you alone, who must decide if he is guilty.'

Harry had to admire the fact that the other two judges were able to keep a straight face while she continued to read out the prepared statement.

'Comrades, first let me ask you if you need to retire to consider your verdict?'

A man seated at the right-hand end of the front row, as befits a bit-part player, stood up and, sticking to his script, said, 'No, comrade chairman.'

'Have you reached a verdict?'

'Yes, we have, comrade chairman.'

'And is that verdict unanimous?'

'Yes, it is, comrade chairman.'

'And what is your verdict?'

Each of the twelve members of the jury picked up a piece of paper from their chair, and held it high in the air, revealing the word *GUILTY*.

Harry wanted to point out that there was only one piece of paper on each chair but, as Anatoly had advised, he looked suitably chastened when the comrade chairman turned to face him for the first time.

'The jury,' she declared, 'has unanimously found you guilty of a premeditated crime against the state, and I, therefore, have no hesitation in sentencing you to twelve years' imprisonment in a labour camp, where you can once again share a cell with your criminal friend Babakov.' She closed her file and paused for some considerable time before adding, 'However, as Colonel Marinkin recommended, I will offer you one last chance to sign a confession admitting your crime and the terrible mistake you have made. Should you do so, your sentence will be suspended, and you will be extradited and never allowed to visit the Soviet Union or any of its satellites again. Should you ever attempt to do so, your sentence will automatically be reinstated.' After a short pause she said, 'Are you willing to sign a confession?'

Harry bowed his head and said, very quietly, 'Yes, I am.'

For the first time, all three judges showed an emotion

– surprise. The chairman couldn't hide her relief, unintentionally revealing what her masters had clearly always wanted.

'Then you may approach the dais,' she said.

Harry stood up and walked over to the three judges. He was shown two copies of the confession, one in Russian and the other in English, both of which he read carefully.

'You will now read your confession to the court.'

Harry read the Russian version first, which brought a smile to the lips of the comrade chairman. He then picked up the English version and started to recite it. From the blank stares he received he wondered if anyone in that courtroom understood a word of English. He decided to take a risk, change the occasional word, and see how they reacted.

'I, Harry Clifton, a citizen of the United Kingdom, and President of PEN, have *in*voluntarily and *with* coercion, signed this *confusion*. I have spent the past three *years* with Anatoly Babakov, who has made it clear to me that he *did* work in the Kremlin, and met Comrade Chairman Stalin on *several occasions, including* when he was awarded his degree. Babakov also admitted that the book he wrote about Comrade Stalin was *fact, and not* a figment of his imagination.

'I shall *continue to* demand Babakov's release from prison, now that I am aware of the lengths *this court* went to, in order to deceive the public with this fraud. I am most grateful to the court for its *lethargy* on this occasion, and for allowing me to return to my own country.'

The chairman handed him a pen and he was just about to sign both copies when he decided to take a second risk.

◄◦►

'Members of the jury,' said Mrs Justice Lane. 'It now falls to me to sum up what has been a complex case. Some facts are not in dispute. Mrs Clifton does not deny that when addressing a packed annual general meeting of her family company, she made the following reply to a question from Lady Virginia Fenwick, and later had it recorded in the minutes of the meeting: *If it was your intention to bring the company down, Lady Virginia, then . . . you have failed, and failed lamentably, because you were defeated by decent ordinary people who want this company to be a success.*

'The defendant, Mrs Clifton, has testified that she believes her words were justified, while the plaintiff, Lady Virginia, claims they are libellous. Whether they are or not is what this trial is about, and the final decision is yours.

'Your biggest challenge, may I suggest, is to make a judgement about the two women involved in this case. You have seen them both in the witness box, and I suspect you will have formed your own opinion as to which you consider the more credible. Do not allow yourselves to be influenced by the fact that Mrs Clifton is the chairman of a public company, and therefore should be given some leeway when answering a question from someone she considers hostile. What you must decide is whether she libelled Lady Virginia, or did not.

'Equally, you should not be overawed by the fact that Lady Virginia is the daughter of an earl. You must treat her no differently than you would your next-door neighbour.

'When you retire to the jury room to consider your verdict, take your time. I am in no hurry. And do not forget that the decision you are about to make will affect both of these women for the rest of their lives.

'But first, you must select a foreman, who will act as chairman. When you've reached your verdict, please tell the jury bailiff that you wish to come back into court so that I can inform all those directly and indirectly involved in this case to return to hear your decision. I shall now ask the jury bailiff to escort you to the jury room, so you can begin your deliberations.'

A tall, elegantly dressed man with a military bearing and wearing what looked like a schoolmaster's gown stepped forward, and led the seven men and five women of the jury out of the courtroom. Moments later, the judge rose from her place, bowed to the court and returned to her chambers.

'What did you make of the summing up?' asked Emma.

'Measured and fair,' Mr Trelford assured her. 'You have nothing to complain about.'

'And how long do you think it will take them to reach a decision?' Giles asked.

'It's impossible to predict. If they are all in agreement, which I think is highly unlikely, no more than a couple of hours. If they are divided, it could be a couple of days.'

'Can I read the letter Major Fisher sent to you?' asked Sebastian innocently.

'No, you cannot, Mr Clifton,' said Trelford, pushing the envelope further down into his inside pocket, 'and nor can anyone else, unless and until Mrs Justice Lane allows me to reveal its contents. I cannot, and will not, go against the express wishes of the judge. Good try, though,' he said, grinning at Seb.

◄○►

'How long are we expected to hang about?' asked Virginia, who was sitting with her counsel on the other side of the courtroom.

'I've no idea,' said Sir Edward. 'If I were to hazard a guess, I'd say a day, possibly two.'

'And why did Major Fisher address his last letter to Trelford and not to you?'

'That I haven't been able to work out. But I confess I'm puzzled why Trelford didn't press the judge more strongly to be allowed to read the letter to the jury, if it was at all likely to benefit his client.'

'Perhaps he was bluffing?'

'Or double-bluffing.'

'Am I safe to take a couple of hours off?' asked Virginia. 'There's something I need to do.'

'Why not? I can't see the jury returning before this afternoon.'

45

HARRY HADN'T EXPECTED a chauffeur-driven car to take him to the airport, and he was even more surprised when he saw who the chauffeur was.

'I just want to make sure you get on the plane,' said Colonel Marinkin.

'How very considerate of you, colonel,' said Harry, forgetting to remain in character.

'Don't get clever with me, Mr Clifton. The railway station is closer than the airport, and it's not too late for you to join Babakov on a journey that won't have a return ticket for another twelve years.'

'But I signed the confession,' said Harry, trying to sound conciliatory.

'Which I know you'll be glad to hear has already been released to every leading newspaper in the West from the *New York Times* to the *Guardian*. It will have hit most of their front pages before you touch down at Heathrow, so even if you did try to deny it—'

'I can assure you, colonel, that, unlike St Peter, there will be no need for me to deny anything. I saw Babakov for what he was. And in any case, an Englishman's word is his bond.'

'I'm glad to hear that,' said the colonel, as he accelerated on to the motorway and put his foot hard down. Within seconds the indicator was touching a hundred miles an hour. Harry clung on to the dashboard as the colonel nipped in and out of the traffic, and for the first time since he'd set foot in Russia, Harry was genuinely frightened. As they passed the Hermitage, the colonel couldn't resist asking, 'Have you ever visited the Hermitage, Mr Clifton?'

'No,' said Harry, 'but I've always wanted to.'

'Pity, because now you never will,' said the colonel as he overtook a couple of lorries.

Harry only began to relax when the airport terminal came into sight, and the colonel slowed to sixty. He hoped his plane would take off before the first editions hit the streets, otherwise he might still be on that train to Siberia, and as he couldn't hope to get through customs for at least a couple of hours, it might be a close-run thing.

Suddenly the car swung off the road, through a gate held open by two guards, and drove on to a runway. The colonel dodged in and out of the stationary aircraft, with much the same abandon with which he had treated the cars on the motorway. He screeched to a halt at the bottom of an aircraft's steps, where two guards, who had clearly been waiting for him, sprang to attention and saluted even before he'd got out of the car. Marinkin leapt out, and Harry followed him.

'Don't let me hold you up,' said the colonel. 'Just be sure you never come back, because if you do, I'll be at the bottom of the steps waiting for you.' They didn't shake hands.

Harry walked up the staircase as quickly as he could, knowing he wouldn't feel safe until the plane had taken off. When he reached the top step the senior steward came forward and said, 'Welcome aboard, Mr Clifton. Let me take you to your seat.' Clearly he was expected. The steward guided him to the back row of first class, and Harry was relieved to find the seat next to him was empty. No sooner had he sat down than the aircraft door was slammed shut and the seat-belt sign switched on. He still wasn't quite ready to breathe a sigh of relief.

'Is there anything I can get you once we've taken off, Mr Clifton?' asked the steward.

'How long is the flight?'

'Five and a half hours, including a stopover in Stockholm.'

'A strong black coffee, no sugar, two pens, and as much writing paper as you can spare. And could you let me know the moment we're no longer in Russian airspace?'

'Of course, sir,' said the steward, as if he got this sort of request every day.

Harry closed his eyes and tried to concentrate as the plane began to taxi to the far end of the runway in preparation for take-off. Anatoly had explained to him that he knew the book off by heart, and had spent the past sixteen years repeating it to himself again and again in the hope that one day he would be released, when it could be published.

As soon as the seat-belt sign had been switched off, the steward returned and handed Harry a dozen sheets of BOAC writing paper and two ballpoint pens.

'I'm afraid that won't be enough for the first chapter,' said Harry. 'Can you keep up a regular supply?'

'I'll do my best,' said the steward. 'And will you be hoping to catch a couple of hours' sleep during the flight?'

'Not if I can possibly avoid it.'

'Then may I suggest you leave your reading light on, so when the cabin lights are dimmed, you can go on working.'

'Thank you.'

'Would you like to see the first-class menu, sir?'

'Only if I can write on the back of it.'

'A cocktail perhaps?'

'No, I'll stick with the coffee, thank you. And can I say something that's going to sound incredibly rude, but I assure you it's not meant to be.'

'Of course, sir.'

'Could you not speak to me again until we land in Stockholm?'

'As you wish, sir.'

'Other than to tell me when we're no longer in Russian air space.' The senior steward nodded. 'Thank you,' said Harry, then picked up a pen and began writing.

I first met Josef Stalin when I graduated from the Foreign Languages Institute in 1941. I was on a conveyor belt of graduates being awarded their degrees, and if you had told me then that I would spend the next thirteen years working for a monster who made Hitler look like a pacifist, I would not have believed it possible. But I have only myself to blame, because I would never have been offered a job in the Kremlin if I hadn't come top of my class, and been awarded the Lenin Medal. If I'd come second, I would have joined my wife Yelena, taught English in a state school and not been even a footnote in history.

Harry paused as he tried to recall a paragraph that began, *For the first six months . . .*

> *For the first six months, I worked in a small office in one of the many outer buildings within the red wall that encircled the 69 acres of the Kremlin. My job was to translate the leader's speeches from Russian into English, without any idea if anyone ever read them. But then one day two members of the Secret Police (NKVD) appeared by my desk and ordered me to accompany them. I was led out of the building, across a courtyard and into the Senate, a building I'd never entered before. I must have been searched a dozen times before I was allowed to enter a large office where I found myself in the presence of Comrade Stalin, the General Secretary of the Party. I towered above him, although I am only five foot nine, but what I remember most was those yellow eyes boring into mine. I hoped he couldn't see that I was shaking. I learned years later that he became suspicious of any state employee who wasn't shaking when they first appeared before him. Why did he want to see me? Clement Attlee had just been elected as the British prime minister, and Stalin wanted to know how it could be possible for such an insignificant little man (Attlee was an inch taller than Stalin) to replace Winston Churchill whom he admired and respected. After I'd explained the vagaries of the British electoral system to him, all he said was, 'That's the ultimate proof that democracy doesn't work.'*

A steaming hot coffee, Harry's second, and more sheets

of paper of different sizes and shapes were supplied by
the silent chief steward.

◄○►

Sebastian took a cab to the High Court shortly after
eleven. Just as he had been about to leave his office,
Rachel had dropped the morning post and three more
thick files on his desk. He tried to tell himself that things
would return to normal next week. He couldn't put off
much longer telling Ross Buchanan that he intended to
go to America and find out if he had the slightest chance
of winning Samantha back, although he wasn't even sure
she would agree to see him. Ross had met Samantha on
the *Buckingham*'s maiden voyage, and later described her
as the best asset he'd ever let go.

'I didn't let her go,' Seb had tried to explain, 'and if I
could get her back, I would. Whatever the cost.'

As the taxi made its way through the morning traffic,
he kept checking his watch, hoping he'd get there before
the jury returned.

He was paying the cabbie when he spotted Virginia.
He froze on the spot. Even with her back to him, it
couldn't have been anyone else. That confident air of
generations past, the style, the class, would have made her
stand out in any crowd. But what was she doing hiding
away in a back alley talking to Desmond Mellor of all
people? Seb didn't even realize they knew each other,
but why wasn't he surprised? He would immediately
tell Uncle Giles and leave it for him to decide if they
should let Emma know. Perhaps not until after the trial
was over.

He slipstreamed in among a tide of pedestrians to
make sure neither of them spotted him. As he entered the

Royal Courts of Justice, he ran up the wide staircase, dodging in and out of bewigged barristers as well as witnesses and defendants who wished they weren't there, until at last he reached the lobby outside court fourteen.

'Over here, Seb,' called a voice.

Seb looked around to see Giles and his mother sitting in the corner of the lobby, chatting to Mr Trelford, killing time.

He strode across to join them. Giles told him there was no sign of the jury returning. He waited for his mother to resume her conversation with Mr Trelford before he took Giles aside and told him what he'd just witnessed. 'Cedric Hardcastle taught me not to believe in coincidences,' he concluded.

'Particularly when Virginia is involved. With her, everything is planned to the finest detail. However, I don't think this is the time to tell your mother.'

'But how could those two possibly know each other?'

'Alex Fisher has to be the common factor,' said Giles. 'But what worries me is that Desmond Mellor is a far more dangerous and clever man than Fisher ever was. I've never understood why he resigned from Barrington's so soon after he became deputy chairman.'

'I'm responsible for that,' said Seb, and explained the deal he'd made with Hakim Bishara.

'Clever, but be warned, Mellor isn't the type to forgive or forget.'

'Would all those involved in the case of Fenwick versus Clifton please go to court number fourteen, as the jury is expected to return in the next few minutes.'

The four of them rose as one and made their way quickly back into the courtroom, where they found the judge already seated in her place. Everyone was looking towards the door through which the jury would make their entrance, like theatregoers waiting for the curtain to rise.

When the door finally opened, the chattering ceased, as the jury bailiff led his twelve charges back into court, then stood aside to allow them to return to their places in the jury box. Once they were settled, he asked the foreman to rise.

The chosen one couldn't have appeared at first glance to be a less likely leader, even of this disparate group. He must have been around sixty, and not an inch over five foot four, bald and wearing a three-piece suit, white shirt, and a striped tie that Giles guessed represented his club or his old school. You would have passed him in the street without giving him a first look. But the moment he opened his mouth, everyone understood why he had been selected. He spoke with a quiet authority, and Giles wouldn't have been surprised to learn that he was a solicitor, a schoolmaster or even a senior civil servant.

'Mr Foreman,' the judge said, leaning forward, 'have you reached a verdict on which you are all agreed?'

'No, my lady,' he replied in a calm, measured voice. 'But I felt we ought to inform you of the impasse we have reached, in the hope you might advise us what we should do next.'

'I will certainly try,' said Mrs Justice Lane, as if she was dealing with a trusted colleague.

'We have taken the vote a number of times, and on each occasion it has resulted in an eight-to-four deadlock. We were not certain if there was any purpose in us continuing.'

'I wouldn't want you to give up at this early stage,' said the judge. 'Considerable time, effort and expense has been invested in this trial, and the least any of us can do is to be absolutely sure we have made every effort to reach a verdict. If you think it might help, I would be willing to accept a majority verdict of ten to two, but nothing less will be acceptable.'

'Then we will try again, my lady,' said the foreman and, without another word, he led his little band back out of the court, with the bailiff bringing up the rear of an exclusive club that no one else would be invited to join.

Once the door had closed behind them, a babble of chattering broke out, even before the judge had made her exit.

'Who's got eight, and who's got four?' was Virginia's first question.

'You have the eight,' said Sir Edward, 'and I can identify almost every one of them.'

'How can you be so sure?'

'Two reasons. While the foreman was speaking to the judge, I kept my eyes on the jury, and the majority of them were looking at you. Juries, in my experience, don't look at the loser.'

'And the other reason?'

'Take a look at Trelford and you'll see an unhappy man, because he will have carried out the same exercise.'

'Who got the majority?' asked Giles.

'Never easy to try to second-guess a jury,' said Trelford, touching the envelope in his inside pocket, although he was fairly sure it wasn't his client who needed the extra two votes to win the action. So perhaps the time had come to allow Mrs Clifton to see the major's letter, and decide if she wanted it read out in court.

He would advise her to do so if she still hoped to win the case, but having come to know the lady over the past few months, he would not have been surprised if she thought otherwise.

◄◦►

While Stalin was serving his first prison sentence in 1902 at the age of twenty-three, like many ambitious party members, he decided to learn German, so he could read Karl Marx in the original – but he only ended up with a cursory knowledge of the language. During his time in jail, he formed a self-appointed political committee of murderers and thugs who ruled over the other prisoners. Anyone who disobeyed him was beaten into submission. Soon, even the guards became intimidated by him, and were probably relieved when he escaped. He once told me that he'd never murdered anyone, possibly true, because he only had to hint, drop a name, and that person was never heard of again.

The most damning thing I learned about Stalin during my time at the Kremlin, and never repeated, even to my wife, for fear it would compromise her, was that when he was a young man and had been exiled to Kuneika in Siberia, he fathered two children by a 13-year-old schoolgirl, Lidia Pereprygina, and once he left Kuneika, he not only never returned, but never contacted them again.

Harry unfastened his seat belt and walked up and down the length of the cabin as he thought about the next chapter. He began writing again the moment he returned to his seat.

Another incident that Stalin regularly regaled us with was his claim that he carried out a series of

471

*bank robberies all over the country to raise funds
for Lenin in support of the revolution. This certainly
accounted for his rapid promotion, although Stalin
yearned to be a politician, and not simply thought of
as a Caucasian bandit. When Stalin told his friend
Comrade Leonov of his ambitions, he just smiled
and said, 'You can't carry out a revolution wearing
silk gloves.' Stalin nodded to one of his thugs, who
followed Leonov out of the room. Leonov was never
seen again.*

'We are no longer in Russian airspace, Mr Clifton,' said
the steward.

'Thank you,' said Harry.

*Stalin's arrogance and insecurity reached the most
farcical proportions when the great motion picture
director, Sergei Eisenstein, was chosen to make a
film called 'October', to be shown at the Bolshoi
Theatre to mark the tenth anniversary of the
October Revolution. Stalin turned up the day before
the first screening and, after seeing the film, ordered
Eisenstein to remove any reference to Trotsky, the
man acknowledged by the Bolshevik Party as the
genius behind the October coup, but now regarded
by Stalin as his most dangerous rival. When the film
was screened for the general public the following
day, there was no mention of Trotsky from beginning
to end, because he'd been consigned to the cutting-
room floor. Pravda described the film as a
masterpiece, and made no mention of the missing
Trotsky. The paper's previous editor, Sergei Peresky,
was among those who had disappeared overnight for
criticizing Stalin.*

'We've run out of paper,' said the steward.

'How far are we from Stockholm?' asked Harry.

'About another hour, sir.' He hesitated. 'I have one other source you might consider.'

'I'll consider anything, rather than lose an hour.'

'We have two varieties,' said the steward. 'First class or economy, but I think economy will serve your purpose better – a heavier texture and less absorbent.'

Both of them giggled like schoolboys as the steward produced a roll in one hand and a box in the other. Harry took his advice and chose economy.

'By the way, sir, I love your books.'

'This isn't my book,' said Harry, as he continued writing.

Another persistent rumour his enemies spread was that during his youth Stalin was a double agent, working for the Tsar's secret police at the same time as being one of Lenin's most trusted lieutenants. When Stalin's enemies found out about his regular meetings with the Tsar's secret police, he simply claimed he was turning them into double agents so they could work for the revolutionaries, and whenever anyone reported him, they mysteriously disappeared soon afterwards. So no one could ever be sure which side Stalin was working for; one cynic suggested whichever side looked like winning. Someone else who was never seen or heard of again.

Harry paused as he tried to remember the opening line of the next chapter.

By now, you will be asking yourself if I feared for my own life. No, because I was like wallpaper. I simply blended into the background, so no one ever noticed me. Very few of Stalin's inner circle even knew my name. No one ever sought my opinion on anything, let alone my support. I was an apparatchik, a junior civil servant of no significance, and had I been replaced by a different coloured wallpaper, I would have been forgotten within the hour.

I had been working at the Kremlin for just over a year when I first thought about writing a memoir of the man no one spoke of unless it was in reverential tones – even behind his back. But it was another year before I summoned up the courage to write the first page. Three years later, as my confidence grew, whenever I returned to my little flat each evening I would write a page, perhaps two, about what had taken place that day. And before going to bed, like an actor, I would learn the newly minted script off by heart, and then destroy it.

So frightened was I of being caught that Yelena would sit by the window whenever I was writing, just in case anyone paid an unexpected visit. If that had happened, I was ready to throw the page I was working on into the fire. But no one ever did visit, because no one considered me a threat to anything or anybody.

'Please fasten your seat belts, as we will be landing in Stockholm in a few minutes' time.'

'Can I stay on the plane?' asked Harry.

'I'm afraid not, sir, but we have a first-class lounge where they serve breakfast, and where I'm sure you'll find an endless supply of paper.'

Harry was the first off the plane and within minutes had settled down at a table in the first-class lounge with a black coffee, several varieties of biscuits and reams of typing paper. He must have been the only passenger who was delighted to learn that the flight had been delayed because of a mechanical fault.

> Yakov Bulgukov, the Mayor of Romanovskaya, faced a potentially dangerous situation when he decided to build a massive image of Stalin, twice life size, using convicts from a nearby prison to build the statue, which would be erected on the banks of the Volga-Don Canal. The mayor was horrified when he turned up for work each morning to find his leader's head covered in bird droppings. Bulgukov came up with a drastic solution. He ordered that a constant electric current should be run through the statue's head. A junior official was given the job of removing the little corpses every morning before the sun rose.

Harry gathered his thoughts before he began the fourth chapter.

> Stalin had a hand-picked cadre of security guards led by General Nikolai Sidorovich Vlasik, whom he trusted with his life. He needed to, because he'd made so many enemies during the purges, when he'd eliminated anyone and everyone he considered to be a possible rival, at that time or in the future. I lost count of how many people were in favour one day and disappeared the next. If a member of his inner circle so much as hinted that someone was plotting against him, that person was never seen or heard of again. Stalin didn't believe in early retirement or a

*pension plan. He once told me that if you kill one
person, you're a murderer; if you kill thousands,
it becomes a mere statistic.*

*Stalin boasted that his personal security
protection was in a different class to anything the
President of the United States was getting from the
American Secret Service, and that wasn't hard to
believe. When he left the Kremlin for his dacha each
evening, and when he returned to the Kremlin the
following morning, Vlasik was always by his side
ready to take an assassin's bullet, although the
nine-kilometre route was permanently patrolled by
three thousand armed agents, and his bullet-proof
Zil limousine rarely travelled at less than eighty
miles an hour.*

Harry was on page seventy-nine of the manuscript when
all passengers on the flight to London were requested to
re-board the plane, by which time Stalin saw himself as
something of a cross between Henry VIII and Catherine
the Great. Harry walked up to the check-in counter.

'Would it be possible to change my flight to a later
one?'

'Yes, of course, sir. We have one going via Amsterdam
in two hours' time, but I'm afraid there's no connecting
flight to London for another four hours.'

'Perfect.'

46

GILES READ William Warwick's signed confession on the front page of *The Times* the following morning and couldn't stop laughing.

How could they have failed to notice that it wasn't Harry's signature? He could only assume that the Russians were in such a hurry to get the confession into the hands of the international press before he arrived back in England that they'd made a cock-up. It had happened often enough in the Foreign Office when Giles was a minister, but it rarely got beyond the press department. Mind you, when Churchill was visiting America just after the war he asked the embassy to set up a meeting with the distinguished philosopher Isaiah Berlin, and ended up having tea with Irving Berlin.

Photographs of Harry dominated most of the morning papers, while leaders and opinion pieces about the popular author and his long-standing battle to have Anatoly Babakov released from prison filled many column inches on the inside pages.

The cartoonists had a field day, depicting Harry as either George slaying the dragon or David felling Goliath. But Giles's favourite was one in the *Daily Express* of

Harry fencing with a pen against a bear with a broken sword. The caption read: *Mightier than the Sword*.

Giles was still laughing when he read William Warwick's confession for a second time. He assumed heads would be rolling, perhaps literally, in Russia.

'What's so funny?' asked Emma when she joined him for breakfast, still looking as if she could have done with a good night's sleep.

'Harry's done more to embarrass the Russians in one day than the Foreign Office could manage in a year. And there's even better news. Just look at the *Telegraph's* headline.' He held the paper up so she could read it.

WILLIAM WARWICK ADMITS TO BEING A SPY

'It's not a laughing matter,' said Emma, pushing the papers aside. 'If he'd still been in Russia when the first editions came out it would have been a completely different headline.'

'Well, at least look on the bright side.'

'There's a bright side?'

'There most certainly is. Up until now, everyone's been asking why Harry wasn't in court supporting you. Well, now they all know, which is bound to make an impression on the jury.'

'Except that Virginia was brilliant in the witness box. Far more convincing than I was.'

'But I suspect the jury will have seen through her by now.'

'Just in case you've forgotten, it took you a little longer.'

Giles looked suitably chastened.

'I've just come off the phone with him,' said Emma. 'He's been held up in Stockholm. He seemed preoccupied and didn't say a great deal. He told me he's not expecting to land at Heathrow until around five this afternoon.'

'Did he get his hands on Babakov's book?' asked Giles.

'His money ran out before I had time to ask him,' said Emma as she poured herself some coffee. 'In any case, I was more interested in trying to find out why it had taken him almost a week to do a journey that most other people manage in under four hours.'

'And what was his explanation?'

'Didn't have one. Said he'd tell me everything as soon as he got home.' Emma took a sip of her coffee before adding, 'There's something he's not telling me, that hasn't made the front pages.'

'I bet it has something to do with Babakov's book.'

'Damn that book,' said Emma. 'What possessed him to take such a risk when he'd already been threatened with a jail sentence?'

'Don't forget this is the same man who took on a German division armed only with a pistol, a jeep and an Irish corporal.'

'And he was lucky to survive that as well.'

'You knew what kind of man he was long before you married him. For better or worse . . .' Giles said, taking his sister's hand.

'But does he begin to understand what he's put his family through during the last week, and just how lucky he is to have been put on a plane back to England rather than on a train heading for Siberia along with his friend Babakov?'

'I suspect there's a part of him that will have wanted to be on that train with Babakov,' said Giles quietly. 'That's why we both admire him so much.'

'I'll never let him go abroad again,' said Emma with feeling.

'Well, as long as he only heads west, it should still be all right,' said Giles, trying to lighten the mood.

Emma bowed her head, and suddenly burst into tears. 'You don't realize just how much you love someone until you think you might never see them again.'

'I know how you feel,' said Giles.

—◄○►—

During the war, Harry had once stayed awake for thirty-six hours, but he was a lot younger then.

> *One of the many subjects no one ever dared to raise with Stalin was the role he played during the siege of Moscow, when the outcome of the Second World War still hung in the balance. Did he, like most of the government ministers and their officials, beat a hasty retreat to Kuibyshev on the Volga, or did he, as he claimed, refuse to leave the capital and remain in the Kremlin, personally organizing the defence of the city? His version became legend, part of the official Soviet history, although several people saw him on the platform moments before the train departed for Kuibyshev, and there are no reliable reports of anyone seeing him in Moscow again until the Russian army had driven the enemy from the gates of the city. Few of those who expressed any doubts about Stalin's version lived to tell the tale.*

With a ballpoint pen in one hand, and a slice of Edam cheese in the other, he carried on writing, page after page. He could hear Jessica remonstrating with him. How can you sit in an airport lounge writing someone else's book, when you're just a taxi ride away from the finest collection of Rembrandts, Vermeers, Steens and De Wittes in the world? Not a day went by when he didn't think of Jessica. He just hoped she'd understand why he had to temporarily replace Rembrandt with Babakov. Harry paused again to gather his thoughts.

Stalin always claimed that on the day of Nadya's funeral, he walked behind the coffin. In fact, he only did so for a few minutes, because of an abiding fear of being assassinated. When the cortege reached the first inhabited buildings in Manege Square, he disappeared into the back of a car, while his brother-in-law Alyosha Svanidze, also a short, stocky man with a thick black moustache, took his place. Svanidze wore Stalin's great coat so the crowd would assume he must be the grieving widower.

'Would all passengers . . .'

━◦━

Mrs Justice Lane released everyone from court number fourteen at four o'clock that afternoon, but not until she was convinced that the jury wouldn't be able to reach a verdict that evening.

'I'm off to Heathrow,' said Emma, looking at her watch. 'With a bit of luck I'll be just in time to meet Harry off the plane.'

'Would you like us to come with you?' asked Giles.

'Certainly not. I want him all to myself for the first few hours, but I'll bring him back to Smith Square this evening, and we can all have dinner together.'

Taxi drivers always smile when a fare says Heathrow.

Emma climbed into the back of the cab, confident she could be at the airport before the plane landed.

The first thing she did on entering the terminal building was to check the arrivals board. Little numbers and letters flicked over every few moments, supplying the latest information for each flight. The board indicated that passengers arriving from Amsterdam on BOAC 786 were now in baggage reclaim. But then she remembered that Harry had only taken a small overnight bag, as he hadn't planned to be in Leningrad for more than a few hours, one night at the most. In any case, he was always among the first off the plane as he liked to be speeding down the motorway on his way back to Bristol before the last passengers had cleared customs. Made him feel he'd stolen time.

Could she have missed him, she wondered, as several passengers passed her, with bags displaying Amsterdam luggage tags. She was about to go in search of a telephone and call Giles when Harry finally appeared.

'I'm so sorry,' he said, throwing his arms around her. 'I had no idea you'd be waiting for me. I thought you'd still be in court.'

'The judge let us go at four because it didn't look as if the jury were going to reach a verdict today.'

Harry released her, and said, 'Can I make the strangest request?'

'Anything, my darling.'

'Could we book into an airport hotel for a couple of hours?'

'We haven't done that for some time,' said Emma, grinning.

'I'll explain why later,' said Harry. He didn't speak

again until he'd signed the hotel register and they'd checked into their room.

Emma lay on the bed, watching as Harry sat at a little desk by the window, writing as if his life depended on it. She wasn't allowed to speak, turn on the television or even order room service, so, in desperation, she picked up the first chapter of what she assumed must be the latest William Warwick novel.

She was hooked from the first sentence. When Harry finally put down his pen, three and a half hours later, and slumped on to the bed beside her, all she said was, 'Don't say a word, just hand me the next chapter.'

Whenever I was required at the dacha (not that often), I always ate in the kitchen. A real treat, because Stalin's chef, Spiridon Ivanovich Putin, would give me and the three tasters exactly the same food as was being served to Stalin and his guests in the dining room. That should hardly come as a surprise. The three tasters were just another example of Stalin's paranoia, and his belief that someone must be trying to poison him. They would sit silently at the kitchen table, never opening their mouths except to eat. Chef Putin's conversation was also limited, as he assumed that anyone who entered his domain – kitchen staff, waiters, guards, tasters – was almost certainly a spy, me included. When he did speak, which was never before the meal had been cleared away and the last guest had left the dining room, it would only ever be about his family, of whom he was inordinately proud, particularly his most recent grandson, Vladimir.

Once the guests had all departed, Stalin would

retreat to his study and read until the early hours.
A portrait of Lenin hung above his desk, a lamp
illuminating his face. He loved reading Russian
novels, often scribbling comments in the margins.
If he couldn't get to sleep he would slip out into the
garden, prune his roses, and admire the peacocks
that wandered through the grounds.

When he finally returned to the house, he didn't
decide which room he would sleep in until the last
moment, unable to shake off past memories of being
a young revolutionary, always on the move, never
certain where he was going to rest. He would then
grab a few hours' sleep on a sofa, the door locked
and his guards outside, who would never unlock
the door until he called. Stalin rarely rose before
midday, when, after a light lunch, no drink, he
would be driven from his dacha to the Kremlin in a
convoy, but never in the same car. When he arrived,
he immediately set to work with his six secretaries.
I never once saw him yawn.

Emma turned the page, while Harry fell into a deep
sleep.

When he woke just after midnight, she had reached
chapter twelve (the opening paragraph of which was on
the back of a first-class menu). She gathered up several
sheets of paper and put them as neatly as she could into
Harry's overnight bag, then helped him off the bed,
guided him out of the room and into the nearest lift.
Once Emma had paid the bill, she asked the bellboy to
hail her a taxi. He opened the back door and allowed the
tired old man and his girlfriend to climb inside.

'Where to, miss?' asked the cabbie.

'Twenty-three Smith Square.'

◄◦►

During the journey back into London, Emma brought Harry up to date about what had been happening in the trial, Fisher's death and Giles's preparations for the by-election, Virginia's performance in the witness box, and the letter from Fisher that Mr Trelford had received that morning.

'What did it say?' asked Harry.

'I don't know, and I'm not sure I even want to know.'

'But it might help you win the case.'

'That doesn't seem likely if Fisher's involved.'

'And I've only been away just over a week,' said Harry as the taxi drew up outside Giles's home in Smith Square.

When the front doorbell rang, Giles quickly answered it, to find his closest friend holding on to his sister with one hand, and the railing with the other, to make sure he didn't fall over. His two new guards took an arm each and guided him into the house, past the dining room and up the stairs to the guest bedroom on the first floor. He didn't reply when Giles said, 'Sleep well, old chum,' and closed the door behind him.

By the time Emma had undressed her husband and hung up his suit, she became painfully aware what the inside of a Russian prison cell must smell like, but he was already sound asleep by the time she pulled off his socks.

She crept into the bed beside him, and although she knew he couldn't hear her, she whispered firmly, 'The furthest east I will allow you to travel in future will be Cambridge.' She then switched on the bedside light and continued to read *Uncle Joe*. It was another hour before she finally discovered why the Russians had gone to such lengths to make sure that no one ever got their hands on the book.

Comrade Stalin's seventieth birthday was celebrated across the Soviet empire, in a manner that would have impressed a Caesar. No one who hoped to live talked of his retirement. Young men feared early preferment because it often heralded early retirement and, as Stalin seemed determined to hold on to power, any suggestion of mortality meant your funeral, not his.

While I sat at the back of the endless meetings celebrating Stalin's achievements, I began to form my own plans for a tiny slice of immortality. The publication of my unauthorized biography. But I would have to wait, possibly for years after Stalin's death, for the right moment to present itself, before I approached a publisher, a brave publisher, who would be willing to consider taking on Uncle Joe.

What I hadn't anticipated was just how long Stalin would cling on, and he certainly had no intention of releasing the reins of power before the pall bearers had lowered him into the ground, and more than one or two of his enemies remained silent for several days after his death, just in case he rose again.

A great deal has been written about Stalin's death. The official communiqué, which I translated for the international press, claimed that he died at his desk in the Kremlin after suffering a stroke, and that was the accepted version for many years. Whereas in truth he was staying at his dacha, and

*after a drunken dinner with his inner circle, which
included Lavrenti Beria, his deputy premier and
former secret police chief, Nikita Khrushchev and
Georgy Malenkov, he retired to bed, but not before
all his guests had left the dacha.*

*Beria, Malenkov and Khrushchev all feared for
their lives, because they knew Stalin planned to
replace them with younger, more loyal lieutenants.
After all, that was exactly how each of them had got
his own job in the first place.*

*The following day, Stalin still hadn't risen by late
afternoon and one of his guards, worried that he
might be ill, phoned Beria, who dismissed the man's
fears and told him Stalin was probably just sleeping
off a hangover. Another hour passed before the
guard called Beria again. This time he summoned
Khrushchev and Malenkov and they immediately
drove over to the dacha.*

*Beria gave the order to unlock the door of the
room in which Stalin had spent the night, and the
three of them tentatively entered, to find him lying
on the floor, unconscious but still breathing.
Khrushchev bent down to check his pulse, when
suddenly a muscle twitched. Stalin stared up at
Beria and grabbed him by the arm. Khrushchev fell
on his knees, placed his hands around Stalin's throat
and strangled him. Stalin struggled for a few
minutes, while Beria and Malenkov held him down.*

*Once they were convinced he was dead, they left
the room, locking the door behind them. Beria
immediately issued an order that all of Stalin's
personal guards – sixteen of them – were to be shot,
so there could be no witnesses to what had*

happened. No one was informed of Stalin's death until the official announcement was made several hours later, the one I translated which claimed he'd died of a stroke while working at his desk in the Kremlin. In fact he was strangled by Khrushchev and left lying in a pool of his own urine for several hours before his body was removed from the dacha.

For the next fourteen days, Stalin's body lay in state in the Hall of Columns, dressed in full military uniform, wearing his hero of the Soviet Union and Hero of Socialist Labour medals. Beria, Malenkov and Khrushchev, heads bowed, stood in respectful silence beside the embalmed corpse of their former leader.

These three men were to become the troika who grabbed power in his place, although Stalin hadn't considered any of them worthy to succeed him, and they knew it. Khrushchev, thought of as no more than a peasant, became secretary of the party. Malenkov, whom Stalin once described as an obese, spineless pen-pusher, was appointed prime minister, while the ruthless Beria, whom Stalin regarded as a sordid sex addict, took control of the nation's security services.

A few months later, in June 1953, Khrushchev had Beria arrested and later, not much later, executed for treason. Within a year, he had removed Malenkov and appointed himself prime minister as well as supreme leader. He only spared Malenkov's life once he agreed to announce publicly that it was Beria who had murdered Stalin.

Emma fell asleep.

47

WHEN EMMA WOKE the following morning, she found Harry kneeling on the floor, trying to sort out various different bits of paper and arrange them in neat piles: BOAC writing paper, the backs of a dozen first-class menus, and even lavatory paper. She joined him, concentrating on the lavatory paper. Forty minutes later, they had a book.

'What time do we have to be in court?' asked Harry as they made their way downstairs to join Giles and Seb for breakfast.

'Ten, in theory,' said Emma, 'but Mr Trelford doesn't think the jury will return much before midday.'

Breakfast was the first real meal Harry had eaten for the best part of a week, but despite that, he was surprised how little he could manage. They sat in silence as he regaled them with everything he'd experienced since they'd last seen him. They were introduced to the taxi driver, the old woman in the bookshop, the KGB colonel, the tribunal chairman, the chief prosecutor, the defence solicitor, the jury and, finally, Anatoly Babakov, whom he'd liked and admired. He told them how that truly remarkable man had spent every hour he could stay awake telling Harry his story.

'Won't he be in considerable danger if the book is published?' suggested Giles.

'The answer must be yes, but he was adamant that *Uncle Joe* be published before he died, because it would allow his wife to live in comfort for the rest of her life. So once the trial is over, I plan to fly back to the States and hand over the manuscript to Harold Guinzburg. I'll then travel on to Pittsburgh to see Yelena Babakov, and pass on several messages from her husband,' he added as Big Ben struck the first of ten chimes.

'It can't be that late,' said Emma, leaping up from the table. 'Seb, go and find a cab while your father and I get ready.'

Seb smiled. He wondered when mothers stopped treating their children as if they were perpetually fifteen years old.

Ten minutes later, they were all heading up Whitehall towards the Strand.

'Are you looking forward to being back in the House?' asked Harry as they drove past Downing Street.

'I haven't even been selected as the candidate yet,' said Giles.

'Well, at least this time Alex Fisher won't cause you any trouble.'

'I wouldn't be so sure of that,' said Giles.

'You must be a shoo-in,' said Emma.

'In politics there are no shoo-ins,' Giles assured her as they drew up outside the law courts.

The cameras began flashing even before Emma had stepped out of the cab. She and Harry walked arm in arm through the phalanx of journalists and photographers, most of whom seemed more interested in her husband than in the defendant.

'Are you relieved to be back home, sir?' shouted one of them.

'Is London colder than Siberia?' quipped another.

'Is it good to have him back, Mrs Clifton?' yelled a third.

Emma broke Giles's golden rule. 'Yes, it most certainly is,' she said as she squeezed Harry's hand.

'Do you think you'll win today?' persisted another, which she pretended not to hear. Seb was waiting for them, and held open the massive door to allow them through.

'Are you hoping to be the Labour candidate in the Bristol by-election, Sir Giles?' But Giles simply waved and smiled, giving them a picture but no words, before he disappeared into the building.

The four of them made their way up the wide marble staircase to find Mr Trelford occupying his favourite corner bench on the first floor. Trelford stood the moment he saw Emma approaching. She introduced him to Harry.

'Good morning, Detective Inspector Warwick,' said Trelford. 'I've been looking forward to meeting you.'

Harry shook the barrister warmly by the hand. 'I must apologize for not being here sooner, but I have—'

'I know,' said Trelford, 'and I can't wait to read it.'

The tannoy crackled. 'Would all those involved in the Lady Virginia Fenwick versus . . .'

'The jury must have reached a decision,' Trelford said, already on the move. He looked round to check that they were all following him, and bumped into someone. He apologized, but the young man didn't look back. Sebastian, who had walked on ahead, held open the door to court number fourteen so his mother and her silk could resume their places in the front row.

Emma was too nervous to speak and, fearing the worst, kept glancing anxiously over her shoulder at Harry, who sat in the row behind her as they waited for the jury to appear.

When Mrs Justice Lane entered the courtroom, everyone rose. She bowed before resuming her place. Emma transferred her attention to the closed door beside the jury box. She didn't have to wait long before it swung open, and the bailiff reappeared followed by his twelve disciples. They took their time finding their places, treading on each other's toes like late-arriving theatregoers. The bailiff waited for them to settle before he banged his rod three times on the floor and shouted, 'Will the foreman please rise.'

The foreman rose to his full five feet four inches and looked up at the judge. Mrs Justice Lane leant forward and said, 'Have you reached a verdict on which you are all agreed?'

Emma thought her heart would stop beating as she waited for his reply.

'No, my lady.'

'Then have you reached a verdict on which you are agreed by a majority of at least ten to two?'

'We did, my lady,' said the foreman, 'but unfortunately, at the last moment, one of our number changed his mind, and we have been stuck on nine votes to three for the past hour. I am not convinced that will change, so once again I am seeking your guidance as to what we should do next.'

'Do you believe you could reach a majority of ten to two, if I gave you a little more time?'

'I do, my lady, because on one particular matter, all twelve of us are in agreement.'

'And what is that?'

'If we were allowed to know the contents of the letter Major Fisher wrote to Mr Trelford, we might well be able to come to a decision fairly quickly.'

Everybody's eyes were fixed on the judge, except for Sir Edward Makepeace, who was looking closely at Trelford. Either he was a formidable poker player or he didn't want the jury to know what was in that letter.

Trelford rose from his seat and reached into his inside pocket, only to find that the letter was no longer there. He looked across to the far side of the court, to see that Lady Virginia was smiling.

He returned her smile.

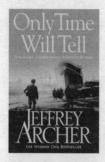
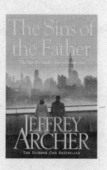
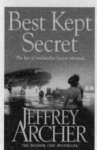